ELIZABETH LONSETH

To Janet,
Peaceful Reading.
With love from
Elsie's Godsis,
E Lonseth

The Things Hoped For

A NORTHWEST NOVEL
NORWEGIAN LEGACY

The Grand House
Lillesand

The Things Hoped For

by Elizabeth Lonseth
Cover Photo and Illustrations by Stan Lonseth
Capistrano Beach Photography
www.capobeachphotos.com

ISBN: 978-0-578-31101-2

Dedication and Thanks

This book is dedicated to my daughters, Meredith Ellis, Lindsey Milligan, and Witney Barnett. Each one of you amaze me with your incredible achievements, your gifts, and your love for the Lord. There are so many wonderful memories of celebrations, adventures, and trips we have shared together. Thank you for being there for me in the hard times. I am blessed and privileged to call you my daughters. Thank you for all your support and encouragement with my writing.

Thank you to my longtime and long-distance friend, Carol Lee Clayton, for keeping me in line.

Thank you to Norwegian Historian, Harald Skjønsberg for his historical input; to Carla Caldwell for her research on the Port Townsend area; to Kevin Peterson for his sailing expertise, and Anna Sophie Høegh – Omdal, museum curator of Lillesand Town – and Maritime Museum for the valuable in-person interview. A special thanks to my daughter Meredith Ellis for her medical advice.

A big thanks to my husband, Stan Lonseth for the fabulous cover photo of the lighthouse on Oksøy Island on the southern coast of Norway near Kristiansand.

Table of Contents

BOOK THREE: CHALLENGES

BOOK ONE

Courage

August of 1913

Rowing Home

CHAPTER 1

Survival

Early August 1913, Lillesand, Norway

Crash! As the china serving platter splintered into a million pieces, with the sound still reverberating through the Grand House, Gudrun's last hope shattered also. All aspirations of approaching the mistress about a live-in position disappeared. She stooped down to pick up the larger pieces. *This is my life,* she thought. *It cannot get any more shattered than this.*

"Gudrun Sagen! Now what are we supposed to serve the meat on? The General and his wife will be here in an hour," Mrs. Olsen whispered, but nineteen-year-old Gudrun wished she had yelled. She used an intense, intimidating tone to convey to the staff they were in trouble, spoken quietly so no one would know things were not running smoothly. It gave the master and mistress the illusion of a happy, perfect staff, securing Mrs. Olsen's position as housekeeper.

"I...I don't know ma'am," Gudrun stuttered. "I will clean this up. Can we use the oval silver tray?"

Mrs. Olsen's raised eyebrow let Gudrun know the idea had been rejected.

"How about using another set of china?" As she said the words she knew that solution would not work. As an entry housemaid keeping the fires she had watched the English butler and under butler setting the table. Measuring with a ruler the distance between each place setting and the proper placement of each piece within the setting, took hours. They did not have enough time to change the table service.

"The mistress carefully selected this china pattern two days ago. She will notice any changes," the housekeeper answered.

Abby, the part-time kitchen maid, found a simple platter that went with the china pattern being used that night.

Hovering by the butler's pantry door Gudrun held her breath as the butler and under butler served the dinner, hoping that Mistress Iversen would not say anything. When the door opened she could see the women in their elegant gowns and the men in their tuxedo coats. "So English" Gudrun overheard Mrs. Simonsen, the cook, say.

"Did she notice?" Gudrun whispered as the door swung shut behind the under butler. Since her promotion to the kitchen eight months ago she had only spoken to him twice.

"Yes, she gave me a funny look when I served her the meat. She did not say anything. You will be hearing about it tomorrow," he replied. "Please fill this again, apparently the General has a big appetite tonight."

Letting out a big sigh, Gudrun took the platter to the kitchen.

∽

"What a mess!" Gudrun yelled at the moon. She stopped rowing and watched drops of water slide off her oars creating silver rings in the smooth water that glimmered in the moonlight. The warm summer breeze ruffled her hair and she pulled her skirt up to her knees. She let the oars rest in the oarlocks, and took the clip out of her platinum blonde hair. Leaning back, bracing her arms on the seat behind her and taking a deep breath she felt her six-foot long body relax.

Gazing at the stars she began to pray, "Thank you Lord, for this beautiful evening. Thank you for loving me…thank you for comforting me."

She gazed back at her town of Lillesand and a tear slid down her cheek. Viewing the white homes and the inns where her father used to sell fish made her miss him more. The deserted shipyards looked like ghosts in the moonlight. Some of the docks were being dismantled. Master Iversen's shipyard and one other were still in business. For how long though? Especially after tonight. The talk throughout the kitchen had been that the general had been invited for dinner to help land a military contract for several new wooden ships.

Moonlight bathed the schoolhouse which held so many memories. Gudrun had done well in school. She even had a few friends. Friends whose families moved to America with the promise of good jobs. When her mother passed away it had been difficult to stay in school and take on the household duties. For three more years her father insisted she attend, but he gave in when she turned twelve because she had gotten a job as a maid. God had blessed her with a better job in the Grand House four years ago, a prestigious place to work.

"Please, Lord, let me keep my job. You blessed me with this new position in the kitchen and now I ruined it. She was right, Lord. It is all so fleeting, temporal, always changing. This place at this time will never be exactly like this again," Gudrun prayed, remembering her mother's words a few months before she passed away. As a nine-year-old those words seemed strange to her, but now she understood.

She picked up the oars and started rowing to her cabin on Lamholmen Island. Would Trygg, her large Halden hound, be waiting for her? Perhaps the warm August day had loosened up his old joints so that he could make the jaunt to welcome

3

her. The wind picked up as she left Lillesand harbor and entered Tingsakerfjorden, the fjord she had grown up on. She brought the old skiff into the dock and watched the sweet white and black spotted dog lumber slowly across the wooden planks. He had been her dearest companion since her mother's death almost ten years ago. Many nights she had cried herself to sleep with her face buried in his short thick fur, especially since her father's passing, a month ago.

"Hello, Trygg. Did you have a good day? Better than mine I am sure." She patted the hound. "Feeling better?"

He nuzzled her hand hoping for some sort of treat. Gudrun dug in her knapsack and found a small piece of dried venison to give to him. Together they sauntered down the path to the cabin.

Settled in front of the fire with her nightly cup of tea, she could almost see her father sitting across from her, his long legs stretched out, slowly puffing on his pipe. His pipe looked lonely sitting on the mantle. She massaged Trygg's fur around his neck. "He would have understood, ol' boy. He would have encouraged me like he always did. He would have said the Lord has good things for me."

Glancing toward the bedroom she continued, "Maybe on Monday, we can work on clearing that out? Do you want to help me go through Papa's things?"

Venturing into her father's room seemed a daunting task, one she had not been able to face. Even sleeping up in her loft had been too much to handle. The first few nights after her father had disappeared at sea, Gudrun had fallen asleep in her chair or slept on the floor next to Trygg's bed by the fire, hoping for news from the search team. After they found her father's body off the east side of Auesøya Island, she had dragged her small mattress out of the loft and placed it next to Trygg's.

෬

Shivering, Gudrun watched the sun rise as she rowed toward Lillesand the next morning. Blowing into her cupped hands she wished she had not left her lightweight gloves in the cabin. Overnight the weather had changed, providing a distinct chill in the air and requiring a coat for her row to work.

"God is our refuge and strength, a very present help in trouble. Therefore I shall not fear, though the earth should change, and though the mountains slip into the heart of the sea…" Gudrun cited her adapted version of Psalm 46, then let her thoughts roam to her job situation for a second. "Thank you, Lord for giving me a job. You made it possible. Please soften Mrs. Olsen's heart toward me. Please let me keep my job."

For a moment she thought about the good-looking under butler. She had caught his dark eyes glancing her way at times. She needed to avoid any involvement with him as it would give more credence to her reputation as the town floozy, ending any hope of a respectable marriage.

She rowed past the dock where it had all happened, three years before. It seemed only her father believed her…she had no idea the visitor from America was married. If she had known that Americans wore their wedding rings on their left hand, she would have never agreed to a walk after church. It had seemed innocent enough; they had been introduced before church and he kept smiling at her throughout the service. She recalled his arm around her shoulder as they walked and his warm lips pressing against hers. She wiped her lips and shuddered as she remembered Mrs. Thorsen's piercing shriek as she descended upon them, declaring Gudrun a harlot and accusing her of seducing her poor nephew. Within a few hours Mrs. Thorsen had spread the news of Gudrun's misconduct throughout Lillesand, demanding Gudrun be banned from church. The parishioners were not willing to take any action other than shunning her when she attended services.

"Thank you, Lord for your forgiveness. I know you have an answer to the mess I have made of my life. Give me strength as I face Mistress Iversen today. Help me to respond in grace," Gudrun prayed as she brought her boat into the landing. She tied down her lines, grabbed her rucksack and headed up the hill lined with small white houses to her work.

∽

Orcas Island, Washington, USA

"Ouch!" Arvik Johansen yelled. "Burned vafler again!" He tossed another waffle on the plate, added the last of the jam and went outside to the newly laid stone patio to eat. The first bite was barely recognizable. Nothing compared to the crisp-edged yet light Norwegian waffles his mother had made. The six-foot-six, blonde, twenty-seven-year-old Norwegian forced himself to finish the waffle out of necessity. He went back into the one room lean-to and rummaged through the shelves next to the stove. He found an old can of sardines and a question-able looking apple behind the flour and sugar. Sitting down on a stump on the patio, he placed the items on the rough table. *Will this be enough to quiet the hunger pains? I better take time off tomorrow and go into Eastsound to pick up supplies and go fishing for a few salmon.*

Arvik noted clouds building over Sucia and Matia Islands. *Maybe a storm?* As he finished the sardines and most of the apple he reflected on the larger problem — his loneliness.

Constant chatter did not appeal to him but the days and weeks of solitude as he worked on his house were beginning to bother him.

Coming to America had been the best choice of all his options. The only child of sharecroppers on Sørfjorden, there had been no fruit farm to inherit. He had given up school at fourteen to take a carpentry job, right after his mother died. Despite the 1899 crash of the Norwegian building industry a local carpenter had a large project and offered him an apprenticeship. A few years later the project ended and his childhood friends encouraged him to come with them to America. Yes, he had made the right decision coming to the Pacific Northwest.

After a few years of fishing in Alaska, he had found work both in the fishing industry and as a carpenter here on Orcas Island. Financially he had done well, not rich but at least comfortable. Comfortable enough to take the time to build the house of his dreams on a ten-acre farm he owned along the north shore of the island.

Over the years a few of his married acquaintances occasionally invited him for a good home-cooked meal. That only made him more aware of his solitude. What seemed to be lacking was an available woman to marry. She didn't have to be exceptionally pretty...but her being Norwegian had become his big priority. *Someone to share the same language with, someone to keep the old traditions with, someone who understands the customs from the old country.* He spit out the last mushy piece of apple. "And someone that can cook," he shouted at the brewing storm, as Matia and Sucia Islands disappeared behind dark, ominous clouds. He had checked his sailboat sitting offshore earlier that morning. The anchor seemed set tight enough to withstand a storm.

Turning toward the foundation of the new house, Arvik determined what needed to be done before the storm hit. He quickly fastened down a pile of rough 2x6's left over from framing the floor and picked up loose tools. He would not be able to start framing the walls this afternoon as he had hoped. He checked the small horse barn. Surefoot, his workhorse, had taken shelter inside. He gave the gelding some hay and shut the doors. A few raindrops hit Arvik's face as he opened the door to his large storage shed full of building materials. He took a quick inventory. Toilets, sinks, and faucets all left over products he had purchased from the head contractor when the large residential project he had worked on ended. A mansion so big it demanded a name — Rosario. He loved the quality of the work the owner expected. He had also purchased brownstone for the entry floors and milled white oak flooring from Rosario's surplus. Someday he would install all of this in his home. He headed to his lean-to just as the pelting rain began.

༄

Stepping out into the morning sunshine, Arvik noted *Himmel,* his boat still bobbing off shore. He surveyed the building site. Though the winds had howled through the lean-to all night, it did not look as if there was any significant damage. That surprised him, as twice he had to relight the candles as he sketched the interior trim details for the house. Rumbling in his stomach overcame the urge to grab two by fours out of the storage shed to start framing. He went back inside for another cup of coffee and looked over the sketches that he had drawn during the storm. *I have to take the day off; without food I cannot get any work done.*

A small familiar boat coming into shore from the west caught Arvik's eye as he closed the door to the lean-to, rucksack over his shoulder. As the short figure jumped off the bow onto the shore and pulled the skiff in, Arvik laid the rucksack on the patio table and went down the path to meet him.

"Good morning, Zhou. How are you?" Arvik asked. He had worked for several years with this man on the Rosario project on East Sound. Zhou Yamaguchi worked quickly and came up with ingenious solutions when problems arose.

Lifting two large salmon and a basket out of the bottom of the boat, Zhou replied, "I good. I come — gifts."

Arvik took a step back. "For me?"

"Yes, missus worry you not eat enough. I have big favor to ask."

Picturing Mrs. Yamaguchi fussing over the basket and mumbling in Japanese about her tall, skinny neighbor brought a smile to Arvik's face. "What can I do for you Zhou? Come, have coffee." Arvik swung his arm toward the patio.

"Thank you," Zhou said as Arvik handed him a large cup of coffee. "My favor — is project over — near West Sound. Some man from mainland building vacation home. He need two good carpenters — now. The missus and I need money. Will you work with me?"

Looking down at the table, Arvik's heart sank. He did not want to disappoint his neighbor. But he needed to get his house framed in by winter. He had to get this house done for his future wife. He couldn't expect a lady to live in the lean-to, not his wife.

∽

Gudrun finished hanging her coat and sat down on the servants' entry bench to brush off her shoes just as the under butler hurried past for a smoke outside.

"You are wanted upstairs. As expected by the mistress," he mumbled.

"Mrs. Iversen requests your presence immediately upstairs in her office," Mrs. Olsen said as Gudrun walked into the kitchen. The housekeeper put her morning coffee cup next to the sink as Gudrun washed her hands. Giving Gudrun a glare she turned and walked out.

Mrs. Simonsen, joined Gudrun at the sink, and said in a low gentle voice, "I can handle things here. I will be praying for you."

Quickly glancing down at the middle-aged cook, Gudrun found kind eyes meeting hers. *Someone who understands! Lord, thank you.* Gudrun resisted an urge to hug the sweet middle-aged woman, and instead whispered, "Thank you."

Slightly out of breath after climbing three flights of stairs so quickly, Gudrun paused in front of the office door. Running her hands over her hair to calm her wild curls, she anticipated the view on the other side of the door. When lighting fires early in the morning, she had often lingered in that room relishing the view of the town bathed in a pinkish light as the sun rose. She could feel her heart pounding so loudly she pressed on her chest, then ran her hands over her worn dress trying to press the wrinkles. *I should have mended the hole by the hem last night. Oh Lord, I am not presentable. Lord, please give me strength and grace.*

Hearing "Come in," in response to her knock on the door Gudrun stepped into the room.

Mrs. Iversen sat at her desk giving her both a view of the door and the harbor below. "Please sit." She motioned to the chairs in front of her desk. As Gudrun complied, she continued, "I am sorry that our first meeting is concerning last night's dinner accident."

"Yes, ma'am," Gudrun replied. She gazed at the mistress a bit in awe of her beauty but more in awe of her position at such a young age. When she married the master six months before, it had been whispered that the strawberry blonde beauty was only twenty-two.

"My husband requires an exact account of all household expenses." Mrs. Iversen looked down at the large leather-bound account book on her desk. "These days every penny counts..." As she glanced across at Gudrun, her eyes seemed kind, almost forgiving. "I would like to replace the platter, but the cost." She shook her head. "I think I have a plan, if you're agreeable. My dresser would like a month off to visit her ailing mother. Could you work a few extra hours? I am quite capable selecting suitable outfits and dressing myself. It is those horrible dresses with hundreds of tiny buttons down the back I need help with."

A sigh of relief escaped from Gudrun's lips. "Yes, ma'am, oh yes, ma'am."

"That will save me the cost of hiring someone else and I can replace the platter with the savings. My predecessor had exquisite taste..." the mistress mused glancing out the window..."high standards for me to meet."

"If I might be so bold as to say ma'am, I think you meet those standards quite admirably."

Mrs. Iversen stood and walked around her desk, extending her hand to Gudrun. Gudrun rose and met her eye to eye; not many women were as tall as she. They shook hands. "Thank you," Gudrun said, and hurriedly left the room.

CHAPTER 2

On Hold

"*T*his is slavery!" Captain Hans Torvik pounded the desk. "I won't take any more passages like this."

"That is too strong a word. It is not slavery. It is a second chance for these women," Mr. Dahl insisted. "You know as well as I do that some are ladies of the night. In a new country, where no one knows their mistakes, they can have a new life. Besides, most of our passengers are families, looking for new opportunities. It is not your job to play father to the single women and children."

Captain Hans' dark eyes blazed. "Since I became a deckhand at sixteen I have observed that every trip has its victims to carefully laid mail schemes or some lies clothed as promises. A young boy brags he will get a free education and a prestigious career, or the young lady so excited about marrying a wonderful man. As a young deckhand there was nothing I could do about it…and not all the single ladies have a sordid past. It happened again this last trip. The sweetest one, not a lady of the night, was picked up at the dock by a drunken, stinky, old man. I tried to stop it, but he had all the paperwork in order."

"Don't the officials at Ellis Island check things?"

Leaning in further on the desk, Captain Hans explained, "Not completely. He had papers declaring he was her uncle and that he had a job at a factory for her. She told everyone on board she had a proposal of marriage and she spent the crossing dreaming of the big American house she would be living in."

Rubbing his chin, the manager of the Norwegian Steamship Line said, "I see, then we need to check their agreement before we allow passage. I will look into this."

"Please do, I cannot stand by and watch. I might end up married myself just to rescue one of them." The middle-aged sea captain relaxed a bit.

Mr. Dahl's eyebrow raised. "You, married? But you are already married to that ship of yours!"

"Not that ugly tin can...but *Marianne*, yes." The captain stared out the window to the docks of Bergen. His eyes became misty as he thought about the beautiful wooden schooner he had braved the seas with for fifteen years. He would never forget standing on the dock in Lillesand watching her slide into the water for her maiden voyage. Made by the best wooden ship builders in the world, she took his breath away. She had never disappointed him, not even sailing the rough seas around the Horn.

"Hans, I wish I could turn back time. We have had this discussion before, it is not economical to use the wooden sailing ships to transport passengers across the Atlantic any more," Mr. Dahl said. "You know as well as I do that the steamers have cut the travel time in half. And the wooden ships were more dangerous."

Shifting his large frame in the chair, Hans grimaced. "I do understand. But the trips to and from New York are so fast and uneventful I feel like a trolley driver."

The manager chuckled. Taking a thick Norwegian Steamship Line envelope out of his desk drawer, he offered it to Hans. "First of all, please stop getting so involved with the passengers; their safety is only your responsibility while they are onboard, not their happiness. You do not have to escort them through customs. Secondly, I want you to take a month off. You need the rest. Do not try and talk me out of this. You take time away, and I will try and find something a bit more interesting for you than New York."

"A whole month? What am I going to do for that long?"

"You have not been on land that long in years, have you?" Hans shook his head.

"Go see your mother, take a trip somewhere inland, maybe Telemark. It will do you some good." Mr. Dahl stood up and shook hands with Captain Hans. "Oh, just a minute I have a letter for you that came the day after you left on the last crossing."

Walking along Bryggen gata Captain Hans looked down the street at the old buildings built in the eleven hundreds. The old wooden structures tilting with age in distinct contrast to the new motorcars touring the street — another unwanted reminder of change. He hurried through the August mist to his favorite inn for lunch. He ordered potetballer with extra bacon on the side. This place made the large bacon grease soaked ball of potato the way his mother did.

Hans took a look at the address on the letter Mr. Dahl had given him. The shaky handwriting seemed familiar...his mother's? He quickly opened the envelope. The salutation confirmed it was from her. He finished reading the letter as the petite ball arrived. *Now I know how I will be spending my month off.* He glanced at the date - three weeks ago. *What condition will she be in now? Better or is she even still alive? I won't be staying here tonight. Best to catch the evening boat to Rosendal.*

∾

Skillfully slipping her needle into the seam, Gudrun caught the other edge and pulled the fabric tight. *No one will ever know it came apart.* For a moment she thought about her mother who taught her to sew at the age of six. Remembering her mother's beaming face the first time she sold some of Gudrun's work to the tailor made her eyes a bit misty. Those were the days. Joining her father after school going house-to-house selling fish. Then picking up piecemeal work from the tailor for Mother on their way home. For years her mother only allowed her to mend their own clothes, but at age eight she graduated to helping with the piecemeal work. *Mother would be proud.*

She hung the dress back up on the ornate display hook, checking it for wrinkles. *None. Good. I should have enough time to peel potatoes and make the salad before Mistress Iversen needs my help putting this on for dinner.* The official dresser had written she could not leave her mother and the young mistress had decided her arrangement with Gudrun worked well. Mistress Iversen picked out what she wanted to wear for dinner each morning and hung it on the hook at the end of a wardrobe. Between meals Gudrun made sure the outfit was presentable, took outfits to the cleaners, or stopped at Mr. Bisset's shop, the French tailor, to pick up new creations.

Often the mistress would engage Gudrun in conversation and after several weeks Gudrun realized the strawberry blonde really had no one to confide in. She alluded to the marriage arrangement not being for love but financial security and position. Not her idea but her parents'. *Must be a lonely existence being a showcase wife,* Gudrun thought, glancing around the large dressing room. *Such luxury.*

Beautiful wooden wardrobes lined all the walls, one with the display hook on the end, another wardrobe had mirrored doors. A lounge chair sat in front of a window, and a bench sat centered in front of the other window. *All this for just one season of clothes.* Gudrun knew at the other end of the second floor hall an offseason clothing storage room existed, a room she had never entered. *And all this does not bring happiness.*

She skipped down the servants' stairwell to the kitchen, eagerly anticipating talking to Mrs. Simonsen as they worked. Over the past month they had become friends. Mid-afternoon usually gave them privacy as the maids were scurrying to finish up before they left, which kept Mrs. Olsen busy checking their work. The housekeeper seemed to be everywhere throughout the day, often stopping in the kitchen to make sure the maids did not take too long of a coffee break. She also loved to subtly remind Mrs. Simonsen that she worked for her, with constant questions on how much she spent on food, preparation time, and checking the state of the spotless kitchen.

"The menu is still the same?" Gudrun asked cheerfully, brushing past Mrs. Simonsen sitting on a stool. She grabbed a bag of potatoes and headed to the sink. "Just four for dinner?" When she received no answer she glanced back at the middle-aged lady intently reading a letter. "Are you alright?"

"Uh? Oh yes, just a bit preoccupied," Mrs. Simonsen answered. She waved the letter and continued on. "This is from my youngest daughter. The one in Minnesota. They have a good crop this year and are doing well." She folded the letter and slid it into the envelope, carefully placing it in her apron pocket.

Gudrun knew it had been months since Mrs. Simonsen had heard from her daughter. "I am glad you have finally heard from Ingeborg. Is she happy in America?"

The plump cook nodded. "Yes, very. It must be a beautiful place, Minnesota. She writes of lakes, and lots of trees, snow in the winter like here but much warmer summers. She and her husband want my husband and I to come and live with them." "You should!" Gudrun blurted out without thinking. "I am sorry. It sounds like such an adventure." "Adventure is not what I need at my age. It is for the young. Besides we cannot leave our son and daughter here and my man will not leave his store. I miss Ingeborg, but I am staying here, no matter how bad it gets."

Gudrun looked at her, one eyebrow raised.

"Oh, you have not heard. They let the under butler go last night after you left. Not enough in the household budget to merit keeping him. Master Iversen demanded that the Mistress let someone go. Poor Mr. Smith will be busy. Though they are not entertaining with big fancy dinners like they used to."

Shaking her head, Gudrun concentrated on the potatoes. "That is too bad. What is he going to do?"

Mrs. Simonsen shrugged. "He mentioned going to America...along with everyone else. He has an older brother in Seattle."

"America...must be wonderful. A new start..." Gudrun stopped peeling and stared out the window.

"Enough daydreaming. The potatoes will not peel themselves."

Gudrun jerked as her mind came back to reality. "We all know that you and Mr. Smith will be the last to go. How many times have we overheard the Master brag about his English butler and your fabulous cooking?"

The plump cook blushed and then shook a dish towel at Gudrun. "Trying to keep your job are you?"

"I heard it whispered that the son might take a job in Oslo. If he moved that would help the budget." Gudrun referred to the oldest child from Master Iversen's first marriage. In his mid-twenties, he worked for his father at the shipyard and still lived at home. "He eats enough for two men."

"Hush now, no gossip. That is their business. We must be respectful and thankful we have jobs. Want to sit with me again at church tomorrow?"

"Yes, thank you." Though it meant another day of rowing into town, Gudrun had been braving the scorn of Mrs. Thorsen and attending church again. Sitting with Mrs. Simonsen and her husband made her feel accepted. Last Sunday Mistress Iversen had even stopped at their pew and publicly acknowledged her, resulting in piercing glares from Mrs. Thorsen. As she continued peeling, Gudrun smiled. *That really rankled Mrs. Thorsen.*

∽

Letting his thoughts roam to the house project he and Zhou were working on, Arvik saddled up Surefoot, his gelding. *Two weeks has turned into four weeks and it is the beginning of September! No progress on my house. I do not want to spend another winter in the lean-to. Hopefully we will finish up tomorrow.*

"Good morning, Zhou. Think we finish putting windows in today?" Arvik asked as he tied the gelding to a long lead in the field next to the building site. Like Arvik the owner of the new house wanted it closed in before winter.

Zhou grimaced and said, "Sorry this take you away from your house too long. I work three weeks for you." He referred to the arrangement they had made. Arvik would give the Yamaguchis half of his pay in return for help on his house.

"It not your fault they change design and add rooms," Arvik replied. "Extra workers help." The owner had hired two carpenters, from the mainland, a week ago, making things move quicker. George and his son Albert were a strong team. Zhou and Arvik worked quickly together all morning, barely talking, each knowing what they needed to do. Carrying the windows upstairs together, placing the window into the opening, shaking their heads and pointing to tight places or gaps and nodding then taking the window out. They would make the adjustments almost in silence or sketch on a piece of left over wood to solve the problem.

When working together on Rosario they found sketching took them to an understanding that their limited English could not. Arvik had picked up a few words of Japanese and Zhou a few in Norwegian. On lunch breaks they laughed at their attempts to learn the other's language, but kept trying. Or they would correct the other's English, filling in adjectives, pronouns, and little words they had recently learned that made sentences flow better. The correct tense still eluded them from time to time, and Zhou had trouble with the letters R, L and V.

I will miss Zhou's company when my house is framed in, Arvik thought. He glanced at his watch. "Lunch?" he asked Zhou.

Nodding, Zhou headed for the open stairwell, tripping over a tool belt left on the floor. He fought to regain his balance and Arvik tried to reach out for him but the momentum flung the wiry Japanese man into the air, his own tool belt letting loose an arsenal of screwdrivers, hammers, and nails to the floor below. A quick shout, an unsuccessful attempt to bring his small frame into the fetal position, and Zhou landed with a thud on the first floor.

Thundering down the stairs, Arvik knelt down next to the limp body. "Zhou! Zhou!" Arvik felt for a pulse. *Good, there is one. Water...oh no, his leg!* A bone stuck out of Zhou's torn pant leg. "Help! We need help," Arvik yelled.

George quickly joined them. "That is a bad break. He needs a doctor. I will get the wagon."

Albert poured water from a canteen onto his bandana and passed it to Arvik, then disappeared outside.

Arvik held the bandana to Zhou's head. *He is still unconscious. Maybe a good thing. It could be a painful trip to Eastsound. Hopefully one of the Drs. Harrison are around.*

Orcas had benefited greatly when Dr. Agnes Harrison and her husband, Dr. Isaac Magnus Harrison, affectionately called Dr. I.M. arrived in Eastsound in 1907. Both highly skilled, the islanders held them in high regard, grateful for their services.

Returning with a board wide enough to act as a stretcher, Albert laid it next to Zhou. He helped Arvik slide the Asian man onto it. Zhou's eyes fluttered. "We are getting help, Zhou. Taking you to Dr. Agnes," Arvik whispered. Arvik rummaged through his tool bag finding a small bottle of scotch which he slid into his pocket, before helping Albert carry Zhou to the wagon.

Sitting in the wagon with Zhou, Arvik winced at every bump, imagining his friend's pain. He rubbed the scotch on Zhou's lips in case he woke up enough to lick his lips; but the carpenter remained unconscious. *Lord, you know I don't pray much. Don't ask for much either. Please keep my friend alive. Please.*

CHAPTER 3

Hopeless

*L*etting out a string of curses Arvik threw the empty scotch bottle across the patio and into the bushes. It clanked against the one he had thrown there earlier in the afternoon. He hung his head, *this is all for naught. No hope of finishing my house by spring or next summer. Another two years without a wife? It is hopeless.*

He watched a fuzzy sunset and vaguely recounted the events of the past two days. Dr. Agnes Harrison had set Zhou's leg and made sure he was awake and stable before her husband and Arvik loaded Zhou into their more comfortable carriage. Arvik followed behind the carriage on his gelding, trying to remember Japanese words so he could explain to Mrs. Yamaguchi what had happened. By the time they arrived he had concluded that none of the words he knew fit the situation.

As expected, she was distraught at first, but quickly made a comfortable bed in the living room and tended to her husband. Zhou stayed awake long enough to relate the events of the accident to her. After an hour, Dr. I. M. Harrison and Arvik said their goodbyes with a thankful Mrs. Yamaguchi following them to the door. According to the doctors, it would take months of healing before he could attempt to walk.

Arvik spent the next morning and part of the afternoon at the job site. George and Albert had arrived extra early and by mid-afternoon they officially had the house closed in for winter. On his way home he stopped at the Yamaguchis' to give them almost the entire payment for the work he and Zhou accomplished. They needed the money more than he did. He explained to the couple that he kept out twenty dollars for groceries. But then at the store he not only got groceries, he stocked up on his favorite Scotch Whiskey. He should have given all the money to them.

"Never give up. Never give up." His father's words haunted him as he stumbled to the lean-to.

၁၀

Walking toward church that Sunday morning Gudrun noticed a group of Mrs. Thorsen's friends gathered near the entry door. Mrs. Olsen had joined the group. Fear overwhelmed her. *Should I leave or go inside? No, Mrs. Simonsen is meeting me here with her husband. God wants me to go to church. You are God's daughter. Put your head up, walk tall, and walk in with a smile.*

Drawing near the entry Gudrun heard Mrs. Olsen voice. "Yes, it is shameful. A young woman living all alone."

Another woman said, "Who knows how many men she entertains at night out there on that island in that cabin...all alone at night?"

The women's cackling laughter seemed to cut through Gudrun's heart. She wanted to run. How could they think up such lies? She only had time to sleep at the cabin.

Head down, she started to turn when a gentle hand touched her arm.

"Shall we go inside, sweetie?" Mrs. Simonsen asked.

၁၀

Rowing out of Lillesand harbor that Sunday afternoon, Gudrun noted the two remaining shipyards. She paused for a moment, pulling a pair of thick winter mittens over her summer gloves. One of Master Iversen's docks sported a new thirty-foot pleasure boat. Which supported the talk throughout the town and the Grand House that he had decided to produce smaller sized boats. There seemed to be a market for them. His son had suggested that they outfit the new boats with fancy, high-powered engines and full yardage so the owners could choose between motoring or sailing depending on the sea conditions or their mood. At lunch Mr. Simonsen had shown her a half page ad in the Oslo Sunday newspaper with beautiful sketches designed to entice those with money to enjoy the sea in style.

Hopefully there will be enough orders to keep his business alive, Gudrun thought. *My job depends on it. What would I do if I lost my job? That is if I can get to my job this winter.*

In previous winters her father had dropped her in town and picked her up in his fishing boat. Even then some of the dark winter mornings and evenings had made the trip difficult with storms and the harbor occasionally icing over. Determined to get his daughter to work on time, her father always found a way. Sometimes that meant docking near the mouth of the harbor and walking with her a few miles into town; dutifully holding a lantern to light their way in the dark.

How am I going to make it this winter in this rowboat, Lord? Should I approach the mistress about taking one of the empty rooms in the servant's quarters? What would I do if I lost my job? I have no other options. Please Lord let me know what to do. Thank you for today's sermon on your provision. I needed the reminder. Thank you for the Simonsen's generosity in providing me lunch. Thank you for providing most of my meals at the Grand House.

A stiff wind picked up as she crossed Tingsakerfjorden making it hard to row. She remembered Paul's claim in his book of Philippians, "I can do all things through Christ who strengthens me." Claiming that promise, she put her back into it and pulled hard. A current caught the boat for a moment taking her the wrong direction. She skillfully turned the boat and got back on course. The wind stung her cheeks as she rowed. She hummed a few choruses of "How Great Thou Art" fighting against the current and wind as she rowed. She wanted to cry as she remembered her father building the sturdy old wooden boat. His design gave her an advantage despite the adverse conditions. It quickly responded to each pull of the oar. "Thank you, Lord!" She exclaimed as she arrived at the island, tying up to dock.

"Trygg. Trygg," Gudrun called, hoping her dog would appear out from the rough doghouse near the dock. She peeked inside. "Nope. Can't blame you old boy. It is nippy for the first week of September. I bet you have only braved the flop door once all day," she mumbled to herself. A knapsack full of leftovers from the Simonsen's on her shoulder and a bundle of firewood from the shipyard under her arm, she headed down the path to the cabin. *Maybe I can make some progress on the paperwork in Papa's desk.*

She had spent the last month slowly going through the bedroom on her limited time off. The long twelve-hour days she spent at work did not give her much free time. First she had gone through her father's clothes, giving his two nice shirts and a coat to the Salvation Army and burning the rest. Next she went through the large trunk, in which she found her mother's bunad and several beautiful silver serving pieces.

Besides a few sketches of her grandparents, her mother's ring and locket, and a wedding photo of her parents, the rest had been junk not worth keeping. A limited amount of possessions to go through, but the emotions that each item brought out slowed her down.

The desk was a different story — the large locked drawers were full of paperwork. At first glance she found a bill for parts to repair the fishing boat engine. Carefully scrutinizing the ledger she had determined it had not been paid and had scrimped together enough to pay it last week.

Gudrun dumped the firewood in the box on the front porch. Opening the door she sang out, "Good afternoon Trygg, ready to...No! No! Trygg!"

Kneeling down next to the hound's bed she started to sob. Touching his cold body confirmed what she already knew. Her beautiful Halden hound — gone. Stroking his head and ears, she thought about the day, Per, one of her father's fishing buddies came to the cabin with eight-week old, Trygg. She recalled his gentle words of condolences about the loss of her mother and how he hoped she would enjoy the puppy. Per had explained about Trygg's special breeding. A first generation of a new Norwegian hunting breed, that would be a good family dog, too. And he had been — a member of the family. Trygg became her shadow and would usually wait at the dock when she left the island.

�◌

Running his fingers through his dark hair, Hans strolled up the lane toward the Baroniet Rosendal with his sister, Sissel, by his side. The mid-September sun bathed the mountain behind the manor house with streams of light bringing out colors so vivid they seemed surreal.

He paused, taking in the white manor house built in the mid-sixteen hundreds for the wealthiest heiress in Norway and a Danish nobleman. The waterfall cascading off the mountain beyond captivated him. "It is magnificent," he whispered.

Nodding, Sissel said, "It is one of her favorite places. I wish her health would allow her to visit one more time. When the current owner visits in the summer she likes to sit and chat with Mother in the garden."

"Maybe we can bundle her up and bring her in Rolf's carriage," Hans suggested. "The doctors don't seem to know how much longer. Maybe she has more time than we think and she might as well enjoy her last days. You know what irks me?"

Sissel shrugged, giving him a quizzical look.

"When people say 'She has had a good long life'...what does that mean? Is sixty-six years too much to ask for? So I am supposed to be alright with her death because of her age?" Hans started walking faster this time, but Sissel's long legs easily kept up with his. This past month had been a mix of emotions from sadness to gratefulness that he had the time to spend with her.

His siblings had done a good job taking care of his mother. His older brother, Rolf, ran the family farm, providing for her all these years. Sigrid, his older sister who lived close by, doted on their mother. Sissel, his younger sister, took time off from her nursing job and made regular trips from Stavanger to help out. Her husband, Dr. Karl Rogland, had come up for a few days to confer with the local doctor. For the past three weeks Sissel had been at their mother's bedside nonstop. At times he felt in the way, a man with no responsibilities, but he treasured the time spent with his mother.

"I have not the answer, Hans," his sister replied.

"The doctor does not know how fast the cancer will grow."

Sissel nodded. "Karl agrees with him, we have no idea how long she will last."

Hans stopped. "I do wish you would tell me which kind of cancer it is. I understand it is one of those subjects only discussed among women. But I am your brother."

"Sigrid and I want to tell you. You know how private mother is. She made us promise not to tell anyone."

The siblings walked on in silence, the noise of several seasonal waterfalls making conversation more difficult for a moment. As they headed back to the farm on a shortcut through the woods, they watched the sun set over the fjord.

Sissel broke the silence, "How are you doing being away from your ship?"

Hans smiled at her. "You remember my yearning to be out on the water headed for some new destination?"

"Oh yes. You made quite the impression on me at fourteen, leaving to follow your dream. I seldom look at the fjord or the ocean without thinking of you."

Chuckling, Hans responded, "Even after all these years, you know me so well. It is hard looking out at the fjord each morning. The desire to jump on a ship is still there. Somehow the sea mesmerizes you and captures your heart."

He did not tell her what really bothered him — her and Sigrid's incessant referral to the Lord and heaven. *How can they be so sure Mother is going to heaven? And this Jesus hypothesis...I have sailed ships around the Horn and never needed Jesus.*

❦

"It is so kind of you to come in earlier this morning. This dress is impossible!" Mistress Iversen looked at Gudrun in dismay. The dress in question had been purchased in Oslo by

27

Master Iversen for a special luncheon in the neighboring town of Grimstad. "Why do they make contraptions like this? To keep us tied down? Do they think we are stupid? This one had to have been designed by a man." The young mistress giggled.

Gudrun forced a laugh, sitting down to undo a difficult clasp on the absurd dress while fighting back tears.

"I need dresses that set me free, not tie me up like a mummy. Oh, listen to me complain. Not with all that I have." She glanced at Gudrun. "Are you alright?" The strawberry blonde sat down on the bench next to Gudrun, putting her hand over hers.

Her kindness broke the dam inside of Gudrun and the tears began to flow. Her tears quickly turned into sobs and Mistress Iversen held her in her arms. Minutes seemed like hours before Gudrun started to regain control.

The mistress pulled a hankie out of her pocket and handed it to Gudrun. "Now you tell me what is going on. I want to know everything. After all what are friends for? Especially sisters in Jesus we are to share each other's burdens. You know or have observed most of mine."

"Trygg, my beautiful..." Gudrun stopped to blow her nose, before continuing, "Halden Hound...died."

"Oh my dear. I am sorry. Those are beautiful dogs. He was your only companion at the cottage, yes?"

Gudrun paused. *She knows I live alone?* "Yes, and..."

Nodding, Mistress Iversen asked, "Go on, what else?"

She stood up and unwound the wide sash designed to wind three times around the mistress's mid-section and clasp in the back.

"After I buried Trygg, I went through my father's paperwork..." eyes wide, Gudrun looked at her mistress. "It is confusing but I think my father took out a loan from Mr. Thorsen's bank. I did not know about it. My father might have been skipping payments. I might not own my cabin! Oh Mistress Iversen what am I going to do?"

"That is grave news. Hmm...bring the paperwork to me tomorrow. Do not panic, we need to know the truth."

Gudrun proceeded to help the young mistress out of her dress and into the new one. Once they had the strawberry blonde looking like the showcase her position required, the mistress took Gudrun's hands in hers. "No more Mistress Iversen when we are alone. Please call me Karoline."

"I...I am not sure..." Gudrun stammered.

"Karoline it is. Now in the meantime I will go and pretend to be grand," she stopped. Her face took on a solemn look. "Both of us will pray. 'A prayer to the God of my life.'" She quoted the last part of Psalm 42:8.

After her mistress left the room Gudrun went over and read the same verse on a plaque hanging above the display hook. *Dear Lord, I am praying and you are the God of my life...it seems so hopeless. I feel like I should just disappear. But your word tells me that I am your child and in Jesus I am special and I have value. You have promised to take care of me. How are you going to work this all out, Lord?*

CHAPTER 4

God's Provision

urefoot? Arvik sat up in bed, the morning sun streaming into the lean-to. *That is not his snort.* Several more neighs and men's voices caused Arvik to jump out of bed, grab his shirt and attempt to put it on as he hurried to the small window. *Yes, several men. Am I awake, still hung over? No, I stopped drinking Wednesday night. Can hangovers last two days?*

Grabbing his pants he struggled to put them on as he headed to the door. *Friendly men?* He stopped and peeked out the window once more. He recognized George and Albert and several carpenters whom he had worked with on Rosario.

"How can I help you?" Arvik asked as he joined the men outside. He quickly counted – eight men.

George stepped forward, "We have come to help you with your house. To get it closed in for the winter."

Arvik's eyes widened.

"It was my tool belt that Zhou tripped over. I should not have left it there. Zhou told us you had a bargain with him and now he can't keep his part of the bargain," Albert explained. "We went to visit him and he told us how good you were to him. Then Dad and I came up with a plan. We can work for free on the weekends and we have a few days off this week and next."

Two carpenters from the Rosario project stepped forward and one said, "Do you remember the extra time you worked and gave your pay to us so we could take care of our mother?" Arvik lowered his head, as he began to fathom the gift these men were offering.

"We will never forget it. You have our help for a week."

A man he did not recognize stepped up. "You helped my wife one rainy night and fixed her wagon wheel."

Each of the men had various stories of how Arvik had helped them or their family members and they were there to help him, to repay his favors.

Clearing his throat, Arvik finally found his voice, "I..." he cleared his throat again and said gruffly, "I being good neighbor. Thank you."

"So tell us what to do, Arvik. You're the foreman," George shouted out.

After an hour of scurrying around and showing the men the barn full of timbers, the milled 2 x 6's, and the plans for the house, he looked up to see a man coming up the trail from the beach.

Holding out his hand, the man said, "Hi, I'm Thomas McGregor. I own property in Doe Bay. Thought I would come learn from the best carpenter on the island and when I decide to build my place I will know how."

"Thank you for coming," Arvik said. "All help — welcome."

❧

Laying the papers on Karoline's desk, Gudrun stood still, her eyes riveted on her mistress.

Glancing quickly at each paper, Karoline pushed them together and tapped them straight on the desk. "This will take awhile to read so no need to wait. I will let you know what it all means this afternoon." Her eyes narrowed. "Remember we are going to go over my fall and winter clothes this afternoon. One-thirty at the off-season storage room?"

"Thank you. Yes, Karoline, one thirty," Gudrun replied, and turned to leave the room. She stopped suddenly, "Excuse me," Gudrun mumbled, keeping her eyes low she hurried past Mr. Iversen who stood just inside the door. *Oh, how much did he hear? He cannot know of my financial woes.*

Master Iversen cleared his throat, "Excuse me, miss, what is your name?"

"Gudrun, Gudrun Sagen." Gudrun felt her knees shaking as she answered the head of the household. She had never spoken to him before.

"Was your father a fisherman?"

"Yes, sir, he was."

"Very well. That is all."

Hurrying down the back stairs to the kitchen, Gudrun played the little scene over and over. *How much did he hear? Calling Mistress Iversen by her first name could be a firing offense. What on earth will I do, Lord, if I lose my job? I have no skills. What if the mistress cannot help me with the cabin paperwork?*

Once in the kitchen she seemed to be all thumbs. She came close to spilling the egg basket, almost sliced her finger as she prepared cucumbers, and she slid and fell on a wet spot on the floor.

"My, my someone needs to calm down this morning," Mrs. Simonsen said. "At this rate the kitchen will be a disaster by lunch. What has gotten you out of sorts?"

Concerned that Mrs. Olsen might pop into the kitchen, Gudrun replied in a whisper, "The walls might have ears."

In a loud voice the cook declared, "Grab the scissors, and follow me, please. I think the egg salad could use some herbs." Once in the small greenhouse adjacent to the kitchen, Mrs. Simonsen shut the door and said, "Now tell me, what is going on?" She took the scissors from Gudrun and began cutting parsley.

Fighting tears, Gudrun informed the cook of Trygg's death and the possible loss of her home, but sharing the recent encounter with Master Iversen caused her to sob. "I'm so scared."

"Now there." Mrs. Simonsen put her arm around Gudrun. "Who has control of your life?...Are you forgetting to take all this to the Lord?"

Blowing her nose, Gudrun said, "You are right. Thank you."

"I will be praying for your future," Mrs. Simonsen said.

૭౿

"Abby can finish those dishes and help with the dinner preparation," Mrs. Simonsen said. "Now you get yourself upstairs."

"Thank you," Gudrun replied. "I am looking forward to this. Seeing all the beautiful outfits will be a good distraction."

Mrs. Simonsen shook her head. "Not my idea of fun. Lifting heavy woolen garments and coats. Now scoot."

Smiling at Mrs. Olsen on the landing on the servants' stairs, and receiving a blank stare in return, Gudrun wondered, *is she alright?*

Karoline had already unlocked the off-season storage door and turned on the gas lamps, when Gudrun arrived. Walking in Gudrun gasped. "This is a warehouse."

"It is a bit overwhelming. This section is mine." Karoline pointed to rows and rows of rolling clothes racks. "And the back corner is my husband's. There are still some of the late Mrs. Iversen's clothes in that corner. I have not decided what to do with them. Grab those empty racks for me." The young mistress pulled ribbons out of her pocket tying them around hangers. She gave Gudrun a look of dismay, then kept tying ribbons as she talked. "I thought this would be fun, you and I going through the clothes together. But I have a bookkeeping project that is urgent. So the yellow-tagged clothes go in my wardrobes. Put the blue ribbon ones aside in my dressing room, folded nicely. I already pulled the summer clothes out of my wardrobes in my dressing room. There are piles labeled, cleaners, off-season storage, give away, and a few with blue ribbons to go with these. Have I made myself clear?"

Gudrun nodded. "Yes, ma'am, you have."

What about my cabin? Gudrun thought as Karoline hurried off.

Mrs. Simonsen is right. Lifting these outfits from rack to rack is hard work.

An hour and a half later after numerous trips with the rolling racks between the off-season storage room and the dressing room, Gudrun sunk into the chair when Mistress Iversen brought in tea.

Putting the tray down and looking around the room, Karoline said, "You have made fast work! I am impressed. I thought this would be a three-day project. It seems you will make it to the cleaners and Salvation Army tomorrow afternoon." Karoline poured Gudrun a cup of tea.

"Yes, ma'am. I am sorry about this morning calling you by your first name in front of your husband. I did not see him," Gudrun apologized.

"Please do not worry. If he heard he did not care. He and I have bigger problems to solve these days. I have been helping him with a bookkeeping problem. He needs my results by this evening."

Gudrun could not hide her relief, letting out a sigh.

"We did have a chance to discuss your living situation. How would you like to live here in the servants' quarters? No more rowing back and forth."

Staring at her mistress, her eyes wide, Gudrun could not find words. Finally she stammered, "it...it would be...it would be...perfect. Thank you..." Taking her handkerchief out she dabbed her eyes. "So your husband knows about my cabin?"

"No. l made my case on how much I depend on you, the bad winter conditions for rowing, the fact your father is no longer here to bring you in his boat. My husband readily agreed that it is too dangerous for you. He is requiring me to lower your wage a little since you will have a free room and food. I am sorry."

"Don't worry about the money. This is a huge answer to prayer. I am so grateful."

"After tomorrow I should have time to properly look at your paperwork on the cabin. In the meantime pack up what you want to keep and make plans to move this Monday. I guess you will need someone with a larger boat."

Gudrun nodded. "I know someone who can help me, my father's fishing chum, Per. Thank you again for this gift."

ᘒ

It had taken days of planning and then days of waiting for a clear sunny day, but here they were, all bundled up in Rolf's carriage on the way to the Baroniet Rosendal. Hans reflected on how the preparation and planning had taken longer than the event itself would take. So many details; getting permission from the doctor, how to keep Mother warm, contacting the caretaker at the old manor house for permission to eat lunch there, invitations, food preparation and transporting everything plus the people. It had taken all four siblings working together to make this day happen.

At first there had been a disagreement about the wisdom of the excursion, but Sissel and Hans had finally won Sigrid and Rolf over.

Last night he lost his temper when his sisters kept talking about Jesus. *Why do they have to ask if I want to believe? They know the answer. I need to keep the peace for Mother's sake. Now we are finally underway.*

Glancing at his mother bundled in layers of blankets and reindeer skins, her smile met his. *We are creating a lifetime memory. One I will always remember. This is a celebration of her life.*

"The Lord is definitely blessing us with great weather. Oh, there are the stables," Mrs. Torvik said.

"Look, Mother. How beautiful the trees are with the morning frost." Sissel motioned to the tree-lined road, which provided a grand entry to the manor house. "Now we need to be quiet so that you can hear the waterfall."

Rolf stopped the horses near the manor for a moment to enjoy the symphony of Hattebergfossen waterfall. As they drove past the manor house, Hans reminded his mother. "We planned enough time to go up to the road to your favorite viewpoint. We won't stay long, just long enough to enjoy the view." Hans carefully laid another reindeer skin over the others and Sigrid placed an extra scarf over her head.

At the viewpoint Hans noted the excitement in his mother's eyes. *This is worth the risk. She is happy.*

"Now home we go?" The matriarch asked.

Sigrid leaned in. "No Mother, we are stopping at the manor for lunch, remember?"

Rolf's teenage son, Vetle, met them at the manor entrance with Mrs. Hague's wheelchair. Once inside, extended family members and a few of her friends surprised her. Her delight reassured the four siblings, this had been the right decision. She praised the neighbor ladies for the beautiful table settings. The luncheon only lasted an hour as their matriarch tired easily and needed to return home.

Slowing the team of horses, Rolf prepared for the turn from the lane onto the main road along the fjord. "Doing alright back there?" he asked.

"Better than alright," Mrs. Torvik replied. "All my children and grandchildren together, along with friends. Having a perfect lunch at the Manor house. This has been a day of God's provision. I could not be happier. Thank you all."

"It has been special, Mom." Sigrid gave her mother a hug.

It has been special, Hans thought. He noticed how pale and tired his mother looked.

Looking down the main road as the carriage made the turn, Hans saw an object coming toward them at a high speed. "Watch out Rolf! A car!"

Whizzing past them at a terrific speed the new contraption barely missed the carriage. A loud blast of the horn and an explosion out of the back tailpipe scared the horses and they took off at a full gallop.

Hans threw his arms around his mother, drawing her close along with the many blankets and skins.

"Whoa, whoa!" Rolf yelled, pulling on the reins.

Taking the turn into town at high speed the carriage lurched around the curve, jostling everyone off their seats. Hans held his mother tighter, making sure she did not hit against the back of the carriage.

Gaining speed, the horses quickly galloped through the three blocks of the town refusing to slow down for the next turn. A large hay mound loomed directly in front of them.

"Jump for it!" Rolf yelled, as they entered the curve. "Now!"

Sissel, Sigrid, and Rolf all jumped into the hay, but Hans could not lift his mother in time. Instead he held her tight covering her head with a blanket, as the carriage flipped over, missing the hay and sliding down a hill.

༄

Tying down her skiff, Gudrun continued her prayer of thanksgiving to the Lord. *And you have given me a place to live. You have answered my prayer in the most unbelievable way. How can I ever thank you enough, Lord? Only a few more days of rowing.* She looked out to the mouth of the harbor toward her island. *It means saying goodbye to my home. Please give me wisdom and strength."*

Letting out a big sigh, Gudrun turned and walked up the hill to the grand house. She opened the servants' door to find Mrs. Simonsen sitting on the entry bench, her finger to her lips.

Gudrun caught the door, closing it quietly as loud voices echoed from the kitchen. She sat down next to Mrs. Simonsen and whispered, "What is going on?"

While the cook scribbled in her kitchen notebook, Gudrun focused in on the voices. *Mrs. Olsen? And who is the man?*

Mrs. Simonsen passed her notebook to Gudrun. The note read – Mr. Iversen just fired Mrs. Olsen. She is refusing to leave.

The master's voice took on a deeper tone. "You will leave on your own this morning or I will call the police."

"You have no proof. I have rights." Mrs. Olsen retaliated. It sounded like something slapped against the kitchen counter. Gudrun jumped, Mrs. Simonsen shook her head at Gudrun, putting her finger to her lips again.

"This, this document is proof. My wife has been suspicious ever since I asked her to take over the books a few months ago. This could put you in jail. We have more than enough proof. You pack your things and leave without references or I will call the police. It is your choice."

Motioning to the servants' door, Mrs. Simonsen grabbed her coat off the hook. Gudrun carefully opened the door and they both quietly crept outside.

"Oh my!" Mrs. Simonsen blurted out. "What a shock."

Nodding in agreement, Gudrun stood there in disbelief. "Stealing? How?"

"Until a few months ago I gave my budget, receipts, all my accounts to Mrs. Olsen and she handled all the bookkeeping. Then the mistress wanted me to give it all to her. I have been wondering why the mistress kept asking me if certain amounts were correct. Maybe Mrs. Olsen padded the books?"

୭

"Such beautiful work, Mr. Bisset. Especially the blue one," Gudrun said running her hand lightly over the embroidery along the edge of the collar. "Mistress Iverson will be very happy."

"Thank you, Miss Sagen," the tailor replied. "Do you have time to do some piecemeal work for me? The dress shop in Kristiansand wants more of my dresses and I am short on time. You could do the collars for me. Your work is the best in town."

Gudrun smiled as she laid the dresses carefully in the canvas dress bag. Oh her mother would have been so proud. "Perhaps. One or two small projects a week?"

"That would help. I need the work from Kristiansand. As you know there is no longer enough business here for me to survive."

"Let me ask my mistress for permission. I usually have my evenings free." Gudrun left the shop thanking the Lord for the opportunity. It would be nice to save a little bit of money.

Sitting down on a bench in front of the church, Gudrun began to pray, thanking the Lord for taking care of her. *A place to live and now possibly extra work? I will have time in the evenings since I will not be rowing to the island.* She leaned back against the church wall and closed her eyes for a moment, letting the early afternoon sun warm her face. She could hear women's voices in the church basement hall. *Oh yes, the Ladies Missionary Society. I wonder what project they are working on now? A quilt or food baskets for the less fortunate?* Gudrun checked a thought of resentment. She had not received anything when her father died. Why would she, when Mrs. Thorsen ran the committee with an iron fist?

The high-pitched screechy voice of Mrs. Thorsen broke into her thoughts. "The rumor is that she will be living at the Grand House! What are the Iversons thinking of, letting a harlot live in their home?"

Gudrun put her ear in closer to the basement window straining to hear a reply from another woman, but the lady spoke too softly.

"Compassion? Forgiveness? I say she got that when she was not kicked out of town! That tramp has more than enough forgiveness when she comes through these doors on Sunday. Kissing a married man. You know I have made it my mission to warn every eligible young man to stay away from her," Mrs. Thorsen screeched.

Through the thick wall Gudrun could hear a chorus of "Amen."

Red-faced, Gudrun fumbled for the canvas dress bag and her errand bag. *I will never be accepted in this town!*

CHAPTER 5

Dreaming

Morning sunshine made the Yamaguchi house gleam like a jewel. Arvik pulled Surefoot to a stop for a moment, enjoying the peaceful October scene. Light shimmering off the water gave the Japanese style house the perfect backdrop. Beautiful yellow roses welcomed friends and strangers to the cozy front porch. The smell of grilled salmon and rice floated toward him.

This is it....This is what I want. What the Yamaguchis have. They are a team, there for each other. Arvik recalled how Zhou would respectfully speak of his wife. No derogatory remarks about her as he often had heard from other men speaking about their wives on construction sites. Now with the progress that had been made on his home maybe his dream seemed possible.

"Aik, Aik. Come. Tea." Mrs. Yamaguchi's voice interrupted his thoughts.

Arvik waved to her on the front porch, dismounted Surefoot and tied him to the horse railing. Far enough away from her yellow roses.

"Zhou, shop, get." She pointed to Zhou's shop. The face she made told Arvik how hard she was struggling for words. He also knew at this early hour she meant breakfast not just tea.

"l understand. I will get Zhou for breakfast."

Mrs. Yamaguchi nodded and smiled.

In the shop? How did he get there? Opening the shop door, Arvik had his answer. There sat Zhou in a custom wheelchair, working on a lathe at his workbench. Noticing the wheelchair's large wheels, and the extension of the high seat for Zhou's leg to rest on, Arvik had to wonder where Zhou got such a contraption. He stood and watched his friend work for a moment. *The rhythm, the expertise, such a talented man. Must be stiles for a staircase he is working on...there are so many of them.*

Zhou broke into a smile when he saw Arvik. "My friend. Welcome." He stopped pumping the machine with his good leg. "Come sit."

"Not now. I have orders from wife to bring you for breakfast. Are you at a good stop point?"

"Yes. You push me?"

Not only did the breakfast include rice and grilled salmon, but also miso soup and a few other interesting dishes that Arvik did not dare try. He did not want to insult his gracious hostess if he did not like them.

"Please tell your wife this is delicious," Arvik said.

"You understand, Nana?"

Mrs. Yamaguchi smiled and nodded.

"Like you and me she understand more than she speak. How is house?" Zhou asked.

"We are almost closed in for winter. Roof on, no gutters yet. All windows in except bay windows. Thank you for telling George and Albert I need help."

Zhou shrugged his shoulders, "You help us, we help you."

Arvik continued, "It seems like the whole island come to help. Wives are... bring food for lunch...enough to eat leftovers for dinner. Men I never meet come help for four hours or more. Yesterday I let most men know I do not need more help. George and Albert will help me put bay windows in next weekend.

Where did you get wheel chair? Did the doctors say you can work?"

"The owner of the house we worked come here. He had chair made for me. He asked for me to do millwork. Things I do sitting down. Dr. Agnes say me good to work."

"I hear you were doing millwork, but I could not believe. The accident only five weeks ago. How you do the long pieces?"

Zhou reached over and patted his wife's hand. "Nana help me. I not make crown or stair rail yet. I need to be stronger. Next week maybe." He patted his wife's hand again. "Nana big help."

Arvik smiled. Not wanting to break the peaceful scene he sipped his tea and finally asked, "Later on you do millwork for me? I will pay you well."

"Yes, I do work, we see about pay."

"Anything you need in Seattle? I go next week. Getting hardware, some lighting, things I cannot make, and stock up for winter with Norsk food."

Zhou laughed. "We fine. We let you know." He waved his finger. "No Norsk food." He laughed again.

∞

Looking out her new window to the garden, Gudrun whispered, "no more rowing, no more cabin...no more water view." Tears formed and she caught them with her handkerchief. Sitting down in the lounge chair she reflected on the range of emotions she had experienced the past week. Happiness, gratefulness, fear, sadness, all interwoven as she moved out of her cottage into the Grand House.

"Yes, Lord, I am grateful for your provision of this place, I am so thankful I will not have to row across Tingsakerfjorden this winter, however, as you know I will miss my home. I miss Trygg, and especially my parents. Thank you for providing a lovely place for me to live. Please help Karoline and I know what to do about the cabin." Her trip to work now meant walking down the hall to the kitchen.

Looking around the sitting room, Gudrun felt like pinching herself. Last summer she had hoped for one of the small maids' bedrooms with a shared bath down the hall. God had provided abundantly. Once Mrs. Olsen had left, Mistress Iversen had the maids give the set of rooms a good cleaning, she had the walls painted, and assigned the apartment to Gudrun. It had a sitting room with a view of the garden and a small bedroom with its own bathroom. She and Mr. Smith, the butler, were the only staff left living at the house. For budget reasons the live-in staff had been phased out and part-time maids and kitchen staff lived in their own homes.

Gudrun continued praying, "Thank you Lord that Per and the rest of my father's fishermen friends helped me move out of the cabin and that I was able to bring a few pieces of furniture."

Most of the furniture in the cabin did not merit saving, but she did save her parents' bed frame along with the old dining table. Those had been her grandparents; and of course she brought the trunk, which held her few belongings. The round table comfortably sat six when the sides were up, and the history behind it made her cherish it. "Maybe someday, if I ever get married, my family will sit around this table. You know my future, Lord." For now the table sat against the wall under the window, with one side down, giving her the option to use it for a desk or a place to eat. Her Bible sat in the middle of the table.

"Knock, knock," sang out Mrs. Simonsen.

Gudrun quickly opened the door wide. "Welcome. Are you going home this late? You know I can finish up on late nights now and let you go home early."

"How sweet of you, no need for you to work extra hours. My man has to work late, too." Mrs. Simonsen's husband's grocery store also required long hours. "Looks like you have settled in nicely."

"It is quite comfortable. Would you like a cup of tea?" Gudrun nodded at the kettle simmering on the small cast iron stove.

"No, thank you." The cook tilted her head and gave Gudrun a sheepish smile. "I really want to see your new clothes, if I may?"

Giggling like a schoolgirl, Gudrun led Mrs. Simonsen to her wardrobe. "I have a wardrobe!" she said as she opened the cabinet door.

"Indeed you do! Look at these dresses. So wonderful of the mistress to give you these and that you are close to the same size. Looks like you have four very suitable work dresses and five more you can wear to church. All fancy you are!"

"Yes. All fancy. I threw out my two old dresses. Now I will look the part of a proper dresser. I am making a new apron to use in the kitchen, and she gave me a beautiful coat." Gudrun led Mrs. Simonsen back into the sitting room showing her the coat on a hook. "Look at the soft nap on this wool. So thick...I think they call it camel hair. Such a generous lady." Gudrun recalled her feeling of elation when the mistress announced that the blue-ribbon folded dresses and coat were to be hers!

"And here is my apron project."

The cook scrutinized the apron for a second. "Beautiful work. All by hand...do you know how to use a sewing machine?"

"No. I have noticed one at Mr. Bisset's."

"Mrs. Olsen had one. You should ask the mistress what happened to it. It would fit nicely in here. So you have never had a wardrobe?"

Gudrun blushed. "We had a small cabin. I slept in a loft with hooks for the few clothes I had. I have never had a real bedroom before. God has been so good in giving me all of this. Best of all I have you as a friend."

The plump cook shook her head. "Now don't make me cry."

&

Gliding through the glassy sea *Marianne* seemed at peace. Her bow dancing over the softly undulating swells as if she were performing for a large audience. The sun warmed Captain Hans' face as he stood at the outside helm. *This must be heaven. No land in sight, just the sea and my best girl, Marianne. Marianne the lady who never disappointed me...but I, I deserted...*

"Hans, Hans, wake up."

Sissel? Sissel? How did she get on board, where is she? It is her voice...

"Hans, Hans, wake up. Wake up!" Sissel gently squeezed his shoulder.

If I roll to my side I will see her? Shearing pain shot through Hans as he tried to roll over. The loud moan from his own lips jarred him awake. His hand went to his side. Large cloth wrapping encased his torso. The accident! Opening his eyes Hans asked, "Sissel? Are you OK?"

"Yes. Do you not remember? The carriage rolled over. Rolf, Sigrid and I only have minor scrapes. You have the worst injuries. You saved mother's life."

Hans sighed. "She is alive?" He closed his eyes. Everything seemed foggy and heavy.

Sissel nodded. "She is doing well, considering. I think all the blankets helped protect her. Only a few bad scrapes and bruises. She has a slight concussion, but she is recovering from that quickly. You will take time to heal. You have three broken ribs, a nasty cut on your forehead and your left arm is broken."

"I'm so tired...that darn car..."

Sissel patted his hand. "It is the medication the doctor gave you. You rest. Mother will come to your room later."

"Marianne, Marianne..." the captain whispered.

৶

Sliding into the public slip at Eastsound, Arvik timed his jump onto the dock just right, grabbing the line and tying down his boat in one fluid motion. Glancing up to the shore he saw Albert with Surefoot and his wagon stacked full of boxes. *All according to plan. I hope Albert listened to what I said and did not hit too many ruts on the way from the farm. I can't sell bruised apples.*

Mrs. Yamaguchi had picked and carefully packaged each apple in his orchard so they could survive the boat trip unscathed. Arvik had provided the packaging and wooden boxes. In return Arvik had promised her half of the profit. Early this morning, he had broken anchor and sailed his forty-five-foot sailboat, *Himmel,* around Orcas and up East Sound to the town of Eastsound.

Arvik hoisted the last wooden box onto his shoulder and carried it down the dock to his boat. Albert laid his box next to the boat.

"How long did you say you would be in Seattle?" Albert asked.

"Not more than a week. It depends on the sailing conditions. It is nice for late October. If we get storm..." Arvik frowned and shook his head.

Albert smiled. "I understand you might have to hunker down for a few days. Your English is getting so much better. It takes time."

"Thank you for taking care of Surefoot, and staying at the house, Albert. I appreciate it," Arvik said.

"I appreciate the place to stay and the work. I should have the rest of the walls framed in upstairs by the time you return." The young man shook Arvik's hand and headed up the dock to the wagon.

The owner of the big house had hired Albert and his father only for framing and had recently brought in a team of finish carpenters. A week ago, George returned to Seattle to work and be with his wife, but Albert liked the island life and wanted to stay on. Arvik enjoyed the company, especially the free English lessons from Albert as they worked together. New words like 'appreciate' were now part of his vocabulary. Words seemed to flow better, but there were still times he got stuck.

Heading out of the harbor Arvik felt like singing. *A joyous occasion, going to Seattle to mail my letters to Norway to find a bride.* As *Himmel* sailed out of East Sound into Lopez Sound, the mainsail caught a good wind. Arvik played with it a bit before tying down the mainsheet to enjoy the sun sparkling off the water, the white billowy clouds dancing across the blue sky. "This is heaven. That is why I named you that, my girl," Arvik sang out and patted the helm.

It will be so good to see the Lundes again. Speak my own dialect, eat good Norsk food, with people that share the same customs. Arvik thought about his good friends from home, Anna, the personification of the perfect Norse woman and Nils his buddy since grammar school. He anticipated the good sleep he would be getting in their guest room. He could not forget to find out where they bought the mattress. He would need several of those next spring. Only the best for his wife. He went below and checked his cargo.

After clearing Thatcher Pass he turned south in Rosario Strait. With this good weather and the decent wind he would be making it into Kingston by nightfall. If there were bad currents off Point No Point he might be slowed down. He might be forced to come in after sunset.

The letters. Are they good enough? Will a lady want to come to America to be my wife? Will the exterior sketch of the house, the floor plan, the map of Seattle and the San Juan Islands, the offer of a return ticket to Norway and a separate bedroom make her feel secure enough to say yes? Should I ask Anna to help me with it? She will know if anything is improper. Should I pray about it? What will she look like? Perhaps I cannot expect too much in looks or she would already be married.

CHAPTER 6

Plans

Waiting in the parlor of the Grand House, Gudrun paced the floor. She stopped in front of the mirror and ran her hands over her hair to smooth down her curls. She pinched her pale cheeks to give herself a bit of color. Taking her handkerchief out of her best dress she started to pace the floor again. Stopping at the window she watched the snowflakes coming down. *Thank you, Lord, for this place to live. Here it is late October and things have gotten so cold. You have provided. Please Lord, please work out all the details for this meeting.*

Karoline walked into the room and over to Gudrun putting her hand on her shoulder. "We shall pray." She bowed her head.

"Thank you, Lord for Karoline's help. You know I would be lost without her," Gudrun prayed.

"Please give us wisdom and discernment," Karoline continued, "We ask —"

Mr. Smith cleared his throat in the doorway and announced, "Mr. Thorsen, ma'am."

The short, dark-haired man nodded toward the ladies as he entered the room. "Good morning. Will Mr. Iversen be joining us this morning?" he asked.

"No. He has business in Grimstad today. Besides I am the one who has been advising Miss Sagen on the matter."

Gudrun noticed the surprise on Mr. Thorsen's face.

Walking toward the game table near the window, Karoline said, "Please sit Mr. Thorsen; we have all of Miss Sagen's papers regarding the cabin right here."

Glancing at the deed on top of the pile, Gudrun felt her stomach churn. *My family's home, Lord please help me through this.* A week ago Karoline had confirmed her worst fears, her debt on the cabin was almost more than it's value. Such an amount she could never hope to pay. Plus with almost eight months of missed payments the cabin belonged to the bank according to the loan papers.

"I am glad you ladies called this meeting," the banker said. "I have been hesitant to address this delicate issue. Miss Sagen, I would like to again express my condolences on the loss of your father. He was a true gentleman whom I admired."

"Thank you, sir," Gudrun said.

"When your father approached me about another loan on the cabin so he could pay for boat repairs I knew I should have refused him. He already owed so much on the cabin, but I could not turn him down. He made me promise not to tell you or anyone else. Just before he died he claimed he would be making a big catch and make up all the payments...when he died I did not have the heart to approach you with the issue."

Karoline said, "We are so grateful for your generosity."

"Our Lord showed kindness and grace to others when He lived here on earth and when I can, I try to follow His example," Mr. Thorsen replied. He turned to Gudrun. "I assume you do not have the money to make the back payments."

He is the opposite of his wife, Gudrun thought. She paused for a moment. "No sir, I do not. I know you have been more than gracious to let this go so long. I understand that action must be taken. I cleaned everything out of the cabin a week ago and locked it up. Here is the key."

"Thank you. I see you have the deed. Please hold on to that for a day or so. We must do an assessment and there will be paperwork to be signed before the bank will officially take possession. I will get back to you as soon as possible. Oh, and by the way no one knows about this yet, not even my wife. I will be discreet."

The young women thanked him and Karoline showed him to the door.

∽

"So it is final then," Karoline said.

"Yes, I gave Mr. Thorsen the deed and I signed the papers. He had copies for me. I made sure one of the pages absolved me from all debt like you told me. Do you want to take a look at them?" Gudrun asked. She finished buttoning the last of the thirty quarter-inch diameter buttons on the back of Karoline's dress. The middle two buttons were the hardest and she could not help but notice that the dress seemed tighter than the last time Karoline wore it.

Karoline nodded. "Yes. How are you feeling about it?"

Gudrun went over to the dressing table and picked up a necklace. "I feel sad, relieved, and grateful. A part of my family's history has ended. But I have no more debt and for that I am grateful. Mr. Thorsen has been so nice." She put the necklace on her mistress. "Thank you for all that you have done for me."

Grabbing Gudrun's hands Karoline said, "It is the least I could do. You have been the best dresser. Your sewing is exquisite and you have such good taste. And best of all you are my friend." Her hand went to her belly. "I have a secret. Promise you will keep it if I tell you?"

Gudrun's eyes widened as she nodded.

"I am pregnant," Karoline whispered.

"Pregnant? But I thought you had separated bedrooms... that the marriage was not for love?" Gudrun could not hide her confusion. Should she be happy or sad?

Karoline's eyes had a twinkle in them. "Let's just say things have changed in that department. We got to know each other better when I took over the bookkeeping last summer. We worked as a team when I became suspicious of Mrs. Olsen's embezzlement."

"Then congratulations. When will the little one be joining us?"

"May."

℘

Anna's laughter resounded through the dining room making Arvik blush. "Oh, I am sorry, Arvik. Now I have embarrassed you...but the idea brings comical images to mind. I see rough signs on the top of Trollstigen or Geiranger or on Bergen's wharf saying 'Wife wanted' in red paint." She winked at Arvik and laughed again.

"Be nice, my dear, this is a sensitive subject for our dear friend. You can't blame him for wanting a wife," Nils gently scolded.

Arvik could not help but smile. Anna's version did seem a bit ridiculous. "You are funny. That is not how I plan to go about it."

"Go on, we are listening," Anna said.

"I have written several letters. One to our friend in Stavanger, Oskar Nilsen, one to my cousin near Bergen, and another to my second cousin in Molde. I am asking them to recommend me to suitable single women. I have sketches and floor plans for the house. I am offering passage here and back home again in case she changes her mind once she sees me." Arvik paused and blushed again. "I have explained the marriage will be one of convenience. The lady will have her own bedroom and bath. I only require housekeeping, most meals made, and conversation."

With a serious face, Anna replied, "That is a generous marriage offer. Better than many women receive. And no woman in her right mind would turn you down based on your looks."

"Now, now, are you reconsidering your current situation my dear?" Nils winked at his wife and chuckled.

Rolling her eyes at her husband, Anna asked Arvik, "Do you want me to review your letter?"

"Yes, please," Arvik said. He blushed again, "It needs to be proper but clear I will not require physical intimacy."

"Understood. You need a photo of yourself. I know just the place. We can go there tomorrow," Anna said.

Arvik smiled and shook his head. "Maybe. I must meet with Mr. Gibson at the market about my apples. I have saved the best box for you."

"Thank you," Nils said. "When do you expect to have the house done?"

"I am not sure, maybe by June or July. I would not want the lady to come until it is done. I need your advice on the best way for her to travel. Coming into New York would mean coming across the country on a train by herself. If she does not know English, that could be dangerous. I have read that the Panama Canal might open next spring or summer. Perhaps it would be best for her to come by ship where a Norwegian captain could look out for her."

Anna placed her fork upside down on her dinner plate and rang a small bell. A young lady appeared. "Emily, thank you for the delicious meal. We would like dessert now. Once you serve it you are free for the night. I will take care of the dishes." She turned toward Arvik. "Maybe you are getting ahead of yourself, Arvik. Find the lady first. Then work out how she travels."

"I know she will not be taking the trolley to a hotel when she arrives here in Seattle. Not suitable. I will hire a car."

"Why would she stay in a hotel?" Nils asked.

"It seems it would be best if we stayed in Seattle for a week in separate rooms so we can get to know each other. She could back out of the agreement and return home at the end of the week if she wants. Leaving from Seattle is easier than from Orcas."

"She will stay here and so will you. We have lots of space and we will chaperone." Anna winked at her husband. "Right, Nils? You will protect Arvik from any gold-digger?"

Arvik laughed. "I am fine if she marries me for my money, the little I have, because I am marrying her for her cooking and conversation."

"Have you considered God's plan for your life, my dear friend? Oh I am not doubting the Lord would like you to be married. God created the institution. But have you prayed about His timing?" Nils asked.

Concentrating on his cherry pie, Arvik took his time answering. "You bring up a good point, Nils. Now I heard on the trolley on my way here that they are building a Ford Motor Assembly Plant down on Fairview Avenue. Sounds like cars are here to stay."

Nils nodded. "Oh yes. The architect, John Graham designed it. They hope to open in February. Back to the subject of your wife...there are eligible Norwegian women here in Seattle. There are several nice young ladies that attend Denny

Park Lutheran Church. We can introduce you on Sunday. You are staying through Sunday?"

"Yes. As to my wife, she must come from Norge."

༄

A twinge of pain shot through Hans' torso as he settled into the dining room table.

"Still hurting, Uncle Hans?" Vetle asked as he slid into his seat at the table.

"Yes." Hans opened his copy of *Moby Dick*. "Remember where we left off yesterday? You tell me what happened." The sea captain listened and nodded as his nephew recounted what he had read the day before. "Very good. Your understanding of English is improving. Let's start here. If you do not understand the meaning of a word, ask."

"Have you ever seen a whale, Uncle Hans?"

The captain smiled. "Yes. Several times."

"What was it like? Where?"

"The most stunning were the gray whales off the coast of California —"

"California! You have been there?" the sixteen-year-old asked.

Hans laughed but stopped, the pain from his ribs not letting him enjoy the moment. "Yes, I sailed to California when I was not much older than you. Early February we landed in San Diego and laid over for a few days. That area has mild weather with warm breezes. From San Diego to Dana Head we followed pod after pod of grey whales heading north, pods of five to seven breaching and playing with each other. Dolphins followed along when the whales were not there. Dana Head had lots of harbor seals..."

Hans remembered the days of riding horses from the harbor to the mission. He enjoyed those wonderful playful days of respite after the long, dangerous journey around the Horn.

"Is that where you learned English?" Vetle asked.

"My English improved along the West coast of America and I learned some Spanish. The first mate on my first voyage to Africa thought I needed to learn English. Why are you learning English? Are you wanting to go to sea?"

The teenager looked past his uncle and out to the fjord beyond. "Maybe. I don't know. I feel restless, like I am being called to something, but I do not know what."

Nodding, Hans fixed his gaze on his nephew.

"My mother and father think I should be a pastor. I have no idea. It is confusing, so I am staying put. It seems like a good idea to be prepared by learning another language, staying fit mentally and physically. I do know the Lord will show me the way."

Hans winced. "We will get back to your English lesson."

The next hour seemed to fly by as they explored another chapter of *Moby Dick*. The lesson helped Hans ignore his pain. Their session ended when Vetle needed to go feed the cows and horses and make sure they were secure for the night.

Moving to a comfortable chair in the living room Hans lightly massaged his ribs with his right hand. The smell of fish cakes permeated the air. He could hear Sigrid working in the kitchen preparing middag, the late afternoon meal. Snow glistened and the water glimmered across the fjord to the islands as the sun lowered in the sky. The doctor had said it would be two more months before he would be completely healed. *Two more months! Can I handle it? At least it answers the question about being here for Christmas. My last Christmas with Mother.*

The sounds of a wheelchair interrupted his thoughts. Without turning he said, "Hello, Mother. Shall we enjoy the sunset together again?"

"Oh yes, dear. I was hoping you would be here. It is becoming a routine..." Mrs. Torvik's voice trailed off.

"Thank you, sis," Hans said to Sissel. "We can manage by ourselves."

Sissel set the brake and smiled at Hans. "I am counting on that. I am going to rest before Sigrid calls us to dinner."

"Did you sleep good?" Hans asked his mother.

"Yes, thank you. I have to rest up so I make it to Christmas in eight weeks."

Hans squeezed her hand. "According to the doctor you will. He's still in awe that you are still here."

"So am I. God is keeping me going."

CHAPTER 7

Rumblings

Mid-March 1914

"**W**ar!" Mrs. Simonsen declared. Slapping the newspaper down on the kitchen table. "That is all we need. One more thing to upset the apple cart."

Gudrun walked over and looked at the headline. "It says War Brewing. That does not mean war. Many of the articles say times are good in Europe. All the new inventions, the economy is good there...not like here. It is like the world has gone on ahead and forgotten about us here in this little corner of Norway. Do not worry, the war talk is just talk."

"I know but it starts with words. It is a coming. More changes."

"Yes, changes. She is still not eating?" Gudrun asked.

Mrs. Simonsen shook her head. "Poor dear, still not eating more than a bite or two. With the master gone off again to Grimstad — I only have the nurse, you, Mr. Smith, the day maid, and myself to cook for. What is to become of us?"

"The Lord has a plan, He will provide. Now stop your fretting. Anything for me to do?"

"You are right. I am sorry. Letting a bit of fear take over, yes?"

Gudrun agreed. She sipped her coffee and opened the paper. None of it was good news. She picked up an old copy of *Popular Mechanics* that Mr. Smith had been reading. She glanced at the date, a December copy. The cover portrayed a beautiful wooden sailing ship going aground on a sunny October day. A magnificent wooden vessel the kind of ship that had been built right here in Lillesand. She finished the article. "Did you read this?" Gudrun flipped the magazine around for Mrs. Simonsen to see.

"Yes, very interesting. The vessel was not worth anything with all the new steamships taking over, so there is suspicion they ran it aground to get the insurance money. What state? I cannot remember." Mrs. Simonsen started peeling potatoes.

"Oregon, the West coast of America. Oregon..." Gudrun mumbled, "Beautiful..." Remembering recent photos and sketches of Oregon and Washington she had seen at the local Bakeri.

"Now, now, daydreamer. We are here and there are a few things to do today. The nurse said the mistress would like to see you. More errands for you to run."

∽

"Ahhhh!" Gudrun yelled as she slipped and slid down the snow packed street to the village. She could feel herself falling backwards. Flinging her arms to keep her balance, her bag slid off her shoulder and onto the ground. She did circles with her arms and regained her balance for a second...then another patch of ice sent her sliding again. Her foot hit something hard. Suddenly she flew through the air but ended in a perfect belly flop in the middle of the street. She lay there for a moment trying to catch her breath. Then glanced around to see if anyone had witnessed her lack of gracefulness.

"Ma'am! Ma'am, your bag and letters," a young boy yelled from up the hill.

Slowly picking herself up, she brushed off her coat, "Thank you," she said as the boy reached her.

"Are you alright, Miss?" he asked as he handed her the bag and letters.

"I think so. It is dangerous out here with the ice hidden under the snow."

The young boy sympathized. "Yes. Maybe you should sit down and rest for a minute at the Bakeri?"

"I will after I get these letters to the Post. Thank you again for your help."

At a slow pace Gudrun proceeded to the post office. Once in the door she leaned up against the wall and counted the letters. *Only six? There were eight! My bag.* She opened her bag and to her relief, the missing two sat safely inside.

"Will these letters make the boat to Oslo?" Gudrun asked the postmaster.

The postmaster stamped the letters. "Yes. The boat is a bit late today. I have a large envelope for Mrs. Iversen. Will you take it to her, Miss Sagen?"

As she slid the envelope into her bag Gudrun noticed the return address — Mrs. A. Jakobsen. *Ah, Karoline's sister in Stavanger. That might lift the mistress' spirits.*

Selecting the most private table with a view of the harbor, Gudrun sat her coffee and vaffel with goat cheese on the table. Taking off her coat made her aware of twinges in her arms and torso. *I might be bruised. All this snow. When will it end?* It had been a rough winter, record snows and low temperatures had kept the whole household cooped up. The harbor had iced up for over two months. She could not see over the piles of snow from all the shoveling. There would have been no way she would have been able to get to work if she had lived on the island. She stirred her coffee, played with her vaffle and began to reflect on the changes in her life since Christmas.

The end of November Mr. Iversen announced that he had purchased several old buildings on the waterfront in Grimstad and planned to renovate them into a hotel. His research showed Norwegians from Oslo and other countries wanted to enjoy the warm summer weather. His son moved to Grimstad to oversee the construction and since the first of the year the master only came home for weekends. Karoline's pregnancy had been a difficult one. Her morning sickness kept her bedridden and had extended well into her third trimester. That meant very little work for Gudrun. Karoline dressed herself in loose gowns and robes that Gudrun picked up from the French tailor, Mr. Bisset.

Finishing her coffee, Gudrun grabbed her bag and hurried off to the tailors with new sketches from Karoline for new dresses. Dresses she would wear once the baby arrived. From the look of the sketches Karoline would not need a dresser. Instead she had Gudrun place an ad for a nanny at the Post. She had groceries to pick up for Mrs. Simonsen, and piecework from Mr. Bisset. He paid her a decent wage. She had been sewing neutral baby clothes on Mrs. Olsen's old sewing machine. It would be nice if they knew if it was a girl or a boy.

෴

Snap! Arvik's fishing line went limp, creating ripples across the still water. He pictured some fish enjoying the herring, which had been on his hook. "Again?" Arvik yelled, his breath showing in the mid-March air. He reeled in the remaining line, fumbled in his tackle box on the floor of his skiff and proceeded to hook and bait his line for the third time. *Tricky salmon today.*

Looking up at his home he let out a sigh. "Sure is a beauty if I say so myself. But still no lady to make it a home." The white paint gleamed in the early afternoon sun. The second story and living room tall bay windows gave the house elegance. He had captured the feeling of the house he had admired in Norway. He had gotten the proportions right. *My miniature mansion situated perfectly, just as peaceful and beautiful as the Yamaguchi home, far away from the hustle and bustle of humanity. Far from the rumors of war in Europe dominating the papers.*

By Thanksgiving he and Albert had all the interior walls framed and the plumbing done. Not only a competent carpenter, Albert kept up with Arvik's pace. Quickly picking up the basics of plumbing, Albert helped push the project ahead of schedule. To Arvik's dismay, Albert announced the week before Thanksgiving that he felt cooped up on the island, 'island fever,' and wanted to return to Seattle to be with his family.

Arvik had enjoyed Thanksgiving with the Yamaguchis. Zhou seemed almost healed, barely limping around his home and complimenting his wife on the fabulous feast. Though grateful for the good food and company, Arvik knew from his past experiences with other island residents that nothing Mrs. Yamaguchi prepared resembled a true American Thanksgiving.

Tube and knob electrical wiring got finished up in December and he even took a break to attend church one Sunday. On December 25th he paid extra to take a private passenger ferry to Seattle to celebrate Christmas with Anna and Nils. He had bemoaned his lack of response to the letters he had sent to Norge. Anna seemed sympathetic but insisted on introducing him to every single girl over the age of fifteen, at Denny Park Lutheran Church. None of them appealed to him; his lady would be coming from Norway.

In January, the heat ducts were installed and it took all of February to nail the lath and apply the plaster on the walls and ceilings of the house. Zhou spent several weeks helping him with the crown moldings, baseboards and finishing the staircase. One of the newel posts had a distinct Japanese flavor. A bit odd but he could not offend his friend. There seemed to be a good chance he would have the house presentable by the end of June.

A letter had arrived in early February from his second cousin in Molde. She had talked to every single lady she knew and none of them were willing to take the risk of coming to America. The sinking of the *SS Norway* in which 582 Norwegians died in 1904, and the 1911 sinking of the *Titanic* still remained fresh in their minds. Secondly, none of the ladies wanted to travel so far to marry a man whom they did not know. Her response discouraged him for a few days. However, he attended church the following Sunday with the hope that the Lord would answer his prayers.

Arvik let the fishing line fly and watched it break the surface of the water about thirty feet from his eight-foot tender. "Dear Lord, please answer my prayer. I want a w—"

Suddenly the bow of the tender jerked, almost knocking Arvik off his seat. The fishing pole bent toward the water, he could barely hold on. "Must be a big one!" Arvik yelled. The boat began to move away from the shoreline, picking up speed as he held onto the pole for dear life. Chills went down Arvik's spine as the fish surfaced for a second, then turned, almost overturning the boat. *A shark! A big one.*

Quickly Arvik let go of the pole allowing it to drop into the water. The shark surfaced again, making a sharp turn it headed straight toward the boat. Arvik grabbed the oars and started to row toward shore, the shark surged toward him, fishing pole in tow. He rammed the boat hard enough to put Arvik on the bottom of the boat. The oars broke loose from the oarlocks. He grabbed one oar just before it slid into the water but the second one disappeared. The gigantic shark surfaced a few feet from the boat — it's angry, evil eye focusing in on Arvik. Out of its bloody mouth hung the remnants of previous lines. A tip of the hook still attached to the fishing pole, poked through his jaw.

Grabbing the remaining oar, Arvik got on his knees and began to paddle to shore. *I must hold onto this. Please God, get me close to shore!* The white shark made another run for the boat. With his back close to the surface he looked about fourteen feet long. *A great white?* Arvik thought as he kept paddling frantically. *They rarely come into these waters.* Faint recollections of stories on the fishing boats he had worked on when he first came to the islands flashed through his mind. *It is possible. There are several accounts of them coming into the Salish Sea.*

The next hit by the shark almost overturned the boat. Arvik regained his balance and kept paddling. *No matter what — do not let go of the oar!*

Out of the corner of his eye, Arvik watched the shark circle around the boat. *Here he comes again!* Arvik put all his strength into each stroke. Coming straight at the boat the large fish dove as he approached the bow. A big bump followed by a ripping sound warned Arvik of incoming water. Immediately a fountain gushed from the bottom of the boat. Looking at the shore about eighty feet away Arvik knew he had to swim. He took off his coat.

In one fluid motion he stood up, jumped high, propelling his long body out over the water, the oar clenched close to his chest. As soon as he hit the icy water he started to kick while holding the oar tight. *Four minutes, I have four minutes.* Arvik knew he would not last long in such cold water. *Don't look, just swim! This is too slow. Too slow.*

Reluctantly Arvik stopped for a second and looked around. There — coming straight at him, the formidable great white. Grabbing the oar tighter, Arvik started to tread water, preparing to swing the oar, when his foot touched something. He could touch bottom! He took his stance, raised the oar high in the air and as the shark came close he landed blow after blow on the head and nose of the predator. The shark's blood ran into the water staining it crimson. The shark retreated. Arvik turned and using the oar to stabilize himself he scrambled to shore. He stood there shaking, looking out over the water, no boat, no fishing pole, no tackle box, no coat, only one oar...and his life. A hundred yards out he could see the surface churn, one very mad white shark going without dinner.

৩

War Brewing, the headlines on the front page of the Bergen paper shouted in large type. Captain Hans shook his head as he read the article. It seemed everyone was mad at everyone else. Tensions were high. *Not good for the steamship business. Norway should be alright as a neutral country,* he thought. *Who would have dreamed in 1905 when we finally gained our independence from Sweden and we were granted neutral status that it might come into play so soon.* He folded the paper, took one last sip of coffee, left money to cover his bill and headed down Bryggen gata toward Mr. Dahl's office.

He stopped to gaze at the ships across the harbor and the pleasure boats rocking in their slips directly below. *Such beautiful boats. That would be the life. A sail boat big enough to brave the sea but small enough for one to handle.* His eyes honed in on the fancy private ships. "Ahhh," he murmured as he read the name *SMY Hohenzollern. Kaiser Wilhelm II's boat! She is a beauty, all two hundred and eighty eight feet of her.* Hans knew the Kaiser loved to visit Norway, Bergen especially. For over twenty-two years the German King had vacationed along the western shores. *I am sure the Kaiser does not want war.*

Hans stopped his sightseeing and hurried off to Mr. Dahl's office.

"Hans, it is good to see you," the manager of the shipping-line said. "You look well. Are you completely healed?"

Han's shook his boss's hand. "Six months older and almost as good as new. Do you have a moment?"

"Yes, come, please sit." Mr. Dahl waved at the leather-bound chairs in front of the window overlooking the harbor.

"These are new...business must be good," Hans said.

"To be honest, recently it is a bit shaky with the talk coming out of Europe." Mr. Dahl settled into a chair and lit a pipe. "I wanted to extend my condolences, I heard about the passing of your mother. About a month ago, yes?"

Hans' eyes misted over and he paused. "Yes, thank you. It has been a long six months. We, my siblings and I have settled the estate this past week. That is why I wanted to come and talk to you."

"Wanting to become a farmer, Hans?"

Hans could not help but chuckle at the wry joke. "Never." Wagging his finger at Mr. Dahl, Hans continued, "And you know that. No. I am hoping you can put me back to work soon."

"Still holding out for a more exciting route than New York?"

"At this point I would be grateful to be at sea again. I will take anything you have."

Gazing out the window Mr. Dahl puffed on his pipe. "...
three weeks. In three weeks I will have something for you.
And there might be something more exciting than New York
coming up this summer. I cannot promise, but I will try."

CHAPTER 8

The Proposal

Stopping at the first landing of the servants' stairs, Gudrun ran her hand over the large envelope from Karoline's sister. *Perhaps this will cheer up the mistress. Please Lord, please let it be good news.*

Gudrun paused in Karoline's bedroom door. *She is sitting in a chair! She must be feeling better.*

Karoline turned, and said, "Good afternoon, Gudrun. How are you?"

"Very well, thank you. You look so much better than this morning. Is that little one treating you better?"

A smile spread across Karoline's pale face. "Yes, much better. I actually feel hungry. Would you be a dear and let Mrs. Simonsen know that I would like some tea and dry toast?"

Gudrun nodded. "Yes ma'am. Here is the mail. It looks like a letter from your sister. I will be back as soon as I can."

"She is eating," Gudrun sang out as she entered the kitchen. She helped Mrs. Simonsen fix the toast and the tray and carefully carried it upstairs. Placing everything on the end table next to Karoline, she sat down on the window seat across from her mistress.

Gudrun watched Karoline for a moment, her eyes carefully reading the pages in her hand, the opened large envelope still on her lap.

Looking up Karoline said, "This is interesting. You should read it."

Gudrun carefully read the introduction note from Karoline's sister while Karoline sipped her tea and tried a few bites of toast.

I think you should give this letter from Mr. Johansen to Miss Sagen. Mr. Johansen is a friend of Mr. Oskar Nilsen, an acquaintance of my husband's here in Stavanger. Mr. Johansen moved to America eleven years go and he is looking for a wife. It is a generous offer. The original mailing included a photo of him, which disappeared as it has been passed amongst several eligible single women here in town. The rumor has it that he is good-looking. A friend of mine says that she knows a couple in Seattle that know Mr. Johansen, so she has written to her friend, Anna Lunde to ask about him.

Karoline pulled out folded papers from the envelope. As she opened them Gudrun caught a glimpse of a sketch and she gasped.

"Such a beautiful house!" She whispered as she took the drawing from Karoline. "So beautiful and on the water in Washington State?" She continued to stare at the sketch as Karoline unfolded more pages.

"These are the floor plans. It is a big house. Look, the bedroom labeled Mistress has its own bath. Not as big, but fancier than my house. Oh, Gudrun what a wonderful place. You have to consider this offer." The pregnant mistress unfolded a letter, which she handed to Gudrun.

Reading two pages of a carefully written marriage proposal out loud to Karoline, Gudrun's hands began to shake. She finished reading and looked at her friend. "This is a gentleman's offer. If he is true to his word it is an offer to take seriously. But how do we find out if what he says is true?"

Taking the letter from Gudrun, Karoline read the proposal again. She passed it back to Gudrun. I will write my sister and tell her to let us know immediately what Anna has to say." Karoline paused for a minute. "I think it is worth praying about and considering. What do you think?"

"I know you cannot promise me a future here. You have been so kind and generous, but you need a nanny not a dresser. I can see in Mr. Bisset's fashion magazines from Paris that clothes are changing and you will not be requiring help."

"True. However, you are such a blessing to me. All the errands, helping out in the kitchen and wherever needed. I can find something for you to do for awhile." Karoline grabbed Gudrun's hands and looked her straight in the eye. "You, my friend should be married, not a servant all your life. You would make a great wife. You meet all of Mr. Johansen's qualifications. You are a good cook and baker, you sew, you know how to keep house." She let go of Gudrun's hands and leaned back in her chair with a sigh, her face looked pale.

Gudrun jumped to her feet. "You have done too much this afternoon, ma'am. Let me help you back to your bed. I will be praying about this and we can talk later. May I keep the letter and the drawings?"

"Yes, please. I will be praying for you." Karoline mumbled as she lay back on her pillow. "Stay with me until the baby comes, please."

"I will."

∽

Clang! Mrs. Simonsen dropped her glass measuring cup into the mixing bowl. "No. You would not!" she exclaimed. "Leave Norway?"

Gudrun hid a smile as the plump cook scrambled to clean up the flour that had landed all over the counter and even onto the kitchen floor. "Yes. I am considering it. What chance do I have here to be married? I have no future in this town."

"I understand leaving Lillesand, but stay in Norway."

"Where to? Oslo? Spend my life going from servant's job to servant's job? I would not make head cook like you. You have a husband," Gudrun replied.

"What about family?" Mrs. Simonsen asked. "You have to have aunts, uncles, cousins, someone, somewhere."

Running her finger through a patch of flour on the counter, Gudrun drew a flower, then lifted her head and in a steely voice said, "Not a single relative. My mother had a sister who died when she was twenty. Married but no children. My father was an only child. His parents had siblings but I have no idea who or where they are. I do not know my mother's maiden name. I never thought to ask. I have no reason to stay." She walked to the kitchen sink. Staring out the window she let tears run silently down her cheeks. *Though I love this town I have no future here. No reason to stay.*

ॐ

Tightening his tie Captain Hans recollected how he dreaded this part of the passage. Steamships created the first-class section and that required proper dining rooms and his presence at one of the tables. He hated how the elite prided themselves in being assigned to his table. He would rather eat with the people in third-class.

Invariably there was the annoying passenger. A lady with a voice like nails on a chalkboard, the young playboy trying to impress the ladies with his father's money, or a drunkard that never stops talking. Maybe this passage would be different, a group of interesting, well-behaved people.

Opening his cabin door he took a large breath of the salt air. *This is the life, the swells, the smell, the mist, the sea. Here it is the first week of April but I am finally back where I belong.*

Hans stopped in at the Bridge. The first mate, Mr. Anders Knobloch, came up and showed him the list of passengers that would be at his table.

"Mr. Pedersen will be happy to say the prayer tonight, sir," Anders said.

"Thank you. Please don't forget that I will be needed at the helm just before dessert is served. It is tiramisu tonight so don't leave me stranded."

The young first mate laughed. "I won't forget, sir."

Hans liked to have an excuse to leave the table especially on the night that the menu included tiramisu. He hated that dessert. He appreciated Mr. Knobloch finding out who would say grace at the table. As the captain he had the prerogative of saying grace himself or asking a willing party. He always chose the latter. What would he say to a god he did not believe in?

Walking into the dining room a few minutes late, he stopped in the doorway and surveyed the group at his table. It looked like a reasonable, pleasant bunch. *This might be a bearable passage after all. It is only for an hour or so each day. I can endure anything to be out on the water again.*

☙

Arvik sat down on the bench right outside the post office in Eastsound. *A letter from Anna? It is always Nils that writes. I hope everything is alright.* Turning the letter over he checked the postmark. April 2nd. *I need to come to town more often; it has been sitting here for four days.*

Opening the letter Arvik skimmed through it quickly. No bad news. A little bit of good news. Apparently a friend of Anna's in Stavanger had written asking her about the legitimacy of his marriage proposal.

"I wrote back and told her that you were a lazy, ugly, fat slob and that no woman in her right mind would marry you."

Arvik could not help but laugh at his friend's teasing but grateful to see that she had written a glowing report. She also explained that her friend wrote inquiring about him on behalf of a young woman who lived in Lillesand. He had heard about the tough times in that town. It had been such a hub of prosperity, the wooden shipbuilding capital of the country. Recently he had read an article that mentioned there were only two struggling shipbuilders left.

He sat there for a moment. Then went over and untied Surefoot. "We might have a lady of the house, old boy. I will have to get her a horse too. I suppose you want some pretty young mare."

CHAPTER 9

Decision Making

*E*yes shining bright, Gudrun smiled at Karoline and asked, "Shall I open it?"

"No. Take it downstairs, put it under your pillow and see what it says by osmosis." Karoline laughed at her own joke.

Her laughter made Gudrun smile. The past few weeks her mistress had gained physical strength, eating more, and even walking a bit. Karoline sat in her chair looking at Gudrun sitting on the window seat, enjoying the mid-April sunshine, playing with the envelope.

"Open it," Karoline demanded.

Staring at the return address one more time, Gudrun felt goosebumps on her arms. *Mrs. A. Jakobsen. A letter from Karoline's sister to me. A few months ago I would never have believed this possible,* Gudrun thought. Turning the envelope over, her hands shook as she slit it open with the letter opener. As she slid the letter out a small note fluttered to the floor. Picking it up, Gudrun began to read.

My Dear Gudrun,

This came from Anna Lunde in Seattle. A friend of my friend, Berit, and a friend of Mr. Johansen. She writes a glowing report of Mr. Johansen. She mentions his faults as well as his strengths. No husband is perfect. However I find life better because of my man. Who knows you might even find love.

Anna also mentions Mr. Johansen has spoken in the past that he hopes the lady that accepts his proposal will travel by boat to Seattle through the Panama Canal. If you do accept, and I suggest you do, and from what I read in the papers, passage would happen in July or August. We live a few miles from the steamship dock. You are welcome to come and stay with us before your passage.

I am praying that you will make the right decision.

Hilsen fra,

Marit Jakobsen

Passing the note to Karoline, Gudrun began reading the letter from Mrs. Lunde. Something in her words felt like a long lost friend writing from her heart. Warm, friendly sentences quieted Gudrun's soul. She gave not only a glowing report of her friend Arvik Johansen but also spoke of her prayers that God's will be done.

Happy tears formed in Gudrun's eyes as she finished the first page. She looked up and smiled at Karoline. "This is a woman who walks closely with the Lord. I feel like she is already my friend. I might be going to America."

A tear slid down Karoline's cheek. Smiling she said, "I am so happy for you Gudrun, but sad that I will be losing a friend. You will stay until the baby comes?"

Giving her friend an understanding look, Gudrun said, "I promise."

"What are Arvik's shortcomings?"

"Be patient. I have not read that far," Gudrun laughed.

Skimming over the next page, Gudrun read snippets out loud to Karoline. For the next twenty minutes the two friends giggled like schoolgirls, reading and rereading the three-page letter. Gudrun blushed as they reread the part about his looks. "He is tall and thin. A bit too thin, but some good cooking will solve that problem. His hair is golden like a wheat field and his eyes the bluest of blue."

"He has two shortcomings," Anna wrote, "Arvik can occasionally have a bit of a temper and though he claims to be a Christian he does not always attend church."

Hearing Anna's words aloud Gudrun grew solemn. "His not attending church bothers me. I think I could deal with the temper."

"My man can be curt with me at times, too," Karoline explained. "As Anna said no man is perfect. Marriage involves a lot of forgiveness and some compromise. I know you have been praying and will continue to do so. My advice is to walk through the door God has opened for you."

ᔕ

Wide-eyed, Mrs. Simonsen sipped her coffee while listening to Gudrun reading Anna's letter. "I cannot believe this." She shook her head. "You are seriously considering putting your life at risk just for a man? You young girls have stars in your eyes."

"Not for love, I cannot expect that. For a way of life. A better life. My own house to keep, not someone else's."

"What if you hit an iceberg? Or the ship sinks for another reason?" Mrs. Simonsen shook her head again and shuddered.

Gudrun tossed her long platinum hair over her shoulder, smiled at the cook, and sipped her coffee before answering. "I know how to swim. Besides, it is an open door. I have been praying a lot over the past three years about my future. Especially since February when it became evident my position here is not secure. I have been asking the Lord to guide me, so that

I might do His will. Before Anna's letter came I asked Him to show me the character of this man. The letter gave me peace. It seems like the right thing to do."

"The right thing...leaving your home..."

"What home? A servant's set of rooms, dependent on a job that is disappearing, no blood relatives. That is the negative side. The positive side here is two dear and precious friends, you and Karoline. I have not decided for sure. I am writing Anna directly, asking her to report to me about the condition of the house when she and Nils visit Arvik on the island the beginning of May."

A knock at the outside servant's door interrupted their conversation. Gudrun scurried off to the entry to answer it. "Per, what a surprise. Come in, how can I help you?" Gudrun asked.

The old fisherman stepped inside carrying a small cedar box. "Mr. Thorsen said I should bring this to you. I found it at your cabin. He hired me to clean out the place and fix it up a bit so the bank can sell the property."

Taking the box Per handed her Gudrun sat down on the entry bench and nodded to the chair across from her. "Please sit."

She fumbled with the box for a moment, trying to figure out how to open it.

"It slides, the top slides," Per said.

Quickly sliding the top back, Gudrun looked inside noting the silver cloth lined interior. She pulled out a beautiful woven scarf. "So blue...where did you find the box?"

"In the bedroom floor. Under the rug. I rolled up the rug and discovered lines in the floor. With a crowbar I lifted up the section of floor and found a cedar-lined two foot square space with this box inside."

Gudrun laid the scarf next to her on the bench, noticing three envelopes on top. "Letters." Scanning the addresses, she noted they were to her mother from a lady named Signe Hansen. Below the letters sat eight tiny silver teaspoons the handles decorated in the most intricate filigree. "Such beautiful dessert spoons."

"Mr. Thorsen said they were valuable. He wanted me to tell you no one else knows about them. He wanted you to have them."

A small leather book caught Gudrun's eye. She opened it and realized it was her mother's journal. Finally in the corner of the box lay a silver bracelet with a detailed pattern representing the Viking days. She picked it up. "This must have a lot of history."

"I am sure it has. Maybe the letters or the journal will explain. Now I must be going."

Putting the box on the bench, Gudrun stood up. "Thank you, Per. You have been such a dear friend, like the uncle I never had. Can you keep another secret?"

Per nodded.

"I might be going to America, to live in Washington State."

He stood there for a moment staring at her. Wiping his eye, Per gave her a hug. He whispered, "I wish you the best, my dear."

☙

Arvik sat down at the desk overlooking the water. *Will Miss Lillesand like this room? It seems like an ideal reading room or a study. I must finish the window seat and the shelves before Anna and Nils arrive. So much to do before Miss Lillesand arrives. I don't even know her name.*

It had been three weeks since he had heard anything from Anna and nothing at all from Lillesand. He stared at the blank paper. *What should I say? How can I convince her to come?*

Please Lord, I need your help. I do not want to look like a mouse hiding behind Anna's skirt. I am not going to allow Anna to decide my life. I need to show Miss Lillesand I am a man. You know I am not good with words. He stopped praying for a moment, staring at the water. *Please Lord, guide me,* he pleaded. He picked up the pen and began to write.

"Dear...dear what? To whom it may concern is too impersonal." Arvik could hear Zhou's words — write from your heart. "To the Lady from Lillesand," he wrote, and the words began to flow. "I have heard you are considering my proposal. Hopefully a summary of life on Orcas Island will help you make up your mind."

An hour later he saddled up Surefoot and rode into Eastsound to mail the finished letter. He had a week to get everything ready for the Lundes visit.

∾

Turning his carriage into the lane, Arvik watched Anna as they proceeded up the slight hill and his house came into view. Anna's hands went to her face, a quiet "Oh!" escaped her lips.

"Stop the carriage, Arvik. We want to take this in," Nils commanded.

"It is beautiful, Arvik. Just beautiful!" Anna exclaimed.

Beaming, Arvik replied, "Thank you. I hope Miss Lillesand will like it."

"Her name is Gudrun, Gudrun Sagen," Anna whispered, "If she does not like this house, she is crazy."

"Gudrun. A good solid name," Arvik murmured.

Nils put his hand on his friend's shoulder. "It is bringing back memories of home. I can picture that house near Uskedal, the house you use to sketch when we spent summer vacations at my parents' hytte on Hardangerfjord."

"Nothing escapes you, Nils. I still have those sketches. That house has been my inspiration." Arvik picked up the reins and snapped them. Surefoot responded and continued on to the house.

As he stopped Surefoot in front of the house, Arvik turned to Anna. "Tell me, what else do you know about Miss Sagen?"

"Not much. She knows how to keep house, she can cook and sew. Also that she has a strong faith. We can discuss that over dinner. Let me see the inside of your wonderful house." Anna accepted Nil's hand and hopped down from the carriage.

∼

"Are you going to have dark bookcases like these in your library?" Anna asked as she ran her hand over the detailing on the display shelves in the entry at Rosario. Arvik had obtained permission from the butler to show his friends the mansion.

Arvik shook his head. "No, I have a different detail in mind and we will not be using mahogany. It will be white oak instead. Zhou and I were working on setting the knives to mill it this past week. I didn't design the interior, here. I am just one of many carpenters that built it."

"You are being a bit modest. Mr. Moran just told us a few minutes ago how you were a major contributor." Nils contradicted his good friend, choosing to believe the owner. He knew how Arvik had always downplayed his accomplishments. "He explained how you played a big part in the public spaces."

Before Arvik could come up with an excuse, the butler led them into the formal dining room.

"Oh this view," Anna exclaimed. "It is almost as good as yours, Arvik."

"Thank you. I believe this is the end of the public tour," Arvik said.

A half hour later they sat down to dinner in the Eastsound Inn. Arvik asked if there were any specials and spoke with the waiter off and on as they ordered in English."

"My, how your English has improved, Mr. Johansen," Anna said.

"It is thanks to the Norwegian to English grammar school book you gave me last time I visited you in Seattle. Albert's lessons at dinner helped the most."

CHAPTER 10

Courage

"I know you are talented, but this will take courage," Mr. Dahl said. "It is a new route for our company. New technology to deal with and possibly poor weather conditions. Who knows what you will be facing."

"That is the thrill of it all," Captain Hans replied. He gazed out at the Bergen docks, his mind imaging tropical beaches and warm breezes. "The Panama Canal...this will be another voyage to remember. This is an adventure..."

"Your experience with the West coast of the Americas makes you the most qualified. You must be willing to be flexible. The date may change several times before the canal opens. We are researching which port in the Caribbean you could lay-over in for a day or a week if things change."

Hans got his head back to business. "The passengers must be made to understand that the arrival dates are uncertain. I cannot have them clamoring to arrive at their destination when there is nothing I can do about it."

"We will make sure that is explained. Along with the possibility they might end up in New York and need to take the train to complete their journey."

"So today is June fourth. How many more times must I drive 'the trolley' to New York before the Panama trip?" Hans asked.

Mr. Dahl laughed. "Once or maybe two times. We will need to have some meetings with you before you leave on the Panama trip, and you will need some time to train your crew. With the canal opening at the end of July you will need to plan to leave around July twenty-sixth."

"You mentioned a layover harbor, may I suggest Saint Thomas or Saint John? I have been to both. Spent almost a month on Saint John when I was nineteen. Beautiful place, perfect climate and the Danish language is so close to ours, almost like another dialect."

"I thought most people spoke English there. I need to do a little more research on current conditions on both islands."

"They are the Dutch West Indies. May I ask a favor? I would like Mr. Anders Knobloch assigned to the ship as first mate."

"Done."

∽

I am not going to cry. Please Lord...help me to be strong. I believe this is your will for my life. You have assured me so many times this is the right thing to do. Thank you for making the way clear. Gudrun clutched her shoulder bag tighter and glanced at Karoline standing on the pier with her, holding her baby daughter, Bjørg. Karoline smiled and placed her hand on Gudrun's shoulder.

A bustling, out-of-breath Mrs. Simonsen joined them. "I was so afraid I would be late. I want a hug, not a wave from the boat."

Gudrun laughed and gave the cook a big hug. "I would have made them hold the boat, just for you. Look, they are loading my furniture. That is the crate, just like Mr. Smith and Per marked it."

The large red painted letters GS could be seen from a block away. She would recognize her crate anywhere. The two men had helped her take apart the table, marking each joint with a number on each piece so it could easily be put back together again. She had carefully wrapped the pieces of the bed frame and table with rags and newspaper so they would not be damaged when they arrived on Orcas Island.

Rubbing her arms, she tried to make the goosebumps disappear. "This is an adventure," she declared. "There is my trunk. I should be boarding soon."

"We will be praying," Karoline said. "Please write me often from my sister's home and once you arrive in Seattle."

"Yes, I will be praying. You could not drag me on board. Praying for your safety!" Mrs. Simonsen shook her head. Once again letting her displeasure with Gudrun's choice be known.

"I am looking forward to being back out on the water. It is a short trip to Kristiansand. The leg from there to Stavanger will be longer. Mr. Johansen is so generous in procuring first-class for me on the Stavanger boat and the steamship. At least on this boat I am still a fisherman's daughter." Gudrun hugged Mrs. Simonsen again. "I will be just fine. Do not worry."

"You are the most courageous woman I know," the plump cook said.

The horn tooted and the captain of the mailboat yelled out, "All aboard."

Karoline asked Mrs. Simonsen to hold Bjørg. She took Gudrun's arm and led her towards the boat. "I know you will be just fine. You are courageous and can face anything. You have been such an inspiration to me and others in this town. You have walked close with the Lord while facing hardships, loss, and others persecuting you for no reason. Go with God my dear friend."

Gudrun hugged Karoline. "I can never repay you for all that you have done for me. You are a true friend."

"I will miss you so much. I am very happy for you." Karoline kissed Gudrun on the cheek.

As Gudrun turned toward the boat, both ladies called out in unison, "Write."

Gudrun stood out on the aft deck as the mailboat left Lillesand harbor trying to take everything in. The smells of the fish and saltwater, the white shops, the church, the houses, the Grand House and Karoline and Mrs. Simonsen waving their hankies, it all tugged at her heart. Memories flooded over her. The boat left the harbor and turned west, giving her a full view of her island and the cabin. Per had informed her that there had been a few offers for the cabin.

The view of the cabin overwhelmed her and she began to sob into her handkerchief. Once the island disappeared from view she regained her composure. A warm June day made staying out on the deck bearable. As the mailboat closed in on Kjobmannsvig the waterway became unfamiliar. The goosebumps returned under her long-sleeved dress and jacket. *This is so exciting! Thank you, Lord for a new beginning.*

Staying out on the deck Gudrun watched the shore and the exchange of passengers at each town. Two got off at Kjobmannsvig, the only other passenger got off at Ulvøysund. From Ulvøysund to Stangenes they experienced a bit of rough water. This section had no outer islands to protect them, leaving them at the mercy of the open sea. The captain came out once concerned she might be seasick.

The up and down motion had quite the opposite effect on her. She found it exhilarating. The large swells helped her keep her mind off what she had left behind. *Memories. That is what I left behind. A person cannot stay in one place and live on* memories. *Memories can be taken anywhere and no one can take them from me.*

At Stangenes a couple got on, excited to see their grand-children in Kristiansand. The mailboat followed the channel between several islands and the mainland. When they rounded a peninsula Gudrun felt her jaw drop as she caught her first sight of Kristiansand.

"It is so big!" she exclaimed. The city seemed to spread for miles and miles. Buildings taller than she could have ever imagined and tall church spires interrupted the skyline. The swells seemed close to four feet. As the mailboat crested each swell she got a great view of the city. In the trough it disappeared. Each view of the city made her shiver. "It is so big," she repeated.

The other female passenger joined Gudrun. "You have never been to Kristiansand?" she asked.

"No, I have not. I have always lived in Lillesand. Once I visited Grimstad." Images of entering Grimstad harbor in her father's fishing boat flashed through her mind.

"This is much bigger, I hope you have arrangements for the night, my dear."

"Yes, thank you. I do," Gudrun replied, grateful that Karoline had arranged for a room in a respectable inn close to the docks.

By the time they landed in Kristiansand Gudrun could only think of food and a warm bed. All the salt air and excitement made her crave both. First she had to make sure her crate made it into the locked storage, ready to be loaded onto a ship, early in the morning.

∽

Lying awake in her bed in the hotel, Gudrun recounted the day's adventures. Everything had gone like clockwork. The deckhands were so kind, going out of their way to immediately lock up her crate and delivering her trunk to the hotel. The extra money Arvik had sent came in useful for tipping.

A generous man, that Mr. Johansen. Not only has he sent enough for my trip to Stavanger - the hotel and boat trips - he asked if I had furniture I wanted to bring with me.

Karoline wanted a friend of her husband's to escort her to dinner and the inn. Gudrun had refused, brandishing her ten-inch long "porcupine stick" as her mother used to call it. The three-inch diameter solid oak stick embedded with sharp metal spikes would do some significant damage if anyone sought to do her harm. Her mother had trained her on how to use it, even informing her of the vulnerable area to aim for on a man. With her height and the porcupine stick in hand as she walked, any man would think twice before approaching her. The thought made her smile as she set the alarm on new Baby Ben brass alarm clock that Karoline had given her and placed it on the nightstand.

Dinner at a place near the Inn had filled her up. It tasted good but not to be compared with Mrs. Simonsen's delicious fare. She picked up the journal Mrs. Simonsen had given her for Christmas. Before she started writing she re-read 'the letter,' the first one directly from Arvik to her. It spoke to her heart and made her decision easy. The way he called her the Lady from Lillesand made her feel special. His concern that she knew what kind of life she would live on the island showed his caring side. He wrote of all the drawbacks — times of isolation, no stores nearby, the need to be strong, not afraid of hard work, and the need to solve problems with what they had available. They did not seem like drawbacks to her. Instead they seemed favorable circumstances. After all, she understood island life. The recent letter from Anna describing the almost finished house made it sound like a luxurious island life.

Arvik had also informed her that almost everyone on the island spoke English. He included the words for 'hello', 'goodbye', and 'thank you' in the letter. He said he would help her learn the new language. *Another exciting challenge.*

ᘐ

The fog hung heavy as Arvik left Kingston. *Himmel's* sails were barely catching any wind. He pulled out his chart again. Maybe he should have stayed at dock in the safe harbor. *You know I need to wire the money for her passage, Lord, today. Please guide me, Lord. Help me see any oncoming boats.*

Once out of Apple Tree Harbor he caught a nice breeze, visibility increased so that he could see about two hundred feet in every direction. Arvik steered the boat toward the east shore of Puget Sound, sounding his horn at three-minute intervals. Once he got close enough to see the shore he headed south. His plans seemed to be working until he reached what he believed to be Golden Garden Point. The fog closed back in again. He took down the sails and started his engine to give himself better control of his speed and direction, still sounding his horn every three minutes.

West Point lighthouse at Fort Lawton blared every two minutes. How close was he? He kept checking his compass, continually readjusting his direction southwest. The thought of going aground on the Point put a chill through his body. *One day earlier, I should have left one day earlier. That last cabinet took so long and I needed that final measurement to order the stove. Lord keep me from the shipping lanes. I have no idea where I am. I promise I will go to church more often, please direct me.*

The fog seemed to thicken. A large dark object loomed ahead. It disappeared again. He slowed his engine. He could hear another engine for a moment. Then his pounding heartbeat became the only thing he could hear. Suddenly he heard a loud horn off his port side. For a split second visibility improved, giving him time to see the barge looming a hundred feet directly in front of him. He turned due west then put the engine in full throttle, missing the barge by twenty feet. Cold sweat broke out all over his body. Through the fog he could see the West Point light flashing off to the southwest.

Shilshole Bay, I must be in Shilshole Bay close to the entrance to Salmon Bay. Thank you, Lord for keeping me safe.

Arvik turned *Himmel* towards the new Fishermen's Headquarters. He would dock there and take a streetcar into downtown Seattle. Gudrun's fare to America would be paid in time.

CHAPTER 11

To Stavanger

*J*erking awake Gudrun panicked for a moment. She looked at the small brass alarm clock. *Four forty-nine. Whew! I did not oversleep.* She enjoyed the luxury of lying in bed for a few minutes, then started her prayers asking the Lord for protection. She marveled at the privilege of selecting a clean traveling dress for the day. A year ago she had only owned two dresses.

At six o'clock she arrived at the boat dock according to her plan. The dockhand she had met the evening before arrived a few minutes later. He assured her that her crate would be loaded at seven-thirty onto the boat to Stavanger and that they would be at her hotel room at eight to pick up her trunk.

While she ate breakfast she recalled all the things Karoline had shared with her about her hometown of Stavanger — the large busy harbor, several large churches, museums, theaters, even a fotball team. It sounded overwhelming and a bit scary. In contrast the boat ride to Stavanger, watching the coastline riding the waves and watching for sea life promised fun and safety, the opposite of living in a big city.

How long she would stay at Karoline's sister's place was unknown, perhaps a month. She glanced at her alarm clock before putting it in the trunk. The dockhands would be there soon.

The partially sunny morning gave her a clear view of Kristiansand as the steamship left the harbor. Harbor porpoises played alongside the vessel, surfing the waves from the steamship. The captain had welcomed her and the other first-class cabin members aboard. He had warned them he anticipated large swells throughout the day and a possible storm. He mentioned points of interest to watch for, such as Lista Lighthouse and the reconstruction of Lindesnes Lighthouse.

As they proceeded out of the harbor toward Oksøy Island, dark clouds over the channel island parted and sunshine bathed the lighthouse. *It is a perfect picture of my life, Lord. I am leaving the dark clouds of losing my father, the cabin, and gradually my job and moving toward the sunshine of hope for my future. The glowing light highlighting the rocky ground seems like approval from you, Lord.*

Gudrun left the stern and walked to the bow as the ship made the right turn to the west. Though the stiff breeze made it a bit difficult to walk, it made her feel alive. Securing an optimum place at the railing she pulled out the precious binoculars that she had splurged on as her remembrance of Lillesand. For years she had admired the elegant lady-like pair sitting in the jeweler's window. Finally she had the money to purchase them. A useful item for her adventures, especially now as the larger steamship had to stay further away from the rocky shore. She fingered the solid woven chain before slipping it over her head and allowing the binoculars to rest on her chest.

You are so powerful, Lord! Gudrun prayed. *Your creation is so magnificent, so beautiful. Thank you for allowing me to experience a minuscule part of your raw power. Thank you for your provision, your love, for caring about the smallest detail of my simple life. I love you, Lord.* Gudrun continued to pray for safety and for Karoline's adjustment to the new nanny.

Little Bjørg's entrance into the world had taken what seemed to Gudrun a long time — six hours. Gudrun could hardly bear the screams and sounds coming from Karoline's bedroom. However, according to Karoline's mother, the midwife and Mrs. Simonsen, she had a fairly easy and short delivery. Karoline quickly regained strength, taking on the duties of motherhood with ease. As the month of May came to an end, so did Gudrun's time at the Grand House.

Watching the waves crash over the bow as the ship followed the coastline, Gudrun recounted all the little dresses she had made for Bjørg in all sizes. She tried to anticipate which size she would need in each season. Mr. Bisset had given her enough yardage for an elegant dress for herself. Karoline reminded her that as a first-class passenger she would need to dress for dinner. Looking down at her new shoes she had purchased, Gudrun thanked the Lord she had enough money to purchase them.

Two pairs of shoes. My mother would be shocked at such extravagance. Neither of my parents could have imagined this adventure. Thank you, Lord for providing for me. Give me courage to face the big city of Stavanger. The thought of so many people and streets scares me. I am looking forward to going to church where no one knows me, just you.

The ins and outs of the coastline entertained Gudrun the rest of the morning. The large rounded rocks disappearing into the water, deep inlets with an occasional red cabin. They passed the town of Mandal, similar to Lillesand with white painted houses stacked side by side, but unlike her hometown, Mandal had plenty of boats bobbing off the hook in the harbor. The construction on the new Lindesnes Lighthouse seemed to be moving along. She had focused in on the site and counted at least thirty men working on top of one of the massive rounded rocks. Suddenly they were scrambling for safety and a large boom could be heard throughout the ship. A sizable puff of white smoke confirmed that they were blasting out rock.

The morning flew by and as noon approached several humpback whales entertained passengers on the starboard side. They drew squeals of delight from the children each time they surfaced. A deckhand informed her that lunch would soon be served.

By two o'clock the weather had made a drastic turn for the worse. The size of the waves had increased, causing several passengers to spend time hanging out over the railing, encumbered with seasickness. The temperature dropped as clouds obliterated the sun. Dark clouds started building toward the north.

Gudrun hung onto the railing, relishing the up and down motion of the swells, the smell of the salt air, and the jumping dolphins off the bow. She tucked her precious binoculars inside her coat to keep them from banging against her chest.

For a moment the sun broke through the clouds, shining rays of light on Lista lighthouse. The reddish-brown stone glowed, standing out in vivid contrast to the dark blue sky behind. She continued to stare at the unforgettable scene until the sun disappeared.

Even with her coat buttoned tight Gudrun shivered. She could see heavy clouds ahead, the falling rain creating a dark line on the water ahead. She decided it might be a good time to retreat to her cabin.

Lying on the built-in sofa, the repetitive rocking motion of the large waves put Gudrun asleep for a time. The howling wind and rain against her porthole kept waking her up off and on. After a few hours she awoke from her restless nap. The rain seemed to have subsided so she returned to the deck. Out on the horizon she could see a hint of light blue. The swells were much smaller and the steamship cut through the water with only a minimum splash of waves against the hull.

Smooth sailing as they say. Too bad I missed seeing Eigerøy Lighthouse. That would have been something to see. She could picture the painting that hung in her favorite Bakeri in Lillesand of the red and white striped lighthouse standing tall, up high on a point overlooking the North Sea. *Now on to meet Mr. and Mrs. Andreas Jakobsen. What will they be like, Lord? Help me to get along with them. May I be useful, not a burden as I stay with them. May I develop another friend in Marit. Will I meet the friend of Anna Lunde, Berit? So many questions, Lord, all of which you already know the answer. Take away my fear Lord. Help me to trust in you.*

Blue sky appeared for a short while just before they passed the town of Tanager. Gudrun noted the captain stayed off shore well away from the dangerous rocks close to the mouth of the large harbor. Per had told her about the area since he used to catch lobster there. Built on a flat area with lakes and water all around, this city began at the end of the Viking era.

Butterflies filled her stomach as the ship made the turn that evening toward Stavanger. *Another adventure awaits. May it be a good one. Oh my, what a large, busy harbor. Karoline's description does not do it justice!*

Gudrun wanted to do a little song and dance as the crate with her initials on it swung onto the dock about two hundred feet from her. She glanced around hoping to catch a glimpse of Marit. She had seen pictures of the dark-haired beauty on Karoline's dresser. The two sisters had similar facial features but their hair and eyes were opposite. According to Karoline, Marit was the shorter, older sister. But no one looking like Marit appeared. People all around her were hugging and greeting each other. Minutes kept ticking away and no one seemed to be there for her.

"No, stop." Gudrun heard herself shout. She could see a man dressed in black, directing two of the dockhands and they were loading her crate onto a dolly. Edging herself through the crowd she finally broke free enough to run. "It is mine!" She shouted as she neared the crate. "It is mine."

"Are you Miss Sagen?" the man asked.

"Yes. That is my crate. Please leave it there."

"I am Mr. Engen. I am the Jakobsen's chauffeur, Miss. I am here to pick you up. Mrs. Jakobsen could not make it tonight. I saw your initials on the crate and I have made arrangements for it to be stored here in the Jakobsen's private storage unit."

Instinct moved Gudrun's hand to her bag, grabbing her porcupine stick, she took it out of her purse in plain view for the man to see. "How do I know what you say is true?"

The butler shrugged, "If you want a ride home you must come with me. Oh. Would my driver's license help?" Mr. Engen pulled his billfold out of his inner jacket pocket and handed her a slip of paper. It had his name and next to occupation it said chauffeur. "When we get to the car I will show you the owner's registration. It has Mr. Jakobsen's name on it."

Gudrun paused for a few seconds. "That would be good. Yes, please store the crate. I will be over there standing next to my trunk."

I am sitting in a car! A real automobile! Gudrun ran her hand over the leather back seat. Then she pinched herself. *I am awake.*

The registration helped to calm her nerves enough that she put her porcupine stick back in her bag. The chauffeur had given her a written receipt for the crate storage that she could use to pick it up at any time. Despite the reassurances she paid careful attention to landmarks as the car wound through the narrow streets. For the next month or more she would be living in this city and she must know her way around.

CHAPTER 12

Waiting

"All it needs, Zhou, is Mrs. Arvik Johansen singing as she cooks over the stove," Arvik declared. He and his friend had just put the last upper cabinet in place.

"Some dishes. Pots and pans." Zhou's eyes twinkled as he replied.

Arvik's loud laughter resounded through the kitchen. "Yes. She needs those. Mrs. Lunde suggested I wait and let Gudrun pick them out in Seattle."

"Good plan. I go home now. Come for dinner?"

"Yes, thank you. Can you believe it? Ten months and it is all done, except for the library and the refrigerator. It should be here next week."

"You a hard worker. It is well made. A refrigerator?" Zhou shook his head. "Like the one that I helped take to Rosario last week?"

"Yes."

"You spoil your wife."

After Zhou left, Arvik grabbed the letter he had received a few days ago from Gudrun, dated the seventeenth of June and took it out to the patio to reread it. The mid-July sun warmed his body as he read. She had been in Stavanger for a week. She thanked him for the first-class passage on the ship to Stavanger and wrote one whole delightful page about the boat trip. "Sounds like she loves the water as much as I do," he mumbled. She informed him that she understood island life and enjoyed being a fisherman's daughter. "Maybe she will like being a fisherman-carpenter's wife. Thank you, Lord. Give me the patience to wait. One more month."

Her last paragraph gave him hope for a good relationship. She confided in him how hard the transition to the big city of Stavanger had been. Her rich host family seemed too busy to have time with her during the day, so she explored the huge house and gardens on her own. Twice at dinner they attempted to help her with basic English words. She believed they were giving up because of her struggle with the correct pronunciation. Dinner topics usually evolved around their busy lives. The husband owned several large businesses; the wife headed up a local charity. At the time of writing the letter she had made friends with their nine-year old daughter over a sewing project. She had several invitations to the symphony, a play, and to a large dinner, all which she turned down. She did not like feeling out of place socially, especially when she did not know anyone. She even shared how she did not foresee a close friendship with Marit like she had with Karoline. She eagerly anticipated meeting Anna's close friend, Berit, the next day.

Please, Lord, I have another request. Help Gudrun adjust to the big city. May she enjoy Anna's friend Berit. Protect her. Help her learn English. I only ask so much because that is what Pastor said last Sunday...you have not because you ask not.

ꙮ

Picking up the small container of urtesalt Gudrun smiled. She grabbed two more. One would be a gift to Anna Lunde. *Urtesalt as a present?* Standing in the middle of a grocery store in Stavanger it seemed like a crazy idea. It would take several years of consistent baking to use even one container, but both Anna and Arvik had informed her that when you could find it in Seattle it was an expensive commodity. *Such a tiny package, it will be easy to transport.*

Standing in line to pay she could overhear the cashier speaking with the customer in front of her.

"Three ladies! Three ladies pushed down and their belongings taken. What is this world coming to?" the cashier said.

"We can only hope the police will find the man soon," the customer said.

"Please be careful. One of the attacks happened in broad daylight," the clerk said.

Gudrun paid the clerk in silence and stepped out into the mid-July sunshine. Only two weeks to go, she mused as she walked towards Breiavatnet. This lake in the center of town had become one of her favorite places to come. The Stavanger Cathedral built in 1150 stood near the north end. Often she walked around the lake, praying and dreaming about what Orcas Island would be like. She had a favorite bench she liked to sit on to write in her journal or read letters from Karoline and Mrs. Simonsen. On several occasions, her new friend Berit had joined her for walks.

A scarf in the dress boutique caught her eye and as she turned she saw a dark-haired bearded man hurrying toward her. She started toward the lake again quickening her pace. Her thoughts roamed back to Berit whose personality seemed twice the size of her small frame.

Berit, her answer to prayer. On their first meeting at church they immediately understood each other. Berit had invited her to a women's Bible Study, where she found other like-minded ladies. Women who wanted to know God's word and allowed their lives to be guided by it. Not that the Jakobsens spurned the Bible, they attended church every Sunday, prayed before meals, and spoke about the Lord regularly. The pressure of their commitments and fund-raising events for the poor and various other causes seemed to make it impossible to attend weekly studies. She enjoyed their company at dinner and sometimes after dinner they would socialize for awhile.

Berit's nursing job at the hospital kept her busy so they had not spent as much time together as Gudrun would have liked.

Gudrun looked back over her shoulder again. He was still there, the dark-haired man heading straight toward her. She dashed into a shop and exited out the back door before the shopkeeper could say anything. She slowed down. She had lost him. Still her hand found the porcupine stick in her bag. Back on the main street she felt secure. Brains over brawn.

Suddenly in the reflection of the shop window she saw him reaching for her shoulder! She turned, raising the porcupine stick high to get the best swing. Instead he grabbed her wrist and pushed her up against the shop's stonewall.

"Calm down, Miss. I do you no harm. I have your package. The one you left on the counter at Olsen's Food Store."

Gudrun relaxed and he let her go graciously offering her the package of urtesalt. Red-faced, she realized her mistake. "I am so sorry. Thank you. I am so sorry." She noticed his kind brown eyes.

The gentleman acknowledged her apology and said, "I sincerely hope you have a good day."

Sitting down on a bench by the lake, Gudrun rubbed her hands over her warm cheeks. *I guess I need to relax a bit and not jump to conclusions.*

She opened her bag and took out a thick envelope that she had picked up from the Post before she shopped for the urtesalt. The shipping company's return address gave her hope that her passage to Seattle would be inside. She opened the envelope to find her ticket and additional instructions on what to expect on the voyage. She noticed that they warned that temperatures on Saint Thomas, in Panama and even California would be much warmer than Norway. Thanks to Marit's previous warning she had already sewn two lighter-weight dresses that should work for that part of the journey.

∽

"Only for you, sis. Only for you. I can barely sit through the formal dinners on my boat." Hans walked over and helped Sissel on with her coat. "You look lovely by the way. It is too bad Karl could not join us tonight."

"Thank you. Poor Karl, his fourth night in a row being the on-call doctor. I so appreciated you being here. You would be amazed how much people will give to the cause just because they got to speak with someone important or famous. Keep focusing on the fact you are doing this for a good cause," Sissel reminded her older brother.

Hans chuckled. "Good cause. Yes, the hospital is always a good cause. Famous or important, I am neither."

"I beg to differ. People still remember the Bergen newspaper article about your heroics around the Horn twelve years ago on *Marianne,* saving all those people. And with all the people going to America...a captain is a very important position. Especially one that will be going through the Panama Canal."

"Your husband's and your work is more important. Each week and maybe every day you and your staff are saving lives at that hospital." Hans opened the door for Sissel and they continued their banter as they walked toward the museum. "Now you said that there are other 'stars' this evening."

Sissel smiled at her brother. "Yes, an opera singer from Oslo. She is a cousin to one of the doctors. There is one of the leading scientists from Trondheim, and even Sigrid Undset, the author. You may find times when there is no one clamoring to talk with you."

"That would be nice. A fundraiser is not as bad as the formal dinners on ship. Tonight I will be able to move around avoiding the obnoxious types. You seem to like everyone. How do you do it?"

"It is not me, dear brother. People can be disagreeable, as I can be too...it is the Lord giving me the ability to love them."

Hans fell quiet for a block. Nearing the steps of the large building, Hans stopped. "Look, Sissel, the tall blonde in the dark blue dress and short black jacket. That is the woman who almost hit me..."

"Her?" Sissel asked. "She is gorgeous. So stylish — you don't know her name?"

"No, but I am going to find out tonight." Hans set his jaw. He had a mission.

Hans kept scanning the room, occasionally getting a glimpse of the mysterious blonde. Each time he started her direction Sissel or another nurse would come up with someone else for him to meet or a waitress would intercept him with more appetizers. After an hour of struggling to speak with the lady he gave up and walked out to the balcony. Despite the clear evening the temperature remained warm and the stars were out in full force. Someone walked up to the balcony railing a few feet away. The captain turned. *It is her! Her curls are so beautiful. Those blue eyes are captivating.*

"Good evening, ma'am. We have met before, in fact, just two days ago near Breiavatnet," Han's said.

The young lady blushed once she recognized him. "It is you!" she blurted.

"I am Captain Hans Torvik. And you are?"

"Captain, oh Captain there is someone you have to meet before you give your speech." One of Sissel's nursing friends interrupted the exchange and swept the captain off to the main gathering.

He turned as he entered the museum, but the young lady had disappeared.

∽

"Berit, Berit, we have to leave," Gudrun whispered in her friend's ear.

Berit shook her head. "Not now. I want to hear the Captain. He has been assigned command of one of the first ships that will go through the Panama Canal. We have to stay."

"No. The captain is the man I almost hit with my porcupine stick! I have to leave."

"Oh my!" Berit started to giggle. "The captain is your attacker? Oh this is funny. That...that means..."

"Yes. He is the captain of the steamship I am going to America on. But the ship is so big he will never see me right?"

"Shush, they are introducing him."

A red-face Gudrun tried to hide behind Berit as the crowd continued to ply Captain Hans Torvik with questions about his days on *Marianne*, his thoughts about steamships, and his upcoming trip through the Panama Canal. As the questions wound down, Gudrun succeeded in pulling her friend away, moving toward the door of the museum.

"Berit. Oh Berit," Sissel called out as she walked hastily toward the two friends. "You are not leaving, are you? We still have the raffle prizes."

"I am afraid we must, something has come up," Berit said. "I hope your brother has a great trip through the Panama Canal."

"He will. His only concern is a special first-class passenger that he must babysit. Some young lady who is too privileged to manage traveling by herself. So pampered." Sissel turned to Gudrun. "I am afraid we have not met, I am Sissel Rogland and you are?"

Gudrun stammered, "I am —"

Berit interrupted, "She is my friend from Lillesand...her name —"

A young woman rushed up grabbing Sissel's arm. "Sissel, we have an emergency with the raffle. We need you now!"

Donning their coats the two young women hurried outside.

"This is so embarrassing! I cannot get on that ship. I am the pampered passenger. Arvik is so concerned about my safety he recently decided to pay extra for the captain to keep an eye on me. The money is due when I arrive, so if I do not go... oh Berit...what am I going to do?"

Berit reached up and grabbed Gudrun by the shoulders and looked her sternly in the eye. "You are going to swallow your pride and get on the boat. You are not letting a little pride get in the way of a wonderful future. Besides, that is almost two weeks away. Captain Torvik might forget about the incident all together."

໑

"Mr. and Mrs. Jakobsen would like to see you in the formal living room," the butler informed Gudrun as she came down the stairs for lunch.

Surprised, Gudrun followed the butler down the hall. *What is going on? Have I done something wrong? I have not seen either of them this morning. Did they hear about last week at the hospital bazaar? Please Lord, calm my thoughts?*

Mr. Jakobsen stood up as Gudrun entered the living room. "My dear, we have something we must discuss. Come, please sit."

Marit patted the seat next to her. Gudrun noted concern in her eyes as she sat down next to her.

Pacing the floor for a moment, Mr. Jakobsen spoke, "We have been discussing all the commotion in Europe between Hungry and Austria and Serbia at dinner time."

"Yes, sir. The last news I heard is that Britain had called a conference with the major European powers," Gudrun said.

"Unfortunately, Germany did not agree to participate and we just got news this morning that Austria and Hungary have declared war on Serbia. We are concerned about your safety, going to America on a ship."

Marit grabbed her hand. "We think you should extend your stay here until things settle down. You are welcome here for as long as you need."

"I appreciate your concern, very much so. Let me pray and think about it. I have not been alarmed because we are a neutral country and our ships can go anywhere."

Mr. Jakobsen said, "Yes, we are neutral. In war even the neutral ships could be mistakenly attacked. We are just expressing our concern. We wanted you to know you have a safe place to stay."

Gudrun stood up. "Thank you. I will let you know. Thank you for your generosity in allowing me to reside here as long as you have."

"It has been our pleasure," Marit said. "You have heard that Karoline and Bjørg are moving to Grimstad?"

Gudrun nodded. "She told me the hotel is doing well. And that she will have a smaller house to run there."

"Yes, smaller, but she said they would still need a staff of two. She said she has been cleaning out and giving away things." Marit continued, "Big life changes for you two friends. She mentioned she appreciates your letters."

"And I hers. I will let you know my decision soon," Gudrun replied.

∾

"Hmm…" Gudrun smiled at her friend. "I think you are right, Berit. I must get on the ship. It is God's will for me to go to America. If I had family here that might keep me, but I do not."

The two friends walked in silence for a moment as they continued around Breiavatnet. "We will keep praying. The shipping line will cancel the boat if they think it is dangerous. Norway is neutral so you will be safe onboard. Once in Seattle and out on Orcas Island you will really be safe.

"Yes, and I read this morning that they think it will all be over very quickly. So they will have no time to blockade our ships."

"I will miss you," Berit sighed. "I am so happy for Anna that she will have another friend. She gets lonely sometimes, even in the middle of Seattle."

Gudrun stopped and gave her friend a hug. "I will miss you, too. I will have three people to write to...you, Karoline, and Mrs. Simonsen."

A little twinkle appeared in Berit's eyes. "At least with all this war talk you have a distraction from your problem with Captain Torvik."

Gudrun blushed. "Yes."

BOOK TWO
America

Sognefjord

CHAPTER 13

Hiding Out

*C*aptain Hans Torvik stood on the Bridge of *Sognefjord*. There seemed to be an affinity building between him and the ship. Like *Marianne* he had taken command of her as a new ship, but the comparison ended there. *Sognefjord's* five hundred and ten foot long steel hull would have dwarfed *Marianne*. All the new instruments and inventions made *Sognefjord* easier to navigate. The larger vessel presented new challenges and at the same time eliminated many of the old. It would be a much safer journey as they no longer needed to go around the Horn. *At my age less danger is probably a good thing.* He gazed at the empty Stavanger dock. *Tomorrow it will be full of people. One hundred first-class passengers, two hundred and fifty second-class and eight hundred and fifty third-class. One of those passengers is Miss Gudrun Sagen. What will she be like? Apparently not able to fend for herself or her fiancé would not have paid for the extra attention.* He pictured a small frail lady unable to make a decision, someone that needed continual guidance. Hopefully, she had not bought into another scam. Something about the letter from Mr. Johansen, however, told him not to be too concerned about the arrangement.

The new ship's first-class dining room sported circular tables that sat eight. The idea seemed to be that this allowed flexible seating. It also meant that every night he would have new people at his table, except for Miss Sagen. He would have the pleasure of her company every night. *Hopefully it will be a pleasure.*

For a moment he thought of Miss Lillesand, as Sissel had named her. Would he ever see her again? Over the past week, the image of her tall slender figure and curly platinum blonde hair had been playing off and on in his mind. Before saying goodbye, Sissel mentioned she had tried to make contact with Berit, but to no avail. He would have to visit Stavanger after he returned from this voyage. Right now he had better stop daydreaming and meet with Mr. Anders Knobloch.

෴

Gudrun waved goodbye to the Jakobsen's daughter and Marit standing in the front door that afternoon. They had been gracious hostesses. She hoped the dresses she had sewn for both ladies would be appreciated. Indeed it had been a strange six weeks, with so much to adjust to. Especially now. Two days ago Germany had declared war on Russia. There were rumors about France also being their target and about England getting involved. The mass of people on the docks and the noise level overwhelmed her. As Mr. Engen opened the car door shouts of "War" from young men holding up newspapers filled the air. *I do not care what is going on — I must get on the ship.*

Berit had rearranged her work schedule so she could wish her farewell. *How will I find her with all these people?* Gudrun stood by the car looking around at the crowd. The chauffeur had gone to claim her crate for her. Someone tugged at her sleeve. She looked down to see Berit.

"My friend the world traveler," Berit said.

Gudrun gave her a hug. "My dear Stavanger friend. I will never forget you. I appreciate you being here."

She heard a loud whistle and someone yelling "Miss Sagen" over the noise. She saw Mr. Engen waving his arms toward the gangplank. She saw her crate going up the gangplank into the hull of the huge ship. He pushed through the crowd and handed her another receipt. "I am going to arrange for your trunk to be taken to your cabin. Stay here, I will be back," he said.

"You have my present for Anna?" Berit asked.

"In my trunk. Do you have anything else for her?"

Berit took an envelope from her bag. "Do you mind? It has a photo in it, so please do not put it next to your porcupine stick," she giggled.

"Excuse me, Miss Sagen. I got permission for Miss Berit to go aboard with you," Mr. Engen said. "It is another hour and a half before the ship will leave. Here is a temporary pass for you, Miss Berit, you must be off the boat in an hour."

Gudrun could not help herself and gave him a big hug. "You are so kind. Thank you for all you have done." She presented him with a small package. He seemed delighted with the personal monogrammed handkerchiefs she had made for him.

The ladies strolled up the gangplank and up to the first-class deck. They made their way down wide luxurious paneled halls to cabin number forty-two. Opening the door Gudrun caught her breath. "Look Berit, how beautiful! My own sink and closet, even a built-in sofa."

"Yes, and you have a porthole. Down in second-class they do not." Berit looked the cabin over again. "It does seem small. I heard up on the Promenade deck the private rooms are larger."

"I cannot complain one bit...a year ago...a year ago I slept in a loft in a cabin out on a remote island. By my standards this is luxury."

Berit nodded. "I remember. How about if we unpack your dresses and make you at home."

"Only a few, I want time to explore the first-class public spaces on the Promenade deck together."

Arm and arm the two friends walked the Promenade deck. They oohed and exclaimed at the extravagant dining room, the luxurious lounge and the wide decks.

"All these wonderful spaces for you to enjoy. You will be spoiled by the time you arrive in Seattle," Berit commented.

"Oh look up there, Berit." Gudrun pointed to a ladder and the top deck. "Large lifeboats hanging off the sides."

"I know what you are thinking. What is the view like from there?" Berit laughed. "You might not be allowed in that part of the ship."

"Maybe not, there is only a rope railing. Look, we can see the clock tower in Breiavatnet...and the church...I will miss this place, especially the ladies in Bible Study. Please tell them again how much I appreciated our time together."

"I will. We will all miss you."

The ship tooted a warning and they hugged one more time, before Berit scurried off the boat.

After waving goodbye to Berit from the first-class deck, Gudrun made her way to the stern. She used her binoculars to get final looks at her favorite places in Stavanger. She hung out there for a while watching the coastline disappear. Glancing back at the ship she noted Captain Torvik striding along the side deck. She quickly headed for the opposite side of the ship as she could not face him yet.

Gudrun finished hanging her clothes in the cabin closet. She closed the trunk and slid it under the built-in sofa. Looking out the porthole of her cabin, the reality of the journey sank in. Gudrun sat down on the bed and began to cry. *This is goodbye, goodbye to my parents. Leaving my country, a country with no more ties for me, a country that will hopefully sit on the sidelines while war rages throughout Europe.* She had seen the headlines of one of the papers as she boarded. Germany had declared war on France. *What will be next?*

After drying her tears she opened an envelope she had received as she boarded. It explained dinner would be served at six. *Such an odd time. I have heard that Americans eat late. Will Arvik want to eat late or at the normal time of four thirty? Oh no, I am requested to sit at the Captain's table. No! Not tonight. I cannot face him tonight.* All of a sudden the world's problems seem to evaporate. She had one big problem, avoiding the captain.

Lying back on the bed the lull of the ship helped her nod off. She woke an hour later, put on her coat, grabbed one of the cheese sandwiches the Jakobsen's cook had made for her and proceeded to the Promenade deck. She walked both the starboard and port side, then settled in at the stern on a bench to eat her sandwich.

❧

Captain Torvik waited until nine the first morning before going to Gudrun Sagen's cabin. According to the ship records she had boarded yesterday afternoon. Her empty chair at dinner had piqued his interest and some concern. So far the seas had been smooth so he could not imagine she was seasick.

As he walked toward the cabin he recalled how he thought he saw Miss Lillesand on the stern, last night. By the time he got there she had disappeared. *I must be imagining things.*

Hans knocked and waited for two minutes. He knocked again. No answer. "Miss Sagen. This is the Captain." Still no answer. A cabin maid walked by and he asked her to open the door. She checked, stepped back and allowed him to peek inside. Personal belongings verified the cabin had been used and the cabin maid confirmed a young lady had spent the night there.

Hans went to the bridge just in time to see Miss Lillesand out on the bow. By the time he arrived there, she was gone. *Have I gone mad? Am I imagining things? I must get my mind back on my duties.*

He checked in with his first mate, Anders Knobloch. Everything seemed to be running smoothly. He would spend the rest of the morning walking the outside decks, checking each station.

∽

Twenty-four hours and I have not had to face the captain, yet, Gudrun mused, leaning over the railing. *In six more days we will arrive at Saint Thomas Island. How long can I keep this up? The whole trip? By tomorrow I will run out of cheese sandwiches and have to show up for a meal.* One of the maids had been kind enough to bring her breakfast in her cabin. Twice today she had caught the silhouette of Captain Torvik coming towards her and she had slipped away. She longed for a nap, but that would mean staying at her cabin, trapped where he could find her.

She looked out at the horizon and took a deep breath of salt air. Oh she loved being at sea. Finally she gave in and went to nap in her cabin.

Gudrun woke an hour later to a growling stomach. She washed her face and looked at herself in the mirror. Berit's words about swallowing her pride hit home. I guess I am acting like a skittish schoolgirl. Sitting down on her bed she began to pray. "Lord, you know my pride has gotten in the way of common sense. Arvik has paid good money for my passage so that I have the best meals and accommodations. To waste it would be a shame. It is not just pride but fear that is keeping me from dinner. I know both are sins. Please, Father, help me act with dignity."

Standing up, Gudrun went to the closet and picked out an appropriate dress for dinner. She fixed her hair, slipped on the mother's bracelet, and her new pair of shoes. Looking in the mirror a wave of shyness came over her. "I cannot do this," she cried out. Tears began to flow. "No, my mother taught me to be strong. I will not cry." Dabbing her eyes she looked at the Baby Ben clock. Six o'clock, I will be a few minutes late. She walked out the door and headed for the first-class dining room. Another wave of shyness overtook her just before she arrived and she fled back to her cabin.

For twenty minutes she sat there, twisting her handkerchief, claiming promises, praying, but still unable to move. A knock on the door put a chill down her spine.

"Miss Sagen, this is Mr. Anders Knobloch, the first mate. Are you there?"

"Yes, one moment please." She looked in the mirror and pinched her cheeks. She hoped the first mate would not notice how red her eyes were and opened the door.

"We have been very worried about you. This is the second dinner you have missed. May I escort you to a private dining location?" The first mate held his elbow out for her to take.

Gudrun nodded and placed her hand on his elbow.

The first mate continued, "Captain Torvik would like to meet you if that is alright."

Gudrun nodded again.

"Here is the private dining room." The first mate stopped in front of glass French doors and opened one for her. "Are you hungry enough to eat? Salmon is the main entree tonight. Or we can fix something special if food is an issue."

"Thank you. You have been so kind. Salmon sounds wonderful," Gudrun said.

"Make yourself at home. I will bring your meal and the captain will be joining you in a bit."

She sat down with her back to the French doors so that she could enjoy the view. The beautifully carved table sat six and the walls were paneled mahogany decorated with delightful tapestries. *I will be meeting the captain. No more hiding.* Her stomach growled several times as she waited. *I am glad the food will arrive before the captain does.*

CHAPTER 14

Amends

Striding down the hallway Captain Hans eagerly anticipated meeting Miss Gudrun Sagen. His curiosity had been growing all day. The first mate had given him her passenger information but his duties had kept him from reading it.

He reached for the private dining room door handle and froze. There, at the table eating her dinner sat Miss Lillesand! *Are they one and the same?* He took a moment to regain his composure. *Wait...if she is Miss Sagen then she is engaged to Mr. Johansen.* It surprised him how much the thought disturbed him. She turned as he opened the door. *Yes, Miss Lillesand is indeed Miss Gudrun Sagen.*

"Good evening, Captain Torvik," she said rising from her chair. "I wish to apologize for my behavior."

He took off his captain's cap and laid it on the table. "No need to apologize for our earlier encounter in Stavanger. A single lady has to be careful when a man is following her. I should have shouted out that I had your package. Let us forget that now. What concerns me more is how we, here on the ship, can be doing our job better."

"I do not understand, sir."

"Obviously we have done something wrong to make you skip two dinners. I know you are not ill, I have seen you on deck. How can we help you?" the captain asked.

Gudrun sat down again, looking at her hands. "I have been thinking about why I have behaved the way I have since I came aboard. It is no one's fault but my own..."

Hans pulled out a chair so that it faced her and sat down. "I am listening."

"It started with the fact I did not want to see you, because of our encounter over the package. My pride got in the way. But it is much more. You see, I am a poor fisherman's daughter. Never really accepted by the people in Lillesand. Now I am here, with fine clothes and first-class passage. I do not belong and the idea for conversing with rich and famous people frightens me."

Hans could not help but smile. "I totally understand, Miss Sagen. Do you know what the worst part of my day is?"

She shook her head.

"Eating dinner in the first-class dining room."

Wide-eyed, Gudrun said, "No!"

"Oh, yes. You see I do not belong there either. I would rather eat with the passengers below. I am a farmer's son. We are alike in that regard, stuck in first-class." The captain started to laugh and Gudrun joined him. "I have a big favor to ask you."

Relief written all over her face, Gudrun said, "Anything, sir."

"Please help me get through this trip by joining me for dinner every night."

She hesitated, then said, "Yes."

"Good. That is settled. If you are finished eating, shall we take a stroll around the deck? I know that you like it out there, as I have caught glimpses of you standing by the railing. You might find I do not bite. Only occasionally growl."

❦

Lying in her bunk that evening Gudrun thanked the Lord for working out all the details. The captain seemed so genteel, forgiving, and he reminded her of her father. In fact when she confided in him about how she felt about the first-class dining room, it reminded her of conversations with her father.

Images of the dining room flashed through her mind. The thought of eating there tomorrow evening scared her, but she calmed down by remembering the captain's description. "All the conversation is about the war, not about where people are from or what they do. Everyone is concerned the Panama Canal might not open or if we will get torpedoed across the Atlantic. The worry level is very high and no one is concerned about your background."

She let out a big sigh. *It seems I have not been trusting you, Lord. Not since I heard about the robber in Stavanger. I have let my emotions control everything. It is emotional, Lord, leaving my country. A bit scary when nothing is familiar. So much bigger than Lillesand. If I am honest I have been afraid these past few days that I might not be making the right decision. Getting on the boat made it all so final. Before I walked aboard this trip was a dream, a gift...from you, Father. The reality is huge. Guide me Lord. Help me to trust you.*

❦

Breakfast in the first-class Lounge took place between seven and nine. A pleasant affair, with a long table loaded with various breads, rolls, meats, cucumbers, tomatoes, and cheeses. Gudrun enjoyed a small table near the window and watched the people come and go. She wondered why she had been so scared. They were people. Like anyone else, only in fancier clothes. Well, most of them, a few wore plain ordinary attire. Some seemed self-assured, others lonely, others reserved. Simply people.

The waiter filled her tea cup one more time and took the plates away. She pulled out the three letters from Signe to her mother. With so much change in her life she had put off reading them until now.

Who is this lady, Signe Hansen? How come I never knew her?

The first letter answered her questions. Signe referred to her mother as her sister part way through. Her aunt wrote of being grateful that she finally found her sister. Gudrun kept reading, then gazed out at the ocean. *So my mother had been hired at fourteen as a nanny to a large family in Vingnes... that is near Lillehammer, up north. My aunt refers to Vingnes as their home town. Apparently when the family moved away, Aunt Signe and Mother lost track of each other.* Her mother had moved along with the family several times and ended up in Lillesand. Gudrun looked at the envelope one more time. The address surprised her. She knew the house in Lillesand— one of the large houses on the west side of Lillesand across the harbor from the Grand House. Her mother must have lived in the house, a house she and her father use to deliver fish to after school.

So much to learn. Lord, I am grateful for this opportunity to learn more about my family.

She put the letter back in the envelope and wandered out on the deck. No more hiding out. "Thank you, Lord," she whispered.

"What are you doing? Are you alright?" Captain Hans asked as he approached Gudrun hanging on to the railing, her head down.

"Praying," she responded. She felt happier than she had in days, completely at peace. "Do you find peace praying to our Lord each morning?"

The handsome captain looked down at the waves below. "No. He is not my God."

Gudrun reviewed the hard lines of his face. Maybe not all the lines were from the sea, some might reflect his hardness toward God.

Interrupting the silence Hans said, "I have someone from second-class that I would like you to meet. She has a similar situation as you. She is traveling to San Francisco to marry her cousin's best friend, whom she has never met. She is very young. Would you like to meet her?"

"Yes, I would."

൜

"Look, another one," Åse exclaimed, pointing to a humpback whale breaching off the bow. "So powerful. Have you ever killed a whale, Captain Hans?"

"No, never. Had a few incidents with them. Ramming the ship or us accidentally hitting them. This time of year we do not usually see whales in this part of the Atlantic. Sometimes the whales use the mid-Atlantic to get from one ocean to another, but only at certain times of the year."

"Interesting, so this is their pathway," Gudrun commented.

"Yes. Now that you two ladies have met I will leave you. I have a ship to run. Miss Halvorsen, remember you are welcome on the first-class deck to be with Miss Sagen. Miss Sagen, I will see you at dinner." The captain turned and strode toward the bridge.

"Oh, he is so handsome. I wonder what my husband will look like," Åse murmured.

For the next hour Åse and Gudrun walked the first-class deck, watching the waves, sitting on the benches, and comparing notes on what they knew about their future husbands and future living situations. When Åse went back down to second-class for lunch, Gudrun reflected that she had a better situation than Åse. No "getting to know you time" for Åse, they would be married the day after she arrived in San Francisco and travel north to a secluded ranch.

After a nap in her cabin Gudrun took one more stroll on the deck before getting ready for dinner. *It is so beautiful Lord. I love watching the waves crest in such a peaceful rhythm. It calms my soul.*

Looking at herself in the mirror, Gudrun could feel the panic starting. *No, I promised the captain. I am not going to give into fear, Lord. Give me courage, give me strength. Help me remember that they are just people. Please calm my soul so that I can be a witness to the captain. I can do all things with your power Lord. Help me keep my head up and help me be gracious.*

Gudrun noticed a look of relief on Captain Torvik's face as she walked into the dining room. He met her in the doorway and said, "I am so glad you are here. The Sandneses are dining at my table tonight. He is one of the owners of the shipping line. He and his wife thought it would be special to be on one of the first ships through the Panama Canal."

"Oh, so an important night, just when I got up the courage to attend," Gudrun laughed.

"True." The captain smiled and held out his elbow. "You just be your charming self and we will be fine. It is me we have to worry about," he said as he guided her to the table.

The Sandneses turned out to be the most genuine people. They immediately put the Captain and everyone else at ease.

Gudrun marveled at how her theory rang true. *They are simply people, nothing to be afraid of. We are all simply people.*

ᘐ

At breakfast on day six Gudrun opened the last letter from Signe to her mother. Bits and pieces were beginning to fill in the puzzle. Apparently her mother and Signe had been born on the outskirts of Vingnes to a sharecropper. When they were children the family moved several times from farm to farm. When her sister turned sixteen she married a shopkeeper and lived in town. Her aunt referred to having miscarried twice and bemoaning the loss of her children. The letters referred to her mother meeting her father when he came to sell fish at the house where she worked in Lillesand.

So now I know a bit more about my heritage, she mused. *Time to meet the captain for our morning walk. Hopefully Mrs. Sandnes will join me for lunch again today. She knows her Bible so well and she is pleasant to talk to.*

"One more day to Saint Thomas. Between spending time with you, Åse, and Mrs. Sandnes the past six days have gone so quickly," Gudrun murmured to Captain Torvik.

"Maybe too fast." The captain gave her a smile. "How are the English lessons with Mrs. Sandnes and Åse going?"

Shaking her head Gudrun paused. "It seems that Åse has a knack for languages. I am still working on the basic words. Like hello and goodbye. My pronunciation is so bad no one can understand me."

"You will figure it out once you hear other people speaking it all the time. I am sure you will be fine."

"Maybe I should just stay on board so I can speak Norwegian all the time."

The captain laughed. "As much as I enjoy your company and our talks about the sea I doubt the Norwegian Steamship Line will allow you to be a permanent passenger. Because you understand and love the water our conversations have been interesting. We have been fortunate to have pleasant weather and relatively calm, smooth seas. You have experienced the best of being at sea."

"God has been good to us," Gudrun replied.

The captain winced and continued walking, looking out at the ocean. "I have even begun to enjoy dinner time."

"I also...are we always going to disagree on belief? When you ride the great seas of the world and see all this power in nature, how can you not believe in God?"

"It is a subject we will never agree on. You are like my sisters. Attributing everything to God. They have explained to me many times that I am a sinner, that Jesus died for my sins and that I must believe in him to be saved. It is all too mystical!"

Praying for the right words, Gudrun paused for a moment, then said, "Believing is just simple faith."

"I must get back to the bridge. At dinner we will talk about St. Thomas."

Gudrun stood and watched the two to three foot swells breaking against the hull. Standing still she could barely feel *Sognefjord* gently rock. *It is so peaceful Lord. I love the colors of the water and sky. Thank you for all the beauty you have given us. The dark, dark blue water, the contrast in the white crest of each wave, the turquoise as it hits the ship. Just beautiful. Please help me to be a good witness to Captain Hans. He has been told the truth, but he is rejecting you. It is obvious he is not at peace.*

CHAPTER 15

Saint Thomas

"**B**lackbeard's castle, just as the captain described." Åse pointed to the stone cylinder-shaped fortress up on the hill.

"I love the way the sunset is making it all rosy-colored. I do hope we can take a walk up to it while we are here," Gudrun said. "This is a big harbor. Look at the shops in Charlotte Amalie. Maybe we can explore those tomorrow."

"Good idea. Not that I have any money to spend. Look at the palm trees and the tug boat is bringing us right into dock."

The ladies walked to the port side and watched the deck-hands tie down the ship, marveling at the size of lines. Captain Torvik had explained that they would have at least four days to explore the island. All the passengers had been briefed on proper procedures for leaving the ship and what to expect on land. Gudrun stayed on deck after Åse left, enjoying the warm breeze, the fading light on the island, and the swaying palm trees. *Yes, this is an adventure.*

"There you are getting every last bit of light?" Captain Hans asked as he walked toward Gudrun.

She laughed. "It is beautiful here. Just like you said."

"It is. Tomorrow you will have to explore the island on your own. There will be excursions to Magens Bay, the town to explore and on Thursday we could walk to Blackbeard's Castle. For the next two days I will be working with the crew.

We have a lot of preparation to do for the locks in the Panama Canal. Plus some training and drills. Will you be alright?"

"I understand. This is not a vacation for you. Åse and I will be fine. We plan to go shopping tomorrow."

"Mrs. Sandnes is planning to venture into town, maybe you could include her?"

"Of course. She will be a delightful companion."

Hans offered her his elbow and walked her back to her cabin.

∽

A waiter brought Gudrun a note as she finished her breakfast. Upon reading it, Gudrun hurried off to the second-class deck to find Åse who only nodded as Gudrun approached. "Look," Åse said pointing below, her eyes wide.

"Yes, they are coaling the ship. Women too…my, that is hard work, shoveling the coal, carrying it in buckets. What a beautiful song they are singing…look how strong they are." Gudrun replied. *I hope they are happy. Like I was at the Grand House.*

"But their skin — it is so dark. It is black. What odd people."

Gudrun paused trying to repress her shock that Åse would even say such a thing. "Beautiful people, like us inside. Remember, the Captain told us that many of the people on this island are descendants from Africans being taken to the Americas to be sold as slaves. We will see a lot of people here with dark skin."

Åse stared at the women shoveling coal and loading it onto the ship. "I have never seen people like that."

"We will be meeting people from all over the world. All sizes and shapes, different colored skin, and facial features.

We have to remember that they are like us. People, wanting to be treated with respect," Gudrun said, remembering Arvik's explaination that the West coast, especially Seattle, consisted of people from every race.

"Mr. Johansen has wonderful neighbors who are Japanese. An educated Black man financed and led the first wagon-train into Washington State. Chinese laborers were brought to the West Coast to finish the railroads, and there are many Indian tribes in the state. The people I stayed with in Stavanger mentioned the people of Saint Thomas could be of Danish, African, or of Jewish descent."

"I didn't know people could be so different. It is getting warm out. Shall we go into town?" Åse asked.

"Yes," Gudrun agreed. "I have some letters to mail that I need to pick up in my room. Mrs. Sandnes is going to join us. She said she would meet us on the dock at nine."

"I will also meet you there. A letter to Arvik?"

"Yes, and to friends in Norway."

∽

Red-faced and out of breath Anders burst into the bridge. "They are taking over the ship!"

"Who?" Captain Torvik asked.

"The women of first-class. They have taken over the lounge. Sewing machines, fabric bolts, cutting out dresses on tables they moved in from the dining room. You have to get them under control."

The captain put down the chart he had been studying. "As long as they do not set up shop in here we are safe. Though I do know one of them that could take over the helm if needed."

"I told them they could not move the furniture around and they ignored me."

Smiling, the captain grabbed his cap. "I will go check on things." On his way to the lounge he passed a group of male passengers relaxing and playing cards under a makeshift awning on the deck. Hans waved at Mr. Sandnes who sat amongst the men. He found the lounge exactly as the first mate described it. Women chatting, laughing, cutting cotton fabric, sewing on machines or hand sewing and Miss Sagen in the middle of marking the hem of a new creation worn by Mrs. Sandnes.

Noticing the captain, the women suddenly became quiet, all but Miss Sagen who had her back to Captain Torvik as she pinned up the hem. "This cotton is so soft, so easy to work with. I cannot believe we got the whole bolt for the price of a yard of wool."

Mrs. Sandnes replied, "That is why we paid the pretty shop owner twice her asking price. We could not steal it."

"Now turn to the right," Gudrun said, and continued to measure the hem. "Yes, the shop owner was so sweet, we had to give her a decent price. I wish I had her beautiful smile. Her teeth gleamed against her beautiful dark skin."

Mrs. Sandnes looked toward the door and blushed. "Gudrun, Gudrun." She reached down and tapped Gudrun on the shoulder. "We have company."

Gudrun turned and stood. She broke into a smile when she saw the captain and walked toward him. "Look what we found in the most delightful shop in Charlotte Amalie, all these bolts of fabric. The deckhands were so nice and brought up several of the ladies' sewing machines from the hold. We all need lighter weight clothing. It is hot out."

"That is wonderful, Miss Sagen. May I speak with you outside?" Following Gudrun onto the deck he continued. "I am sorry to break into your productive afternoon but you have my first mate in a stew. He is worried you will take over the ship and he does not know how dinner will be served without tables." Hans failed to conceal a smile.

Gudrun laughed. "I am sorry to cause trouble and interrupt your work. It is so much fun designing and sewing with the ladies here. We have the best view and the sea breezes are delightful."

"It is alright. Please keep it contained to the lounge. Can we get our tables back for dinner?"

"We only took four tables, but we will return them. Will you be at dinner?"

"Yes, will you be wearing a new creation?" he asked.

"Maybe."

The captain patted her shoulder. "You behave. And I will inform the first mate the uprising is under control."

ဏ

Finishing the hem on another dress, Gudrun glanced across the harbor to the beach. Families from the ship were playing in the warm water, their children running along the sand. She could hear their screams and shouts of delight. *That would be fun.* She ate the last of her breakfast sandwich Åse had brought her an hour before. They had been up most of the night sewing. Åse had retired to her cabin for a nap.

"We have done well, Miss Sagen. You should start a dress shop when you get to Seattle. Your designs and work are excellent," Mrs. Sandnes commented, sitting down on the lounge chair next to Gudrun's. "It is so peaceful here."

"You have been a big help. Now all the ladies have cotton dresses appropriate for this heat." Gudrun started to giggle. "We do look like we are members of some club. All the dresses cut from four bolts of fabric. We all match."

"The *Sognefjord* Women's Club." Mrs. Sandnes declared, raising a glass of juice.

Gudrun laughed. Then in a demanding tone she said, "Vi trenger badedrakt."

Mrs. Sandnes looked at Gudrun with curiosity written all over her face. "Tell me...why do we need swimsuits?"

"Look at the beach. How fun is that? Running up and down the sand and wading is great. It would be so much better to swim."

The ship owner's wife shook her head. "Oh to be young. I admire your energy and spirit, but we need time to relax and enjoy the island. They say we will be leaving the harbor on the sixteenth for the Panama Canal."

Gudrun blushed. "...I am sorry if I have gone too far. I doubt I will ever have the chance to swim in such warm water in this lifetime. My mother and I used to swim in the cove near our cabin. Do you know how to swim?"

Mrs. Sandnes stood up, grabbed Gudrun's hand and pulled. "The day is young! God gave us this wonderful day to play. We shall go to town wearing our new dresses, wade in the water, eat lunch, and ask about badedrakt for you and me. I love to swim."

∽

"Watch your step, we are almost there." Captain Torvik encouraged Miss Åse Halvorsen. "One more short flight and we will have walked up the ninety-nine steps." He kept an eye on Mr. Sandnes ahead of him. It would not do if the owner of the shipping line died from heat stroke on his watch.

Åse paused, fanning herself, then grabbed the captain's arm again. "It is so hot, I feel faint. May I have another sip of water?"

Skipping up the steps ahead of the Sandneses, Gudrun walked along the path toward the castle. She paused, looking at the view of the town below. "There is the beach we swam at yesterday," she called out to Mrs. Sandnes as she walked up the stone path.

At dinner Hans had heard all about how Gudrun and Mrs. Sandnes had found a small shop near the beach that had a few swim dresses. The shop owner let them change in her dressing room. Mrs. Sandnes had procured extra towels for them from the ship. Gudrun had carried on about how she enjoyed having another woman to swim with and what a fantastic feeling it was floating in the clear warm water.

Gudrun glanced straight up at the castle next to them, as Captain Hans helped Åse to the railing. "Will we be able to go inside?"

"Yes," the captain replied. "We will rest a bit here. The steps inside are steep."

"A rest would be appreciated," Mr. Sandnes huffed, completely out of breath. He took a sip from his canteen.

His wife piped up, "Though it is called Blackbeard's Castle he did not build it. Our cousins the Danes built this in 1679, right, Captain?"

Pleased to see someone had done their homework, Hans said, "You are right — the Danes built it and called it Skytsborg. Blackbeard used it for a short time in the early 1700's. In fact, in the 1700's there were more pirates living on ships in the harbor than there were locals living on land."

"Amazing!" Mr. Sandnes exclaimed. "Imagine that harbor full of pirate ships. Colorful times."

The captain chuckled. "Dangerous times. The English could not get their large war ships into the harbor to eradicate the pirates, because of the shallow harbor. They have done a lot of dredging over the years to make it a deep enough port for trade. Are you ready to hike up the stairs inside? It is worth the view."

Hans kept a close eye on Gudrun as they enjoyed the view from the top of the castle. She seemed quiet today, maybe because Åse demanded all his attention? The young teenager did not have Gudrun's physical strength and agility. He would rather be walking alongside Gudrun.

"We can see for miles in every direction. Oh to be a pirate's wife and live here in seclusion." Gudrun started laughing as soon as she finished her sentence.

"He would not have been that civilized to marry anyone. This would have been a dangerous place back then," Captain Hans said.

"I know. I am just being silly. It is easy to forget the cares of the world in a place like this and romanticize everything." Gudrun smiled at the captain. "Do not take me so seriously. I am grateful for gentlemen like you in this world."

CHAPTER 16

Making History

*T*he sound of the engines woke Gudrun. *We are moving! It is happening! Just like Captain Hans said.* She glanced at her Baby Ben, four o' clock. *We are on time. Lake Gatun here we come!*

At dinner last night, Captain Torvik had announced to the whole dining room they would be leaving early, crossing the Caribbean Sea and arriving in Colon late in the evening. The next day they would be the first Norwegian passenger ship to go through the Panama Canal. She slipped out of bed and quickly got dressed. She grabbed a shawl to ward off any coolness on deck.

Standing on the stern she could see a few twinkling lights in Charlotte Amalie. After their morning outing to Blackbeard's Castle yesterday, she and Mrs. Sandnes had taken a long swim in the mid-afternoon. They swam back and forth, floated, chatted and thoroughly forgot the world and all its problems.

Last night's dinner had brought them back to reality with all the talk about the war. Not only had England joined the fight, but they had landed troops in France. Despite England's presence, the French army had suffered severe losses. The Germans were standing strong. *It feels odd Lord. Like I am running away from the world's troubles. Fleeing to safety. But you know it did not happen that way. Please protect the Sand-*

neses when they return to Norway. Keep them safe when they sail across the Atlantic again.

Gudrun knew she would miss Mrs. Sandnes when they got off in San Diego. *Hopefully she will be willing to write to me.*

Moonlight streamed across the harbor as they sailed past Hassel Island and out to the Caribbean Sea. The moonbeams seemed to follow the wake, dancing off the edge of the waves.

This is so exquisite, Lord. Thank you for giving us such a magnificent and gorgeous world to live in.

Thank you for caring for me, for providing for me. A year ago I broke the platter, my father had died a month before, and I was so scared I would lose my job. My future has been in question until now. I might have a secure future, as secure as things can be in this life. I know my future is secure in you... even if there is never love between us, I ask that Arvik and I will respect each other. That we will get along. That I will be able to cook, clean and converse up to his expectations.

Please open Captain Torvik's eyes to his need for you. Help him understand the gift of salvation you have for him.

Guide me today, Lord, help me to be what you want me to be.

In your Son's name, Amen.

Ending her prayer she could feel *Sognefjord* pick up speed. She continued holding on to the railing, all alone, mesmerized by the slight rocking of the ship, the wake, and the occasional mist from the ocean below. Gradually the sky to the east began to lighten. More and more color began to creep into the sky. Finally the sun made its entrance and she stood in awe as the glorious sunrise unfolded.

∽

Concrete walls seemed to close in and gigantic gates loomed ahead as *Sognefjord* inched her way into the locks.

"Look, Åse. The doors are opening. How symbolic — the doors to our new future," Gudrun said.

"How can you be so excited?" Åse asked. "We have no idea what is ahead for us. They seem like jail doors locking us in."

Giving Åse a curious look, Gudrun replied, "First of all, God the Father loves to give good gifts to His daughters. Whatever lies ahead will be for our good. And secondly I believe what Anna and Arvik have written is true. Would your cousin purposely suggest you marry someone that is not a good person?"

"Well, that is where you and I are different. I do not see the good. I have to admit I am dreading the boat docking in San Francisco."

Gudrun refused to allow Åse's mood ruin the magic of the moment. "Oh look at the boats with the lines."

"They are coming toward us. What are they doing?"

"Oh, they are going to tie *Sognefjord* to the small railroad cars called mules. See one on each side of the locks?"

"Are the mules going to pull the ship with those lines?" Åse asked.

"Yes, clear through the channel to the other side."

Åse gave Gudrun a funny look. "How do you know this? From Captain Torvik?"

"No, Mr. Sandnes has been explaining how the locks work in the first-class lounge."

The ladies watched as small boats came alongside the ship to tie the lines to *Sognefjord*. Once the lock hands had the lines secured the mules led the ship into the lock chamber. The tall concrete walls made them feel insignificant. The gates closed and the water began to rise.

"So amazing," Gudrun mumbled. "The locks were designed big enough to handle the Titanic. It is so sad it will never happen."

A scared-looking Åse agreed.

ᕫᕬ

Hans surveyed the bridge as they left the locks and continued on into Lake Gatun. His crew could easily navigate the twenty-three mile long lake. It seemed to be a good time to check on his "ward" as the crew had come to call her. Each member would alert the captain as to where and when they had last seen Miss Sagen. With so many firsts jammed into the day this might be the only time he would have to talk to her. He had missed dinner last night as they had arrived in Colon quite late. The last sighting of the platinum blonde had been on the starboard side of the bow.

He mused over the reports of her being up yesterday morning to witness them leave Saint Thomas. Anders had spotted her at forty-thirty out on the stern. Several crew members kept an eye on her off and on until sunrise. As they did their duties they were careful not to disturb her solitude.

Hans came alongside one of the lifeboats on the first-class deck when he heard Miss Halvorsen's higher-pitched voice. "Please, please keep away from the captain. I need time with him. I do not want to get married to a stranger. Maybe I can make the captain fall in love with me."

He strained to hear Gudrun's calm voice, and took a few steps closer, well hidden by the lifeboat. "Åse, it does not work that way. You cannot pick a man and claim him as yours. You are not thinking correctly, relationships do not work that way.

Besides, you are engaged. You told me you signed a contract to marry for the price of your ticket."

"Well, you are the self-righteous one, Miss 'I get to choose at no expense to me.' Not every woman has your arrangement. My parents told me to leave. This is my only choice. The man waiting for me could be horrible. He could beat me or be mean verbally. If I marry the captain before we land there is nothing anyone can do about it," Åse declared.

Gudrun continued calmly, "Captain Hans is old enough to be your father. Besides I am sure he has had many chances to marry, but he loves the sea too much to give it up."

"If you treat them right you can change any man's mind. My only problem is you. Please, stop talking to him, please," Åse pleaded.

"No. He is my friend...look how dark it is ahead. I am going to my cabin to avoid the rain. You should do the same. You should go below," Gudrun retorted.

"You want him all to yourself. Is that why you are sending me below?"

Gudrun snapped back, "Stay here and get drenched if you want to."

Hans quickly retreated several yards back and then started walking toward the women as if he had just arrived. Gudrun's hurried pace slowed when she saw him.

"Miss Sagen, I had hoped to find you. Unfortunately, the weather is changing. It seems we will be getting one of the infamous Panama downpours. May I walk you to your cabin?"

"Yes, please, quickly."

He paused as Åse stepped out from the railing. "Good afternoon Miss Halvorsen. It is best if you go to your cabin, it is going to rain," the captain said. He held out his elbow for Gudrun and she slipped her hand through.

As they walked in silence, Hans mulled over what he had just heard. *Feelings for Miss Halvorsen I do not have. I have extended to her the courtesy I would any female passenger. What I can do is secure Mr. Sandnes' help in checking out her arrangement in San Francisco.*

Looking at Gudrun, the captain continued to analyze the situation. She smiled at him, holding his arm a little tighter. *Feelings for Miss Sagen?...I do admire her. Who could not be drawn to this beautiful, genuine young lady? Feelings? Possibly, otherwise why did her description of me sting? Father and friend sounded insulting when she said those words.* He said a quick goodbye to Gudrun and headed back to the bridge.

∽

The deluge of rain outside her porthole seemed to match her feelings, Gudrun reflected as she wiped another tear away. *Why am I crying Lord? Because Åse and I had words? I was not very nice? You want me to love others. Not act like I did. But I felt like I had to protect Captain Hans. Why? He can take care of himself.*

It has to be bigger than that Lord. Am I really afraid of the future? It seems like a fairytale unfolding before my eyes. Maybe I am afraid. Afraid it will all disappear. Or that another version of Mrs. Thorsen will appear and ruin my new future, my fresh start. I should have been nicer to Åse, Lord. I am sorry.

Gudrun's tears subsided and she watched through her porthole as they entered another set of locks. They had made it across Lake Gatun. She washed her face, grabbed her shawl, and headed down the hall and up the stairs to the lounge to watch.

Mr. Sandnes stood next to the window explaining to fellow passengers that the distance they would be descending in this set of locks would not be as dramatic. They would follow a wide channel to a third set of locks before they got to the Pacific Ocean.

Gudrun wished she could be out on the bow watching everything unfold, but the rain kept coming down hard.

෧

Through the mass of passengers on the second-class deck Gudrun searched for Åse. *I need to apologize for walking off with the captain like that. And I should not have reminded her of her second-class status. That was snobby! You know I did not mean to be snobby, Lord. So silly of me to want to protect Captain Torvik. Give me the right words Lord to mend things with Åse.*

The rain had stopped and the decks were full of people eager to watch *Sognefjord* descend through the third locks. Gudrun continued to wind through the crowd, to no avail. She stopped along the railing just as *Sognefjord* leveled out with the Pacific Ocean and the gates began to open. The lock hands untied the lines as a tug started to pull the ship out of the locks. They would land in Panama City before dinner. Hopefully the captain could join them tonight.

A hand on her shoulder startled Gudrun. She turned to see Åse's dark eyes glaring at her.

"Are you slumming? Why are you on this deck?" Åse asked.

"To apologize to you," Gudrun said.

Åse's eyebrow raised. "Apologize?"

"Yes. For the way I left things early today. I am sorry I was not very nice."

"I did feel snubbed. You have a great opportunity in Seattle. Though I do like the captain, I would not use him to get out of getting married in San Francisco."

Gudrun watched Åse's face change from quiet surrender to an almost sinister look.

The sixteen-year-old continued on, "I have no chance of getting to know him because you are in the way."

Gudrun stiffened. She quickly asked the Lord to give her the right words. "As I said, the captain and I are friends. He is like an uncle to me. I value his friendship and will do what I can to protect him from people taking advantage of his kindness."

"So that is how you ease your conscience. I see the captain look at you. Listen to my warning," Åse sneered. "Stay away from him."

Gudrun turned, bumping into Anders as he passed by. She apologized to him and headed to the stairs. She had tried. The conversation did not make sense.

Back in her cabin she tried on two different dresses before deciding what to wear to dinner. "This is ridiculous. They have already seen every appropriate dinner dress I have at least once if not twice," she said to the mirror. "I do not have or will need a wardrobe like Mrs. Sandnes'."

Dinner turned into a celebration party marking their place in history, which continued on into the lounge when dinner ended. "The first Norwegian passenger ship to make it through the locks," Captain Torvik toasted their accomplishment. "I would like to thank everyone for joining me on this journey."

Watching him from across the room Gudrun could see why Åse liked him. His confident manner, proper etiquette, and good looks, she could not blame her. She wondered about

Åse's stability — burning the only bridge she had to get to the captain.

The more rational route would have been to be sweet and nice to me, so she could be up here all the time.

After the toasts, Gudrun and Mrs. Sandnes sat in a corner of the lounge chatting about fashion, their adventure, and the Lord. Gudrun longed to ask for her friend's advice on Åse, but did not want to gossip so she did not bring up the subject.

༄

"You are missing one of your friends," Captain Hans said as he came alongside Gudrun out on the bow of the first-class deck.

For two days *Sognefjord* had been sailing north along the coast of Panama, Costa Rica and now Nicaragua. From the bridge he had watched Gudrun point out porpoises and whales to Mrs. Sandnes. He had purposely tried to avoid Miss Sagen while still keeping an eye out for her safety. He needed to sort out his feelings.

"I know. I am beginning to wonder if she really is my friend. We had a bit of a spat. I have apologized. She is holding to her position and has not forgiven me."

Hans grabbed the railing with both hands staring out to sea. Then turning and looking directly at her said, "I must be truthful. I overheard the spat that day on Lake Gatun. A lifeboat hid me from your view as I came to meet you."

Gudrun's mouth dropped. "Oh my."

"Over time people can show their real self. Maybe she is overwhelmed by her situation. I do not believe you are to blame for anything."

"From her point of view and mine I was haughty, leaving with you that way and reminding her of her status on this ship. It was wrong. I came from nothing. There were women in town that treated me in the same manner. I know how it hurts." Gudrun twisted her handkerchief. "...the way she talked about you..."

"She is jealous. In her eyes you have everything. She does not know what you have been through or the challenges you will be facing. She is so focused on herself she cannot be happy for you," the captain explained.

"My, you are quite the psychologist." Gudrun laughed.

"All the years of watching people...one learns."

"I am sure. Maybe I should apologize again or invite her up to this deck."

The captain smiled, "Warn me if you do. I need to get back to the bridge. I will see you at dinner." He started to walk off, then turned and said, "From what I overheard you do not owe her another apology. That is my humble opinion. Anders said he saw her reaction when you spoke with her on the second-class deck. He said she seemed upset, even nasty. I would give her time, let her come to you."

As he walked toward the bridge he noticed Mrs. Sandnes coming toward him. He smiled, tipped his cap and nodded in response to her cheery hello.

The middle-aged lady immediately started waving at Gudrun. The captain heard her call out, "Time for another English lesson, Gudrun?"

CHAPTER 17

Stormy Days

*I*t seemed as if *Sognefjord's* rocking and rolling would never end. The first large waves had hit around midnight, waking Gudrun up. She had tried watching the storm from her port-hole, but darkness kept everything hidden. The occasional flash of lightning gave her glimpses of the large waves pound-ing the sides of the ship. Taking the small torch out of the pocket of her night-robe, she glanced at the watch on her wrist. Three-thirty.

Captain Hans had warned everyone at dinner that they would be facing a large storm. He told them to stay in their cabins, to put anything not tied or bolted down in their clos-ets, trunks, or dressers, and not to panic. They were expecting fifteen foot waves or larger. He warned them to stay off the decks as the rain would make the decks slippery and that in this storm they would not be able to go back and rescue any-one swept overboard. He reassured them that he had experi-enced storms of this size many times and though it would be an uncomfortable night, they would be fine if they obeyed the rules. Life jackets were handed out.

Gudrun had been an obedient passenger packing up her belongings, going to bed early so that she would have some sleep, and praying for their safety. She appreciated the captain giving her a small torch and Mrs. Sandnes lending her one of her watches.

The howling outside her porthole intensified along with the rocking and rolling. Suddenly the ship swayed to the starboard side and Gudrun found herself on the floor. *Sognefjord* jerked back in the other direction and flung her toward her bunk. As she crawled back into her bunk, her hand automatically found the sturdy leather strap attached to the wall near the head of her bed and she hung on tight. "Now I know what you are for," she said to the strap. "I had been wondering." She had noticed it when she had first walked into her cabin. Lightning struck as her cabin tilted toward the sea and through the porthole she watched a wave break over the deck, sending water toward her cabin. It struck with a thud. Swoosh! She could hear the water rush back out to sea as the ship righted itself. Praying seemed like the best course of action and pray she did. Praying for safety, for the storm to cease, and especially for wisdom for Captain Torvik, Mr. Anders Knobloch, the crew, and for the passengers below deck. The howling and the rocking seemed to decrease a little. The peace in her soul and the consistent rhythm of the waves lulled Gudrun to sleep for a moment.

Shouts and loud banging on her door jolted Gudrun awake. She recognized Åse's voice.

"Gudrun! Gudrun, please let me in."

Gudrun opened the door, clicked on her torch, to see a wide-eyed, panic-stricken Åse. She stepped back and motioned to her built-in sofa. Åse sat down, wringing her hands.

"I cannot stay in that tiny tin box anymore," Åse said in a deadpan voice. "No windows, being hurled all around the cabin. I will not do it."

Recognizing Åse's spirit seemed completely broken, Gudrun replied, "Alright. You can stay here until the storm subsides. We might be in the center of the storm. It seems calmer. Or it could be the end of it."

They sat in silence, rocking back and forth. Gudrun turned on her torch again four-fourteen. "In a little over an hour we will begin to see daylight. That will help."

Åse shook her head in agreement, staring at the floor.

Sognefjord lurched to her starboard again as a new set of large waves tossed the ship around. Åse screamed.

"Quiet now. Screaming does not help, it only makes it worse," Gudrun whispered.

"I cannot take this." Åse stood up. "We have to get off. We have to get off the boat. Then it will all stop."

Standing and grabbing Åse by the shoulders, Gudrun commanded, "Sit down. We will be alright."

Åse sat back down. Gudrun sat next to her, with her arm around the terrified teenager. "We need to think about the Lord, about scripture. We can recite Psalm Twenty-Three...the Lord is my Shepherd, I shall not want..."

Åse joined in and Gudrun could feel her body relax as they finished the Psalm. For a few minutes calm seemed to be restored to the cabin, then another set of waves hit.

Jumping to her feet Åse gave Gudrun a terrified look and stumbled out the door. Gudrun followed her cautiously across the constantly pitching floor. As she closed her cabin door she saw Åse heading up the stairs to the promenade deck. Despite the rolling of the ship she caught up with her in the lounge. Tables were sliding toward her one moment and going the other direction the next. Chairs were strewn about. The sofas were out of place. Åse wandered through the maze heading for the door to the deck.

"Åse, stop! This is not safe! Come back to the cabin."

Turning toward Gudrun, Åse gave her a blank stare. "I cannot do this. I have to get away from this rocking, the noise, and you!" She struggled to the door, just as a sliding table knocked Gudrun down.

Adrenalin surging, Gudrun picked herself up quickly, navigating her way through the lounge. She had the rhythm of the current set of waves down and leaning into each wave she danced along accordingly, dodging moving furniture on the way. The torrential rain stopped her at the door. *I have to keep her from jumping overboard! Help me Lord!*

Turning on her torch, Gudrun found Åse climbing up the ladder to the upper deck. *The lifeboats! Is she going after one of the lifeboats? Too dangerous with only poles and cables for a railing.* Reaching the top of the ladder Gudrun saw Åse struggling against the wind and driving rain, attempting to cross the wooden deck. Åse fell sliding toward the ladder as Gudrun stepped onto the deck. The ship crested on a wave before diving down toward the trough again, sending Åse in the other direction before Gudrun could grab her.

Ꮼ

"Outstanding job, Mr. Knobloch. Your understanding of how to approach these swell waves is excellent," Captain Torvik said as he watched Anders guide the boat over another fifteen-foot wave. "Though I would hate to lose you, I know you are ready to command your own ship."

Anders smiled. "Thank you, sir." The smile faded as he saw the next wave coming.

"Captain, look!" The second mate yelled pointing to the deck behind the bridge. "Two women on the deck! Are they fighting?"

Turning, Captain Hans saw Åse sliding across the deck and Gudrun scrambling to grab her. "First Mate, Anders Knobloch, *Sognefjord* is officially under your command, until I return to the helm." He grabbed his raincoat and a lifejacket and made his way to the deck.

Hans could feel the ship level out for a second as he stepped onto the deck. He grabbed the top cable at the same time Åse stood up and stumbled to the edge. Instead of holding on tight she attempted to climb over the railing but her dress prevented her from succeeding.

Sognefjord started to climb the next wave and Hans slid toward Åse, grabbing her around the waist. "What are you doing?" he yelled. He could see Gudrun struggling to reach them, leaning toward the waves. She slipped and fell up against a lifeboat.

Åse pounded on his side and pulled on his arms, almost breaking free. "I am getting out of here," she screamed. "Let me go!"

A deckhand came alongside Hans, and gave Åse a punch on her jaw and she collapsed in the captain's arms.

"I have her. I will get a doctor." Another deckhand joined him and Hans let go of the teenager.

"Gudrun!" Hans yelled. Lightning flashed just as the ship crested the wave, giving him a view of her lifeless figure next to the lifeboat, blood dripping from her head. Her limp body started to slide toward him as the ship descended the wave. "Gudrun!"

Suddenly the ship shifted and Gudrun slid away from him. Hans feared she would go overboard. Another wave changed the tilt of the ship turning her back toward the railing. His hand grabbed hers as she bumped up against the shallow railing curb. Still holding onto her he sat down holding tight to a pole with his other arm, anticipating the next swell. Hans struggled to hold onto Gudrun and the pole as another set of waves battered the ship.

During a brief lull between sets, he pulled her close, getting a better hold on her. He checked for a pulse, though faint, it seemed steady. He noticed the cut on her forehead did not look too bad, a few stitches at the most. Another set began to rock the ship; however the wind and noise were lessening and the waves seemed smaller and smaller. A gleam of light broke over the horizon of Guatemala and southern Mexico. He sat there dabbing her head with his handkerchief as *Sognefjord* gently swayed. "Gudrun, Gudrun wake up. The storm is over. It is all over."

He continued to lean against the railing post staring at the morning light breaking across the sky and the calmer sea below.

Finally, he stood, picked up Gudrun and stumbled towards the ladder to the promenade deck. Two more deckhands arrived with a stretcher to carry Gudrun's unconscious body.

One of the deckhands reached out for Gudrun. "We have her, sir."

"Thank you for coming so quickly. First Mate Knobloch's orders?" Hans asked.

"Yes, sir," the other deckhand answered. "He also ordered the crew to set up a hospital in the first-class lounge."

"Good."

Gudrun's eyes began to flutter as they entered the lounge. Hans observed a doctor attending Åse and several deckhands were picking up chairs, righting tables, and setting up cots. As they slid Gudrun onto the first one, Hans kneeled down next to her.

"Miss Sagen, Gudrun, can you hear me?"

Her eyes fluttered again and she mumbled, "Yes."

∽

Despite the fogginess in her pounding head, Gudrun recognized the ornate ceiling of the lounge.

Mrs. Sandnes sat down next to her. "The doctor will be with you next," she said, daubing Gudrun's wound with a damp cloth. "He is a gentleman that sat at our table earlier in the week. Did you know I used to be a nurse in a hospital in Bergen? Many, many years ago, before I met my husband."

"Oh, I am in the hands of a professional," Gudrun mumbled.

Mrs. Sandnes laughed. "Yes. It is all coming back to me quickly. It looks like two or three stitches will take care of this."

Gudrun put her hand on Mrs. Sandnes's arm, and asked, "Åse?"

"She is sedated. She woke up yelling and screaming about getting off the ship. She even tried to punch the doctor. We will be keeping a close eye on her until we arrive in San Diego. Once we are at dock we can look further into Åse's situation. You rest. The doctor will check you for a concussion."

"Were others injured?"

"Yes. One man has a broken leg, a few others with concussions or cuts. The crew is still taking inventory of the damage. As long as people obeyed orders they were not hurt."

Gudrun sat upright. "I did obey orders!" Her hand went to her head trying to stop the dizziness.

"You sat up too fast. You must take things slow," Mrs. Sandnes said, lowering Gudrun back down on the cot. "I did not mean you. We know you were trying to help Åse."

"She came to my room. She wanted off the ship. Please let Captain Torvik know I did not want to disobey orders."

"He knows. Here is the doctor, once you are fixed up you can rest."

CHAPTER 18

Confusion

Looking up from his report, Captain Hans looked across San Diego Bay at Point Loma. *Just as beautiful as the last time I stopped here. The warm breezes are perfect.* He looked back down at his report, continuing where he had left off —

...Despite the crosscurrents and waves pounding from every direction First Mate Anders Knobloch kept control of the ship. Some of the waves were higher than fifteen feet. He stayed calm and navigated *Sognefjord* through difficult seas. Through careful observation on this, and other voyages, I believe First Mate Knobloch is ready to command his own ship.

However, having someone with his skill as second in command, kept us from having any more damage than occurred from the storm, or losing any passengers.

The only injuries were sustained when passengers did not obey orders, except one. Passenger Miss Gudrun Sagen heroically left her cabin to keep another female passenger from jumping overboard. She sustained a cut to her head that required three stitches, and is recovering from a slight concussion.

Without the utmost confidence in First Mate Knobloch's abilities I would not have been able to leave the helm and assist Miss Sagen with the difficult passenger.

My conclusion is that when navigating the West coast of the America's, a strong, experienced crew is needed.

Hans glanced at his watch, closed his logbook and stepped out on deck. To the south he could see the newly constructed Coronado Bridge. His thoughts returned to Gudrun. *I have been avoiding her since the storm. We started this journey with her avoiding me and now I have been avoiding her. Why does my heart beat faster when I see her? I cannot fall in love. I cannot give up the sea. Besides, she is engaged. Why all this turmoil. Would she even have me? Should I tell her how I feel?...enough daydreaming, I need to change for dinner.*

Since he and Miss Sagen had been invited to dine with the Sandneses at their hotel up on the hill near the newly named Balboa Park, he would have to face her.

The couple had made arrangements for Miss Halvorsen to leave the ship, obtained a room for her adjoining theirs at their hotel, and found a doctor to help her. Mr. Sandnes had sent a telegram to Miss Halverson's fiancé, explaining the situation and invited him to visit his intended.

৽

Finishing up the last embroidery stitch on the handkerchief, Gudrun glanced out at Point Loma with the lighthouse standing tall up on the hill. She leaned back, enjoying the warm breezes coming from the shore. She could understand why people wanted to live in this glorious country. She folded the handkerchief, rolled it and tied it with a ribbon. All finished. Handkerchiefs for the Sandneses and Åse. She had made over thirty handkerchiefs during her stay in Stavanger out of the best material she could find. She had the rest of the voyage to finish the embroidery on the ones for Arvik and the Lundes.

"Excuse me, Miss, this letter just arrived for you." Anders handed her an envelope. "It is from Seattle."

"Thank you. Have you been able to take some time off?"

"Yes, ma'am. It is beautiful here. Enjoy your letter."

The familiar handwriting told her the letter was from Arvik. *How thoughtful of him to write — Sunset Lane, Orcas Island, Washington. Will that be my address?*

Enjoying the breeze, Gudrun read and reread the letter from Arvik. He had received her letter from Saint Thomas and expressed his delight that she found the trip an adventure. He ended the letter with:

> The summer has been warm this year. I do hope you arrive in time to enjoy the balmy weather. It looks like we will have a good apple crop.
>
> The shipping line has been keeping me informed of *Sognefjord's* progress. I will be there to pick you up in Seattle and have arranged for transportation to the Lundes' home. Please, please do not leave the ship until I arrive. With so many passengers it will take time to unload. It might be best to meet when things calm down and most of the passengers have left.
>
> Anna is also looking forward to meeting you.
>
> Every morning and evening I pray for your safety.
>
> Until we meet,
>
> Yours,
>
> Arvik.

Running her finger over the words "every morning and evening I pray for your safety," she knew they had two connections, their belief and their culture. *Lord, thank you for this letter. It feels so right. Like you have guided me to this time. Please help me with my decision to marry. I ask for your strength and the right words as I meet Åse this evening. Please*

heal her. Guide her too. Thank you for your provision. In your
Son's name, Amen.

As she reread the letter one more time, her heart warmed.
She knew good things awaited her in Seattle.

Now what to wear? Such a warm evening. Maybe the
dressier cotton from Saint Thomas...with the right accessories
it will do.

∾

"I am nervous about seeing Åse again." Gudrun broke the
silence as she and the captain sat in the back seat of the car the
Sandneses had sent for them. Since the captain had knocked
on her cabin door they had only spoken a few words.

"It could be awkward at first. We must make sure she feels
accepted by us," Hans replied. "There is a chance she might
not want to see us. I am sorry your friendship has taken this
turn."

Gudrun looked at him, his eyes so warm and tender. For a
second she felt the urge to kiss him on the cheek like she did
her own father, but stopped herself. She did not want to offend
or mislead him, besides Arvik's words still echoed in her mind.

"You are right. I have been praying things will go well."
She could sense the captain's body stiffen as she referred to
prayer. The car came to a halt and the driver helped her out of
the car. Hans offered her his arm and they walked up the stairs
and through the entrance of the grand hotel. They found Mr.
Sandnes waiting for them in the lobby.

"We are so glad you both could come." He shook the captain's hand. "Åse would like to meet with both of you in the
parlor. She does not feel up to dining with us."

Mr. Sandnes led them to a room off the lobby. As he opened
the door Gudrun got a glimpse of Åse and restrained herself

from gasping. A thinner, drawn-looking Åse stood and came to meet her friend. She took Gudrun's hands and said, "I am so sorry."

Instinctively Gudrun reached out and gave the teenager a hug, then guided her to the sofa to sit down.

Looking up at Captain Torvik, Åse said, "I am sorry for all the trouble I caused, sir."

"It is in the past. We are grateful you are alive and being cared for."

"The Sandneses have been so gracious. The doctor here is helpful. He says I am claustrophobic. On board *Sognefjord,* each night below deck became a nightmare in such close quarters with three ladies I did not know. Then with the storm it became too much. The stress regarding my arranged marriage added to everything."

"That is understandable." Gudrun put her arm around Åse.

Nervously rubbing her hands together, Åse continued, "… the doctor also recommended we limit our visit. I believe I must return to my room now. Thank you for coming."

She stood and Mr. Sandnes walked her towards the door just as his wife entered the room. Nodding to Gudrun and Hans she took Åse's hand to lead her upstairs.

"We will be dining out on one of the hotel's private patios. My wife will be down in a minute. We have employed someone to stay with Åse."

Warm breezes played across the patio as the friends enjoyed the meal, the view of the harbor and each other's company. Gudrun could not help but notice that every time she looked at the captain his dark smiling eyes met hers. After dessert and a brief exchange of presents, Mrs. Sandnes asked Gudrun to join her for a walk in the garden.

They wandered the path through exotic plants and various palm trees, commenting on the strange shapes and colors. Several of the species were the same as on Saint Thomas.

Taking a small box out of her purse, Gudrun handed it to Mrs. Sandnes. "Thank you for loaning me the watch during the storm."

Mrs. Sandnes handed the box back to Gudrun. "I meant to tell you I want you to keep it. Think of me as you wear it. I have several watches and I plan to purchase a new one here to remind me of San Diego."

Gudrun gave her a slight hug. "You are so kind. I will never forget you."

"I will be praying for your journey to Seattle," Mrs. Sandnes said as she bent down to smell a unique orange boat shaped blossom. "It smells like grasses or a tomato. Odd scent yet so beautiful. Also I have been praying that the Lord will make your choice clear to you."

"Thank you. I value those prayers. I will be praying for your protection as you travel back home."

"We appreciate that. I have written down the hotel address and our home address. Please write to me. I will be eagerly waiting to hear your decision." Mrs. Sandnes handed Gudrun a card. "You might have more than one suitor in Seattle. You are a beautiful young lady. Remember, the Bible tells us to marry in the faith. Our common love of the Lord has gotten me and my husband through the hard times."

Gudrun shook her head. "More than one suitor? That would be confusing. I am praying the Lord keeps it simple, clear and direct."

"So will I. Please promise you will write?"

"I will."

⁓

Through her binoculars Gudrun strained to follow the coastline north of San Francisco. Due to slightly submerged large rocks the ship kept a few miles offshore. When they were sailing from San Diego towards San Francisco, Captain Hans had allowed the ship to follow the coastline a bit closer. She had to agree with him that the Mission at San Juan Capistrano had a special beauty. The cliffs at the nearby harbor below Dana Head also intrigued her.

Goosebumps formed up and down her arms as she thought about *Songeford's* landing in Seattle. Soon she would be meeting Arvik.

Gudrun watched the silly young girls giggle as Captain Hans walked past them towards her. At their stop in San Francisco she had watched the exchange of passengers.

The parade of new first-class passengers included a group of young women who were allegedly from a house of ill repute. The rumor that police had raided and shut down the house quickly spread throughout the ship. Business must have been good for them to secure such a passage. Apparently this group had decided they wanted new lives. She had to admire their courage to do so. What would Mrs. Thorsen think about them? She would have probably thrown them all overboard, one by one. Gudrun smiled at the thought.

"What is so humorous?" Captain Hans asked as he arrived next to her. She turned toward the railing and looked out at the ocean.

Letting out a sigh, Gudrun explained in hushed tones about her past encounter with Mrs. Thorsen's nephew and the repercussions of being shunned and gossiped about. It felt like someone else was sharing this intimate story. A secret she had only wanted to talk about with her father.

Hans placed his hand on her shoulder. "Your secret is safe with me. However, it sounds like an honest mistake to me and that he took advantage of your innocence. Do not blame yourself."

"I used to. However, I trust in the fact that God has forgiven me."

A dark cloud covered the captain's face. He mumbled quickly, "I am needed at the helm." And left.

CHAPTER 19

Introductions

*E*arly Monday morning sunshine silhouetted tall mountains to the south of *Sognefjord* as she sailed down the Straits of Juan De Fuca towards the town of Port Townsend. Gudrun had given up trying to sleep around five o'clock that morning and gone out on deck to do her morning prayers. All night she had tossed and turned, thoughts of finally meeting Arvik keeping her awake. As she finished her prayers the captain joined her.

"Good morning. What was the town we passed a bit ago?" Gudrun asked.

"Port Angeles. We are looking at the end of the Olympic Mountain Chain and that mountain is Hurricane Ridge," Captain Hans explained.

"I thought so, thank you, now I am oriented," Gudrun replied. "Anders lent me a chart a few days ago which I have been studying."

They stood in awe of the sun breaking across the little town of Sequim, both looking through their binoculars.

"I have instructed Anders to stay a half mile off shore in this area. Do you see all the fishing boats?"

Gudrun nodded. "It looks like a long point?"

"Yes, there is a two and a half mile long spit there, called Dungeness Spit. Reason enough to stay off shore and for them to build that lighthouse. "

Just before the steamship passed Fort Worden, Captain Hans disappeared to the helm. He had explained to her that intense shoaling off the sandy point would require his full attention. He did not want to add to the number of ships that had gone aground there. The August sun hitting the newly constructed Point Wilson Lighthouse took her breath away for a second. The white octagonal tower shone in the morning light. The serene sandy beaches called out to her. *Now Lord, now. We will be turning south into Puget Sound. It is starting — my new life. There is Whidbey Island. Give me wisdom Lord. Guide my choices. Please protect me.*

Binoculars in hand she scanned the shoreline and Port Townsend. Blocks and blocks of brick two and even four story buildings lined the waterfront. Fort Flagler eventually blocked her view of the city.

At the south end of Whidbey Island a forty-five foot sailboat also heading south caught her attention. She zoomed in with the binoculars and her heart began to pound. At the helm stood a handsome, tall, blonde man. She dropped the glasses against her chest, blushing. She picked up the glasses again. The sailor must have gone below. She noticed the name of the boat - *Himmel. A Norwegian name...hmmm.*

Sognefjord passed the sailboat, it's course set for Seattle. Gudrun walked up and down the deck, looking through her binoculars at the shore. The green trees reminded her of the forests inland from Lillesand and Puget Sound reminded her of a fjord. *This looks like home, definitely more familiar looking than the palm trees and foliage of San Diego. This could be a great place to live,* she thought.

∽

Fighting the urge to find Miss Sagen and propose to her, Captain Hans held onto the wheel. Skillfully guiding *Sognefjord* past West Point toward Seattle. He needed to stick to his plan. He needed to talk to Mr. Johansen first, as it seemed the right thing to do. Miss Sagen had informed him of Arvik's request that she wait on the boat until most of the passengers had left. A wise man and a wise request.

Hans knew the dock where *Sognefjord* would moor for a week. It sat north of Yesler Way and next to the public dock where Arvik would be docking his boat.

Anders went on deck to ready the crew. As they rounded the area called Magnolia, a tug came out to guide them into dock. He could feel the excitement rising. With so many Norwegians living in the Seattle area of Ballard, many of those on board were reuniting with family. Even with the best systems in place it would be chaos for the next hour or more. He could see Miss Sagen standing along the railing, away from the first-class passengers lining up to disembark.

Once the lines were secured and *Sognefjord's* engines turned off, Captain Hans left his post to help with the disembarkation. He said goodbye to the first-class passengers, while keeping an eye on the staff. He waved to Miss Sagen before heading down to the second-class deck.

Over an hour later the captain climbed the stairs back up to the first-class deck to talk to Gudrun one more time. There she stood in a beautiful blue dress, her long curls dancing in the breeze, speaking with Anders. His heart skipped a beat as he walked along the railing toward her. A sailboat caught his eye as it came into the public moorage.

Hans spotted his rival immediately as Arvik sailed into a slip below. This could be the man he had to beat out to win Gudrun's heart. He glanced at Gudrun saying her final goodbye to Anders. She turned to him and then glanced down at the dock directly at the stranger in the boat called *Himmel*. The surprise, then delight, and finally the rosy blush that spread across her face told Hans he might have lost the war.

Coming up to Gudrun, Hans took her hand. "I will go down and find Mr. Johansen and bring him up to the lounge and introduce him to you if that is acceptable to you?" He could feel her shaking slightly.

"That would be nice. Thank you." She withdrew her hand from his.

"You can stay on board as long as you need to. If for some reason you are afraid to go with him, please let me know."

Gudrun smiled. "I appreciate the offer. I doubt it will be necessary. I will meet you in the lounge."

Hans noticed she hung by the railing looking down at *Himmel* as he started down the stairs.

∽

"It is finally here! This moment when I will be meeting my Gudrun...well, hopefully my Gudrun. Hopefully she will accept me." Arvik said to *Himmel* as he stepped out onto the dock. He straightened his sports jacket and looked up at *Sognefjord*. The tall slender blonde and the captain standing next to her had disappeared. "Perhaps that is she." He walked towards the ship, his anticipation building.

He found himself standing in front of *Sognefjord*, not sure he heard the captain correctly. "You do not want payment for looking after Miss Sagen? Does that mean you did not do your job?"

Captain Hans took off his cap and wiped his brow. "I did as you requested and kept a close eye on her...as I got to know her I realized what an exceptional young lady she is. I must

163

confess I have developed feelings for her, feelings that she is not aware of. She thinks of me as a father figure. However, I must warn you that during the week *Sognefjord* will be at port I plan to let her know how I feel. That is why I cannot take your money."

No. This cannot be happening. I have a competitor? Arvik could feel his blood pressure rising. "You have caught me off guard."

"I do apologize. It seemed only fair to be honest with you. Please come on board. I will introduce you to Miss Sagen."

As he followed the captain up the stairs Arvik sized up his competition. *Dark haired, good looking, definitely an older man. Nice physique, limber as he is climbing the stairs quickly, and honest. All qualities a young woman could be drawn to. I do appreciate the warning and that he arranged a private place for us to meet.*

Arvik could not help but notice the beautiful paneling on the walls and the luxurious carpet beneath his feet. Miss Sagen had traveled in the style that he hoped she would. Suddenly the captain turned, motioning him through a door. There, standing next to a window stood a vision in blue. It felt like a dream. He kept walking closer, unaware of anything else but her.

In the distance he vaguely heard the captain say, "Miss Sagen, I would like to present Mr. Arvik Johansen. Mr. Johansen this is Miss Gudrun Sagen." Arvik took her hand and kissed it. "It is my pleasure to meet you."

☙

After Captain Hans left to meet Mr. Johansen, Gudrun paced in the lounge, then stopped and started praying. *Arvik, Lord. I think Arvik is the sailor that took my breath away up by Port Townsend. Even though he changed his clothes I am sure it is the same man. But looks are not everything Lord. Give me clear thinking. Please do not let my emotions take over. Guide me to do your will. My heart is pounding...finally I am going to meet the author of those letters. The man who paid for my passage. May he be half the man I imagined him to be. Thank you for keeping me safe. Thank you for knowing what is best. In your Son's name, Amen.*

Hearing footsteps, Gudrun turned. Her knees began to shake as the handsome man she had seen aboard *Himmel* walked across the lounge toward her. He took her hand and kissed it. He spoke and she replied, "The pleasure is mine."

Smiling blue eyes met hers. Eyes she had to look up to, such a rare privilege to look up at a man. She felt like a school-girl.

"I have matters to take care of. I will leave you two alone," Captain Hans said.

"Thank you, Captain," Arvik replied. Turning to Gudrun he gestured toward the chairs by the window. "Shall we sit?"

Following his lead, Gudrun sat. Did she dare look at him? Could he tell she found him attractive? Words she had been practicing the past two days fell from her lips. "I wish to thank you for the generous passage to America that you provided for me. I am grateful. I appreciated the protection and amenities of first-class."

"You are welcome. I could not ask you to come and expect you to suffer hardship. The representative for the Norwegian Steamship Line here in Seattle explained the conditions below deck. I am not rich but well enough off to provide such passage."

Gudrun looked at Arvik. "Such luxurious passage took some getting used to. I am just a poor fisherman's daughter. Again, I thank you for your provision."

Arvik nodded. "The captain seems nice. Did you get along with him?"

"Oh, yes. He and the crew took good care of me. His understanding and love of the sea is unmatched. One of the younger second-class passengers took a liking to him. I know he is in love with the sea. He would never marry," Gudrun explained.

"Shall we walk around the deck?" Arvik asked. "We can see the city better up here than on the crowded streets. We should enjoy the sights at this vantage point."

Gudrun nodded.

Arvik offered her his arm. Gudrun placed her hand inside his elbow and they walked to the deck. To the north they could see Pike Place Market. Looking straight ahead, Arvik pointed out special areas of Pioneer Square and beyond to the newly constructed Smith Tower, the tallest building in Seattle. By the end of their walk they were on a first name basis.

This is comfortable, Lord. Can it really be this easy? she thought.

ᕳᖇ

The motorcar turned off Highland Drive, then into a narrow drive that led to a circular turn around in front of a large brick mansion, surrounded by lush gardens. Arvik opened the car door just as a medium height, red-haired lady came running down the entry steps.

"You are here, finally! I began to wonder if this day would ever come. I am Anna Lunde. Please call me Anna." Anna reached up and gave Gudrun a hug. "I am so glad you are here. Come on in, you must be tired." Anna grabbed Gudrun's arm, leading her up the steps, totally ignoring Arvik.

They passed a man coming down the steps who smiled and nodded to Gudrun. As they entered the home Gudrun turned to see Arvik, the man, and the taxi driver unloading her trunk. "Oh. I should have introduced you to Nils. The main floor washroom is down this hall, the parlor is on your right. Please join me for tea in there." Leaving Gudrun at the washroom door the pretty redhead hustled on down the hall.

This is not what I expected. The house is huge and luxurious. I expected a nice suitable home, something much smaller. So far nothing has been like I imagined it.

Finding the parlor again, Gudrun walked to the windows to admire the view of Puget Sound. About four hours ago *Sognefjord* sailed right past this part of Queen Anne Hill.

"There you are. Please sit and have some tea. I have smørbrød and småkake. The men should be down in a minute." Anna laid a tray of open-face sandwiches and cookies on the table. A young lady followed with the tea service and laid it next to the tray. "Thank you, Emily. Oh I am afraid I am doing all the talking. It is just that we have waited so long for your arrival—"

Arvik and Nils' entrance into the parlor interrupted Anna's chatter. She introduced Nils and began to serve tea. As she served the tea Gudrun kept stealing glances at Arvik when he was not looking.

After twenty minutes of small talk Anna stood up and said. "Let me show you to your room, Gudrun. You must want to rest before dinner after such a long day."

"Thank you, it sounds wonderful. Do you have other plans, Arvik?" Gudrun asked.

"Please relax. Nils and I are going back down to *Sognefjord* and get your furniture moved onto *Himmel*," Arvik responded.

"Thank you. Inside the crate there is a bed frame and table in pieces. It would be easier to transport those without the crate," Gudrun suggested.

Following Anna up the wide, winding staircase, Gudrun said, "Your house is so perfect."

"Thank you," Anna replied. "Your room is at the end of this hall. We are at the end in the other direction. I hope you find everything comfortable." She opened the door to the guest room. "Arvik is staying on the main floor at the other end of the house." A twinkle formed in her eye. "We must keep things proper. Oh I am so sorry but I have to ask, what do you think of him? He is handsome, right?"

Gudrun blushed. "Handsome. Yes he is that...and tall."

Anna giggled. "I feel like a schoolgirl." She sat down on a bench at the end of the bed and patted the seat next to her. "Any woman would have to admit Arvik is handsome, however being attracted is a different thing. I hope someday there will be an attraction between you two. Nils is not as handsome but the moment I saw him I knew...the attraction was so strong."

Sitting next to Anna, Gudrun bowed her head and looked at her hands. "I understand what you are saying. There is much to take in, so many new things. I am not sure how I feel about anything."

"You poor dear." She squeezed Gudrun's hand. "And here I am prattling on. One more thing and then I will leave you in peace." Anna walked over to the closet and opened it. "I took the liberty of purchasing a few dresses for you. I thought if I had been traveling for weeks all my clothes would need cleaning. From Berit's description I guessed at your size. Now I think I bought a size too big around. Such a thin waist you have. If they do not fit we can return them."

Astonished Gudrun walked over and pulled each dress out one by one. "How beautiful. I have never had a ready-to-wear dress before. I will repay you."

"No, no. These are your welcome to America gift from me." Anna patted Gudrun on the arm, then glanced at her watch. "Now dinner is in three hours. If there is anything you want to know about Arvik I can fill you in or find out from Nils. They have been friends since they were young children."

As she drifted off to sleep, Gudrun thought of the 1 Samuel passage where Jonathan and David met and their souls were knit. That perfectly described how she felt about Anna. She knew she had a lifelong friend.

CHAPTER 20

Gudrun's Decision

*R*iding with Nils in his car, Arvik fumed internally. While they carried Gudrun's trunk up to her room he had told Nils about the Captain's intentions.

"I have a suggestion," Nils said. "How about we stop down at my lumber mill, grab a truck and bring Gudrun's crate still intact to the house to store? It is safer in my garage than on *Himmel*. Later on, if she turns you down we do not have to re-crate everything."

Arvik chuckled. "So you have me losing this war? Good to know my best friend is rooting for the captain."

Nils laughed. "Not at all. Remember, the more low-key you are about the captain the better. We should invite him to dinner at the house."

"Dinner! You really are against me."

"Knowing your enemy gives you the advantage. Besides, Gudrun is all ready to have you load her furniture on your boat. She is not even thinking of the captain. Also if he comes to dinner, Anna and I can assess the situation."

"Alright," Arvik conceded. "It would help to have your opinion. Not sure I can trust your wife. She is so giddy about having a new girlfriend she will probably try to marry Gudrun off to every bachelor at church. She is pretty, is she not?"

"Pretty and beautiful in a natural way. Also very quiet."

"Give her time to warm up to us. The three of us can be intimidating." *I am glad she is not glitzy or flirtatious or I would have even more men after her. The captain is all I can handle.*"

༓

Noises and men's voices in the courtyard woke Gudrun. She went to her bathroom and peeked through the curtains. Arvik and Nils were unloading her crate onto a dolly. She watched Arvik push it into the garage. He had taken off his dress shirt and she could not help but notice his arm and even his back muscles ripple under his sleeveless undershirt. Blushing, she left the window and went to the closet to select a dress to wear to dinner.

A half hour later she descended the stairs carrying a small basket. She explored the first floor, finding the dining room and putting the basket on a side table. Exploring for a few more minutes, she found a large living room looking over the Seattle harbor. Beyond the harbor stood a tall mountain covered in snow, almost the same view as from her room. She heard someone clearing their throat and turned to see Arvik dressed for dinner in a sports coat.

Hiding her surprise at his attire, Gudrun said, "Good evening. How are you?"

"Well, thank you. I see you are enjoying the view of Mount Rainier. Also I come bearing news concerning Captain Torvik and your crate."

"Good news?"

"I hope you think so. The captain is coming for dinner tomorrow night and has requested that he might come early so the two of you can take a stroll."

Gudrun could not hide her excitement. "Oh. That is nice. And my crate?"

"Nils suggested that we store it here until all the details have been worked out. It is safer. I hope you do not mind," Arvik said.

"Not at all." Gudrun turned to Anna as she walked into the room. "I hope the captain joining us for dinner tomorrow is not an imposition? He is such a wonderful man. He often reminds me of my father."

The redhead laughed. "The more guests we have the happier I am. We are excited to meet him. Dinner is ready, shall we go to the dining room?"

Wanting to minimize questions about herself Gudrun quickly steered the dinner conversation to how the three friends had met. Stories of Arvik and Nils meeting while they were in grade school in Odda dominated the dinner discussion. Arvik shared how Nils' family had welcomed him for dinners when his mother passed away. His father worked long hours as a sharecropper at several fruit orchards along the fjord. Anna shared how she met Nils at the university in Stavanger and she spent a whole semester pining after him before he noticed her.

Gudrun presented each of them with her gift of handmade, monogrammed handkerchiefs. They expressed their appreciation and admired her work. Anna seemed delighted with her urtesalt.

With dinner completed, Arvik pushed his chair back. "Miss Sagen, might I have the pleasure of taking a stroll with you to the nearby park?"

"We can show you the sight—" Nils began.

Anna interrupted, "No, dear. I do not think we are invited on this walk."

"You do need a chaperone, right?" Nils smiled at Gudrun.

Gudrun could feel her cheeks reddening, even though she knew it was all in fun. "Arvik, I would like to go for a stroll.

Nils, thank you, but we are not in need of a chaperone. Thank you for your concern."

"So you will be leaving your porcupine stick in your room?" Anna teased, then put her hand over her mouth as she realized she had overstepped her bounds.

Gudrun gasped. "You know about that?"

"I am so sorry, please forgive me. Berit wrote—oh Gudrun, I did not mean to embarrass you. The men do not know the story."

Nils came and stood behind his wife gently putting his hands on her shoulders. "Please know you are among friends, Gudrun. My dear wife will keep your story to herself until you are ready to share it."

Arvik stood. "Thank you for the lovely dinner, Anna. Gudrun, your stick sounds like a good defense weapon for the woods. Maybe you can tell me about it someday. Shall we go for our walk?"

They walked for several blocks past large homes facing the water, before Gudrun got the courage to speak. She appreciated Arvik's patience. "My mother gave me the porcupine stick for my eighth birthday and she taught me how to use it."

"Please do not feel like you have to explain," Arvik said.

His understanding tone made her want to share the whole story. She found herself not only explaining the construction of the stick, but also how she had unexpectedly met Captain Torvik. Soon they were both laughing.

"I consider myself warned. You are a lady not to be trifled with," Arvik joked. Then he took on a serious look. "I like a strong woman. On the island you will need to take care of yourself at times. Look. See the sun setting over the Olympic Mountains. We can turn back once it disappears."

Once back at the house they said goodnight in the entry. As Gudrun neared the door to her room she noticed Anna standing in the hall in her dressing gown.

"Can we talk?" Anna whispered.

"Yes, please come in." Gudrun opened the door, went over to the bed and sat down.

A subdued Anna sat across from her. "I am so sorry. I can get too caught up in the moment and not think about what I am saying. Can you forgive me?"

Gudrun smiled. "Of course I can. It turned out for the best. It gave Arvik and I something to talk about. I understand. It is easy to say the wrong thing."

"So your walk went well?"

"Yes. He is so easy to talk to when we are walking."

"I wanted to make sure things were good between us. Now I had better get to bed. "

Gudrun gave her new friend a hug. "They are. I do have a question. You do not dress fancy for dinner?"

"We are more casual unless we have a special occasion. For you I would have dressed up, however I know Arvik only owns two sports coats so I wanted him to feel comfortable. He is not one for dressing up. Most of the Norwegian men at church are fishermen or work for lumber companies. Often a sports coat is as fancy as you can expect."

"That is fine with me. It suits my humble beginnings. Because of your beautiful house I expected more formality."

"This is the Pacific Northwest. Everything is more casual here."

❧

Looking in the dresser mirror Gudrun ran her hands over her hair trying to calm her wild curls. She gave up and sat down in one of the bedroom chairs, her thoughts turning to the morning's activities. The four of them had gone to Ballard to shop that Tuesday morning. They had walked along Market Street lined with stores selling Norwegian and Scandinavian goods. They had stopped at Hansen's Bakery for coffee, krumkake and lefse. Anna had her own list to shop for, though she took the time to point out the best shops for pots and pans, kitchen utensils, and china. She quietly let Gudrun know that Arvik did not have any kitchenware or china at the house.

Gudrun heard voices in the courtyard and slipped into the bathroom. Anna and Arvik must be starting on the table project. When Nils reminded everyone at lunch that Captain Hans would be coming in the afternoon, Arvik got a funny look on his face and asked Nils if he needed any wood chopped. Anna had piped up that she had some large log butts in the garage that she wanted made into outside tables. Arvik quickly offered to take on the project.

Gudrun watched him work in a short-sleeve shirt, rolling out the three foot diameter log pieces, getting out the hand saw and cradling the first log in the sawbuck. Anna stepped up and showed him the thickness she wanted for the table tops and Arvik began sawing just as the captain walked down the drive carrying two large bunches of flowers. The captain presented Anna with one bunch and she scurried off toward the kitchen. Arvik stopped working and Gudrun watched as the two men conversed for a moment.

Emily knocked on the bedroom door. "The captain is here."

"Thank you. I will be down in a minute," Gudrun replied. Though it had only been a day since she had seen him she had missed her friend. She skipped down the stairs and pretended to be surprised about the flowers. "They are so beautiful, thank you!"

"How do you know they are for you?" he teased.

"I saw you give Anna hers from the upstairs window. And I doubt that these are for Nils or Arvik." Gudrun laughed and took the flowers he extended to her.

"I enjoyed my walk from the trolley stop along Highland Drive, how about we go for a stroll and explore further?" the captain asked.

"A wonderful idea. Let me give these to Emily to put in a vase."

The pair walked out into the courtyard, waving at Arvik as they passed by and out onto the street.

"Isn't he marvelous? So strong and good-looking." Gudrun remarked as they walked along the street.

Hans asked, "How are you and Anna getting along?"

"Famously. She has told me all about the house Arvik has built, I cannot wait to see it. She says he is very talented."

Walking in silence for a minute the captain changed the subject. "I heard you went shopping in the Ballard district."

"Oh yes," Gudrun said. "Arvik wanted Anna to show me where to find Norwegian food and home goods."

෴

Sitting down to dinner at the Lunde table, Hans had to hide his displeasure with Arvik. He had spent the past two hours listening to Gudrun prattle on about his rival. He watched Arvik seat Gudrun at the table, leaning over and whispering something to her as he slid her chair in. For an island fisherman and carpenter he had the manners of a well-bred gentleman. Hans caught Anna's smile and nod of approval to Arvik. *Ah, so she is coaching him. That makes more sense. I will not give up. I will return tomorrow morning and ask Gudrun to marry me.*

"Gudrun told us you have been to Seattle before," Nils said to the captain after he gave the prayer. "How do you like it here?"

Hans passed the potatoes to Gudrun. "Yes, I have been here twice before, however, it was many years ago. The city has grown. I remember when Queen Anne Hill seemed out in the country. I doubt your house had been built yet."

The conversation went on about the growth of the city. Starting with the Klondike gold rush in 1896, the city had mushroomed. They discussed the new trolleys, the cars, the construction of the locks and the Montlake Cut, the Denny Regrade, and the warm September they were having. The men loved the topic of the leveling of Denny Hill — they all agreed, the expenses and muddy mess it created made the project a folly.

ᴄᴏ

Arvik paced the entry floor glancing into the parlor off and on keeping a close eye on the captain talking to Gudrun that Wednesday morning. He had to admit it rankled him that the man he trusted to bring Gudrun safely to Seattle had become his rival. Nils kept reminding him that by being easy-going and likeable, he would win Gudrun over. He really wanted to deck the guy and send him packing. Anna had been preaching self-control for the past two days.

"What is going on in there?" Anna came up beside him.

"Shh. We have to be quiet. Nothing. Just talk so far," Arvik looked at Anna as he answered.

Anna gasped. "Not just talk. Look, the Captain is down on one knee. Is that a ring?"

"Of all the nerve! I am going in —"

"No, you are not." Anna pulled on Arvik's arm."

Nils walked through the front door. "What are you two up to?" He glanced through the glazed parlor doors. "Spying?" Nils face turned red. "Shame on you both. Into the living room, now."

Feeling like a disobedient child, Arvik followed his friend and Anna into the living room.

Nils turned when they were safely out of earshot. "Where are your manners? In my home acting like children and treating a guest like that? An embarrassment."

Arvik cleared his throat and looked Nils straight in the eye. "You are right and I am sorry I lost control. It is about all I can take having him court the woman I plan to marry, right in front of me. He is old enough to be her father!"

"Yes, I am old enough to be her father."

The three friends turned to find Captain Hans standing in the archway between the entry and the living room. "Mrs. Lunde, Miss Sagen needs your attention."

Anna scurried off to the parlor.

He stepped toward Arvik. "I will no longer be in your way, Mr. Johansen. She turned me down for that very reason. She loves me like a father not as a suitor. She also rejected me because I am not a Christian."

Arvik stood still taking into account what the captain had just said.

The captain walked up close to Arvik and continued in a low guttural tone. "You had better treat her right. If I ever hear that you have hurt her in any way I will come back here and take care of you." Turning quickly he walked out of the room and out the front door.

Regaining his composure, Arvik hurried to the parlor to find Gudrun sobbing in Anna's arms. Anna looked up as he entered the room and gave him the signal to go away.

Arvik shook his head and signaled Anna to leave. *I should be the one comforting her,* Arvik thought. *A hug would be too personal...it is hard Lord to see her this way. Show me what to do or say.*

Gudrun saw him out of the corner of his eye and sat up straight. Anna stood and nodded to him as she left the room. Arvik sat down and placed his hand over Gudrun's. "I am sorry," he said.

She quickly pulled her hand away. She dabbed her eyes with her handkerchief then explained, "I hurt him. I didn't mean to. I had no idea he felt that way. It would not have worked. He is not a Christian."

"I know," Arvik said, "I know."

"Why does it hurt so bad when I know it would never work?" Gudrun's hand went to her forehead. "I must rest before we leave for our outing."

I pushed too hard, Arvik thought as he watched Gudrun walk up the stairs. *We have not known each other that long. I must give her time to warm up to me.*

CHAPTER 21

Courting

*R*ain hit the windowpane so hard it interrupted Gudrun's journaling that Thursday afternoon. She had spent the earlier part of the afternoon writing letters to her Norway friends, to Mrs. Sandnes and one to Captain Hans. Nils had gone to his lumber mill. Arvik had left to sail *Himmel* around to Fishermen's Headquarters, closer to the Lunde home. Anna needed to visit an older friend in the hospital. Originally Gudrun had planned to sail with Arvik, but the weather change had become a good excuse to decline.

Yesterday's outing to Leschi Park on the west shore of Lake Washington might have been the last bit of warm weather for the year. The car ride had been interesting and at times uncomfortable on the rough roads. She had asked to sit in the back with Anna because the Captain's proposal had made her feel like running away from Arvik.

Why? Why such a strange reaction...am I afraid of getting hurt myself? I should not have retracted my hand when he tried to comfort me. It seemed if I left it there, Arvik would be able to tell how attracted I am to him. I do not want him to know, because the terms of this marriage clearly state there will be no physical intimacy. But what if I fall in love and he does not?

She lay down on the bed, staring at the ceiling, reminiscing about the outing and last night's church service. Anna introduced her to so many people. She could barely remember their faces much less their names. Who knew there would be so many single young Norwegian men? Anna kept introducing her to one gentleman after another. Arvik had explained that this would be the only place she would be hearing a service in Norwegian. The pastor on Orcas taught in English.

Enough of the "what if's." I am going down to the kitchen and help Emily with dinner.

᯽

Soaking wet, Arvik came in through the side door of the Lundes' home. He shed his poncho. The smell of his mother's meatballs met his nostrils as he took off his boots and socks. Walking towards the kitchen, barefoot, water dripping off the ends of his wet pant legs, he asked at the top of his voice, "Emily, how did you find my mother's recipe for meatballs?" He stopped when he saw Gudrun working over the frying pan.

She looked up and smiled at him. "These smell like your mother's?" Wearing a light cream dress almost the color of her hair and a white apron, Gudrun pushed her hair back with the back of her hand.

"Oh yes," Arvik said. Walking closer he surveyed the meatballs. "Do you need a taste tester?"

Smiling at him, she picked up the spoon that she had been turning the meatballs with. "There is more than one use for this utensil. You must be patient. This one over here is the most well done, it will be ready in a minute. My, you are wet!"

Arvik looked down at the puddle he had created on the floor. "It is a full blown storm out there. I will go and change and be back to taste test. Do not give the job to anyone else."

She is smiling and relaxed again, no more stiffness be-tween us. She is at ease in the kitchen. Ah, those meatballs... He took a big whiff as he headed down the hall.

Returning to the kitchen, he paused in the doorway, enjoy-ing the sight of her humming as she rolled several new meat-balls from the meat mixture, in cornbread crumbs just like his mother used to do. Rubbing her nose with the back of her hand she accidentally left a dab of crumbs. A long curl broke loose from her barrette and dangled across her forehead. *Thank you, Lord for making her beautiful.*

Stepping into the room, Arvik asked, "Is my meatball ready?"

Gudrun smiled and pointed to a meatball sitting on a plate at the end of the kitchen table. "I just took it out of the pan. It is all yours. Be careful it is hot."

"Thank you." Rubbing his nose, he said, "You have some cornbread crumbs..."

She giggled, her face took on a rosy glow and she went to the sink to wash them off.

Arvik picked up the knife and fork Gudrun had put next to the plate and cut a slice of the meatball. He closed his eyes as the piece melted in his mouth. "This is heavenly...thank you," he said as he finished the first bite. "The spice brings out the flavor of the meat. You even make them the same size as my mother did. Perfect."

He continued eating, watching her rotate the meatballs to brown them evenly then transferring them to a large casserole dish to warm in the oven. *This is better than I imagined. My house will become a home when she moves in. I do hope she moves in, Lord. I pray she will accept me —*

Emily walked into the kitchen with a basket of potatoes from the cellar.

"Potetstappe?" Arvik asked.

"Yes," both the ladies said in unison.

Rubbing his tummy, Arvik declared, "This will be a dinner to remember."

"It looks like you have dinner taken care of," Emily said. "I will go set the table."

Gudrun began washing the potatoes. Arvik joined her at the sink and began to peel.

"Would you do me the pleasure of joining me tomorrow for an afternoon at the Volunteer Park Conservatory and dinner at The Virginia Inn?" Arvik asked. He watched her eyes light up as he finished the sentence. "We will not be out too late."

"That sounds lovely. So we will give the Lundes back their house?"

He laughed. "For one evening."

"It looks like I have new kitchen staff? What did you two do with Emily?" Anna joked as she entered the kitchen. "And what is that wonderful smell? Meatballs?"

Arvik beamed. "Gudrun makes delicious meatballs just like my mother's. She is making dinner for us. Emily is setting the table."

"Oh. Thank you, Gudrun. I have been looking for you two. On the way home from the hospital I got the most fabulous idea."

"Go on," Gudrun said.

"On Saturday we shall have a big open house. I am going to invite people from church and from the neighborhood here." Anna swung her arms to include the whole neighborhood.

Arvik stole a glance at Gudrun. With her back to Anna she gave him the most horrified look and mouthed, "No."

Dropping the peeler, Arvik skirted around the table and grabbed Anna's arm. "We need to talk privately." He guided her out of the kitchen and down the hall to the parlor. Once he closed the door, he let go of her arm. "You, my dear, are going overboard. I...I know you mean well...however it is too much. Gudrun is not like you. She does not thrive on big parties and meeting new people. She is on the shy side."

He paced the floor, then stopped in front of Anna. "Both Gudrun and I have had a lot to take in these past few days, with finally meeting each other. We need time to sort out what has happened."

"How do you know that about her?" Anna whispered.

"She confided her shyness in her letters. I have been watching her. She is still adjusting to us and a new country. At church she seemed very uncomfortable meeting all those new people. By the way how come most of them were single men? Are you trying to sabotage our relationship?"

"No...I want you to be happy...she should see she has options so she knows you are the right choice."

Arvik threw his hands in the air and paced in front of the fireplace. He wanted to yell, but held his tongue and prayed for control.

"So no party on Saturday?" Anna asked. "She will get bored sitting around the house until Sunday."

Arvik shook his head. "No party. She will not be bored. She is in her element right now — the kitchen. Besides we have a date tomorrow afternoon and evening, just the two of us. Do not worry. I have made all the proper arrangements. You have taught me well." Arvik put his hands on Anna's shoulders. "Let it go, Anna. We will figure it out. Please give us time and space. Before you know it we will be heading to Orcas."

∽

Sun streamed through the tall glass ceiling creating a cascade of sparkles on Arvik's blonde hair as he bent over to smell a carnation. "I wish I could pick one for you."

Gudrun giggled. "You might get kicked out and then how would I get back to the Lundes'?"

"You know how to take care of yourself. You would be fine." Arvik gave her a big smile and offered her his arm. They continued on down the center aisle of the main conservatory building admiring the different plants. "That is a pretty dress you are wearing."

"I made it in Saint Thomas. Yesterday I would have never dreamed I would be able to wear it today. This weather is so unexpected. However, I didn't need this sweater in Saint Thomas."

Arvik stopped suddenly. "So you not only excel in the kitchen, you are an excellent seamstress."

Gudrun blushed. "I just happened to have the same meatball recipe as your mother. You might not like my lefse recipe. Potato or flour?"

"Definitely flour. Though my mother made both."

"Oh good...yes, I do sew. I am better at that than cooking."

As they walked through the gardens and around the reservoir she told him about the sewing project in Saint Thomas and Mrs. Sandnes's suggestion that she open a dress shop in Seattle. Approaching the seventy-five foot high water tower, Arvik asked, "Want to climb one hundred and two steps?"

Gudrun's eyes sparkled. "Beat you to the top." She ran into the entrance with Arvik right behind her. His longer legs almost passed her in the foyer. First on the stairwell she had the advantage until she began to tire and he nudged past her.

At the top he turned and gave her his hand to help her up the last few steps.

"You win. I am out of shape!" She bent over gasping for breath.

"No, very few men can keep up with my long legs. You almost beat me." He led her over to the arched windows. "This is why we climbed up here." He gestured to the expansive view. "Look at the city. All those houses, row after row."

They could see the houses below them on Capitol Hill, the houses on the southeast slope of Queen Anne Hill and other neighborhoods Arvik did not know the name of. "Would you prefer to live in the city?" he asked.

Gudrun gave him a sharp look. "Never. I like island life. I do not want to see my neighbor's house. I feel sorry for these people so close together. One thing being in Stavanger taught me is that I could not take the hustle and bustle of the city life."

"Really? Arvik asked. "You could have your dress shop."

"Just because Mrs. Sandnes suggested it does not mean I want to do it. I do not know what I want to do, but I always want to contribute..."

Arvik pulled out his pocket watch. "I agree with you. City life is not for me. It is fun to visit. I think we better go and catch the trolley downtown. We do not want to miss our dinner reservation."

༄

Laying in bed half dozing on Saturday morning, Gudrun thought about their dinner at the Virginia Inn. She had asked Arvik about his fishing and his carpentry. When pressed about the dangers of fishing in the San Juans he told her about his encounter with the great white shark. She shuddered.

Footsteps outside her door and a whoosh sound made her sit up in bed. A white envelope sat just inside the door. Slipping out of bed she recognized Arvik's handwriting as she bent to pick it up. The note inside requested that she join him in the parlor as soon as she could.

Coming out of the bathroom a little voice in her head told her to dress up a little bit. Emily had washed all her clothes from the voyage so she picked her favorite dark blue shirt style dress with the pin tucks down the front that Karoline had given her. She took some time with her hair. *What does he want? Another walk? She could wear this dress if they were walking in the neighborhood.*

Her heart pounding, she slipped down the stairs to the parlor. Through the glass doors she could see him next to the fireplace, fumbling with something in his pocket. He turned as she entered the room.

"Good morning. I hope you slept well."

"Yes, very well. Thank you."

He took her hand and led her to the couch. "Please take a seat. There is something I wish to talk to you about."

She sat but he continued to stand. He took her left hand in his. Suddenly he knelt on one knee. Her hand went to her mouth.

"You started this journey knowing that I wanted to marry you. I had no idea what you would be like. I kept praying and praying. It took so long at times I almost gave up hope. God has answered my prayers and brought me exactly who I hoped for and much more. Now I am asking if you want to continue with our agreement." Arvik fumbled in his pocket and brought out a small jewelry box. He opened it and inside sat a small diamond ring and a wedding band. "Miss Gudrun Sagen, will you marry me?"

Overwhelmed, Gudrun started to shake. A tear slid down her face and across her smiling lips. She wiped it away. "Yes, she whispered, yes."

He seemed relieved as he slid the diamond engagement ring onto her left ring finger. "It was my mother's."

∽

As Arvik waited in the Lundes' garden, his thoughts were on Gudrun and the past few days. *Thank you, Lord for making it possible to walk back into Denny Park Lutheran Church this morning with Gudrun on my arm and a ring on her finger.* He had left her side for a few minutes to talk to Pastor Stoa and arranged for him to come to the Lundes' house for a Saturday afternoon wedding. He recalled Anna's reaction to their engagement announcement. While Nils had congratulated both of them, Anna immediately began planning a big wedding at the church. Anna's grandiose description brought terror to Gudrun's eyes and she left the parlor. He had stood his ground for Gudrun's sake and arranged what she wanted, a simple house wedding with only the Lundes attending. She would wear her mother's bunad, and he would wear a new sports jacket and his best dress slacks.

Turning as he heard footsteps, his eyes met Gudrun's. Her smile melted his heart. Motioning to a bench, he said, "Thank you for coming. I wanted a chance to go over things."

"What kind of things?"

"I wanted to review terms of the marriage and discuss finances," he explained, sitting down next to her.

Gudrun smiled. "That sounds good."

Continuing on he said, "As I outlined in my original letter, my requirements are meals made, housekeeping, and conversation. Our conversation seems natural. You and I are suitably matched. We are more on the quieter side."

Gudrun laughed. "Not like Anna?"

Chuckling, Arvik's eyes met hers. "No. We are not. I know your cooking will far exceed my standards...if you saw what I have been eating these past five years you would be appalled."

"I will do my best. Do promise me that you will let me know what you do not like so I do not make those meals again."

He patted her hand. "I promise. And I hope you realize this does not mean you have to make all my meals. I can warm up soup on the stove, make my own breakfast, we can work it out as we go along. The same with the housekeeping. The house is good-sized, not as big as the Lundes', but do not feel that every room has to be spotless all the time."

Gudrun smiled. "Remember, I was born in a small fishing cottage without a room of my own. It will be a privilege to have a house to clean."

"Home, it is your home. Please let me know if anything I ask is not reasonable. Which brings us to finances." He pulled a small notebook out of his jacket pocket and opened it. "Here is what we have in savings. We could live several years on it if needed. Because I am self-employed I only want to touch this money in an emergency. This amount here is the checking account. Until I make more money this has to last for food and our daily needs. There should be money coming in from our apple crop. I have a few house remodel projects that will tide us over for the winter and there is always fishing. This third account is for you to spend on outfitting the kitchen and furniture for the home."

Taking the booklet out of Arvik's hand she studied it for a moment, briefly recalling what Mrs. Sandnes taught her about American dollars. "All these numbers...it seems like a lot of money. I might have some questions. Hopefully, I will not need that much for the kitchen and furniture."

"The last item is that I will honor our agreement. You have your own bedroom and I have mine." Blushing, he stood up and walked a few steps. "Is there anything you disagree with?" He pulled out his handkerchief and wiped his brow. Then glanced at her, head down with her hands folded on her lap. *Please, please say you hope someday we will share a bedroom, tell me you care. I am so dumb, how do I tell her I want more. What if I scare her off?* Minutes seemed to tick by. He could hear his father's voice, "In tough situations never let your face or body give you away. Start practicing hiding your feelings." This seemed to be one of those times.

Gudrun looked up, smiling, her eyes seemed a bit moist. "It is all good. More than I could ever hope for." She stood up. "I must get back to the house and try on my mother's bunad. But I do have a favor to ask."

CHAPTER 22

Wedding Vows

"Turn! Turn! Slow down! Take your foot off the gas," Nils yelled at Arvik who sat behind the wheel of Nils' Model T Ford.

A stack of logs loomed fifteen feet ahead. Reaching over, Nils grabbed the wheel and the model T made an abrupt turn to the right, almost tipping the car over.

"The brake! Hit the brake!" Nils yelled.

Arvik looked down at his feet. "Which one?"

"The far left. Watch out! The fence." Nils pointed straight ahead.

Arvik fumbled with his feet, moving his foot from the clutch to the brake too late. He hit the brake hard as the car crashed through the wooden fence. It slowed down and he turned the wheel to the right a few feet in front of the railroad tracks and stopped. Breathing a big sigh of relief, Arvik remarked, "Hmm, that did not go so well. I will fix your fence and pay for the car repairs."

Nils wiped his brow with his handkerchief. "Maybe I am not the person to teach you how to drive."

Arvik shook his head. "No, I am the problem. I need to go over the controls while we are sitting still, not just once but several times. Can we get it back through the hole in the fence?"

"No, remember we have a gate down there and a ramp? For taking the lumber out to the trains? Let me drive it back in. You go through the hole and open the gate. It is locked at the top and the bottom."

Nils successfully navigated the car back into his lumberyard, parking it by his office. The two men went over and over the controls. First Nils sat in the driver's seat showing Arvik, and then they traded places.

Pulling out his pocket watch, Nils said, "Enough of the driving lesson for today. We better go and meet the ladies for lunch. Hopefully they have not spent all your money."

Arvik watched Nil's movements and which pedals he hit as they drove toward Ballard. His mind drifted to Gudrun. Her request for a favor yesterday afternoon had thrown him off guard for a moment. She had written a letter to Captain Hans and one for the captain to take to Mrs. Sandnes. She wanted his permission to have it delivered to *Sognefjord* before it sailed for San Diego. Despite instant thoughts of jealousy he had checked his tongue, and had politely replied he would take care of it for her. She had offered that he could read her letter to Captain Hans. He had quickly declined. He reminded himself that she would be saying "I do" on Saturday to him, not Captain Hans.

Early yesterday morning he had kept his promise delivering the letters to the ship. It seemed good that the ladies were off shopping that morning, so they missed seeing *Sognefjord* sail out of Seattle.

༄

Her eyes sparkled as she showed him three different options for china she had laid out on a back table at the kitchen store in Ballard. She had also picked out cloth napkins, silver service, and goblets. "Which of the three do you like? They are all within the household budget."

"They are all very nice. I would be happy with any of them. Do you have a favorite?" Arvik asked.

"Oh, yes. However, this is your house and your money, I want you to pick —"

"Stop right there. As we talked about yesterday afternoon when we went over the budget, this is our house and our money, no matter who makes it. Honestly I would be delighted with any of these options. I want it to be the one that makes you smile. Let me guess which is your favorite...the blue set?"

She clapped her hands together. "Yes. How did you know?"

He laughed. "The way you kept looking at it." He picked up a fork, knife, and spoon and fingered them in his hand. Then he did that with the silver service for the other two options. "Have you held each piece in your hands?"

"No, that is a good idea."

After holding each set they quickly agreed on the service, the napkins and water goblets. Arvik asked the shop owner if they could package everything up themselves. He wanted to make sure the china would survive their trip to Orcas Island.

∾

*It is going to work just fine...I even look like her...*Gudrun thought, taking another long look in the mirror at herself in her mother's bunad.

Bands of green and red close to the hem of the black wool jumper caught the eye first. She ran her hands over the red and white Hardanger embroidery on the bust. *So many, many hours of work...I wish they were here. Would they approve? I think Father would have approved of Arvik. They could compare fishing stories.*

"Knock, knock. It is Anna. May I come in?"

"If you are alone," Gudrun answered.

Anna swung the door open and clapped her hands in delight. "It fits you perfectly. I love the white blouse contrasting with the black. You look beautiful."

"Thank you. I had to take the waist in just a bit and lower the hem a few inches. I did not realize I am taller than my mother. With the alterations, it fits me better. I found out from the letters from her sister that my mother's mistress gave her the materials for this bunad as a wedding present."

Sitting down on the bench, Anna asked, "Are you sure you do not want to wait a few weeks and have a church wedding, with more people there?"

Smiling, Gudrun shook her head. "I am not like you, Anna, I only tolerate large gatherings. I do not enjoy them. I am grateful that Arvik seems to understand me."

"He does. Can I order a bouquet of white roses for you and decorate the parlor?"

Gudrun squeezed her new friend's hand, "If that makes you happy, but please check with Arvik first. He might be planning something."

"Nils is very honored to walk you down the stairs. He thinks you are the best thing that has ever happened to his friend."

The two ladies sat and chatted about Gudrun's china, the silver, and the pots and pans Gudrun had purchased.

"With my belongings and everything we have purchased I hope there will be room for us on the boat."

Anna said, "All important items for your new home. I cannot wait to see how you furnish it. If the weather holds, maybe Nils and I can come visit in late October. Or that might be too soon to intrude on you. We can stay at one of the inns."

"Let us get through the wedding, first," Gudrun murmured.

ɡͻ

Dabbing her lips with her napkin, Gudrun glanced around the table. She wanted to pinch herself. She sat here with two new friends, Nils and Anna, and with Arvik, who would be her husband at this time tomorrow. Such a lovely dinner, only two weeks ago she would never have imagined this. The magnificence of the home seemed to dim compared to the warmth and love in the room. They all had accepted her just as she was, a poor fisherman's daughter, and none of them cared about her past. Despite their university educations Nils and Anna treated Arvik, and now her, as equals. The week had flown by with wedding preparations. Indeed, this seemed to be a beautiful answer to her prayers. Her Lord fulfilling all things hoped for, right here on earth. *Extra blessings besides the eternal ones to come. Thank you, Lord. You are so good —*

Nils stood up interrupting Gudrun's silent prayer. He cleared his throat and raised his glass of apple juice. "To the bride and groom. May our Lord Jesus bless and protect your marriage. May He be Lord of your home. To your happiness."

Anna raised her glass. "Amen. Skål."

Four glasses clinked together in unity.

"Thank you," Arvik said.

"It is time to run through the ceremony." Anna stood. "Nils and Gudrun to the top of the stairs. Arvik and I will wait in the entry and we will pretend Pastor Stoa and his wife will be waiting in the parlor."

Her knees wanted to buckle as Gudrun descended the stairs, holding onto Nils' arm. Twice she looked down at Arvik. *Tomorrow morning at eleven o'clock, this will be the real thing. O Lord, make my legs work.*

"Now Nils, you pass her off to Arvik, you and I will walk into the parlor first and take our places. Then Gudrun and Arvik will enter." Anna instructed. "Pastor Stoa will be standing between the two large bouquets. We will pretend he is there."

Once in place Nils stepped into the pastor's place and pretended to be the pastor. Laughter filled the room as he made up ridiculous commitments in the vows. He stopped laughing and said, "I pronounce you man and wife. Now please kiss your bride."

"No! No! I already spoke with Pastor Stoa and there will be no kissing," Arvik interjected.

"No kiss?" Anna gasped.

Gudrun noticed the sharp look Arvik gave Anna. Her heart sank. *Why do I care? It has not even been two weeks since we met.* Emotions swirling through her, she recalled her mother's advice. "A lady never gives away her feelings. Control is an admirable thing." That control had served her well serving in the Grand House and it would right now.

"No kiss, right, Gudrun?" Arvik asked. "That is what you want?"

She paused, then in her iciest voice she said, "No kiss."

The silence in the room hung heavy. Anna broke the awkwardness with a sigh. "I guess we have practiced enough. I am a bit tired. If you will please excuse me I will see all of you in the morning."

༄

Staring at the ceiling, Gudrun's mind and emotions kept spinning. *Are we only to be friends, Lord? Only friends? He seemed very determined that there would be no kissing. Am I not attractive to him? We get along so well...but do I really want him to kiss me for the first time in front of other people?*

The wind picked up, howling through the trees outside her window. Shadows from the streetlights flickered across the ceiling. She watched the patterns as her emotions calmed down.

You are being ridiculous. It is exactly what you agreed to. You were warned about his good looks. You knew it was a business agreement and it has turned into friendship. It will be a much better life than you could have hoped for in Norge. So trust God and be grateful. Be careful oh heart, do not give me away. He can never know how you feel. Never.

She watched the patterns and dozed off to sleep.

∽

A knock at the door interrupted Gudrun's morning Bible study. "Who is it?" she asked.

"It is Anna. May I come in? I am alone."

"Yes, please."

The bubbly redhead seemed to bounce into the room. "Today is the day! Are you excited? Nervous?"

Gudrun could not help but laugh at her enthusiasm. She patted the bed and Anna plopped down beside her. "Maybe both. I do not know. It is all happening so quickly."

"I know. I forget that this is all so different for you than it was for me. You have not known him for years. And I can see how perfectly matched you two are, so it seems things should move faster."

Gudrun closed her Bible. "It is what it is. Arvik wrote asking for a companion that could take on the chores he was not good at. I am that companion. It may never be more."

"However...you would like more?"

Gazing out the window Gudrun paused. "Honestly I do not know how I feel. It is all in the Lord's hands."

Anna took Gudrun's hand. "You are right. Shall we pray?"

Anna's sweet prayer of blessing put Gudrun at peace. Gudrun prayed for unity with Arvik, before praying for Anna and Nils. They hugged.

"Now the men are gone. You should come down for a quick breakfast before you start getting ready."

ᏨᎤ

Knowing the boundaries were set made it much easier walking down the stairs on Nils' arm that Saturday morning. *Control, control. Please Lord, bless this union. You lead it to what it should be.* Her foot hit the entry floor, Nils walked her over to a smiling Arvik, she took his arm and waited a minute as Anna and Nils walked into the parlor and stood on either side of Pastor Stoa. They walked through the doors and across the room. Emily, the chauffeur, and Mrs. Stoa stood as they entered the room.

Pastor Stoa prayed, read a few verses from the Bible and spoke about God ordaining marriage. The vows were next. As she slipped the thin gold band on Arvik's left hand she realized the pastor only mentioned the word love once, which occurred in a Bible verse. After the vows, Pastor Stoa pronounced them man and wife, the photographer took their picture, they signed the guest book, and everyone adjourned to the dining room for lunch.

A slight sigh escaped her lips as Arvik helped her sit her at the table. *It is over. Done. Help me be me, Lord. It all seemed so mechanical. Something I should have enjoyed is over.*

ᏨᎤ

Everything in order and business-like. Arvik thought. *I wish I felt comfortable enough to at least give her a hug. To whisper to her that it will all be alright and we can take our time getting to know each other. I should not have said "No" quite so loudly about the kiss last night. She seems standoffish since then. Our first kiss should not be in front of others. Plus I do not want to scare her off by being too forward. If only we had more time before the ceremony.*

He snuck a glance at his new bride. *Thank you, Lord.* He came back to reality in time to hear Nils say, "Yes, Mrs. Stoa, they are leaving Monday morning. Arvik is concerned about the weather changing and possible storms. What time are you planning to leave dock, Arvik?"

"I am hoping for seven. Arriving at Orcas Tuesday afternoon. We could make it in one day but with all our cargo it would be almost midnight." He looked at Gudrun. "My plan is that it will be daylight the first time you see your new home."

"I am sure I will love it," Gudrun replied.

ᑀ

Arvik paused at Gudrun's bedroom door that Saturday evening. *Have I given her enough time? She said she wanted to change before I came to look at her trunk. Please, Lord. I have no right to ask, but ease the tension between us. Help me know what to say.*

His knock received a pleasant "One moment, please," in reply. Minutes ticked away, while he played with the tape measure in his hand. Finally she opened the door wearing a simple grey dress he had not seen before.

"My trunk is in that corner. I hope it will fit onboard and not be a burden."

"We will make it fit. I need to make sure I am balancing the boat so we do not run into trouble." He measured the outside and picked up the trunk to guess its weight. Writing it all down he looked up and inquired, "May I sit down?"

Gudrun blushed, "Yes, please." She pointed to one of the chairs before she sat in the one facing him, nervously playing with her wedding ring.

"Are you sure you will be alright without your trunk for one night?"

"I can manage. It is not a problem," Gudrun said. "How is the guard at the boat?"

"He seems to be fine. His name is Benjamin in case you need to know."

Gudrun stood up and walked over to her trunk. She opened it and pulled out her porcupine stick. "It is right here on top, if you need it tomorrow night." She walked over and handed it to Arvik.

Carefully running his hands over the spikes and wood, he said, "Now this could do some damage. Thank you. I doubt I will need it. Most fishermen respect each other's property. But, being such a big city there can be other types hanging around the docks. Nils and I noticed a rough pair watching us load your furniture, and china. Tomorrow after church we will load the rest of the kitchen items, the food supplies, and your trunk."

"Will there be room for us?"

Arvik chuckled. "I hope so. That brings us to the trip. We will take two days if the weather behaves. We will spend the night in Port Townsend. I am willing to put you up in a hotel. Or you may sleep on board in what you are wearing in the stateroom. I will sleep in the main cabin. I want to respect your privacy."

Silence reigned for a moment. Arvik played with the stick, struggling for words. "I...I...it seems best to make sure there is no question of your purity, if you are to change your mind and ask for an annulment." He stood up quickly, handed Gudrun the stick and left the room.

CHAPTER 23

Home

Sunlight started to break through the morning mist as Nils stopped the car at the docks at Fishermen's Headquarters, promising a sunny day ahead. Getting out of the car, Gudrun felt a pleasant breeze. She turned to Anna. "We might make good time if this breeze keeps up."

"True. There she is, beautiful *Himmel*. The third finger pier over and Arvik, tending the lines. Looks like he is ready to go."

Gudrun waved at Arvik. Then tugged at the waist of her new khaki pants. "I hope Arvik approves of me wearing these."

"You look feminine. As we discussed when you bought them, they make sense on the boat and for life on the island...I bet Arvik won't even notice."

Grabbing her satchel out of the car, Gudrun followed Anna and Nils down the docks to *Himmel*. Her heart pumped faster. Goosebumps started to tingle on her arms. *This is the day, Lord. The day we sail toward Orcas. But for Arvik's sake, please Lord, let things go according to his plans. I am so excited about finally seeing this home that Arvik has spent so much time on. I ask for travel mercies, Lord. Jesus' name, Amen.*

Arvik's warm smile turned to surprise as Gudrun approached the boat. "You look like you are ready to help," he said.

She blushed. "Yes, I hope so. Remember, my knowledge of sailboats is limited. You must tell me what to do. Looks like a great day."

"Yes, and a breeze in here will be stronger out on the bay. We should make good time." Arvik took her satchel and sat it onboard. "We are all ready to take off, if this is all."

Anna passed Arvik a lunch basket. "Some food to tide you over."

"You have given us so much already. Are you trying to fatten us up? Arvik gave her a quick hug. "I cannot thank you enough for all that you have done for us. Once Gudrun is settled in and ready you are welcome any time at our place."

Arvik shook Nils' hand. Gudrun squeezed Nils' hand and thanked him. Anna started to cry as she and Gudrun embraced.

"Promise you will write?" Anna insisted when she finally broke the hug. "Promise?"

Gudrun patted her arm. "I promise."

"I want to know what you think of the house."

"You will get full details." Gudrun assured her.

Arvik started the engine. He reached out and helped her onboard. "Nils will get the lines. I put your bag in the cabin. You can sit back here so we can talk."

Gudrun turned and waved to Anna several times as they headed out to the channel that would take them to the bay.

Arvik pointed to the construction site looming ahead. "That mess is for the future locks. Someday we will come in that way."

"It is huge. So much dirt!"

"They are also working on a channel between Lake Union and Lake Washington to connect both lakes to the bay."

"So much construction in this city. I am looking forward to the quietness of the island," Gudrun confided.

Arvik returned a wave to a passing sailboat, then slowed the engine down. "This is a good place to go over a few sailing terms, before we cross into Puget Sound. Only if you want."

Gudrun replied, "Yes. Good idea."

Untying what looked like a main rope that ran toward the mast, he asked, "What do you think this is called?"

"A line?"

"That would make sense, however it is called the mainsheet, it is attached to the mainsail, it is how you control the sails."

She repeated, "Mainsheet."

"See the long pole coming off the mast? That is the boom, which the mainsail is connected to. It controls the direction we are going. When it is going to move I call 'boom.' It can knock a person over."

He gave the engine more throttle and they headed toward the Sound.

As they drew closer she asked, "Do you mind if I go sit on the bow?"

Curls dancing in the wind, Gudrun gave up trying to control her hair and let it fly. She dangled her long legs off the bow, leaning in for each wave as they crossed into Puget Sound. With the light fog gone, the sun sparkled across the water. *This is all so confusing...one minute we seem to get along so well, then I feel awkward and shy...*

Arvik called out, "I am going to cut the engine and put up the sails."

"Do you want help?"

"I can handle it. Your job is to lay low when we turn and the boom changes direction. I will call out when it is moving."

She watched him skillfully pull the mainsail up and secure the jib. Catching a stiff south wind *Himmel* ran quickly north toward Whidbey Island. Later today they would be going along the west shore of that long island.

For the next hour she lost herself in feeling close to the water again, enjoying the lyrical motion, the spray off the waves, and the beauty of the shoreline, the new sailing terms in the back of her mind. *This is so exciting, Lord, sailing on this beautiful boat through this beautiful water. Tomorrow I will have my own home. My home. Help me get used to thinking of it that way. It is so much more than I ever hoped for, marriage and a home. Thank you, Lord. I know life always has challenges. I know you make the impossible happen. Please remind me of that and never let me take all this for granted.*

She could see the south tip of Whidbey in the distance, the area where she had first seen Arvik. At this rate they would be there around lunchtime.

Arvik called out, "Boom." She instinctively ducked even though she sat well out of reach.

Maybe I should move back to the stern. The waves are getting bigger and Arvik might like the company.

Gudrun stood up and began to move along the port side of the boat, the mainsail obscuring her view of Arvik. Suddenly she heard him yell, "Boom." Before she could duck, the long timber swung toward her, catching her at the waist and tossing her into the water.

ᗧ

He swung the boom slightly giving him a full view of the bow. "Gudrun? Gudrun!" Arvik heard a scream off to the port side and turned to see Gudrun bobbing up and down in the waves struggling to breathe in the cold water. Quickly he grabbed a life preserver and threw it towards her. She swam to it and grabbed it.

"Breathe, hold on tight, and kick," he yelled. Silently counting he thought, *she is at one minute. We have about three, maybe four more before the temps begin to get her.*

The strong wind suddenly shifted and *Himmel began* to list severely. As he corrected the sails he knew the quickest and safest way to rescue her, the figure eight maneuver his father had taught him. *Please, Lord help her understand that I am not leaving her.* Experience had taught him this age-old maneuver worked because it embraced the wind and the currents of the sea instead of fighting against them. He had to trust it one more time. *Head over heart, focus on the job, make the turn.*

As he changed course to the right, away from Gudrun, he looked back to see her still bobbing in the waves about several boat lengths to the southwest. At four boat lengths he tacked, positioning *Himmel's* bow due south. Gudrun's head kept going up and down with the waves. Making a broad curve he had positioned *Himmel* perfectly, a few boat lengths to the south of her.

He tied down the mainsheet as he pulled alongside Gudrun, her teeth chattering. He grabbed her under her arms and pulled her onboard.

Another shift in the wind demanded he pay attention to the sails. "Are you alright?" he asked as he adjusted the mainsheet.

Despite her shivering she managed to nod.

"Go below. In the head there are towels. Strip off all your wet clothing —" the boat listed again.

Gudrun nodded. Through chattering teeth she said, "I... know...body temp —" She stumbled below.

"Can you handle it yourself or do you need help?" Arvik yelled as he skillfully fought the wind.

Once he had the sails under control he went to the hatch and called out. "There is a blanket on the bench. Wrap yourself up. In the blue duffel bag I have extra clothes and socks. Are you alright?"

"I...I...am...fine."

"I am sorry," he said.

∽

Gudrun stripped down once she found the towels. As she rubbed her body dry flashes of falling off her father's boat into the frozen waters of Tingsakerfjorden in February ran through her mind. Her mother had panicked, screaming at her father not to leave Gudrun, as he performed the figure eight maneuver. He had ignored her mother and successfully fished her out of the water. Her mother's sobs as she undressed her and rubbed her dry, then holding her tight to transfer her own body heat had been an experience she would never forget. This time of year the waters here in Puget Sound were not quite as cold. Besides, she had a body twice the size as she had back then.

She found Arvik's extra clothes and after trying on his pants she decided to wear the heavy gray dress in her satchel with his long woolen socks, and one of his wool sweaters. Even with a belt his pants slid right off of her. She came above, wet clothes in hand.

"Looks like you are setting a new trend in fashion," Arvik commented, with a twinkle in his eye and relief in his voice.

Gudrun laughed as she wrung out the clothes. She wondered how she could hang them securely to dry.

"We are close to the south end of Whidbey. We will drop anchor for a while, have lunch and I will find some clips so we can hang your clothes. We will anchor a ways offshore as there is a lot of shoaling."

With a funny grin on her face, she said, "I am going to have so much to tell Anna when I write — how you tried to get rid of me this morning."

"Please do not make it too bad. I could not see you. I did not know you were standing."

"It was my fault. I should have alerted you of my plan."

∽

Despite the warm afternoon sunshine kissing her face, Gudrun felt shivers up and down her arms. They were so close to home.

Arvik had taken down the sails and the low hum of the outboard engine echoed across the quiet waters of East Sound.

"That is Rosario up ahead on your right." Arvik spoke in normal tones and she could easily hear him from her perch on the bow.

Not wanting to break the spell she answered in a hushed voice. "It is large. So elegant for a private home." Last night as they ate dinner in a small cafe in Port Townsend, Arvik had shared stories about working on the private home of Robert Moran.

The tall forests lining the shore reminded her of Norway. Arvik had informed her most of the trees were called Douglas Fir, a species native only to the Pacific Northwest and New Zealand. The dense forest looked soft and fuzzy from a distance.

Even though Arvik had offered once more to put her up in a hotel, she had declined. She explained that she felt much safer with him. He arranged a few things so she could sleep in the bunk in the state-room, he slept on the built-in seating in the galley. This morning they left dock at seven and here they were mid-afternoon, close to her new home.

"You can see Eastsound," Arvik called out.

"Yes, I see the dock and a few buildings," she called back. "I will help with the lines." As they glided into dock she jumped off and secured the lines. The sun kept playing peek-a-boo with the clouds.

Pointing to the east, Arvik explained, "The stables are over that direction, only about two blocks away. I will be back in a bit with Surefoot and the wagon."

As she waited, Gudrun walked the dock and surveyed what she could see of the town. The inn, general store, a grocery, post office, a small church, and a few houses seemed to make up the extent of it. From maps she had seen she knew that the isthmus spanned a mile and a half. Her new home would be almost straight north from here, a mere forty-minute walk. She could feel goosebumps on her arms again.

Finally Arvik appeared with a man from the stables to help load the wagon. She helped by lifting the smaller boxes. Soon they were traveling right through town up North Beach Road, heading to Sunset Ave.

"As you can see the town is much smaller than Seattle," Arvik commented.

Gudrun laughed. "A little bit smaller."

"Surefoot will get us home in good time. I am glad the sun is shining. Things look better in sunshine."

Surefoot knew the right turn onto Sunset Ave, a two-wag-on-wheel path with an apple orchard on the right.

"All of this is part of the farm." He pulled the wagon up close to a tree. "Looks like the apples need picking. The warm weather hurried the process. The Yamaguchis will help me harvest them and pack them. They will get half of the profit. That will be our last trip to Seattle before winter. So you might only have a week or two to make a list of everything you want for the house." He slapped the reins and they took off down the lane.

Suddenly she could see it. She let out a slight gasp. "Please." She put her hand on Arvik's arm as he made the turn to the left. "Please stop. I want to take it all in."

They sat there in silence for a moment — the white Norwegian-style house seemed to glow in the late afternoon sunshine with the shimmering water beyond. *It is not as big as the Grand House, but oh so perfect,* she thought. "Oh Arvik. It is wonderful."

CHAPTER 24

Settling Into Sunset Avenue

Sunshine streaming through her bedroom window woke Gudrun. *Lord, thank you for this beautiful house. For getting us here safely. For this perfect location. Help me Lord to know what to do first. Guide me...* She sat up in bed looking at the view of Matia and Sucia Islands, replaying the events of yesterday afternoon.

Walking into the entry with the solid brownstone floors, the commanding view of the water straight ahead, and a powder room off to one side, it seemed like a dream. The kitchen to the left took her breath away with the beautiful cabinetry, the large propane stove, and the most magical item — a refrigerator. It even had a large bay window with plenty of room for her parents' table. The living room, the formal dining and library stood completely bare except for one old chair facing the window seat in the living room.

Her stomach growled, reminding her that breakfast should be the first item of the day. They each had beds to sleep in, and hopefully soon a kitchen table to eat at. Getting the kitchen in order seemed the most important project.

Opening the door to the bath she marveled at the fact she had her own private bath. She had studied the floor plans for this house; however, the reality proved to be better. She stepped out of her room and looked down the long hall past three bedroom doors at the guest bedroom door. The room where Arvik slept. She paused at the study at the top of the stairs that Arvik had presented as hers. What a view. She felt like a grand lady as she descended the stairs. *Is that coffee, I smell?*

Striding into the kitchen she stopped suddenly at the sight of a young pretty Japanese lady pouring coffee into a mug and placing little soup dishes onto a tray.

The lady looked up. "Hello. Me—" she put her hand on her chest. "Nana."

"Hello. Me — Gudrun."

"You no food." She waved her hand at the cabinets. "I bring." The smile on her neighbor's face conveyed an invitation.

"Thank you."

Nana carried the tray into the living room and sat it in the middle of the window seat. Nana motioned to the chair. Gudrun shook her head and sat cross-legged on the window seat next to the tray. She recognized the miso soup from her short time in San Francisco. Another bowl had rice and one piece of salmon. The very Japanese breakfast Arvik had told her about.

Disappearing for a moment Nana returned with a sketchpad, pencil and an apple. She sat across from Gudrun and began to draw. Gudrun lowered her head to say grace. When she finished she looked at Nana and smiled. Both of them sitting on the window bench cross-legged, facing each other. *This is a new world, Lord, with new ways. Non-verbal signals will be so important with my new friend, since neither of us have a command of the English language.*

Nana finished her sketch and handed it to Gudrun. A tall man and a short man were picking round objects off of a tree.

Nana picked up the apple. "Apple," she said. "Many apple."

Smiling Gudrun said, "Men pick apples."

Nana nodded and they laughed together.

"Me go pick," Nana said.

"Me?" Gudrun pointed to herself.

Shaking her head, Nana said, "you kitchen, box...box...es?"

Gudrun laughed. "Yes. Me work kitchen."

Finishing her breakfast in silence, Gudrun soaked in the view. *How will I ever get anything done here? It is so beautiful, Lord. That sunset Arvik and I watched last night was amazing. Thank you.*

Looking around the large living room she wondered what she should do with the space. "Off to today's project — put the kitchen together and procure food, just like the lady in Proverbs thirty-one. I have a man to feed." She picked up her dishes and headed to her "command post" as Arvik had jokingly called it last night.

∽

"You happy." Zhou said.

"Why do you say it?" Arvik inquired.

Zhou pursed his lips and whistled as he picked another apple. "All morn...you." Zhou whistled again.

"Really? I did not know."

Zhou gave him a knowing look as he emptied his basket into a bushel. "You like wife."

Blushing, Arvik smiled. "Yes."

"Good."

Both men turned as they heard Nana approaching. She had been picking at the other end of the orchard.

"Big. Good." She said holding up an apple from the top of her basket. She rubbed her tummy. "Food?"

Arvik pulled out his pocket watch. "Yes, lunch." Something caught his eye as he started to descend his ladder. Blonde, curly hair, blowing in the wind, Gudrun waved with one hand, basket in the other.

Long strides brought her quickly to the picking party. Her blue eyes sparkled in the sunshine. The smudges on her work dress told him she had been working hard all morning. *How did I get so lucky? —She is perfect. I did pray. But Lord, you know I do not deserve her. I did not even hope she would be this special,* Arvik thought as he walked toward her. He wanted to give her a hug, but instead he offered to take the basket.

"I brought lunch. Nana thought we had no food in the house and she brought me the best breakfast. But I found the smoked salmon and boiled eggs in the refrigerator, after I figured out how to open it. We had that extra loaf of bread and the butter you bought. And it looks like we can eat apples." She waved her arms toward the trees.

Laughing, Arvik touched her shoulder, guiding her over toward Zhou. "Zhou, this my pretty wife, Gudrun." Arvik noticed a rosy glow spread across Gudrun's face. *So she likes being called pretty. I must always remember that.*

Gudrun nodded and bowed a bit like she had seen Nana do that morning. "I...happy..." Her face became deep red. She looked up at Arvik. "Oh, Arvik. My English is so bad. Please tell him I am honored to meet my husband's good friend."

Arvik did his best, apparently well enough because his friend smiled and nodded back.

"Please tell Nana that her breakfast was the best present," Gudrun asked.

Arvik translated for Zhou and Nana smiled big as Zhou translated the message into Japanese. Nana spread out a big blanket and opened a container of fried rice. She washed four of the Gravenstein apples. Gudrun laid out her part of the fare. They enjoyed a half hour sitting in the sunshine, the men translating for the women and Nana sketching to get her point across.

"Thank you for lunch," Arvik said as he carried the basket and they walked up the lane toward the house. "We will be picking apples all week."

"I can help," Gudrun offered.

"No, you have the kitchen to get in order."

"All the cabinet interiors have been washed and the dishes, utensils and pans unpacked, washed and put away. I am ready to make meals, but we are low on food."

Arvik stopped and gazed at her. "You work fast! I thought maybe by the end of the week..."

She smiled up at him. "I enjoyed it. Everything is new and clean. I love my china. And the kitchen you designed is easy to work in. I stacked the crates in a corner. Maybe we will need them for the apples?"

"A wise idea," he said, and they continued walking up the lane.

As the path turned Gudrun stopped to stare. "I love this view of the house. It feels like home."

"It is your home."

He held the front door open for her, and followed her into the kitchen. Not only did he find it just like she had described, but parts of her table were laying out in the bay window ready to be assembled.

Gudrun motioned at the pieces and said, "I will put that together this afternoon."

"Do you know how?" Arvik asked.

"Not really. I watched them take it apart; however, I am not good with a screw driver."

"Tonight we will do it together. This afternoon I have a surprise for you. We are going to the store. Mrs. Nesbo will be meeting us there. She is the only Norwegian speaking woman on the island. I have asked her to help you with the shopping as everything is in English. You two can shop while I go check on *Himmel.*"

Running her hands over her soiled dress Gudrun looked up at him in dismay. "Do I have time to change?"

"Yes, I must change too. Not too fancy. This is a small village."

⁓

"Flour?" Gudrun asked. The word seemed so foreign.

"Yes, mel is called flour," Mrs. Nesbo retorted. "We have the local ground kind, and Gold Medal to choose from." She bent over some strange-looking packages.

Gudrun paused, needing a moment to soak in what the older woman said. Arvik had explained she came from Volda, a small coastal town northwest of Bergen. Her Romsdal dialect sounded foreign to Gudrun's ears.

"I would never have guessed that was flour. I am so glad you are helping me." Gudrun gave the older lady a big smile and got none in return, only a long cold stare.

Gudrun looked at her list. As soon as Arvik had introduced them, Mrs. Nesbo had grabbed the list and not said a word as she wrote the English word next to the Norwegian. *Odd words. Sukker becomes sugar and honning — honey, at least those make sense. You can hear the similarity. But meat for kjøtt? That makes no sense at all.*

All sense of accomplishment from that morning left Gudrun as she and Mrs. Nesbo went up and down the aisles shopping for items that should have only taken a short time. Could she do this? Run a house and learn the local language? Waves of inadequacy began to drown her and she wanted to run out the door, back to the house and hide in her luxurious bed. *No, Arvik did not bring me here to be a princess. I must do my share. Please, Lord help! Peace returned and she remembered. "I can do all things through Him..."*

"This is the best place to purchase meat, unless you know of someone butchering a cow and is willing to sell you some. One of the farms along North Shore Road sells lamb and your husband is one of the best suppliers of crab and salmon. He catches his salmon right off your place." Grabbing the list from Gudrun she scanned it and handed it back without a smile. "Mrs. Wright has chickens. You passed her farm on the way into town. For a small charge, she delivers eggs, milk, and butter from the dairy her husband runs."

Mrs. Nesbo's words brought Gudrun back from her pity party and she scribbled down notes on what the aloof lady had just said.

"With winter coming you will want to purchase large quantities of the basics. When we get a bad storm or it snows you will be hunkered down for a week or more," Mrs. Nesbo explained.

"These items you wrote an "S" next to?"

"Seattle. You cannot purchase them here on the island. Seattle. Have you been to Ballard?"

Gudrun nodded. "Yes I have. Seattle..."

An hour later they had the list completed with a few extra items added in. Gudrun felt overwhelmed with all the new names she had just heard. They stood in silence on the store porch waiting for Arvik to return.

Finally Gudrun asked, "What about a store that sells furniture?"

"There is no store, but there are several men who make furniture. Two blocks to the south is an upholstery shop and another man works out of his house on the east side of town, if you need sofas or chairs. Your own husband makes tables. Mr. Samuels makes dining tables and chairs."

"That is wonderful news. Bringing everything back from the mainland would be expensive and it would not all fit into Arvik's boat. What about rugs?" Gudrun asked.

"There is a weaver a few miles south of the Yamaguchi home that makes beautiful, sturdy rugs. She is half-Lummi Indian so her work is unique."

Arvik pulled the wagon up to the store.

"Thank you so much for helping me." Gudrun wanted to add something about how valuable her translating had been, but Mrs. Nesbo quickly turned and without a goodbye marched down the street.

After helping Arvik load the food, he helped her into the wagon and handed her two letters. "I think it is a good day for you."

౸

"That is the final screw. Shall we turn it over and use it?" Arvik asked.

Eyes shining, Gudrun declared, "Yes!"

They turned the table over and placed it in front of the bay windows in the kitchen. Her family table, exactly where she wanted it. Arvik wiped it down and sat the table. He grabbed the plate of vafler and goat cheese, Emily had sent with them, from the kitchen island while she served up the soup.

"Tomorrow we will have a proper middag." Gudrun sat down in the only dining chair they owned and Arvik sat on the upright end of an old apple crate. After he said grace she continued, "No proper middag or kveldsmat. We are eating like Americans at six o'clock."

"I am grateful for the meal. You did a week's project in one morning and got groceries in a foreign language in the afternoon. I do not expect a proper middag when you have worked so hard. My meal times were all messed up when I worked on the house."

"I can make meatballs for tomorrow," Gudrun offered. "Or is that too soon? We just had them at the Lundes'."

"Meatballs would be delightful. I am the one that is sorry you only have a week or so to decide what you need to furnish the house. We could wait until next spring."

"No. We cannot live like this until spring. I think I have an answer for furnishing the house. You explained that shipping the furniture here from Seattle could be expensive, right?"

"Yes..." Arvik gave Gudrun a curious look.

"And we know it will not all fit on *Himmel*. Mrs. Nesbo told me about the upholsterers and the weaver here on the island. She said you make tables. Would you make me a dining room table?"

Smiling, Arvik asked, "How soon do you need this order by, Mrs. Johansen?"

"Christmas?"

"Maybe. I suppose I could make special concessions for you." He gave her a wink.

Ignoring his innuendo Gudrun continued, "My thought is that I will visit all the tradesmen and women here on the island

and see if I like their work, see how much can be made here, then I will know what to purchase in Seattle. When do you think we will leave?"

"Monday...maybe next Wednesday. Depends on how fast we can pick and package the apples."

"I can help."

"The furniture comes first. Then if you have time you could help with the apples," Arvik said. "I have some work in the shed. I hope to go to bed early. See you in the morning?"

"Yes. I am going up to the study to read and answer Berit and Karoline's letters."

Sitting down at her desk, she opened the letter from Karoline first. Karoline and Bjørg had made the move to Grimstad. The Hotel had done well that summer. Mr. Iversen's son had taken over the Grand House and Mrs. Simonsen had stayed to cook for him. The butler had gone to Grimstad. Most of the letter detailed Bjørg's accomplishments as a four month old.

Berit's letter told about her busy summer with work. She had taken a week to join her sister and her family at their cabin near Rosendal in July. A warm spell made it possible to swim everyday. At work Sissel had inquired about Gudrun and smiled when Berit informed her that Gudrun had left on *Sognefjord*.

CHAPTER 25

To Market

Sitting down next to a pile of furniture magazines in the middle of the empty living room, Gudrun bowed her head. "Lord, please guide me as I make decisions for this house. Help me pick the right furniture, the right colors. Keep me within budget, Lord. May it be furniture my husband likes. Please Lord, may it come together quickly. Amen."

She had sent her Baby Ben alarm clock for five-thirty that morning, so she would have time to make Arvik breakfast before he headed to the orchard. She had sat at the kitchen table for her Bible study before venturing into the living room.

Flipping through the pages of the first magazine she murmured, "I have this morning Lord. To plan..." A room with wooden floors and white painted walls caught her eye, similar to her house. The elegant but welcoming cream and blue color scheme spoke to her. She marked the page and continued to flip through the magazines. She marked two other color schemes and several pages for the style of furniture. *Anna did say I could cut these magazines up.* She stood up to get scissors from the kitchen but stopped and looked around the room. She could see it. She knew exactly what she wanted.

Three hours later she walked toward the orchard, a basket swinging slightly on her arm, hoping the Yamaguchis and Arvik would like the lunch she had made. *Thank you, Lord. It has all come together so quickly...You prepared me for this...*

working for the Iversens, staying at the Jakobsens' and the Lundes' homes, all preparation for decorating and running my own home —

"Hey, over here. We are in this part of the orchard," Arvik called out.

Turning into the orchard Gudrun waved to Nana picking high on top of a ladder. Gudrun spread out the blanket and started placing open-faced sandwiches, raw vegetables, and cookies out for everyone.

"How is the apple picking going?" she asked Arvik as he joined her first.

"Good. It will be Monday or later before we will go to Seattle. So many apples...I think we have a bumper crop. So you will have more time to plan the furniture. How is it going?"

"I have the planning phase all done. It is time to go shopping."

"Already?"

"Yes. I used clean ropes from the storage shed to lay out the placement of the furniture on the living room floor. I know the sizes I need. I have a color scheme." Gudrun grabbed the catalogue pages she liked from the basket. "What do you think? This page is just the colors. Not the furniture style."

"Looks fine to me. You have my approval."

The Yamaguchis joined them and with lots of translation by their husbands Gudrun and Nana cooked up a plan. Nana would drive Gudrun in the wagon with Surefoot during the next few days to the studios and workshops. Gudrun would in turn help pick and pack apples for the same amount of time.

Two hours later Gudrun walked into the weaver's studio with Nana, tape measure and photos in hand. After rough broken English introductions Gudrun began looking through the pile of rugs in the middle of the studio. Nana touched her arm and pointed to a small room. "Come." Gudrun followed her and stopped. There on the wall hung her rug. She immediately fell in love with it. The intricate pattern definitely had a native feeling like it belonged in the island, but somehow the ethnic pattern reminded her of the early Viking patterns from her homeland. Woven carefully with the blue and cream yarns she loved, she felt a sense of peace looking at it. She checked the measurements and within half an hour loaded it into the wagon with Nana's help. The weaver graciously provided her with tufts of the yarn she had used in the rug so that Gudrun could match upholstery to the rug without toting it all over the island.

"You — drive," Nana said as they sat down on the buckboard and handed Gudrun the reins.

"Me?"

Nana laughed. "You." Nana held her hands as if she was holding the reins, then jerked her hands.

Gudrun copied her motions. The reins slapped Surefoot on his rump and he took off down the lane toward Eastsound. Throughout the ride Nana kept coaching Gudrun with her hand motions.

"We stop — there." Gudrun pointed to the upholstery shop. "How?"

Nana gently leaned back a bit, pulling with her hands. Gudrun did the same and Surefoot stopped a block too soon. Nana and Gudrun broke into laughter. Then Gudrun regained her composure, slapped the reins bringing Surefoot up to the shop, and stopped the horse.

༄

"I could not believe my eyes. We pulled up to the upholstery shop and there in the window sat the exact chair I want for in front of the fireplace. Nana and I measured it but it was too small. I wrote down the measurements I wanted and the upholsterer gave me a price for two chairs," Gudrun explained to Arvik as she put a serving bowl full of meatballs next to the salad already on the table.

Arvik struggled to keep his eyes open and concentrate on her words as she added a large bowl of potetstappe. He longed for his bed. What had she said? Something about the perfect cream fabric? "Seems like everything is coming together quickly," he interjected as she took a breath.

"It had been up to that point. The sofa and the other fabrics could be a problem. Did I tell you Nana is teaching me how to drive the wagon?" Eyes sparkling, Gudrun sat down at her place and bowed her head.

Prayer. Prayer and then I get to eat like a king, Arvik thought. He gave a halfhearted grace and waited for Gudrun to pass him the meatballs.

"Nana and I will go and visit the other upholsterer tomorrow morning. So I should be able to help out in the orchard tomorrow afternoon and all day Friday."

Finishing a bite of meatball, Arvik said, "It might be best if you ladies started washing and packing them. We will set that up in the storage shed."

∽

Himmel surfed up and down over the two-foot swells as they crossed the Straits. Gudrun sat up on the bow in a pair of his refitted jeans and one of his old sweaters, the sunshine bouncing off her platinum curls. Occasionally she turned and smiled and waved at him. They had left the dock in Eastsound at five that Wednesday morning and if everything went according to plan they would be at Fishermen's Headquarters by ten tonight. They would sleep amongst the boxes of apples and sell them from the boat the next morning.

A larger swell brought spray all over the bow. Gudrun stood up and waved at him. He waved back and she made her way back to the stern.

"Getting a little wet up there." She laughed as she sat down next to him. "I have been thinking...only ten days ago I arrived at Orcas. It seems like a month or more. That was one full week and a half."

He grinned. "Yes, busy." He tightened the jib sheet keeping the boat close to Whidbey as they made the gradual turn into Puget Sound. They could see Port Townsend across the bay. No time to stop this trip. "I am afraid the next few days will be just as busy. Selling the apples and shopping. We could stay longer but the closer to October it gets we are taking chances with storms."

September twenty-third. A bit early for selling apples, however I am glad. When he only had to be concerned about himself he did not care if he ran into a storm. Now with Gudrun it had all changed. Her safety had become his number one concern.

"I understand. I have asked the Lord to guide me quickly to the right shops. It would be nice to have more time with the Lundes, but better to be safe. May I ask why we wash and wrap the apples so carefully? Yesterday while we were loading the boxes on the boat, I noticed other growers dropping off bushel baskets of loose apples at the commercial boats."

"And they get half the price we will. It is worth the extra work. Those growers sell to a middleman on the mainland who sorts out the bad or damaged apples for applesauce. We sell direct to the Seattle grocers."

Gudrun nodded. "That makes sense. And because you own your own boat it all works."

"Yeah."

"Or as Nana would say 'Hai'." Gudrun started to laugh as she pronounced the Japanese word for 'yes'."

Arvik gave her a quick look. "Are you learning Japanese or English?"

"Japanese and Nana is learning Norwegian." She continued to giggle.

Arvik shook his head and gave her a big smile. "So much for the English." He watched her face change and wanted to brush the sadness away.

"I try. I am trying, but it is so hard. I keep reading the book you gave me."

"I know." He patted her knee. "You will get there. I am impressed how quickly you have learned to drive the wagon."

Her smile returned and they continued south in a comfortable silence.

&

"Can you take the helm?" Arvik asked. "I will go down and get us coffee."

Gudrun blew into her gloves hoping to warm her hands. "Yes. That sounds good."

The weather had changed that Saturday morning and the temperature had dropped. They were running the in-board-engine as the wind seemed nonexistent.

Now that they were out of the channel and heading North up Puget Sound they were back to being themselves again, friends getting to know each other. During their short stay at the Lundes' things had gotten tense between them again. She knew why. The occasional question in private from Anna about if they had kissed yet, did she love Arvik, and even joking about Christmas mistletoe in front of the men. They had only been gone ten days, what did she expect?

Gudrun knew her new friend meant well, she just saw life a little differently. It had been great shopping with her, and Anna had been very helpful. She appreciated the meals Anna had planned, and being in their warm, cheerful house.

That first morning in Seattle, Nils and Anna had arrived at the boat with pastries and fruit for breakfast. Anna had taken her back to her house to freshen up, change clothes, and then off to shop. They left the men to sell the apples.

It had been a productive two days. In *Himmel's* hull sat a bolt of blue and cream patterned fabric for the sofa that went perfectly with the rug. She would also make throw pillows out of it for the window seat. Her prize, a large hide of leather for the chairs by the window seat, she had wrapped carefully in blankets to keep the soft leather from being scuffed. She had found drapery fabric, fabrics and linens for the current guest bedroom and throw rugs for the kitchen, baths, and entry. Still she had not found a solution for the window seat fabric or the guest bedroom rug.

"You look deep in thought," Arvik remarked as he handed her a cup of coffee.

Gudrun smiled at him. "Thank you. Yes, still working out the furniture and fabrics."

Arvik sat across from her looking at the sky, checking it out in every direction.

She could sense Arvik's concern about a possible storm. He could be right. Dark clouds hung off in the distance to the South.

"I have been praying...I am not the best at asking the Lord for things. But something does not feel right about this trip... can we pray together?" Arvik asked and he held out his hand.

Gudrun took his hand.

"You go ahead if you want," Arvik whispered. "I can close."

Asking for safety and wisdom, Gudrun kept her prayer short then Arvik asked for guidance. Silently she gave thanks for Arvik's willingness to go to the Lord. She also thanked the Lord for Arvik's kindness. Last Sunday at church on Orcas, Arvik looked up all the scriptures in her Norwegian Bible and pointed out the verses the pastor referred to so she had an idea what the sermon was about.

Continuing north to Whidbey they chatted from time to time about the house, Surefoot, on any subject except the weather. Occasionally Gudrun glanced at the dark clouds behind them, which seemed a bit closer each time she looked.

By noon they had made it to the south-end of Admiralty Bay. *It is so slow without the wind,* she thought. The engine let out a loud, odd noise. It clanked and sputtered some more and then quit. Arvik opened up the hatch and leaned in to take a look.

After several long minutes he sat back up and looked at her, his face looking extremely white and a bit scared. "It is a good thing it quit. We could have caught on fire!"

"Fire?"

"Yes. The clamp on the gasket must be loose. It has been dripping oil and the engine is very hot."

"So we are stuck. Should we drop anchor so we do not float into the shipping lane or go aground?" she asked.

"Let me take another look. Maybe I can fix it." He disappeared into the engine compartment again.

Does Arvik have more oil? A rag to clean up the oil might help. She knew where the rags were and went to the cabin to fetch some.

Arvik appreciated the rags and just as he finished cleaning up the dripped oil a gust of wind hit the boat. Gudrun looked to the south; the dark clouds were closer now.

"I am going to try and get us closer to shore," Arvik yelled and quickly started to hoist the sails.

As they drew closer to shore the dark clouds started to close in. He dropped the sails. Gudrun went to the bow and prepared to drop anchor. As they secured the anchor large drops of rain stung Gudrun in the face and the wind grew stronger.

"You, go below." Arvik yelled over the wind as he donned a poncho.

"I can help fold up the sails."

"Please, inside!" he insisted.

Something in his voice made her obey. *I must remember he knows what he is doing.* As she closed the cabin door the rain began to pound and darkness encompassed the boat. *Trying to sail in this would not be good. It is a good thing we are staying put.*

⌒৩

Surfacing from the engine compartment Arvik called out to Gudrun, "The clamp is on tight. Going to start the engine."

Gudrun stepped through the cabin door all bundled up. "Here is another rag. Wipe your face and hands before you touch anything else."

"Yes, ma'am." He gave her a sheepish grin. In his eagerness to get moving again he forgot. He wiped his face where he could feel the oil and then his hands.

"No, no." Gudrun shook her head, grabbed the rag and started rubbing oil off his right cheek. "You missed several places..."

He grabbed her wrist to stop her. Looking deep into her eyes, he resisted the urge to pull her closer and kiss her. Instead he said, "We need to get going. I do not want to spend another night out off the hook."

She smiled. "Just one more place. I cannot have my husband looking like a ruffian." She gently rubbed oil off his chin.

"Why not?" he asked as he took the rag from her. "Seriously, we need to get moving."

The torrential rain had lasted all afternoon and throughout the night. It suddenly broke mid-morning. It had taken the last few hours to replace the old clamp and refill the oil.

He turned the engine and it started.

"Thank you Lord!" Gudrun exclaimed. "Wish we had wind."

"Agree. Can you help me with the anchor?" Arvik asked. "I will haul it up if you take the helm."

Gudrun took over the wheel. She followed Arvik's commands, rocking the boat forward and back to loosen the hold. Soon they were underway. Gudrun went below to fix lunch.

What a trooper, he thought. *Most women would not have put up with the cold and damp like she did last night. The coffee she had in the thermoses and sandwiches helped. She did not complain once, just found ways to help.* His appreciation continued as her obedience about going inside came to mind. He did not have a second poncho and they did not need another damp body in the hull. The new propane space heater helped dry his pants and boots and gave them a little heat, but he could only run it for short intervals. The salesman at the hardware store had warned him to keep a close eye on it as it could tip over and start a fire.

Layers of blankets became their friend. Without the engine working all of the systems were down. They had played checkers, read the Bible, and Gudrun wrote in her journal to pass the time by the light of the kerosene lantern. Gudrun had suggested that they both sleep in the main cabin to keep warm. A quick conversion of the built-in seat turned it into a large bed. Despite all the blankets she had bundled herself in, with her lying next to him he forgot the rain and eventually fell asleep thinking of her.

"Cheese and crackers?" Gudrun asked as she came through the cabin door. "I have apples and fresh hot coffee, too."

"Wonderful."

They sat in comfortable silence enjoying the late lunch. The clouds began to clear and they could see glimpses of Port Townsend off in the distance. As they finished lunch the sun came out.

"Sol!" Gudrun exclaimed.

"What an answer to prayer. If the clouds clear and the moon and stars are out I am comfortable trolling along after the sun goes down. We could be home tonight."

Suddenly a gust of wind hit. "Maybe even sooner?" Gudrun said. "Although, we do not have a deadline and with the engine working, we could stay out another night."

CHAPTER 26

Secrets

Late October sunshine streamed through the windows as Gudrun sat down at her desk in the study. She thought of Karoline's study in the Grand House. *I never dreamed I would have a room to sketch, journal and write letters.* Running her hand along the grain of the white oak she thought, *Karoline's study was so grand. Mine is more...cozy. I am so grateful to have this...this view of the islands...so beautiful. I must get cushions made for this window seat, too. One project at a time.*

Opening the letter she had received from Mrs. Sandnes, relief flooded over her as her friend reported that they had made it back to Bergen safely. There were a few tense moments where Captain Hans thought they might be near German ships. Mrs. Sandnes mentioned that there had not been very many passengers returning to Norway and she had caught up on her reading during the voyage. She also wrote about Åse's situation. Åse had responded well to the doctor's help during their month-long stay in San Diego. Her fiancé had visited her for a week and during that time Mr. Sandnes had gotten to know him. He seemed a solid young man who would treat Åse well. At the end of the month the fiancé returned and Åse agreed to be married. The Sandneses attended the wedding before boarding *Sognefjord.*

Picking up her journal Gudrun began to write about the events of the first weeks of October:

The upholsterer in town delivered the two light cream chairs for in front of the fireplace the first week of October. The brown leather chairs by the living room window seat arrived yesterday. He has promised me the sofa by Thanksgiving. I still need fabric for the living room window seat cushions. However, I finished the pillows for the window seat early this morning. Arvik has been busy on kitchen cabinets for a bungalow in Eastsound, a small project. For a few weeks he has been home everyday out in the storage shed building the cabinets. It has been so much fun taking him coffee and snacks mid-morning and afternoon and having him home for every meal. This week he will be gone for most of the day as he and Zhou are installing the cabinets.

She looked up from her journal staring at the islands.

Should I write about how seeing him makes my heart beat faster. And sometimes as I am serving him meals my knees go weak. Am I in love? Does he feel...

Bang! The front door slammed. Gudrun jumped to her feet. *I know I locked the front door. It has to be...* inching toward the top of the stairs, she heard a crash in the kitchen, then a curse in a deep guttural tone. *Arvik?* As she quietly descended the stairs she heard a deep moan and a dull thud on the floor. She arrived at the kitchen door to see her husband sitting up against the island, blood dripping from his finger and fire in his eyes. Even from that distance she could smell alcohol.

Hurrying across the hall to the powder room she grabbed the first aid kit. Back in the kitchen she noted the shattered glass in the sink. His head down Arvik did not even look at her. Anger began to build inside her as she knelt down next to her husband and tended to the cut on his finger. *He better have a good explanation for this,* she thought.

Memories of her father coming home drunk and angry after a bad day fishing flashed through her mind. His actions not only scared her but she also felt totally helpless. It never happened when her mother was alive. After the first few times she had let her father know she would not stay with him if he continued to get drunk and it only happened one more time before he died. They had discussed it once. Her father said when you have someone you love so much and things go wrong and you think you cannot provide for them, the weight of the whole world gets to be too much.

Focusing on those words as she finished bandaging Arvik's finger she began to pray for the right words. She did not know this man as well as she knew her father. She did not know what he was capable of. She had been warned of lack of church attendance and the temper...no one had mentioned a drinking problem.

Arvik turned his head and looked at her for a second. His head dropped in shame and he muttered, "Thank you..." He fumbled and got to his feet, leaning on the countertop. "I will replace the glass."

"That is not one of our glasses," Gudrun stated using her iciest voice.

Arvik looked at the pieces in the sink. "I guess it is one from the storage shed."

Gudrun poured him a cup of coffee. As she handed it to him she asked, "Is that where you keep the whiskey?"

Head down, Arvik mumbled, "No, I got rid of my stash over a year ago. I have not had a drop since. I got a bottle in town this morning." Lifting his head he chugged down most of the coffee.

"Do you want to tell me why?" she asked in a level tone.

He fumbled with his coffee cup, took another gulp and looked at her. "She changed everything! The cabinets are all done and she wants it all different." Anger built in his voice as he talked. "I have had difficult clients before, but she is beyond rude. She refuses to pay and I owe Zhou for his work." He slammed the coffee cup down shooting drops of coffee into the air onto the counter. He stumbled over to the kitchen table and sat down, crossed his arms on the table and laid his head down in defeat.

Carefully picking up the glass fragments, her father's word ran through her mind again and again. At least she understood the situation. *Now, how to make sure it does not happen again.*

Arvik's gentle snoring let her know he would be sleeping it off for awhile. She went upstairs to put away her journal and Mrs. Simonsen's letter. *I should not write now, as my words would be harsh. Lord guide me. I do not want to live in fear of my husband. I hate this...should I leave?*

She sat cross-legged on her study window seat and began to sob. Letting her mind wander to packing her bags and leaving for Seattle. *Where would I go? The Lundes'? Could I find a job? How often is he like this?* She stopped crying and wiped her tears with her handkerchief. She wanted to pray but the words would not come.

Psalm 46:10 came to mind. "Be still and know that I am God;..." kept repeating itself over and over, letting the meaning of the verse sink into her soul. A familiar calm overtook her and she prayed a new thought, *I do not have enough information, Lord. Show me your will. Guide me, please.*

Glancing at her watch she realized she needed to make lunch. Food might help both of them. Walking toward the kitchen she could hear Arvik continuing to snore.

⁓

"A month and a half of marriage and I already blew it!" Arvik yelled. The large salmon in the bottom of his boat flopped one more time. He had his fish but he did not want to row to shore and face Gudrun. He stared across the glassy water. Another fish jumped about fifty feet away, causing ripples across the water.

"Everything was so perfect, Lord, and I destroyed it. My temper destroys. But I need to make sure she is secure financially. We needed that money. If anything happens to me she must be secure for the rest of her life..." Fogginess in his head made him stop. Oh his head hurt.

The food and the coffee she had for him when he woke up had helped. He had apologized and told her it would never happen again.

Her reply stung. "Talk to me later when the alcohol is out of your system." Her eyes told him she did not believe him. *Maybe she is right. I might do it again...how come alcohol has such an effect on me, Lord?"*

He had gotten up from lunch ready to return to the bungalow and tear the cabinets apart, but Gudrun had stopped him by asking if he could go fishing so they could have salmon for dinner. *She probably figured I would not hurt myself out here. I could fall overboard.*

He bent over the side and splashed water on his face. The cold water shook the last of the cobwebs out of his brain.

"Ahoy!" Sounded across the water, echoing slightly off the shore. Arvik looked to the west. Gliding across the water towards him, Zhou waved with both arms. Arvik gave a weak wave back.

"Surprised to see you out here. Thought you be in shed drinking, hiding from missus." Zhou said as his boat slid in next to Arvik's.

Head down, Arvik replied, "Why did you think that?"

"You come out store with Scotch Whiskey."

Arvik nodded.

"She need apologi...no apol—"

"Apology, Zhou. Yes, she is waiting for a sincere apology. If she is not packing to leave."

Zhou leaned over the side of his boat to give Arvik a slight punch in the shoulder. He looked down. "Oh. Nice fish." He smiled. "You take to missus now."

Arvik stared at him.

"Go. Now!" Zhou demanded. "You big man." Zhou puffed up his chest. "Afraid?"

Arvik smiled. "Maybe." He picked up his oars and began to row to shore.

Once in the storage shed, he gutted the fish, washed it, and wrapped it in newsprint. Picking up the half empty whiskey bottle he headed for the house.

He laid the salmon on the counter next to the sink just as Gudrun walked into the kitchen. He picked up the whiskey bottle, pulled out the cork and poured the remaining contents down the drain as she watched. Their eyes met. He threw the empty bottle in the trash.

"I am going upstairs to clean up," he said and left the kitchen.

An hour later the aroma of baked salmon wafted up the stairs. He came down and watched her for a second, struggling to get the salmon onto the serving platter. She gave up and looked at him in despair. He walked over, got out a second spatula and helped her move the large fish. He picked up the platter and carried it to the table filled with potatoes, and various side dishes. Once they sat down he knew prayer would be the next thing on the agenda.

He looked her directly in the eye, "I am sober and I am truly sorry. I wish I could promise that it will never happen again but I cannot. I know my flesh can be weak at times. I do promise to do everything I can to keep it from happening. Shall we pray?"

Gudrun bowed her head.

"Our Father, you know my weaknesses, my frailties and I confess my sinful choice of letting my anger get out of control leading to more bad choices. We thank you for your forgiveness. Thank you for this bountiful table of food and especially for the hands that made it. Please, bless it to our bodies. In Jesus' name, Amen."

They served themselves in silence and continued to eat without a word.

"May I ask how many times you have gotten drunk?" Gudrun inquired.

Arvik nodded. "...four times, now."

"Four?" She gave him a look of surprise.

"Yes, when my mother died. I got into Nils' parents' liquor cabinet, drank for several days and went on a rampage through the woods, busted up a few cabins that I had the privilege of repairing, later. I got so mad at God."

"Yes, anger can be a part of mourning. But you were young."

Arvik shrugged his shoulders, "No excuse. And fourteen months ago when it looked like this house would never be built."

"Why would it not be built?" Gudrun asked.

Looking down at his plate, Arvik filled her in on Zhou's accident and how the community came to help out. "Zhou's accident hit me hard as it reminded me of Oddvar."

Arvik took one last bite of salmon, then stood and began pacing the kitchen floor with his head down. He wiped a tear off his cheek and looked at Gudrun. Eyes wide and compassionate she continued to stare at him.

He sat down. "You see there were three of us. The three musketeers, a band of brothers, all three of us without any siblings. Nils, me and Oddvar. Oddvar's aunt raised him from the time he was a baby. We grew up together and came to America together. Because Nils had an education and a wife he stayed in Seattle. Oddvar and I took off to Alaska to make our fortune fishing. Dangerous work but the money was good. After a few years we decided to give it up, we had made enough money. We found this piece of land and we bought it together."

"You do not have to continue," Gudrun broke in. "You can tell me another time."

Arvik took a big gulp of coffee. "No. Now is the time. After a few years of working on Rosario, Oddvar got bored and left for Alaska. He did not enjoy carpentry or construction work. He came home a few times in between fishing seasons, even built a shed to live in. After a few years he had a bad accident on the fishing boat. Nils and I buried Oddvar in Seattle. When he and I bought the property we had a lawyer set up a contract with each plot of land allowing easement to the next. That established Sunset Lane. He bought three waterfront plots. I bought this waterfront piece and the orchard. The lawyer suggested we name each other as our heir since we did not have any family. So I inherited Oddvar's pieces."

"Oh my. I had wondered why we had a street through our property. I am sorry, go on."

"After Nils and I buried Oddvar I came back and started drinking. It went on for almost a month before Nils came and locked me up in the storage shed till I was dry. Then he took me to Seattle and made me work for him for a few months. If you ever find any bottles on the property it is left over from that time. I am told I even dug holes in the ground to hide it."

They sat in silence. Finally, Gudrun leaned over and took Arvik's hand. "Thank you for telling me. I want to help."

"Thank you."

"I do forgive you. My father...well that story is for another time." Gudrun stood up.

"Will you stay...stay married?" Arvik asked.

"It is late now — we can talk again in the morning. I will get up early and clean up the kitchen."

Arvik sat at the table until he heard her bedroom door close. Then he got busy cleaning up the kitchen. It was the least he could do. As he walked up the stairs he could hear sobs coming from her bedroom. He stopped in front of her door. Oh how he wanted to comfort her and promise her a perfect world.

୧୬

Sunshine flooding into her window woke Gudrun before her alarm went off. She thought about the incidents of the night before. It had taken over an hour for her to calm down enough to fall asleep. She kept praying, asking the Lord to heal Arvik, asking the Lord to guide her. Last night at one point she had decided to leave, but she could not even get out of bed to pack.

"Good morning Lord. I cannot leave...I care too much for him. I do not think he has ever hurt anyone...and it has not happened often," she whispered watching the sunlight dancing on the ceiling. "My fairytale world has disappeared. It is the real world now."

As she got dressed she smelled coffee brewing. She hurried downstairs to find Arvik at the kitchen table. The cabinet drawings were spread out and he was sketching new ones.

Arvik looked up, examining her face for acceptance. They gazed at each other for a second and then he said, "Good morning, I made coffee. And I already ate —oatmeal."

Looking around Gudrun exclaimed, "My kitchen is clean! Thank you."

"I think there is a way to give my client what she wants and not lose money, even pay Zhou. There will be no profit."

Gudrun picked up the original drawings and flipped through them. "Did she see these and approve them before you started building the cabinets?"

"Yes. Nils has told me that I should have a statement in ink on the drawings, saying they have reviewed, understand and approve the drawings with a place for them to sign and date. From now on —"

"Look, someone is coming." Gudrun pointed to a single horse coming down the lane.

Squinting at the figure for a few moments, Arvik said, "That is my client's husband. He has been on the mainland. This could be interesting."

Arvik went to the door. Gudrun put a few biscuits in the oven to warm. Arvik ushered the man into the kitchen, introduced her to him, and they sat at the table. After she served the biscuits and coffee, Gudrun went up to her study. She sat and read her Bible and prayed.

A half hour later she heard some laughter and goodbyes then footsteps coming up the stairs. Arvik sat down on the window seat.

Sighing, he said, "It seems like I got all worked up about nothing. Her husband apologized for his wife, asked for one small change, and he paid me three quarters of my bill. He will pay the rest when I make the change and the job is finished."

"Oh, what an answer to prayer. I started praying last night."

"Before or after you cried?" Arvik asked.

Gudrun blushed. "You heard me?"

"Yes. I hope you got some sleep."

"I did. Should we put this behind us?" she asked.

"I would like that." Arvik stood up. "I have work to do."

She put her hand on his arm. "May I make a suggestion?"

"Go ahead."

"Stop putting pressure on yourself. I do not require all this —" she waved her arm around the room. "— I enjoy this house…immensely. However, I do not need it…not to be happy. We do not need the money, do we?"

Arvik sat back down. "You are right. With the sale of the apples we will be fine this winter. I wanted to have enough to take care of you for the rest of your life."

"God will provide, like the manna in the wilderness, one day at a time."

৩

"Enjoy your oats, Surefoot." Gudrun hung up the bridle and opened the stable door to the pasture. She could hardly wait to get back to the house and unpack her groceries. She had picked up two letters in town, one from Berit, and Anna's weekly correspondence.

Once all the perishable groceries were in the refrigerator she poured herself coffee and sat at the kitchen table. She scanned Berit's letter, pausing at the part about Captain Hans:

Sissel had a dinner party and seated me next to the captain.

It seems he still cares about you as he asked me about how you were doing. He seemed to relax when I told him how well things had turned out for you. I hope you do not mind, but he asked me for lunch in a month when he returns to town. Please let me know if I have your blessing. He is such a gentleman.

They are closer in age, but he is not a Christian. How could Berit even consider him?

Looking out the window Gudrun noticed Nana jumping down from her wagon and running toward the house. Meeting her at the front door Gudrun started to ask. "Why such hurry —"

"I found fabric. Window...seat." Nana pointed to the living room.

"Where?"

"Weaver. You little fabrics bring. I drive."

Running upstairs to her study, Gudrun thought, *Could it be Nana has found the solution?* She grabbed her fabric and yarn swatches and her bag and ran back down the stairs.

An hour and a half later she and Nana arrived back home with a bolt of the most beautiful, durable fabric in her possession. "Come." Gudrun motioned to the house. "Tea?"

God is good, Gudrun thought as she carried the bolt inside. She sat the bolt on the window seat draping it across and placing her newly made pillows on top.

"Ah...so good!" Nana exclaimed. She waved her arm around the room. "You, good job," beaming as she spoke.

"You good friend." Gudrun bent down and gave her friend a hug. "Now tea." And she marched into the kitchen to start the water, pulled out the cups, and placed the special box of Japanese tea that Arvik had found in Seattle on the table. "Like?" She asked Nana.

"Oh yes!" Nana's eyes sparkled.

CHAPTER 27

Christmas Plans

*D*usting the end tables in the living room that morning, Gudrun could hardly contain her excitement. *Tonight! Tonight! December twenty-third, the Lundes will be here. Spending the holidays with them will be such a treat. We will bring the Christmas tree in tonight, just like in Norway, Little Christmas Eve. Before we attend the Christmas Eve service tomorrow we will have lapskaus — a light middag. After the service the marsipan cake and some cookies. On Christmas Day the salmon and pork loin.*

She ran through the menus, checking that she had every ingredient she needed, then looked around the room. The rug still spoke to her with its blue and cream colors melded together in an intricate, subtle pattern.

Arvik had finished the dining room table this past week. They still needed a hutch, someday. One corner of the living room waited for the game table she envisioned. Not completely furnished, but they would be comfortable while their company visited. *It will all come together in time. Just like Arvik and my relationship. We have been so busy Lord. The past two months have flown by. Me with the house and Arvik either in the shed working on all the Christmas orders or away working on the remodel project. We have not had much time together. Please make our relationship into what you want it to be Lord.*

Recently Arvik had taken on a remodel project for a couple, two coves to the east of their house. His schedule varied day to day. Some days he came home for lunch and worked the afternoon in the shed; other days he would row to work so she could take the wagon to town. After dinner he would apologize and retreat to the shed to work on table orders. She would sit and sew by the fire in one of the new chairs or write letters or journal, up in her study. Her correspondence with Anna, Berit, Karoline, Mrs. Simonsen and Mrs. Sandnes kept her from feeling lonely. Around nine o' clock Arvik would come and join her for a late kveldsmat and they would sit and chat for an hour. They had put the October incident behind them and she began to feel close to him again. Sometimes the way he looked at her made her wonder if he felt the same way about her as she did about him. Occasionally he would touch her shoulder in church, guiding her to their seats, or their hands would brush up against each other as they worked together. She appreciated the comfortable way they were building their relationship with no pressure.

Church — she loved attending and singing the hymns with the same tunes she sang in Norway. However, the sermon and the social time before and after pointed out her struggle with English. She could properly greet people and say goodbye but much more than that and she got lost. Her inability to learn prevented her from making friends.

Looking out at the view she noticed dark ominous clouds over Matia and Sucia Islands. *A storm coming from the north? How fast is it coming? Arvik warned me they can build quickly.* The islands suddenly disappeared. She dropped the duster and ran upstairs. Opening her north facing bedroom window she closed the outside shutters. Precious minutes ticked away as she shuttered each window on the second floor. She ran down the stairs to the living room window and shuttered all but the bay window. *Where is Arvik? Still out fishing? Yes.* She could see him pulling the dinghy on shore. The ominous clouds were closer. *Surefoot! I need to get him.*

Grabbing a lead rope off the horse corral fence she ran out in the pasture and began to lead the aging gelding toward the barn. A strong gust of wind hit the barn, making it moan under the pressure, which made her quiver for a second. Surefoot felt it too as he balked. Head thrown back, he refused to move. Hanging onto his halter she kicked her feet out from under letting her whole weight hang on his head. He succumbed.

"Come on, Surefoot. Be a good boy." She spoke calmly, rubbing his neck, like Arvik had taught her. "There are oats in the barn." The word oats pricked up his ears and he followed her lead. "Let us hurry. I need to get you taken care of and me in the house before it hits," she called out as they ran. The noise of the impending storm increased so much she could barely hear her own voice. "We are almost there. In the door."

Arvik burst in the other door. "Good. I will feed and water. You get to the house!"

"The storage shed?"

"Go! The upstairs windows?"

"Done. I will get water and the candles out." Arvik had forewarned her that in the event of a major storm they would shut off the generator for safety reasons. He did not know how the machine would behave in such high winds.

As she ran towards the house, the dark wall of clouds seemed almost ready to engulf it. Rain began to hit her face as she ran and she pulled her open coat closed. She glanced at the storage shed and saw the doors were bolted shut. A string of salmon had been dropped by the front door. Arvik's catch.

After she got the candles, matches and water taken care of, she found an old pail in the basement. Arvik burst through the door as she reached the entry with the pail. Holding the dripping string of salmon he looked confused for a second. She held out the large pail and relief covered his face.

"I will take these to the basement," he said. "We should go there too. Grab extra blankets, extra clothes, food, anything you might need."

ᗯ

"This is worse than the September storm, a year ago. That one I rode out in the old lean-to. I planned to tear that down this winter...I might not have to."

The wind continued to howl with loud intermittent crashes and occasional flashes of light coming through the basement windows. They sat up against an interior wall on the tiny old bed Arvik had slept on in the lean-to, huddled in blankets, far enough back from the windows to be safe.

"Do you think any of the large trees will hit the house?" Gudrun asked.

Arvik could feel her body shiver as she spoke. He longed to put his arm around her, but refrained. "I do not think so. I made sure to clear a large area when I built the house. I am more concerned about the wind picking up something and slamming it into the house or through the bay windows."

Shining her flashlight around the north end of the basement, Gudrun asked, "What are we going to do with this huge space?"

Arvik shrugged. "I have no idea."

"Is there a reason you made the house so big?"

"It is exactly like the house I admired in Norway. I wanted that house so I built it...after working on Rosario this seemed rather small. You could set up a dress shop?"

Gudrun's laughter echoed through the unfinished space. "Where would all the customers come from?"

Arvik shrugged again.

"You sir, think differently than other people. It is not bad, just different," Gudrun said.

"Nils has often told me I think backwards. It might be almost noon..." he stopped. *No sense in getting her all worried. The boat the Lundes are on should be crossing the Straits... Please Lord keep them safe. Thank you for Gudrun. She is amazing. Jumping in and helping when needed.* The wind and rain continued pounding against the house. "Are you hungry?"

Gudrun nodded and opened the basket. "We have egg salad we can spread on the bread and we have apples."

"You did a good job taking care of the windows and bringing in Surefoot, Arvik said.

"Thank you. That is island living. Watching out for changes in the weather. I saw the clouds engulf Sucia and Matia so quickly and remembered what you told me about storms from the north."

Arvik smiled. "We are a team against the storm. This will be the real test of how well this house is built." He took out his pocket watch. "Twelve-thirty. This could go on for hours."

"We could sing a few Christmas hymns," Gudrun suggested.

By the third Christmas carol the wind increased so that they could barely hear themselves.

"Maybe we should be praying for the Yamaguchis and others on the island," Arvik suggested.

"The Lundes? Where is their boat right now?" Gudrun's eyes told him she had been thinking the same thing he had.

"I have no idea. I hope they found safe harbor, maybe at Port Townsend."

"It sounds like one-hundred and twenty kilometers per hour winds. What about *Himmel?* Did you secure the dinghy?" she asked. Her thought going back to the wild storms on her island in Norway.

Arvik waited for a loud crash to subside before answering, "The dinghy is locked down, ropes across it, several times, and securely tied to the clamps. I checked *Himmel* yesterday. The lines and bumpers are set to ride out a storm. The way the marina is situated she is protected from the full force of the winds from the north. There is nothing we can do now."

"Like you said we can pray."

They fell silent for a while. After a lengthy prayer, Arvik looked at Gudrun, her head bobbing and lightly snoring. He put her head on his shoulder to stabilize it. She had been working so hard the past three months getting the house ready. The guest bedroom for Nils and Anna looked amazing. She had sewn the comforter cover and decorative pillows by hand. Best of all she had forgiven him...

৩

Pacing the first floor of the house, Gudrun kept inspecting the furniture and floor for dust, peeking out the entry and kitchen windows down the lane. Everything had been taken care of. She could not think of one more thing to do, except worry and pray.

The storm had subsided about three-thirty the previous afternoon. They had quickly assessed the damage. As Arvik suspected, the lean-to did not survive. The dinghy stayed in place, tied to cleats, upside down on a concrete slab that would someday become a boathouse. Surefoot's stable survived, only missing a few shingles on the roof. The same for the storage shed. Miraculously not one of the bay windows had broken. Her prayers had been answered.

After they had assessed the damage at home, Arvik went to check on *Himmel* which made it through with only a few minor scrapes. The boat the Lundes were on had not arrived yet and no one in town had heard anything about it. This morning he took off for town again. She looked at her watch. Almost noon. *Should I make lunsj? Are they alright? Did their boat go ashore, did it capsize? Are they even alive?*

She paced across the living room one more time. Then stopped. *I am sorry Lord, I have been worrying, which is not trusting you. You who brought me here, safely. You who gave me a place to live, a husband. You who made the universe and know everything. You know where the Lundes are and I must trust you. They are your children too, Lord. Forgive me. You have always been faithful. Thank you. Give me faith Lord. In your Son's precious name, Amen.*

Marching into the kitchen she got to work making popcorn for the garlands for the Christmas tree. Arvik had an angel for the top of the tree — one of the few possessions he had from his mother. Sitting at the kitchen table stringing the popcorn she thought about how her perfect Christmas had changed. No Little Christmas Eve celebration with the Lundes. They might not even make the Christmas Eve service at church. She kept a close eye on the lane as she threaded the popcorn. She had imagined the four of them doing this together.

Arvik had brought the tree in that morning and placed it where her future game table would be. The aroma filled the house.

"A wagon!" Gudrun stood up. "Yes, Lord, a wagon..." She looked closely. "The Yamaguchis?"

She hurried to meet them at the door.

Zhou jumped down and came to explain. "Alik came to me house. House had tree on it. Alik say we come here?"

For a split second Gudrun saw her perfect Christmas image shatter into a million pieces. An image of the Good Samaritan flashed into her mind. "Yes, yes. You stay here."

Zhou helped Nana down. Nana carried a few bags, her head down. She stopped in front of Gudrun. "Me sorry. You — guest — Seattle."

Reaching down Gudrun hugged her. "You guest. You friend. Come."

The Yamaguchis followed her upstairs, Zhou carrying two large duffle bags. Gudrun showed them one of the empty bedrooms. "We find bed. Sorry."

"No. We have bed." He quickly unrolled a large straw mat. Then two thicker mats which he placed together. "Bed."

"You need —" Frustrated with her English Gudrun gave up. "Come." She marched into the room she had prepared for the Lundes. The Yamaguchis followed. She pointed to the bed. "Bed."

Both of the Yamaguchis shook their heads. "No." They said in unison and walked back into the empty room. "Bed."

"Hello. Anyone home?" Arvik's voice boomed up the stairs.

Running down the stairs to meet him, she stopped in the entry, surprised to see a very bedraggled Anna sitting on the bench. "Anna. Are you alright?"

"We need to get her upstairs and into bed. I have sent for Dr. Agnes," Arvik said. Nils and Arvik helped Anna up and off with her coat. One on each side of her they half carried Anna up the stairs to the guest room. Nana and Zhou joined them asking if they could help.

Easy-going Nils suddenly took command. "Someone make hot tea, I need warm water and a wash cloth. Gudrun, please find her flannel nightgown and socks in her suitcase. Otherwise, everyone out."

Nana hurried off to the kitchen. Arvik went to get the suit-cases off the wagon and Gudrun got the warm water in a basin and several washcloths. As she carried it into the room she heard Anna moan, "I never get seasick...never."

"The doctor is on her way, my dear," Nils said and began washing Anna's face.

Hurrying back down the stairs Gudrun found Arvik in the entry with Anna's suitcase. "So she got seasick. Did they ride out the storm?" She asked as she opened it up and started searching for things.

"Apparently they were forewarned and laid over in Port Townsend. Anna got sick on the way to Port Townsend. Then today she was throwing up over the railing and the ship's second mate accidentally hit reverse and she fell overboard in Rosario Straight."

"Oh no! Poor dear. I found everything." She started off and stopped. "Thank you. Would you bring their bags up and put them outside the door? I think Nils is undressing her."

"Yes, and I will bring Doctor Agnes up as soon as she arrives."

❧

Dr. Agnes walked into the kitchen and placed her medical bag on the counter and announced in English, "Mrs. Lunde will be fine. She needs rest." She turned to Gudrun, "Your friend has requested your presence."

Noticing Gudrun's confusion Arvik quickly translated for her and Gudrun hurried upstairs.

Nana offered the doctor a cup of tea, which the doctor gratefully accepted.

Putting his hand on Arvik's shoulder, Nils said, "Can we talk in the living room?"

Following Nils to the bay window, Arvik asked, "Is she alright?"

Beaming Nils announced, "Better than alright! I am going to be a father! She is pregnant! It is not seasickness, it is morning sickness!"

Arvik's jaw dropped. "A baby? You seem happy."

"It is not something we shared with anyone but we have been wanting children for a long, long time. We actually gave up hoping. And now the Lord has blessed us. Me, a father at thirty and Anna twenty-eight, we will be older parents."

"And I have the privilege of being the first to congratulate you!" Arvik gave his friend a hug.

"Do you still need help with the crate out on the wagon?" Nils asked.

"Please. Zhou can help, too."

CHAPTER 28

Good Samaritans

Opening the door very slowly, Gudrun peeked into the guest bedroom. Anna sat up against the pillows, eyes closed. Gudrun stood in the doorway for a second not sure what to do.

Anna's eyes fluttered. "Come..." she patted the bed.

Quickly joining her friend, Gudrun sat on the bed. "Are you alright? What did Dr. Agnes say?"

Anna repositioned herself. She grabbed Gudrun's hand and said, "I am going to be a mother!"

Gudrun's hand went to her mouth. "Oh! So that is why you were sick."

"Yes...such wonderful news..." She started to doze. "God has answered my prayers."

"Is there anything you need?"

"No...well, the suitcases?"

Gudrun looked around the room. Three large cases sat between the closet and the dresser. "They are here. Do you want me to unpack them?"

"Just my things...would be nice. Nils would not know what to do with my things...you are so..." and Anna drifted off to sleep.

Finished with unpacking Anna's clothes Gudrun almost skipped down the stairs. *A baby! Such exciting news Lord. Thank you that she is not ill.* Turning at the bottom of the stairs, she stopped short. *What is that next to the Christmas tree? It is huge.* She walked toward the object. *Blue fabric? A rug? I love the rug.* She got close enough to touch it just as a large hand came down on her shoulder.

She heard Arvik's voice in her ear. "Please, leave it alone. You can unwrap it tomorrow."

Turning around she looked up at his smiling eyes. "It looks like a rug and fabric," she said.

"Think what you want but no touching," he said, his hand still on her shoulder. "Of all the responsibilities I have given you this is the most important one. No touching. Agreed?"

She nodded.

"I have been meaning to thank you. I am so sorry about all of this. It is not the Christmas you have been planning. There was no time to warn you that the Yamaguchis were coming, I had to get the Lundes at the boat."

"You did the right thing. No, it is not the Christmas I planned, but it might be better. Did you hear the news?"

Arvik grinned. "Yes, a baby."

"We will be like the Good Samaritan and share everything we have." She liked the way his hand continued to gently rest on her shoulder, the closeness she felt with him.

He nodded. "I agree...Good Samaritans together. There is something else. Nana is in your kitchen putting middag together." He chuckled. "...though she does not call it that and it will be different. She wants to help. Zhou is out chopping wood —"

"But they are our guests. And it is too early for middag."

"They are," Arvik agreed. "However, they are not the kind to sit around and do nothing. It makes them feel better to help so I think we should let them."

"I will." Suddenly she remembered. "Oh, Arvik, we have to do something about a bed for the Yamaguchis. They brought these mats like they are camping. You have an extra mattress wrapped up in the basement, can we set it up for them?"

Trying hard not to laugh, Arvik replied, "No. That is their culture. That is the most comfortable for them. They have the best type of Japanese bed. I remember Zhou bragging about buying the thicker mats for Nana's birthday. Leave that alone. We have to continue to be flexible."

Suddenly she felt Arvik's big arms around her giving her a hug. She felt so safe she never wanted the hug to end. She laid her head on his shoulder for a moment then hugged him back and pulled away. "I need to find out what is going on in my kitchen," she stated.

Gudrun stopped in the doorway to the kitchen. In the middle of the table sat a platter filled with a variety of her crisp Norwegian cookies. *Cookies that will go soft with all the steam coming off the pot on the stove. How did Nana find them all hidden away in their tins? Lord help me be loving. I guess it is acceptable to eat middag so early...* She looked at the clock. *Three o'clock already? It will only be an hour or so early, since no one has had lunch it will be fine.*

Looking up from the pot Nana gave Gudrun a big smile. "Rice," she said. "You make." She pointed to another pot.

Gudrun looked in the pot to see her Lapskaus — the meat, and vegetables simmering at the perfect temperature in the heavy broth. "Thank you." She smiled back at Nana. *Rice with Lapskaus — it is food and that is all that matters.*

Nana opened the refrigerator and showed her a platter of smoked salmon, sliced brown goat cheese and bread.

"Good," Gudrun said.

Arvik walked into the kitchen. "Nils is still upstairs keeping an eye on Anna. How soon shall I get him for dinner?" He asked in Norwegian. He looked at Nana and continued in English, "Sorry, how soon do we eat?"

Nana held up all ten fingers. "Ten," she said.

"Thank you." He walked over to the cookies. "I will take these to the dining table." He winked at Gudrun.

She had understood enough of the English to know he wanted to rescue the cookies. "Yes."

Dinner became a happy affair with lots of translating for Gudrun and Nana. Arvik made a toast in perfect English to the Lundes and their forthcoming baby, then Zhou and Arvik translated for their wives.

Between the main course and dessert Nils had another surprise announcement. He had brought Christmas lights for the tree. After dessert Gudrun sat and watched the men string the lights and turn them on. "So beautiful," she murmured, enjoying the brightness they brought to the room. After a few minutes she started up the stairs to check on Anna. *Yes, Lord this could be the best Christmas ever. Thank you.*

గ్రా

Arvik sipped his coffee as he surveyed the scene before him. Such a contrast to last December when he had spent Christmas Eve sitting on a lifeboat cushion in front of the fire in his empty living room; then spending all Christmas day on a boat to Seattle. At that time he had not heard back from the letters he had sent to Norway earlier in the fall. His hope of finding a wife had begun to dim.

Now here he sat in a comfortable leather chair, listening to his best friend read the Christmas story to Anna and Gudrun. *Thank you, Lord. This is beyond my wildest dreams. My own pretty wife has done such an impressive job with the house. Her cooking will make me fat and she is sensible. Thank you. Please help the Yamaguchis.*

That morning at breakfast the couple had announced that they wanted to spend the day at their home accessing the damage and deciding the best way to approach the repairs. Since the Yamaguchis did not celebrate Christmas, Arvik understood that today could be uncomfortable for them.

Gudrun must have gotten up at four as she had fresh bread for breakfast. Besides the usual brown goat cheese and sliced meats for the bread, she also had made cinnamon buns. Anna joined them stating that she felt much better and found herself a bit hungry.

Here they were, the four of them. Next year there would be five, if all went well. *Yes, Lord, I am truly blessed.*

Nils finished up the story and they took turns praying. Anna proved she felt normal again as she jumped up after they prayed. "Now it is time for the presents," she exclaimed and began passing them out.

They each opened several presents and then only one present remained. Arvik stood, walked over to Gudrun and helped her to her feet. "Now you may take the rug and fabric off and find out what is underneath. It is from me, well most of it...I hope you like it."

Gudrun picked up the corner of the rug. "This is so beautiful, where did you find it?"

"That is from Nils and I as a housewarming gift. I saw it down on Fifth Avenue and knew it belonged to you," Anna said. "I am not sure where you might want to use it."

Gudrun carefully rolled the rug and put it to the side. "Thank you. I know just where it will go." She smiled and winked at Anna.

"The fabric I found in the general store here on the island," Arvik explained. "It had just come off the boat and I grabbed the whole bolt. You look good in that color. A dress perhaps?"

"It is perfect." Gudrun said as she slid the fabric off to reveal a black sewing machine sitting on a beautiful wooden table with wrought iron legs. Her hand went to her mouth. She started to laugh, then cry. She looked at Arvik in total shock then gave him a quick hug and a peck on his cheek. "A sewing machine!"

He loved how she jumped up and down a little bit, how her eyes danced and sparkled. "I wish I could have given it to you sooner. I kept thinking of all the time you would have saved if you had it to make things for the house. It arrived on the boat with Anna and Nils. Is it like the one you used at the Iversens'?"

She ran her hand over it playing with the wheel. "Similar. Oh Arvik, it is perfect."

"You decide where in the house you want it and Nils can help me move it there."

ை

"I am so sorry. I am not aiming for the ruts," Gudrun said as she tried to rein Surefoot through a large uneven patch in the lane. "I am glad that Doctor Agnes gave you permission to ride in the wagon."

"The seat cushion helps. And it is good to get out. Poor Nana. Her house ruined." Anna winced as the wagon bounced over another rut.

Gudrun glanced back at the baskets behind them. It would not be good to have the lunch for the men and Nana ruined. The Yamaguchis had returned for Christmas dinner with the news that they had moved what they needed into Zhou's shop and would live there while repairs were made on the house. Yesterday Doctor Agnes had returned and declared Anna strong enough to do anything she wanted. Early that morning the men had taken off to help get the tree off the Yamaguchis' house.

"I have a crazy business idea," Gudrun said. She tilted the reins to the right, guiding Surefoot around the next curve.

From underneath her layers of blankets and scarves, Anna asked, "What is that?"

"I want to make dresses for your friend's shop in Ballard. I can develop sketches for her to select from and make one of each in her most popular sizes. Can you help set up a meeting with her this Spring?"

"What a fabulous idea. Yes. I will approach Raghild with the idea when I return...how about you and I work on a business proposal during the rest of our stay that I can present to her?" Anna held on tight to the wagon as it went over a few more ruts.

"Yes. I would appreciate your help. This is the last curve before the Yamaguchi residence. I hope they have the tree —" Rounding the corner Gudrun yelled, "Oh no!"

Running straight toward them was a large fox with a chicken in its mouth. A ways behind the fox they could see Nana running with a shovel. Surefoot started, neighed, and the wagon jerked to the right, then the left as the horse nervously sidestepped.

"Hold on," Gudrun warned. Then in a quiet voice she said, "It is alright, Surefoot. It is alright. Calm down." She gently pulled on the reins, stopping the gelding off to the side. She could see Arvik, rifle in hand back by the house. Gudrun jumped down from the wagon and held Surefoot's head. "Good boy, Surefoot, good boy."

The fox sped by them holding tight to his prize. Nana seemed to be slowing down — a bit out of breath. She shook the shovel in the air and yelled something in Japanese. Suddenly Arvik sped by, the ladies watching as he closed in on the fox. He stopped, took his stance with his rifle, aimed and got the fox on the first shot. Picking up the chicken by its feet he walked back to the wagon.

Handing the chicken to Nana he said, "Chicken dinner?"

Nana gave him a horrified look. "No," she said and laid the chicken on the ground and felt its neck. "Alive!" she said. The chicken's eyes fluttered.

CHAPTER 29

Sunshine and Hearts

Spring 1915

"This is my hole to dig." Gudrun tried side-bumping Arvik to get him to move. He did not even budge.

"No." He laughed and bumped her back.

She almost fell over. She picked up the water pail and threatened him with it.

"You better not!" he yelled. Putting down the shovel he took a tackle stance and then began to chase her.

Gudrun threw the pail down, laughing as she ran for the house. Arvik stopped, went back to his shovel and began digging the hole. They had spent the morning laying out the perfect garden patch, a fairly new experience for both of them. Both of their mothers had gardens when they were kids. But the memories of how to garden were dim while the memories of the bountiful benefits were vivid. He knew he needed to build a fence to keep the rabbits and deer out, or the critters would eat it all, if they were successful gardeners.

The flirting and teasing had started a few weeks before. He enjoyed her playful attitude. Looking up he saw her coming out the door with two cups of coffee. She signaled to the patio and he nodded. Her slender frame clothed in blue jeans and a flannel shirt. She had become quite the talk of the island, being so bold to wear pants while working outside and on the boat. No one made jeans look as good as she did. He did not care if some of the old biddies gossiped about her. They were probably jealous. He loved her sensible side yet he found pride in the fact she knew how to dress up for the right occasion. They were becoming best friends, very comfortable together, yet how he wished for more intimacy.

One last shovelful of dirt and then he could put in the post after their break. He put down the shovel and walked to the patio. He sat across from her in the empty lounge chair. Carefully taking his steaming cup of coffee, Arvik said, "After lunch we need to take a ride over to West Sound."

"Why?"

"We need a second horse and Mr. Bellantonio has two for sale," he replied.

She wrinkled up her nose, giving him a quirky smile and asked, "Why?"

He had to laugh. "Because I will not have my wife stranded. I start the Caldwell project with Zhou next week. I will be gone eight to ten hours at a time. We both need to be able to get around the island."

"That makes sense. Thank you for being so considerate. I appreciate it," Gudrun said. "It has been nice having you around the past few months, even though you have spent most of the time in the shed working on table orders. What kind of horses?"

"A Morgan gelding and an Appaloosa mare. You have gotten so attached to Surefoot and he likes you. I think we have to meet the horses and then decide who keeps Surefoot and who has the new horse. Someday we will have a car when the roads are completed." Arvik referred to the one road that Robert Moran had built between Rosario and Eastsound. At this point having a car did not make sense.

"Well then, enough of the break time. We can get a few more posts in before lunch." Gudrun stood up, she offered her hand to Arvik and pretended to pull him out of his chair.

∽

Lightly slapping the reins on Daisy Mae's spotted rump, Gudrun made the turn toward town. "First stop — the Post and mail letters to Karoline, Mrs. Simonsen, Berit, Mrs. Sandnes, and Anna. Maybe, there will be a letter for us," Gudrun said to the perky young mare. "Then to the store to pick up the five bolts of fabric I ordered. We have a lot of sewing to do in the next month."

Daisy Mae seemed to understand and quickened her step. She and Arvik had been planning their spring trip to Seattle. Anna had made arrangements for Gudrun to meet with Raghild Thorp. The shop owner had been impressed with her proposal. Gudrun's dream of designing and producing a limited line of dresses had begun to materialize. The large North basement room overlooking the water had become her studio. Arvik had made her a cutting table, a drafting table for sketching, and a desk for doing business. Her beautiful sewing machine sat by the window where she could enjoy the view. If things went well, she had plenty of room for a second machine if she hired someone.

The long days that Arvik had mentioned had materialized. She would pack him a substantial lunch so that he had enough for middag. He would return home just in time for kveldsmat at seven or eight o'clock. He had made sure that her porcupine stick hung by the front door on one of the coat hooks. He also put clubs by each of the other exterior doors. Arvik had made her promise to carry the porcupine stick with her when she went out for errands.

"Look, Daisy Mae, letters." Gudrun patted her mare as she climbed back into the wagon. One from Mrs. Sandnes and one from Berit. This is a good day." She slapped the reins and they moved on to the general store.

Sorting through the bolts, Gudrun immediately knew one of the bolts would not work. She fumbled through her bag finally locating the receipt with the small cuttings of the fabrics she ordered. *Now to explain to the clerk...Lord, help me communicate...oh how I just want to run and hide. It would almost be worth the price of the bolt...No it is money Arvik worked hard for...I ask that you give me the right English words.*

Gaining the clerk's attention she showed him the receipt with the fabric swatches. She carefully went through each bolt. "This...good. This..." she pointed to the second bolt and then the swatch. "Good." Working her way through the stack she arrived at the fifth bolt. "This...not good." Her face flushed and she looked at the clerk in dismay. *If only my English was better...will he give me my money back? How do I ask for that?*

"Well Mrs. Johansen, this is what arrived on the morning boat. I can see it is not the same." He walked over to the fabric wall. "Will one of these bolts work as a replacement?"

Fumbling in her bag she found her English/Norwegian dictionary and looked for the word replacement. Would she have to purchase another bolt? What did he mean? "I not pay," she stammered.

"No, you already paid. This would be on the house," the clerk explained. "Excuse me one moment. I will see if Mr. James can explain better." The clerk went to get the storeowner.

Words began to run together, the pages kept sticking as she fumbled to find the meaning of replacement. *And what does "on the house" mean? I am so stupid. I am an embarrassment to Arvik. How can I run a business?*

Squeaking loudly the entry door caught her attention. She could hear the clerk say, "Ah, Mrs. Nesbo. I am glad to see you. Perhaps you would be so kind as to help us. Mrs. Johansen and I are having a bit of trouble understanding each other. Oh, Mr. James, there is a problem with the fabric order for Mrs. Johansen."

"Why, Daisy Mae, why?" Gudrun asked her mare as they trotted home. The money for the fifth bolt of fabric in her pocket did not make her feel better. "Why do I have so much trouble with English? And now we only have four bolts to work with. Will four dress styles be enough for the big debut?"

Daisy Mae made the turn onto Sunset Lane quickly passing the newly pruned apple orchard. Gudrun noticed a few buds beginning to form. They reached the top of the knoll and she pulled on the reins. The sun broke through the clouds. She let the reins loose so Daisy Mae could graze as she soaked in the sun and the view of her home. "Lord, I am sorry, I have been complaining again. You have provided so much for me. Thank you for bringing Mrs. Nesbo to help at the right time, even though she is a bit standoffish." Gudrun bowed her head, going over in her mind how the Lord had blessed her, praising God for his greatness. *Lord, I should not ask for more... but Lord I love my husband...please...please...only if it is your will...can we be truly husband and wife? In your Son's name, Amen.* She could not help but blush as she finished her prayer.

Reaching for the letters Gudrun opened Mrs. Sandnes' first. A page from a magazine fell to the wagon floor. Opening the page Gudrun gasped. It was the cover of Vogue magazine with a tall blond wearing balloon style pants. "That is it! Sorry Daisy Mae, we have to return to town. I need that bolt of denim. I can see it now 'Balloon Jeans — what practical ladies wear in the garden,' but will they sell?"

∾

"This is the last one before the grand finale." Gudrun turned slowly in a circle on the patio as Arvik took another bite of dessert. The evening sun highlighted the fabric with a warm glow.

"This is the best one so far and the rest were fantastic. You really look good in that color," Arvik said.

"You remember you gave me this fabric for Christmas?" she asked.

"Of course. The blue had your name written all over it. That one will sell for sure and you have a whole bolt of it. So that makes five dresses. Are you modeling them next Tuesday?"

"Since they are all my size and I cannot afford to pay a model I am the only candidate. Anna is shorter and pregnant...I am afraid it is me. Now don't look toward the studio until I tell you to." Gudrun waltzed back through her studio doors.

Arvik took one last bite of his marsipankake as he sat staring at the islands. *Such a perfect evening. A wonderful dinner and a fashion show put on by my talented wife on a warm May evening. Lord, thank you.*

"Alright, you can turn around. Announcing Balloon Jeans, what every practical lady wears in the garden." The jeans contrasted nicely with her white blouse and her bare feet.

"Wow. There is no mistaking you for a lady. They are beautiful. Those will sell for sure."

"You really think so? It is the softness of the denim that makes it perfect."

Standing up, Arvik gave a slight bow and said, "My lady, would you like to dance?" Holding out his left hand.

Eyes wide in surprise Gudrun gave him a big smile. "It would be my pleasure, sir." She put her hand on his shoulder and took his left hand.

Humming a faint tune, he began to guide her around the patio, trying hard not to step on her feet. Faint memories of his mother teaching him to dance played through his mind. The only other time he had danced was at Nils and Anna's wedding with one of her friends. This seemed much easier, more natural.

Suddenly Gudrun stubbed her toe on an uneven paver. "Ouch!" She grabbed her foot holding onto his shoulder to keep from falling.

"Sit down," he said.

"No, I can't wrinkle or soil the fabric. It has to look brand new," she moaned and continued to rub her toe. After a minute she ventured to put her foot down, gently putting weight on it. "It will be fine. Just painful." And she hobbled back to her studio.

Arvik cleared the dishes and carried them up to the kitchen, rinsed them and stacked them in the sink. He hurried upstairs and took a small box out of his dresser. *Now seems to be the time. I hope she likes it.*

Gudrun came out of her studio, just as he arrived back at the patio, dressed in the modest dress she had worn for dinner.

"I have something I want to show you," he said. "Shall we go to the beach?" He offered her his hand. She held it for a moment but let go as they headed down the path.

She giggled as she followed him to the water. *Arvik* turned back toward her just as she tripped gently catching her in his arms...he pulled her close. "My heart," he whispered. Lifting her head she pulled back slightly. He leaned in and kissed her, his lips lingering for more.

Gudrun laid her head on his shoulder and he could smell the lavender shampoo she used. He took her hand and they continued down the path to the beach.

"Shall we sit on the log?" he asked.

She nodded.

The sun played hide-and-seek with a few clouds near the horizon. "It looks like it will be a good sunset," Arvik said. He put his arm around her.

Gudrun leaned her head on his shoulder. "Is this what you wanted to show me? The sunset?"

"No. I have a little surprise." He took the box out of his pocket and handed it to her. "Open it." He watched her lips curve into a smile. Her eyes sparkled as she gave him a curious look.

Opening the box, she said, "Oh, how beautiful." Picking up the silver heart dangling on a silver chain, she blushed. "I love it."

"I am glad you like it. I saw it at the general store and it seemed the best way to let you know that you have stolen my heart. Here, let me help you put it on."

CHAPTER 30

Business Trip

*P*utting her newest dress carefully on top of her suitcase, Gudrun paused and looked around the room. It would be nice to have matching dressers now that Arvik had moved in. She blushed, as she thought about their first night together. Looking at her wedding ring she thought about how after their first kiss Arvik had given her long kisses at her bedroom door each night. Finally on the third night she got the courage to ask him if he would like to come in and he did not hesitate.

The most precious cargo on this trip had been carefully folded between light blankets, and placed in her trunk. Five dresses, a pair of balloon jeans, and a crisp white blouse to be modeled for Raghild on Thursday. Arvik had suggested that they take two days, stopping at Port Townsend on the way. That would give her Wednesday to do touch-up ironing and prepare, once they arrived at the Lundes. It would also give them an extra day to travel if the weather changed. He had told her with it being almost mid-May that probably would not happen. She knew the weather near bodies of water could change unexpectedly, and appreciated her husband's caution.

Arvik had spent the last week making sure everything, especially the engine, was ready to go on *Himmel*. They did not want a repeat of last fall's journey.

I am so excited to have a whole week with Anna. She must be showing. In her last letter she said the morning sickness *has stopped...*the sounds of the wagon broke into her thoughts. Surefoot let out a neigh. Looking out the window, she watched Arvik carefully load her trunk. Gudrun put the last few things she needed on the side of the suitcase. Then she stashed another pair of pants, a heavy sweater, and a dress in her satchel along with her toiletries so she would not have to open her suitcase on the boat.

Arvik walked into the room. "All packed?" he asked.

"I just finished."

He took her in his arms, giving her a kiss. "Alright then, Mrs. Johansen, we shall be going." Then picked up her suitcase and followed her out of the room. "Your briefcase, trunk and my bag are loaded."

"Thank you. I am looking forward to being back on *Himmel*. It looks like it is nice enough to sit on the bow," Gudrun said as they walked towards the wagon. "Hi, Daisy Mae. I am sorry you are in back today." Gudrun petted her horse securely tied to the back of the wagon. "You will like it at the stables while we are gone. You might get extra oats. We will be home before you know it."

Arvik placed her suitcase in the wagon and helped her up. "Sitting on the bow should work until we hit the Straits, then we will have to see."

༺༄༅༅༄༺

Pulling up to the Lundes' residence, the chauffeur helped Gudrun out of the car. "Miss Anna is very excited to see you, madam. You will find her in the parlor."

Taking Arvik's arm Gudrun whispered, "My, this is different than the first time I arrived here and our other visits. I hope Anna is well."

Arvik chuckled, "She can be quite a whirlwind. I am sure she is fine. Maybe the pregnancy has slowed her down a bit."

The butler opened the door. "It is good to see you again Mr. and Mrs. Johansen. Please, come in."

"I am going to help with the luggage. That will give you a chance to inform Anna about the room situation." Arvik winked at Gudrun.

"Let me show you to the parlor, madam," the butler said.

A much more subdued Anna sat on a lounge chair not even offering to get up and greet her. Gudrun hurried over and kneeled down next to her. "Are you alright?"

Taking Gudrun's hand Anna replied, "I am as good as I can be in my condition. Look how big I am for only five months." She laid Gudrun's hand on her belly. "Can you guess why?"

Gudrun shook her head.

"Twins! I have two babies right here."

"Oh my goodness!" Gudrun gasped. "They will keep you busy. What does the doctor say?"

Smiling, Anna said, "I need to rest more and eat more. I am fine but I do tire easily...I am also bored. Nils does not want me leaving the house —" Sounds of the luggage in the entry interrupted their conversation.

Gudrun cleared her throat and could feel her checks turning pink. "I have a request...well...you see we will only be needing one bedroom."

"Wonderful news. When did that happen?"

Gudrun's cheeks seemed to be on fire. Head down she replied, "Just three nights ago."

Anna patted her hand. "You do not need to say more. I am happy for you. He is a good man. No more drinking?"

"No more drinking. Yes, he is a good husband."

∾

Arvik passed the butter to Nils. Gudrun had filled him in on Anna's condition. She did look a bit bigger than he had expected. *This is going to be a busy house come September. A happy house I hope. Maybe...maybe someday we will have children.* He glanced at Gudrun, giving her a smile. He had not ever thought along those lines until last week. *It would be nice. I wonder if Gudrun wants children?*

"So I am hearing that communities on the east side of the mountains are producing apples," Nils said.

"The east side of the state has been producing apples and other fruit for many years. It seems like they are sending more and more to Seattle now. Several of the orchardists on Orcas have given up this past year. The competition is steep. We have done well only because of our hands-on approach to each apple," Arvik replied.

"It is often said the whole island is one big orchard. It will not hurt to have a few less. Will you keep going?"

"For a while. We will assess the situation each year and then decide. We always lose a tree here or there. I just will not replant. Do you think that the United States will join the war effort?"

"There is a lot of talk here about it. No one knows. I do hope Norway can remain neutral. It might be difficult, as they need to keep their merchant ships going for the country to survive. You heard the news?" Nils asked.

Arvik gave him a quizzical look.

"A German U-boat attacked an English passenger ship, the *Lusitania.* They lost one thousand one hundred and ninety-some passengers. It was traveling from New York to Liverpool. "

"That is shocking!"

"Now enough talk of war. The four of us are not going to change the course of history. Tomorrow is a big day for Gudrun." Anna stopped long enough to give Nils a long look.

Nils cleared his throat. "I have not changed my mind, dear. It is just too dangerous."

"What is dangerous?" Arvik asked.

Anna gave Gudrun a sad look. "I am afraid I will not be able to join you tomorrow as we had planned. The doctor...and Nils have decided leaving the house is too risky for me. With the twins and all. I am so sorry."

"Our chauffeur will take you. If you want help with the negotiations I can come," Nils offered.

Gudrun thought for a moment. "I do not want you to put the babies' health in danger, Anna. Having a ride would be nice, thank you, Nils. However, if you do not mind I would rather Arvik accompany me."

"It is settled then," Nils said.

"Please promise me a fashion show tomorrow night. I want to see the dresses and hear all about it," Anna requested.

⁓

At first Gudrun seemed a little nervous as she modeled the first dress. Raghild's face did not hide her surprise and then grew into unabashed delight as Gudrun unveiled each new creation.

My wife...creative, beautiful, sensible, a hard worker, and now a business woman? Where did this come from? I thought Anna was the brains behind this. Apparently not. The way she seemed to glide across the floor in each outfit. I noticed I was not the only one mesmerized — Raghild Thorp is too. And now look at her negotiating the down payment and working out

*delivery dates for everything that she modeled in five sizes.
Clearly the only reason I seemed to be needed is to carry the
trunk.*

Gudrun turned from the desk and signaled him, then met
him half-way.

Gently grabbing his lapels, Gudrun whispered, "Would
you mind helping me fold up the dresses and pack the trunk
while Raghild writes me a check?"

"I watched you fold them on Orcas. I can handle it. I will
be careful. You stay here and do business, tiger," Arvik whispered back.

Gudrun tried to stifle a giggle. "Thank you."

Once out in the car, Gudrun asked the chauffeur to take
them to the bank. "I am so glad we set up the checking account
yesterday. I will try to be quick and then I hope you do not
mind but I need to get to the wholesale fabric place."

"All that is fine, I just want to know who you are? How do
you know the business side of things?" Arvik asked.

"I have my secrets," Gudrun laughed, "Remember the big
packets from Karoline and Mrs. Sandnes that I received in
February?"

Arvik nodded. "Go on."

"They both sent me information on business practices, the
forms I would need, contracts, money exchange, and on and
on. I have been pouring over them, making sure I understood
everything. Mrs. Sandnes took the time to find information for
fashion designers and manufacturers in the United States, not
Norway."

"So when I could not hear your sewing machine, you were
reading?"

"Part of the time. The machine makes everything so fast,
but there is still some hand sewing. Anna found out which

wholesaler has the fabrics I want before she became a prisoner in her own home."

Grabbing her hand, Arvik said, "I am proud of you. All of this out of the money you saved on the furnishing."

"Yes. I still have money left for the remaining furniture we need. Do you mind if tomorrow we go shopping for a matching dresser for our bedroom? Do you remember where you got that furniture?"

"I do remember and yes we can go as long as you promise to go out to lunch with me."

ᕯ

"Oh, I do agree with you. I am very concerned too," Anna said as she walked slowly down a path in her garden. "How Berit can even be interested in the Captain is disconcerting. Yes, he is a good-looking man and only nine years older than her." Anna sat down, patting the bench for Gudrun to join her. "At thirty-three I can understand Berit possibly compromising. But that is not God's plan to compromise in this area."

Sitting next to her friend, Gudrun asked, "Do you want to be the one that addresses the subject with her? You have known her longer. Or maybe I should write so it does not ruin your friendship?"

"No. I should. She might think you are jealous or regretting your decision. I will write her later this afternoon. We have to remind her of 2 Corinthians 6:14 about not being unequally yoked, before she becomes too attached to him."

"I know that his sister Sissel is a believer. Do you think things have changed with Captain Hans? Our God is the God of miracles."

Anna smiled. "Thanks for the reminder. God does change people. That is how I will approach the subject in the letter.

Now about those balloon jeans. Will you make me a pair when this..." she patted her tummy. "...is all over?"

"I would be delighted. A gift to you for all your help."

"No," Anna insisted, "I am paying full price."

Gudrun wrinkled up her nose and smiled, "We will see."

∞

They watched the sun slide behind the clouds near the horizon. The sky grew into a myriad of reds and pinks. "So beautiful," Gudrun whispered. "The perfect trip and the perfect day to return home."

Arvik gave her a nod in agreement. He wished now that he had shortened their trip by one day. He did not plan to wake up this morning with a headache and stuffy nose. Thankfully they would be in their own bed tonight. Gudrun's desire to sit on the bow most of the day had helped. Not as much chatter when he was so miserable.

"You really do not feel well, do you? Want me to take the helm? You can go below and nap for a half hour until it gets dark. I know what to do," Gudrun said as she returned to the cockpit.

"I better..." everything seemed as fuzzy as her sweater. "... alright, only for 20 minutes. Smith Island—"

"It is right up there. I have watched you every time. I know where it is. I will be careful. Go to sleep. I will wake you in twenty or so."

"Let me take down the sails and start the motor first." He watched her clear the sunken Smith Island like a pro. With only a three-foot draw at mid-tide, the tiny, usually sunken island in the middle of the large body of water had taken many boats down.

Once under blankets the rhythm quickly put him to sleep, rocking away with the swells. He dreamed they were out on a peaceful ocean laughing in the sunshine like school children. Then she started pushing him, demanding that he move. He did not want to move. He woke up enough to realize Gudrun was touching his shoulder.

"Wake up, wake up," she said. "I let you sleep longer as the water is perfectly still here on Rosario Straight. I can get us to Eastsound if you want to keep sleeping."

He sat up and his hand immediately went to his throbbing head. "How close are we to Thatcher Pass?"

"Almost there."

"I need to take that part, the currents. I will be up in a minute."

He navigated through the pass and then asked Gudrun to take the wheel. She turned to the north into East Sound. He sat across from her. Such a quiet evening, the rosy glow to the west disappeared and moonlight shone a path up the sound. *So magical,* he thought. *If I didn't feel so rotten this would be a very romantic situation. Gudrun looks so happy...so peaceful.* The moonlight played across her face. A long lock of her curly hair broke loose from her headband and danced across her face. *If only I had the strength to reach out and touch her.*

Dozing off to sleep he jumped a bit when Gudrun asked if he could take the helm so she could tie down the lines.

"We are all tied down," Gudrun called out. "You do not look well enough to go to the stables. I will go."

A jolt of energy surged through his body, he stood up and stepped onto the dock. "No. I will not have my wife walking there in the dark. You stay here," he commanded.

Looking at her watch Gudrun said, "I will give you forty-five minutes. If you are not back by then, then me and my porcupine stick will head to the stables."

∽

"Well, we officially had our first argument," Gudrun murmured. Waking up in her bed alone, she stared out at Matia and Sucia Islands. *Of course Arvik's cold fueled most of it. I guess you can say we are truly married now. I know Lord that married life is not a fairy tale. But this hurts. I do not like feeling so separated from him. Heal his body Lord. Help us mend our differences soon.*

Arvik had only taken a half hour to return to the boat with the horses and wagon. She had obeyed his order and only grabbed her satchel, her briefcase, and suitcase. They left the trunk and new dresser for another day. She had asked the Lord to protect her creations as she locked the cabin door.

It took some convincing but a very grouchy Arvik finally allowed her to take the reins on the way home. Together they took care of the horses. Once in the kitchen everything broke loose. She made him tea and as he started to drink it, she mentioned that the next day, Kathleen James would be arriving at nine o'clock to help cut out dresses.

Gudrun could still hear him yelling, "Here? In our house?" She had explained that Kathleen would go through the French doors right into her basement studio. Despite her explanation of how her new assistant would only work three hours each morning, Arvik glowered as she talked. Then he demanded, "Why did you not ask me first? This is the first I have heard of it." She had yelled something about not needing to ask his permission. He pounded the counter top and declared, "I am going to bed in my room. I do not want you catching this cold."

I have so much to do before Kathleen arrives. Best to get up and get started. Tea and toast for Arvik.

Freshly cut red roses sat in a vase in the middle of the table when Gudrun walked into the kitchen with a note next to it.

I have made myself tea and toast, sanitized everything and gone back up to bed. I am sorry about last night. Kathleen can come in the front door if you like, however I do not want either of you catching this. I feel rotten. I do love you, Arvik.

She wanted to go and help him but knew he wanted to be left alone. She would check on him at lunch. Hopefully by then he would be able to eat some chicken soup.

She grabbed a biscuit and wrote a note back to Arvik that she had gone to get the trunk off the boat. She picked up her coin purse and the boat keys and ran to the stable to hook up Daisy Mae to the wagon.

"We will stop at the Wright Farm and order chicken breasts, eggs, cream, and milk to pick up on the way home, Daisy Mae. Then to the general store and see if Kathleen's older brother can help me get the trunk and the bolts of fabric off the boat. I need to see if her father can order several bolts of the denim for the balloon jeans." She had not been able to find denim that soft at the wholesalers in Seattle.

Almost two hours later Gudrun and Kathleen carried the trunk through the basement doors into the studio. As they carried in the last of the fabric bolts Gudrun asked in English, "Kathleen, please..." she pointed to the trunk and the garment rack Arvik had made for her. "Take out..." she could feel her face flush.

"Yes, you want me to unpack and hang the garments?" Kathleen asked.

Giving her assistant a smile Gudrun nodded. *How is this going to work Lord? I have no one else that sews like her. And no one else speaks Norwegian except Mrs. Nesbo and I know she will not be popping in here every morning. Please help me to communicate well.*

"I back soon," Gudrun said.

As she put her groceries in the kitchen and unhitched the wagon, she remembered the day when she had ordered the fabrics from Kathleen's father. The teenager had asked why so much fabric? Why purchase whole bolts? Between Gudrun's broken English and sketches, Kathleen quickly got the idea. The young lady went to the back of the store and showed Gudrun a dress and aprons she had made.

"She does amazing work. I know she is the right one, Lord." Gudrun prayed as she hurried downstairs to show Kathleen how to make patterns in different sizes.

༄

"Thank you for the chicken soup. I am sorry I cannot finish it." Arvik said, pointing to the tray he had left near his bedroom door. "Food is not appetizing right now, even your good cooking. Do you have time to talk for a moment?"

Gudrun nodded and sat down in a chair not too far from the tray.

"I am sorry about last night. I should not have yelled..."

Gudrun interrupted, "I understand you did not feel well."

"Still, no excuse. You do not need my permission to have people come to the house. It is just common courtesy to let me know, if you can, in advance. There are times like at Christmas when the Yamaguchis needed a place to stay. No time to warn you. But in this case you must have known for some time." Arvik stopped to cough.

"I am sorry I did not think of it that way. Things were so busy before we went to Seattle I did not think to tell you," Gudrun said.

He watched her bow her head, long platinum curls going in every direction. "Please, do not blame yourself. Do you agree with me, that when we can, we warn the other about people coming?"

She gave him a smile "Yes. I do. Now you need some of Nana's rub for your chest. I will be right back. I am warning you now, I might need to hire Nana a few mornings each week."

CHAPTER 31

The Porcupine Stick

"Gudrun! Gudrun!" Arvik yelled.

Dropping the collar she was hand sewing, Gudrun hustled up the stairs. "Arvik? Are you alright?"

Grabbing her hand at the top of the stairs he pulled her in for a hug. "I am so glad you are safe. A woman has been attacked in Doe Bay. They came in by sailboat. Apparently they knocked her unconscious and stole a sum of money." Arvik walked to the bay window. "Is that Nana leaving in the row boat?"

"Yes, her horse is being shoed today. She rowed over. Kathleen is just about ready to leave. I have been hand sewing and looking out at the water. I have not seen any strange boats. Is the woman alright?"

"I do not know. As soon as we heard about it Zhou and I headed to our homes. A group of men are going house-to-house warning people."

Putting her arm around his waist Gudrun scanned the water.

"I am ready to leave, Mrs. Johansen," Kathleen yelled up the stairs.

"No!" Both Arvik and Gudrun yelled in unison.

Running to the top of the basement stairs Arvik yelled back in English. "I will take you home in the wagon. Give me five minutes. Mrs. Johansen will be down to explain."

Grabbing her shoulders, Arvik said, "I have keys to the front and side doors. Lock all the doors and keep your porcupine stick on you. Get me the rifle but talk to Kathleen first."

Locking the entry door, Gudrun watched Arvik and Kathleen bounce down the lane. Surefoot seemed to sense the urgency, trotting a bit faster than his usual pace. *Please Lord keep everyone safe. Please apprehend the robbers before anyone else is hurt. Protect my husband and give him wisdom.* She went into the kitchen and made herself some tea, then went to the living room window seat to keep watch for intruders. *Arvik should be back in a half hour if Surefoot keeps up that pace. Hopefully Nana is home safe. Lord, they could come in on the empty lots.* She honed in on the waters to the east for some time, praying and claiming verses. Briefly she thought about the safe in the floor of the master bedroom under the rug. *How much do I have in there, Lord? Will they take that and leave me alone?* She looked to the right. *A bow of a boat coming around the point?* Waves broke in front of a large white bow. *Oh Lord! Guide me!*

Running downstairs she checked the landing side door. Locked. Running on down to her studio she closed the drapes and pushed her long cutting table up against the French doors. She took a quick look through the drapes at the water. A white sailboat almost the size of *Himmel* slowed directly off shore. With her binoculars she could see a medium-size, red haired man taking down the sails and a larger stocky man seemed frustrated with the anchor. She ran back upstairs, porcupine stick in hand. She double-checked the entry door then ran into the living room and stood watch out a side window, hidden by the drapes.

ॐ

Relief flooded over Arvik as the wagon came close to the North end of town. He could see a crowd of people and Mr. James came running to meet them.

"Whoa, Surefoot," Arvik called out.

Mr. James held up his arms. "Hurry down, Kathleen, Mr. Johansen needs to get home quickly."

"Thank you for your work, Kathleen," Arvik said. "If the robbers have not been caught by tomorrow morning, stay home." He turned the wagon around.

"Thank you for bringing her home." Mr. James yelled after him.

Surefoot trotted quickly north on North Beach road. He barely slowed down for the turn onto Sunset Ave. At the top of the rise Arvik glanced toward the house. A large sailboat bobbed off the hook in the water beyond. He pulled on the reins. "Shh, Surefoot. You are going to have to stay here," he whispered.

For a split second Arvik watched the two men rounding the corner of the house, heading for the front door. He jumped down from the wagon, grabbed an old dark hat from under the wagon seat, and threw the reins loosely over a fence railing. "Stay. Leave the apple blossoms alone," he told Surefoot.

Running down a path through the woods with his rifle, he circled around to the back of the house, and quietly ascended the outside stairs to the side door. He pulled out his key, inserted it into the lock and slid in the door. Resting his rifle in the corner of the landing for a second, he quietly closed the door and locked it. In the window glass he could see a reflection of the porcupine stick high in the air. Quickly turning he grabbed Gudrun's arm and pushed her up against the wall. He put his finger to her lips. Her terrified eyes relaxed and she leaned up against him. They stood frozen in place listening to the men jiggling the lock on the front door.

"Go downstairs. Hide. Take your stick," Arvik whispered in Gudrun's ear. "Hide in the closet under the stairs."

She nodded just as the front door squeaked and footsteps let them know the robbers were inside.

Arvik tiptoed up the stairs with his rifle. He glanced back. Gudrun remained frozen in place. At the top of the stairs he slid into the library and stood close to the door.

"Nice house. Where do you think they keep their money?" One of the robbers said as they walked into the living room.

"Maybe in the library?" another voice answered. "Maybe there is jewelry upstairs."

Holding his breath Arvik waited as the footsteps came closer. The red haired man cleared the door and Arvik hit him over the head with the butt of the rifle. As the first robber collapsed on the floor the heavy-set robber pounced on Arvik's back beating his head with a club. Blow after blow hit his head and the massive weight of the man made Arvik feel faint. Falling to the floor, Arvik grabbed the second robber's leg. His bulky frame did not budge. Out of the corner of his eye Arvik saw him hoist his club one more time. Suddenly a loud thud echoed through the room and the man collapsed on the floor next to Arvik.

Porcupine stick raised ready to strike again Gudrun stood looking down at the robbers.

"I think they are out for awhile...please find me some rope to tie them up with?" Arvik asked as he slowly picked himself up off the floor.

With a little jerk of her head Gudrun focused in on his face. "Yes...yes. Oh but you are bleeding and bruised."

Taking his handkerchief out of his pocket Arvik wiped his forehead. "Just flesh wounds. Head wounds bleed more. Now off to the barn before they wake up." Picking up his rifle, Arvik stood guard, as Gudrun rushed off to the barn. They worked together tying the men's feet and hands. The intruders moaned as they worked.

"Are you comfortable riding Daisy Mae into town to get help?" Arvik asked.

"Yes. That is a good plan. I do not know how to shoot if they try and break loose."

Arvik chuckled. "Maybe not, but I am thankful you know how to use a porcupine stick. Look at the bruise and the blood on this guy's head. That stick can do some damage. He is out cold."

"Sorry I almost hit you in the stair landing. I did not recognize you in that dark hat. Where did you get that?"

"Under the wagon seat. I thought I should cover my blonde hair so they would not see me coming through the woods. I know it is slow work getting the phone lines in across the island from Deer Harbor, but after today I am going to demand we get a line out here."

෧

"I have two surprises for you," Arvik called out as he walked in the front door.

"Me? Why are you home so early?" Gudrun called back as she ran up the stairs from her studio.

Arvik stood at the top with a big grin on his face. "As I said, I have two surprises for you. One planned and one unplanned."

"I am listening."

"This letter from Berit." Arvik handed Gudrun the envelope.

"Thank you, sir."

"The other one you must come out to the storage shed to see."

Giving Arvik a quizzical look, Gudrun asked, "Why the shed?"

He smiled. "You will see." As they neared the shed he stopped. "Now take my hand and as we get inside you close your eyes."

She followed his instructions and closed her eyes as they entered the shed. It seemed like they were walking to the other side. She wanted to look.

"Now you can open your eyes." Arvik stood there watching her, letting her take in her surroundings. In the middle of the shed sat a medium-size crate, with spaces between the slats.

"Something is moving inside!" Gudrun exclaimed.

"Yes, open the top."

"Such a familiar smell..." she murmured as she removed the lid. Big brown eyes met hers and her heart melted. "Oh... Arvik...a puppy." She scooped up the white and black hound and turned toward Arvik. "A Halden Hound! Where did you find him?"

Putting his arms on her shoulders he said, "I wish I had a photo of your face right now." He kissed her. "This one is a girl."

"Oh," Gudrun said. "Where? How?"

"I remembered all your stories about Trygg and with our scare last spring with the robbers I felt you needed a dog. All summer every time we went to Seattle, I have been inquiring about Haldens. They are rare here. Nils and I found a gentleman in Ballard that knew of a Norwegian farmer near Anacortes who breeds Haldens."

"That fishing trip..."

"Yes, the one three weeks ago. There were only four pups and one did not make it. By the time I got there the two boy pups were spoken for."

Sitting down on the floor Gudrun inspected her furry bundle. "How old?"

"Eight weeks."

"When and how did you get her here?"

Arvik joined her on the floor. He gently took the pup from Gudrun. "You came in on a boat this morning, right?" He asked the pup. He gave the pup a hug and handed her back to Gudrun. "Another farm had beagles but they seemed like too small of a dog up against your long beautiful legs."

Gudrun giggled, her face got warm. "She is perfect. I love that she is a Halden...a true Norwegian...she feels right." She held the pup tighter. "Like when I picked Daisy Mae. What shall I call her?"

"Your choice. She will need training...it seemed like a good time to do it. You have sent the Fall line of clothes off to Seattle and have a bit of a break before the Christmas line."

"Look at her tail, all the black spots. She is about the same age as Trygg was when Per brought him to me. Her fur is so soft now...it will get course." Gudrun continued to pet the hound. "Venninne. Venninne is her name. Venn for her nickname."

Arvik chuckled. "I hope she does become your girlfriend." He stood up and went to the end of his workbench. He pulled out an elegantly carved shallow wooden platform, with tall wrought iron bars and a wrought iron door."

Gudrun smiled. "It is an indoor dog house."

"Yes, I designed it and made it for the Yamaguchis' dog years ago. But the dog died before I ever gave it to them."

"That is sad. What happened?" Gudrun asked.

"He got in a fight with a couple of foxes. It was a smaller dog than Venn will be," Arvik said. "Venn will be able to hold her own."

⤫

"What did Berit have to say?" Arvik asked as they sat on the big log on the beach watching the sun approach the horizon with Venn gently snoring in Gudrun arms.

"It is an interesting letter. She and the Captain are engaged."

"Really?"

Gudrun nodded. "I know. At first I was shocked and disappointed. Then she explained that the Captain has been attending church with her for several months. A couple of weeks ago he became a Christian."

"Wow. That is amazing."

"I know, a true miracle. An answer to my prayers and I am sure Berit's. She is perfect for him. She is not that much younger than him. I guess he is no longer going across the Atlantic because of the war. He is captain on one of the large ferries from Bergen to Stavanger." Gudrun kissed Venn and laid her head on Arvik's shoulder. "I will write her tonight about Venn. Thank you for dinner." She referred to the baked salmon Arvik had fixed in the outside brick oven and a beautiful vegetable salad and fresh rolls Arvik had bought at the store.

Arvik put his arm around her. "I am married to a very famous fashion designer that makes lots of money so I could afford it."

Gudrun laughed. "Not famous and not sure she wants to be. We have to talk about how big this is going to get...I am tired at times, even with Nana and Kathleen's help. How long has Mrs. James been taking orders for her cooking?"

"She always has soup in a pot in the back kitchen area. And as long as I have lived on the island she has taken orders, usually for single men. Oh, there it goes. Another beautiful sunset." They sat and watched the colors spread across the sky. Arvik patted her knee, "Time to get this baby to bed." He patted Venn on the head.

Gudrun glanced up at him. "Thank you. This has been a perfect day. I know Venn will be one special companion."

Arvik leaned in and gave her a long kiss. "All for one special lady. My gift from God."

BOOK THREE
Challenges

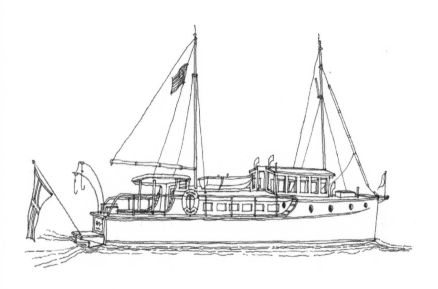

Lundes' Yacht

CHAPTER 32

Disappointment

Early July 1918

"Oh Lord, you are faithful, generous and have provided me so much. Thank you for Arvik. The husband who is better than I ever hoped for. Please guide him Lord, please soften his heart to love you more. Please keep him from drinking when the disappointments come." Gudrun stopped praying for a second and rubbed her belly. Remaining on her knees by her bedside she continued on, "as I have asked every morning, please keep this little one safe. May she or he continue to grow until it is safe outside the womb...if we lose this one like the last time, Lord, please give Arvik the strength to continue on. I pray all of this fervently in Jesus' name, Amen."

A little flutter inside her belly made her smile and dwell on Arvik's reaction last night. As they lay in bed he had felt the flutter for the first time. Oh she wished she could make that moment continue forever along with the joy on his face. They had discussed many times how neither of them had ever dared dream about children. Venn came up beside her and pressed her nose in against her cheek.

"Yes, Venn, now I need to get up and get to work. Three dresses to finish and then I am done. This is Monday...I should be able to ship them all by Thursday."

Lord, thank you for all the fun I had designing dresses and having my own business, Gudrun prayed as she and Venn descended the stairs and walked into the kitchen. *You have blessed me so much.*

The Spanish flu had hit parts of Europe, Norway, and the East Coast of the United States. As a shop owner, Raghild Thorp expressed her concern of it hitting Seattle and did not want to order anything for a while. She had sent a letter last week asking Gudrun to finish the current order, but she would not be ordering for late fall and winter. With the baby coming it seemed like a good time to close down for a while. Kathleen had been planning her wedding to a military man scheduled to return home from the war in the next few months. Nana had quit last January when she and Zhou welcomed a little girl, Kiyo, into the world. *It seems like you are closing down this chapter of my life, Lord.*

Arvik had sliced bread and cheese for her breakfast before he left to fish. Currently he had no carpentry work and fishing had not been good either. With the apple income gone, things were starting to look a bit bleak.

She made tea and then took it downstairs to her studio. She opened the French doors so Venn could go in and out as she pleased. The hound loved sleeping in the sun on the patio.

As she began hand-sewing a collar she thought about the letter she had received from Anna. Her friend wished she could come for their planned visit, but Nils had forbidden her to travel with the children. The twins were just getting over a case of the mumps and they were waiting to see if Edel, their eighteen-month-old daughter would catch them. Arvik did not want them coming due to her pregnancy. So letters and memories of the Lundes' Christmas visit, her visit in the spring to Seattle, and last summer would have to do.

And what grand memories they are. I am thankful we had last summer, Lord. The "cottage" as Nils liked to call it housed all of them with plenty of space left over. She and Arvik had enjoyed luxurious guest quarters separate from the main house. The sandy beaches made a great playground and there were occasional jaunts into the town of Sequim.

Gudrun shuddered as she thought about the close call. One would not expect on such a beautiful sunny day things could go so wrong. The men were coming in from fishing. Holding little Edel she had stood on the beach watching the twins, Alf and Ansgar, play with their mother in the shallow water. Suddenly, Anna screamed. She looked up to see Alf being swept out by a current.

The terror in Anna's voice as she screamed, "I cannot swim! I cannot swim," still gave Gudrun the chills. She vaguely remembered passing Edel off to Anna as she ran through the shallows and dove into the chilly water. The current and her strong stroke had quickly taken her out. Within a few minutes she caught up with the bobbing head of Alf. She approached him from behind as her father had taught her and pulled the toddler in toward her shoulder holding him around his chest well above the water line. He fought her for a few moments.

Tears formed in Gudrun's eyes as she reminisced. Arvik, her hero, pulled up in their tender with Nils holding out his arms to take Alf from her. Even in this last letter from Anna she had thanked Gudrun one more time for rescuing her son.

Her thoughts turned to the war and the Spanish flu. She had not heard from anyone in Norway for some time. She prayed for her friends in Norway, for the Lundes and for the ability to understand English better. She could follow part of the Pastor's sermon at church as her understanding had improved. Arvik continued to tell her the passages and she followed along in her Norwegian Bible. She prayed for the Yamaguchis and for Kathleen.

～

Gudrun heard Arvik walking up the path from the beach as she poured herself a cup of tea that Wednesday afternoon. Those footsteps, the rhythm of his stride, she would recognize his walk anywhere. All the dresses were done. She could ship them off tomorrow. She met Arvik at the front door ready to give him a kiss.

"I am mad. Furious!" His eyes met hers for a moment. "Not at you." He hugged her and for a split second she could feel anger shaking through his body. He let go and stomped upstairs. "That Great White is back and has destroyed my nets. Cut to shreds," he yelled.

She could hear him rummaging around in the hall closet. Coming back down he let out a string of cursing, his rifle in hand.

"Arvik, no. It is too dangerous. I can not lose you!" she pleaded. Stories of the great white had been circling the island. Parts of the story of Arvik's first encounter played in her mind.

"He's taken all our profit — all the money for the baby, and maybe food for the winter."

She reached out for him trying to stop him, but he brushed her aside. She followed him outside onto the patio, crying out. Venn followed him part way down the path. Gudrun watched him march onto the beach and push the dinghy out into the sea. "Arvik! Arvik!" A thought came to her mind, *be still, pray.* Pray she did.

Raising her head she saw the great white, coming straight at the boat. Arvik took aim and missed the shark. It barely missed the boat and almost capsized it. The white circled around again. Arvik stood up towering over the small boat. His feet in a wide stance, his broad shoulders seemed even bigger as he aimed the rifle. Several shots rang out across the water. The great white slowed to a stop and the dark stain in the water marked his death. *I have witnessed a hero, a man storybooks are written about, defending his property and my well-being. And I am the only one here to tell about it.* She watched him row to his nets to survey the damage.

☙

Hot, humid, late August air made Gudrun pray for a breeze. Maybe then she could fall asleep. *Six months along, Dr. Agnes said I am at six months. Hang in there little one. You need a few more months.* A sudden breeze floated in through the open bedroom windows giving her much needed relief. She tossed and turned for a few more minutes and then drifted off to sleep.

A sharp pain in her abdomen woke Gudrun up and she bit her lip to keep from screaming. She glanced at the clock — two-thirty. She could not wake Arvik at this hour. He had come in late from the new project he and Zhou were working on with instructions to set the alarm for five in the morning. He needed his sleep.

Walking into the bathroom she felt the urge to push. She looked down at her nightgown and saw blood. Her legs got weak and she started to faint. A loud moan from her own lips surprised her. Everything went black.

Noises, people talking, covers being laid over her...more talking...Dr. Agnes? Nana? Arvik? *It is so cold. Am I shaking?*

Dr. Agnes' voice seemed far away. "She will need lots of rest. She needs someone with her constantly for the next twenty-four hours. No getting out of bed."

Did she hear Nana? "I stay two more hours, Arvik."

"That would help. Thank you, Nana."

∽

Pacing the beach looking for the largest rocks, Arvik stopped, picked one up and heaved it as far as he could into the water. "Why? Why?" he yelled. He found another large rock and heaved it out about fifteen feet. Finally he sat down on the log, exhausted. He had called Dr. Agnes as soon as he saw Gudrun on the bathroom floor. The loud thud had woken him up.

She is so strong physically and mentally. So healthy. How can this be happening again? She has told me how badly she wants children. Why have you taken another child away from us? Because of my sins? My drinking? My missing church all those years? Please do not punish her for my transgressions Lord...for her sake...

Head in his hands he began to sob. Oh he wanted to fix this. To measure the board correctly and pound it into place, making it better. He felt so helpless. He did not know how to go forward. *My baby, our baby, another baby, gone.*

Dr. Agnes had explained a few things about what had happened, but he had not understood the medical terms. She had tried to simplify her explanation but it all turned to mush in his brain. Something about total bed-rest if Gudrun became pregnant again.

I have to be strong for Gudrun. I have to be strong. How Lord? How? Words from a sermon in 2 Samuel came to mind. How David, mourning the loss of his infant child, stated the fact he would see his child in heaven. Pastor had taught that when a child died before they were old enough to believe in Christ they went to heaven. *My baby is with you, Lord. She is with you. Thank you for reminding me.*

He glanced at his watch which Gudrun had given him last Christmas. *Time to go and relieve Nana. She needs to get back to her family.* He heard a wagon coming down the lane. *A neighbor with food? Like last time?* When they lost their son they had more food than they could eat. *News travels fast around the island.*

∽

Slowly walking into the kitchen Gudrun marveled at how tidy everything was. The past three days seemed like a blur. Arvik had been by her side every time she woke. He had held her when she cried. Venn kept curling up next to her when the opportunity arose. Arvik kept insisting she eat. She liked the coolness of the first floor rooms. Some coffee and the living room window seat sounded good. Dr. Agnes had started her walking two days ago.

Arvik had gone to the job site to explain to the owner that he needed a few more days off. He planned to pick up a few groceries to fill in. Their wonderful neighbors kept bringing food in. Some dishes were very foreign to her, though tasty and much appreciated.

Curling up on the window seat she put her one hand on her abdomen and petted Venn with her other hand. *My little girl. My sweet precious girl...gone...love her for me Lord. Tell her I love her. I wish I had had time with her here on earth.* Tears started to flow.

She picked up her Bible and started to read in Matthew 19 about Jesus defending the little children and reminding the disciples that the children belong to the kingdom of heaven. Psalm 73:26 brought her comfort as she read about the body and heart failing...*oh I feel that now Lord. How can I go on? I have to be strong for Arvik.* She continued to read aloud, "But

God is the strength of my heart and my portion forever." *You will get me through this.*

Remembering a sermon Pastor Stoa taught last spring from Hebrews 11 she turned to the passage. Verse one jumped off the page, "Now faith is the assurance of things hoped for, the conviction of things not seen." As she started to read the rest of the chapter about all the trials the saints of the Bible had gone through, a remarkable peace came over her. *The things hoped for are eternal Lord. You did not promise me a husband and children. Even though you love children and want to bless them. Instead you promised to love me and to some day bring me to heaven. Thank you, Lord, thank you for Arvik.*

Thank you, Lord, that he has been there for me, holding me, drying my tears, encouraging me to come to you with my pain. You know he is in great pain — he wants a child too...he is hurting and hurts more when he sees me hurting. And you know Arvik's weakness...please Lord keep him strong. I plead in your Son's name, Amen.

She could hear Daisy Mae whinny and Surefoot answering her greeting. Arvik was home. Ten minutes later he joined her on the window seat putting his arms around her, and whispering, "How was the journey downstairs? You were careful, right?"

"Yes, very. How did your client take the news?"

"He understood. Zhou will work overtime. He wants to give us some of the money. How many times does he have to pay me back for helping him when he broke his leg?"

Gudrun smiled. She leaned back on his chest. "God wants us to receive grace not just give it. Another subject...how are you doing? I am so grateful you have been there for me. I know it is your loss just as much as mine."

Staring at the water Arvik took a minute, cleared his throat, then answered, "It is hard to get all hopeful. To prepare..."

Gudrun could feel him wipe his eyes. She thought of the crib and dresser he had made. The rocker he had purchased. They were prepared and he had been so excited. "I am here for you," she said. "If things get unbearable, promise me you will let me know?"

"I promise." He hugged her tighter. "Oh, I have several letters for you. One from Karoline."

Quickly opening the letter, Gudrun scanned it and then started to cry.

"What is it?"

"Mrs. Simonsen died. The Spanish flu."

CHAPTER 33

Adjusting to Changes

"**W**hoa, Surefoot." Arvik pulled the wagon to a stop at the top of the lane, that late September morning. "At least the house is the same. Everything else is changing." He glanced over at the orchard. Only ten trees remained, enough for apples for the winter and some to sell to the neighbors. "Everything changes. The orchard gone and now Zhou's news."

After they went over the finished project with the owner, Zhou informed him that he and Nana were planning to move to Seattle to live close to her family. "And this letter —" Arvik reached into his knapsack and pulled it out along with a bottle of whiskey. "Howard Digby wants to buy Lot One, Surefoot. Would Oddvar approve?"

Arvik let his thoughts dwell on his childhood friend. Oh how he missed Oddvar; he missed his potential son and daughter, all of them gone. Arvik could picture Oddvar's house, the kids playing in the field and Oddvar being an uncle to them. Maybe Oddvar would have found a wife by now and have kids of his own. *Can I deal with a stranger living there? We do need the money.* He started to unscrew the whiskey top. Then stopped. *I cannot do this to Gudrun. Bring her more pain. Not when she is just beginning to laugh again. I will take it back to the tavern. No. And shame her? No. I cannot let anyone else know I bought it. A return will be public, as the lunch crowd will start.* The craving to open the bottle, to get rid of his pain, took over and he opened the top and raised it to his lips. "No," he shouted. Screwing the top back on he put it back in the knapsack. *I will give it to the one who understands me. Will she be strong enough, Lord, to do what I need her to do?*

"Well, enough moping, Surefoot, let us go and tell Gudrun the bad news." He slapped the reins.

While taking off Surefoot's halter and brushing him down, urges to grab the bottle and start drinking kept coming over him in waves. He gave both horses some oats and started to grab the knapsack out of the wagon. Somehow his hand grabbed the bottle instead. Slowly he twisted the top, put the bottle to his lips, took a sip, then another. Images of Gudrun crying flashed in his mind and he stopped, put the cap back on and walked to the house, a sturdy rope in hand.

He found Gudrun upstairs in her study sitting in the window seat and reading her Bible. She smiled up at him.

"How did your final meeting go? Is the owner happy?" she asked.

"Yes."

"What is wrong?" She asked.

Placing the bottle of whiskey on her desk he said, "Lots of things. Zhou and Nana are moving to Seattle as soon as the Spanish flu dies down, the orchard is gone, our children are gone, and someone wants to purchase Oddvar's Lot One."

Her eyes riveted on the bottle, Gudrun put down her Bible, stood up and grabbed it. "Is this the only one?"

"Yes. I need you to do something. It will be hard." He struggled not to show any emotion.

Gudrun nodded.

"It worked when Nils tied me up in the shed. Tie my hands behind my back and lead me to the shed. Tie me to the center pole. I do not trust myself right now."

❧

Silent tears slid down Gudrun's cheeks as she pulled on the last knot. Her strong man tied up like a prisoner in his own shed. Battling a demon he could not see. *This is not right! But I will do anything to keep him sober.*

"Thank you. Now you leave. Check on me a few times before you go to bed," Arvik said.

She noticed that he continued in the deadpan tone he had greeted her with upstairs. He had to be using every ounce of strength to give the orders.

"No, I will be bringing you lunch. You are not drunk, you will need food." She knelt down and kissed him. "Remember — I love you."

Standing in the entrance to the shed, Gudrun watched Arvik. He kept jerking and moving as he slept, but he seemed a bit calmer. Maybe all the Psalms she read to him in the afternoon had helped. She put the tray with two bowls of lapskaus down on a table and leaned against the entry wall. She gave a hand signal to Venn to lie down and put her finger to her lips to be quiet. He had eaten lunch four hours before. He jerked and woke up. She grabbed the tray, "I have lapskaus for you and me for middag."

Shaking his head, Arvik, mumbled, "No," and dozed off.

Her stomach growled, so she sat next to him, slowly eating her portion. When he woke ten minutes later he allowed her to spoon-feed him. He even thanked her before he dozed off to sleep. Gudrun grabbed some of the blankets she had brought out earlier and curled up next to him. Venn curled up next to Gudrun. "We need a nap," Gudrun said, petting her hound.

"Gudrun, Gudrun, wake up," Arvik said.

Rubbing her eyes, Gudrun looked around. Light streamed through the East windows. "What time is it?"

"It is morning."

She sat up. "We slept here all night?" Venn stood up and stretched.

Arvik laughed. "I guess so. You know we do have a house and a bed we could go and sleep in. However I am a bit hungry. We missed keveldsmat last night."

"Is it alright if I let my prisoner go?" She leaned in and kissed him.

"Please. Thank you for staying with me." He kissed her back. "The temptation has passed. You are the best wife."

She untied him and said, "I think a big breakfast would be good. And I have a bit of good news."

As he sat at the kitchen table watching her cook, she told him about one of the letters. "A Mrs. Eldridge wrote and informed me that she and her husband bought the big house over on West Sound that you and Zhou helped build. She has some things she would like to change and wants you to do the work. She also asked if I would be willing to make her several pairs of pants and work dresses."

Arvik smiled. "That is good news."

"So maybe we can keep Lot One," Gudrun suggested.

"Maybe. Maybe it is time to let it go. After all, everything is changing. We need to purchase a car. Surefoot is getting old."

∽

Hearing footsteps on the stairwell, Arvik put down his paper, stood up, and watched his wife descend the last flight of stairs. "You look beautiful. Radiant, in fact."

Gudrun blushed. "Thank you. I will need your help today. Promise you will not leave my side."

"I promise. They mean well. They do care. I will whisper complicated answers and remember one tap in your hand means 'yes.' Two is 'no.' And three is 'thank you.'"

She nodded. "I remember. Venn — goodbye. To your bed."

As Arvik walked with Gudrun to the wagon he asked the Lord to help Gudrun understand the Pastor's message and what was said to her. *Maybe they will leave her alone, being her first time back to church since the baby...Oh I know Lord a wishful thought.*

Glancing over at Gudrun during the service she smiled back at him and nodded a signal that she understood what the Pastor had just said. She even turned to Colossians by herself and followed along in her Norwegian Bible. Why did someone who was so smart have so much trouble learning English?

She leaned into Arvik as they stood outside the small church, surrounded by eight ladies all giving their condolences at the loss of their daughter. Gudrun surprised him at how quickly she remembered who brought food and thanked them in her broken English. Next came the compliments on her new outfit. They oohed and ahhed, asking if she was still sewing. She smiled up at him, a confused look in her eyes. So he stepped in explaining she had stopped mass production but she continued to design and sew for individuals.

As Surefoot trotted north toward home she leaned her head on his shoulder. "Thank you for bailing me out. Sorry...I am so dumb. I am an embarrassment to you."

He pulled Surefoot to an abrupt stop. He took both her hands in his. "You are not dumb. You are the smartest and most courageous woman I know. You have never embarrassed me. We all have weaknesses. I help you with yours and you help me with mine. No more! No more talk of being stupid, agreed?"

She nodded.

He gently held her chin and kissed her.

∽

A single tear ran down Nana's broad cheek as she watched Kiyo crawl off the fuzzy blanket onto the cold sand. Kiyo looked up at the two women with surprise. She touched the sand again and settled back in a sitting position on the blanket.

Gudrun and Nana could not help but laugh for a moment. Then Gudrun grabbed Nana's hand. "I pray?" she asked.

"Yes." Nana bowed her head.

"God. Help Katherine, please. Give...her—" Gudrun stopped, struggling to find the word for comfort."

"Help her, please," Nana said.

"Yes, Lord, help her. Amen."

Both ladies sat looking out at the water on Nana's beach thinking about how brokenhearted Kathleen must be. Gudrun had received the news that morning that Kathleen's fiancé had died of the Spanish Flu. Immediately she had saddled up Daisy Mae and rode over to tell Nana since the Yamaguchis did not have phone service.

"No sense!" Nana exclaimed. "They say war over soon. He almost home."

Gudrun threw a pebble in the water. "Yes. No sense. So — three men from island die in war in less than two years we in war."

"Yes."

They sat silently watching Kyio play with pebbles and attempting to put them in her mouth, her mother stopping her every time.

Finally Gudrun brought up the subject she did not want to talk about with her good friend. "You and Zhou...moving to Seattle?"

Nana gave her a sorrowful glance. "Sorry. It right to be with parents. I need help." She patted her abdomen. "New baby."

Smiling with delight, Gudrun asked, "Yes? When?"

"May." She scrunched up her nose. "We no go yet. Spanish flu."

"Yes. Bad." Gudrun thought about the news off the boats that arrived from the mainland. The flu had hit hard. Starting at Camp Lewis near Tacoma and moving up to north to Seattle. At the sign of the first cases, Mayor Ole Hansen required people to wear masks and closed down all large public gatherings even Denny Park Lutheran Church has stopped Sunday services. Seattle schools and theaters were closed. In her weekly letter, Anna explained that they were staying home. Nils only went to the lumberyard for a few hours each morning. He had moved most his business papers home and ordered his bookkeeper and secretary to do the same. They had long telephone meetings to keep things going.

Gudrun had made masks for herself and Arvik to wear when they went to Eastsound.

"In few months, maybe we move," Nana said.

"I need help sewing. New customer. You bring Kiyo and we sew?"

Nana's eyes lit up. "Yes. For who?"

"Mrs. Moran. Big order."

They sat in the October afternoon sun for another half hour, laughing over Kiyo's cute antics and shedding a few tears as they discussed how they could help Katherine. "Her dress beautiful," Gudrun murmured. Her thoughts going back three months before when Katherine came over so Gudrun could mark the hem. Nana had come over to help.

"Beautiful. I agree."

"I go. Dinner make," Gudrun said. "Thank you for time."

On the way home, Gudrun start praying. *Lord, I praise you and thank you for your goodness. Things are upside down and hard right now. However, you stay the same. You have provided for us, given us strength, and comforted us. Thank you. I ask for protection for the Lundes, for Raghild Thorp, those in Norway, and this island from the Spanish Flu. Give Mayor Ole Hanson wisdom. And Lord thank you for the new buyers of Lot One. They seem like they will be nice neighbors. Please ease Arvik's pain, keep him sober. I know these are hard times. You have allowed to make us closer to you and each other. Help us to find the purpose you have in these tests..."*

Her thoughts roamed for a moment, thinking about losing her daughter, Nana leaving sometime in the future, all the losses.

Yes, Lord you are good. Someday it will all be perfection, in heaven. Someday these problems will fade. Thank you. Amen.

CHAPTER 34

Joy

August 1926

*L*aughter, beautiful melodious laughter floated into the shed and Arvik put down his lathe. He strode toward the garden...no, she must be on the patio. He walked around the house and stopped. There in the August sunshine sat Gudrun, her long blonde curls cascading down, hitting the blanket and shielding from view something moving next to her. He heard a cooing sound and Gudrun started laughing again. *The best music I have ever heard.*

He walked over to Gudrun and picked up his ten-month-old son swinging him high up in the air. Arvik sat down on the blanket and handed Dale to Gudrun. For the next fifteen minutes they did not say a word. They played with their son, smiled and laughed together at his antics.

Arvik gave Gudrun a kiss. "I am so sorry. I have that deadline," Arvik said and stood up.

"I know. PaPa must work so you can have food, Dale, and finish his project to take to Seattle." Gudrun tickled her son. "It is time for your nap. Afterwards we can go see what PaPa is making in the shed."

She held out her hand to Arvik. He helped her up and picked up Dale and they walked to the entry door together.

Arvik watched her carry Dale up the stairs. *My son...I have a son. I still cannot get used to the idea, Lord. Thank you. Working the long hours this dining table order demands is worth it, for my family.* His first commissioned piece for a Seattle client. Not just any client but the prominent Mrs. Foss. She had admired the table he had made for Anna and Nils as a Christmas present. Anna's high praise had landed him the job. This had been the furniture and cabinet year. Orders streamed in from people building vacation homes on the island. He heard the mailman's truck and walked out to Sunset Lane to pick up the delivery for Gudrun. There usually was a letter from at least one of her girlfriends.

༄

Humming the tune of 'How Great Thou Art,' Gudrun cut out sirupsnitter for their trip to Seattle. Goosebumps ran up and down her arms as she thought of seeing Karoline and Bjørg again. *Over twelve years since I left. So much has happened Lord. Good times, happy times, sad and difficult times. Thank you for helping me grow during those tough times. Through it all you have been faithful. Thank you. Thank you, again and again for my sweet son. Please keep Karoline and Bjørg safe as they travel.*

She paused and looked at the stack of mail that Arvik had brought to her earlier, Karoline's letter on top. She put the cookies in the oven and as she opened the letter she marveled at the luxury of mail coming to the house.

"I hope this letter arrives before I do." Karoline wrote.

I have a bit of a surprise for you. The people involved wanted it to be a secret but I disagreed so I am forewarning you. Berit and Captain Hans will be traveling with me. I am sure this news is a bit of a shock and I wanted you to have time to adjust to it. I am sure you will want to discuss it with Arvik. We were not sure it would happen because of the captain's declining health. It does make me feel safer traveling with a man in our party.

Gudrun sat down at the kitchen table and reread the letter. *I am so glad my friend knows me so well. Yes, I need the time to take this in.* Gudrun knew that Karoline was still adjusting to being a widow. Her dear Mr. Iversen, 'my prince,' as she called him, had passed away the year before.

Dale's laughter from the library interrupted her thoughts. She rushed in to find him cooing at the mobile hanging above his crib. "How spoiled you are my love, upstairs and main floor cribs and mobiles at each of them, all made by your PaPa. Let me change you and we will go and see him."

"You are really outdoing yourself on this one." Gudrun commented as she entered the shed. She put a plate of sirupsnitter on the workbench.

"You are admiring the wood, not my work."

"No, in the curves, the lines, there is love in this table. Love for the wood. Mrs. Foss will be pleased."

"You found me out. Yes, I am in love with this wood. Like you are with fine fabrics." Arvik's smile had an extra twinkle in his eye. "However, there are two people I love more."

"Can you take a break? There is something we need to discuss."

"Sure, besides these need sampling." He picked up one of the cookies and took Dale from her with his other arm. "What is the problem?"

"Karoline warned me that she will be traveling with two other people besides Bjørg." She watched Arvik raise his eyebrows and then continued, "Berit and Captain Hans are coming too. We need to talk about how we each feel about this."

Arvik's head cocked to the side. "Well..." He put the last bit of cookie in his mouth, walked up to her, put his free arm around her waist and pulled her in close. "Since I am the one married to you and he is married, I do not have a problem with him visiting. How do you feel?"

Putting her head on his shoulder, she said, "You always seem to understand me...since the day we met. I was shocked to read it. And I have not seen him since he proposed...I do care for him and want to see him."

Arvik brushed a curl back from her face. "It is alright. He is the father figure you needed after losing your father. I understand the type of love you have for him. It is Berit that could have the problem."

"She knows that the captain never really loved me. I was the one who introduced him to the idea of love and a wife. I warmed up his heart so he was ready for her."

"So it is solved. Will they come to the island?"

"Yes but only for two days. They are staying at the Eastsound Inn. And they are not traveling home with Karoline and Bjørg. Instead they are going back through the Panama Canal. We will only have Karoline and Bjørg staying in the house as the Lunde children want to sleep on their yacht." Gudrun outlined the plans.

"Yes, Nils asked permission to anchor off our beach. You will have a lot of meals to prepare. Maybe you should hire someone to cook for that week."

"Maybe, the Lundes could bring Emily. She could stay in the house and we could even give her a night off when you bake salmon in the outside oven."

"Good plan."

❧

Pure amazement flooded over Gudrun as she stood in the middle of King Street Station's main lobby. Light flooding in from all directions highlighted the high, intricately coffered ceiling. She noticed Arvik and Nils looking up at the grand architectural detailing. On the ride down Queen Anne Hill to the station Nils had informed them the station had been built in 1906 — a long train whistle in the distance interrupted her thoughts...

"That could be them!" Anna exclaimed. She grabbed Gudrun's hand and squeezed it.

Arvik walked over. "It will be chaos on the platform so we have a plan. Nils and I will go out to the platform and greet them. Nils will bring the ladies along with Captain Hans in to meet you. I will secure the luggage while Nils grabs a taxi for us. Is that acceptable?"

"Yes," Anna replied and sat down on one of the wooden benches. She patted the space next to her for Gudrun to join her."

"How do you think the kids are doing?" Gudrun asked.

"You mean Dale? My three are driving the butler crazy. The nanny is excellent with babies. So relax." Anna patted Gudrun's hand. "I am so excited to meet Karoline. I feel like I know her through you."

"And Berit. I am so excited to see her. Sorry about my nervousness over Dale. It is the first time I have left him with anyone."

Anna laughed. "Oh, I remember those days. Now I can hardly wait to get out and have some time to myself. It is too bad our other car is being worked on. Arvik could have driven it. It is nicer than a taxi."

"We will be fine. I have a feeling we might need two taxis to get all the luggage to your place. If Bjørg is like her mother there will be lots of luggage."

Minutes ticked by slowly as they watched the big clock and the doors to the train platform. Finally the doors opened and in walked Berit, Karoline and Bjørg.

Anna rushed over to Berit hugging her tight. Karoline met Gudrun half way.

Breaking the hug, Karoline exclaimed, "It is so good to see you." And she hugged Gudrun again.

"Yes, so good," Gudrun agreed. "So this is Bjørg." Gudrun smiled at the twelve-year-old. "You do not remember the last time I saw you. You were a tiny baby. What a fine young lady you have become."

"Thank you, ma'am," the dark-haired beauty answered.

Thinking, *she looks a lot like her father,* Gudrun turned toward Anna. "Anna, I would like to present Karoline Iversen and her daughter Bjørg. Ladies, this is Anna Lunde."

Laughing and talking with her friends, Gudrun forgot her surroundings. Arvik's big hand on her shoulder caused her to jump.

He smiled as he looked down at her. "There is someone else who wants to say 'Hello.'" Arvik nodded behind her.

Turning, Gudrun's hand went to her mouth as she recognized Hans leaning on a cane. She rushed over to him, gave him a gentle hug and a peck on the cheek. "My dear Captain, it is so good to see you again."

"It is good to see you, my dear. It seems like life here in the Northwest is treating you well."

A porter interrupted their greeting, wanting direction on where to take the large dolly full of luggage.

Middag that afternoon became full of talk about Seattle's Mayor Berta Landes and the new engine that Arvik was putting in *Himmel*. Occasionally the women tried to change the subject matter. As they finished dessert the nanny brought in Dale fresh from his nap and full of energy. Gudrun excused herself from the table and allowed her newly walking son to roam the hall between the entry and the dining room. Dale successfully negotiated the two steps into the living room by crawling down them backwards. Then he started toddling around the sofas and chairs.

"Looks like he keeps you busy," Captain Hans said.

Gudrun laughed. "He is a full-time occupation." She scooped up her son and took him to the window looking over the garden and Puget Sound. "It is good to see you."

The captain joined her. "And you. I would like to apologize about the last time we saw each other. I should have never proposed. When I introduced you to Arvik I knew you were perfect for each other. I am sorry about muddling up the waters," he said.

She smiled at him. "You did me a favor by proposing. It helped me understand what was going on. At that moment I understood you are like a father figure to me. That is the gift you gave me on that long voyage. You protected and provided for me in so many ways. The proposal left me with only the confusion of how I felt about Arvik. I was so attracted to him but I did not fall in love with him until after we were married."

"It has all turned out for the best, God's plan for each of us."

"Yes. Berit has told me about your coming to know the Lord. I rejoiced when I heard the news," Gudrun said.

"I had a lot of time on the trip home to think about my beliefs. Mrs. Sandnes answered a lot of the questions I had.

After I returned, they shut down most of the passenger routes to the U.S. because of the war and I took the job with the ferry system. I lived with Sissel and her husband in Stavanger and Sissel never gave up on me. Getting reacquainted with Berit became the final way the Lord brought me to my knees."

"I am so glad He did. Your salvation has been an answer to prayer." She sat Dale back down on the floor.

The captain reached down and ruffled Dale's hair. "Looks like a fine boy."

"We have high hopes for him. I keep praying he will be a man of God."

∽

Is this a fairy tale or a dream? Will I be waking up soon and find out it never happened? Gudrun mused as she sat next to Karoline on the back deck of the Lundes' yacht. Swells from another boat gave them a slight rocking motion and caused the twins and Bjørg to squeal in delight as they went up and down in their inner tubes in the waters of Lake Washington. Nils and Arvik, like a couple of school boys were diving off the swim platform that Edel sat on, dangling her legs in the water. Berit, Anna, and Hans sat on the bow while Dale slept securely on the boat crib below.

"What an unbelievable week this has been so far," Karoline said. "Finally, after all these years — getting to hug you, hear your voice and spend time with you. These memories will mean so much to me on long cold days this winter."

"The same for me...I owe you a big debt of gratitude. I would be scrubbing toilets and floors for a living in Oslo if you had not helped me. Your friendship means even more. To have a Christian girlfriend gave me...well, it gave me courage," Gudrun said.

Edel tugged at Gudrun's sleeve. "Auntie Gudrun, will you please come swim with me? Please?"

Gudrun looked at Karoline. "Are you game? Ready to show everyone the two piece suits we bought yesterday?"

Karoline nodded and they slipped out of their sundresses, displaying long sleeveless tunics that overlapped matching swim shorts. Arvik whistled, hoisting himself onto the swim platform and made a half-hearted attempt to throw Gudrun in. Edel grabbed Gudrun's hand and they jumped into the warm lake water together.

"Mother, come swim with me," Bjørg called out. Karoline swam to her daughter leaving Edel and Gudrun to float on the round corkboards Nils had fashioned at his lumberyard.

"This is like a big party, Auntie Gudrun."

Gudrun smiled. "Oh yes. One big party and we are not even halfway through the celebration. A big party with all my closest Norwegian friends. It is a gift, you know, from God."

Edel agreed, "You are right."

They floated in silence and Gudrun's thoughts turned to yesterday's shopping with Karoline in downtown Seattle, just the two of them and going to lunch at the Olympic Hotel. What a special dinner they had at the Lundes' that evening. And the day before, their trip to Snoqualmie Falls with lunch at the Salish Lodge would be a memory to last her the rest of her life.

They still had plans for a play, the Seattle Symphony, and church at Denny Park Lutheran, and many other Seattle sights to take in. The Captain and Berit had a few of his friends to visit so they would not be joining them until they left for Orcas next Monday. *The trip home to Orcas will be fun, with the Lundes taking Hans and Berit on this boat, and Karoline, Bjørg and us on Himmel. Himmel will have her new faster engine so we can make it there in one day.*

❦

"I wish I could stop time and keep you here longer," Gudrun said, as she sat next to Berit on a log. Venn gave up chasing a seagull down the beach and joined them.

Berit patted Gudrun's arm. "I know. But this is a long trip and we cannot stay in America forever. I did not realize Hans has so many friends here. I am thankful that we have had the time we have had. It is wonderful to see where you live. It will make your letters all the more real."

Gudrun pressed her shoulder into Berit's. "And I can picture where you live."

"I am sorry I cannot stay for church this Sunday so I can meet your friends."

Gudrun grimaced. "I really do not have friends at church. It is not the ladies at church who are to blame. It is my inability to speak English. It is such hard work to communicate with them."

"That is sad. You must be so lonely."

"Not really. I have the Lord. Arvik and now Dale are more than I ever hoped for. And I have letters from all of you." Gudrun hugged Berit and nodded to Karoline and Anna wadding close to shore. "I am very happy."

"So not one girlfriend on the island." Berit shook her head.

"Not anymore now that Nana has moved. I never had friends on our island in Lillesand, either. I had Trygg and here I have Venn. There is a new young couple, the Meirs, who started attending a month ago. He used to live here. He has a cabin over on Deer Harbor. His wife seems nice. She makes the effort to converse with me."

"You will have the memories of this visit. Now what can I do to help you with dinner?" Berit asked.

"You can help make the salad. Arvik will bake the salmon. Karoline is going to set the table and Bjørg and Anna all have jobs. I do wish you and the Lundes were not leaving tomorrow." Gudrun gave her friend another hug as she walked up the path to the house. "It will seem like a quiet two weeks with just Karoline and Bjørg visiting."

CHAPTER 35

Himmel

March 1953

Mr. Meir let out a big belly laugh as Luke did clumsy half somersaults across the living room floor. The one year old knew what this party was all about — him. The balloons, the cake, the stack of presents, all for little tow-headed, Luke Johansen.

Gudrun stood in the corner watching all the activity. Several men had joined Arvik at the window pointing to the boats at the Meirs' dock. She knew *Matilda,* the Meirs' new boat, would be the main topic. She had asked Rosa if she needed help in the kitchen. Rosa had suggested she spend time with Luke. Several women sat on the sofa and they had asked her to join them. She had for a moment — however she just wanted to watch her grandson. Such a rare opportunity to have time with Luke. She sat down on an ottoman near where he played.

"Hello, Luke. Me —" Gudrun pointed to herself. "Far Mor. Father's mother."

Luke looked up at her and smiled. He came up to her, putting his hand on her knees. A long grey curl broke loose from her barrette. He reached up and grabbed it.

"Soft," Gudrun said. Then she remembered the word she wanted. "Gentle."

Luke looked at her. "No. Soft." He did not pull as he kept stroking her curl.

"Can you...say Far Mor?"

Rosa came over and sat on the floor next to them. She did not look well. Her normally thin frame seemed even thinner than before, her olive skin had a yellowish cast and she had dark circles under her pretty eyes.

"You get sleep?" Gudrun asked.

"I sleep all the time. I am not sure why I am so tired." Rosa grabbed Gudrun's hand. "I am so sorry we keep turning your invitations down. I get sick or Dale has a long day on the crab boat. I cannot drive myself to your house alone as I am afraid I would crash the car."

Gudrun squeezed her hand. "I understand. You...you get well." Luke pushed himself up against Gudrun and laid his head on her lap.

"I have been seeing the doctor. It does not seem to help."

Gudrun picked up Luke and sat him on her lap. "I can come...help you."

"Maybe. It is a long difficult ten miles for you to come. Arvik would have to drive you. Mom helps out and Dad too. We will manage. I must check on something in the kitchen. Keep an eye on him for me?"

"Yes." She kissed her grandson's head. "You must come to my house," she said in Norwegian. He played with her rings and her bracelet, smiling up at her for a moment, then intrigued with her jewelry again, then another smile.

Rosa announced, "It is time to light the candles and sing to Luke."

Dale came over to Gudrun. "I'll take him, Mom. Thanks for watching him."

As they sang 'Happy Birthday,' Luke's eyes lit up each time they said his name. He gave Gudrun a big smile. They had bonded. Arvik took pictures as Luke tried to follow Dale's lead and blow out the candles. Then they put him in his high chair and gave him a piece of cake to play with. Arvik kept snapping photos. *We will pay a pretty penny to have those photos developed. But completely worth it,* she thought.

Spring 1954

Two-year-old Luke crawled into her lap as she sat on the window seat, looking out at the islands. He nestled into her bosom and said, "You smell good. Flowers."

"Lilacs, it — it the flower lilacs," Gudrun said in English. She grabbed a picture book about Jesus. "We read?"

Luke looked up at her, his blue eyes shining. "Jesus?"

"Yes. Jesus."

"Please. Please." He clapped his hands.

For the next fifteen minutes grandmother and grandson sat in the living room window seat exploring the book. The fact his English skills and hers were about on the same level did not matter. The language of love bound them close together.

Gudrun hugged him tight as they finished the book. "Time for nap. You be good. Sleep. Then play ball with Far Far."

Luke nodded, hopped down from the window seat, grabbed her hand and led her upstairs.

So precious. Please Lord guide this little one to be the man his father should have been. Save him at a young age. Keep him from the addiction my husband and son have suffered with. Help the doctors to know what is wrong with Rosa. She is so special. I know Dale does not deserve her. Thank you so much for this precious time I have had to babysit him today. In your Son's name, Amen. Gudrun prayed as they ascended the stairs.

She went to the kitchen for some tea and grabbed her sewing basket from the corner of the living room and started upstairs to do some handwork. She needed to be alert for noises from Dale's old bedroom. Instead she heard footsteps, Arvik's footsteps, coming toward the front door. She hurried to intercept him. As he opened the door she met him, finger to her lips. He smiled. Put his coffee cup down and took her in his arms.

"This reminds me of the old days when you put Dale down for naps," Arvik whispered. "Looks like you are having fun. Which ferry are they coming home on?"

"They were not sure. It depends how long the doctors take. Rosa said maybe the five o' clock," Gudrun said. "Did you understand anything Dale said about Rosa's illness?"

Once in the kitchen, Arvik poured himself a cup of coffee and grabbed a cookie out of the cookie jar. He gave her a long look. "I understood some of it. She is very tired. Too tired to do anything, which could be anemia, a disease where your blood is missing iron. She also still has times where she cannot deal with being a mother and Mrs. Meirs has to take over. It is a good thing they live in the Meirs' guest house."

"You are right. But I wish I could be more a part of Luke's care."

"Maybe this is the beginning of your babysitting." Arvik paused, then shook his head. "You would think that son of ours could be better organized. Giving you more notice, and allowing time to calmly drop Luke off this morning. Sometimes I wonder where his brain is."

Gudrun nodded. "I agree, but at this point I will stop everything to spend time being with Luke."

"Back to work...bring the little guy out to the shed when he gets up. I can stop and play with him."

॰॰

Fall 1956

"I will be seeing Jesus soon." Gudrun's countenance seemed to glow as she spoke. "I wish I could let you know what heaven is like."

Arvik gently squeezed her as she sat on his lap on the window seat in her study. He cleared his throat, fighting to find words to say. All he could do was hold her, his precious Lady from Lillesand.

Please, Lord, give her more time...I cannot go on without her. Please...I need her. He struggled not to yell 'do not take her from me.' *I have to be strong. I have to make this as happy of a time as I can.*

The past two weeks seemed like a nightmare, so many doctors. Emphysema had been the diagnosis. They both knew something major had a hold of Gudrun's body. Her fatigue, the trouble she had breathing over the past months had kept getting worse. She had procrastinated going into Seattle like the local doctor suggested. *I wish we still had Dr. Agnes. I should have insisted on going to Seattle sooner.*

"Thank you. Thank you for loving me, for being such a wonderful husband, for providing for me. There is so much you gave me. You gave me a beautiful life. One I could have never dared hope for —"

"Hush, hush. You have given me way more. You are tired. You sleep for a while. I will be back with tea in a half hour." Arvik stood up. He laid two comforters over her as she lay back on the pillow.

Gudrun tugged on his sleeve. "Wake me if Nana arrives before then."

"I will."

Once in the kitchen he sat down at the table and started to sob. He could not listen to her goodbye, yet it seemed so important to her, so he must. Sixty-two. Sixty-two is too young to die. Four months ago she had so much energy, it seemed like nothing would ever stop her. The specialist had asked a lot of questions — like if she ever smoked, did she live in a large city, and if she had been around harsh chemicals in closed in spaces? To the last question she had answered 'yes.' Early on in her time as a maid before she worked for the Iversens she had cleaned lots of small rooms without any ventilation. Often the chemicals she had been given choked her. Suddenly she remembered her father's smoking a pipe in the small cabin and informed the doctor. The doctor explained that the chemicals and the smoke caused a small pocket of infection in the wall of her lungs that took years to manifest itself, in this case, over forty years.

He got up to make tea and noticed Nana riding her bicycle down the lane. She had refused a ride from the ferry, as she wanted him to stay with Gudrun every minute. Anna and Nils planned to come tomorrow. It would be good to have Nils here. Dale, Rosa and the boys had come by a few days before. It had lifted Gudrun's spirits to spend time with her grandsons, Luke and his little brother, Adam.

After Nana left, Arvik made his way slowly up the stairs. Gudrun's smile spoke of peace.

"The best visit," she said.

"You liked the miso soup?"

"That is always good. She had wonderful news. A few months ago her parents got saved. Last month they led Nana to Christ. Such a big answer to prayer."

Arvik sat next to her. "That is wonderful news. How is Zhou?"

"He is doing good..." Gudrun paused for a breath. "His furniture and cabinet shop is doing well."

"We need to pray for his salvation. Now you need to rest before dinner. You have a big day tomorrow with Anna coming. You will need your strength." He put his arm around her. "I think I need a nap too." He sat up against the pillows listening to her labored breathing and watching a few boats go by. The fog in the distance parted and Matia and Sucia Islands appeared.

∾

"Here is your breakfast, my lady," Arvik said as he entered their bedroom.

Gudrun had been too weak to get out of bed that morning.

"Some of the miso soup Nana left us and laks on a slice of bread. I can get more if you want it." Arvik put the bed tray down on her nightstand and helped her sit up against the pillows.

"Thank you. I have been laying here thinking about Dale — his graduation from high school and going off to college in Bellingham."

"Yes and then instead of getting some big job in town he came back here to crab. A disappointment." Arvik shook his head.

"I have gone over in my mind time and time again where I went wrong. How I should have been a better mother..."

"You cannot think that way. You were the best. You gave him so much. Your time, you made sure he had everything he needed, you patched him up physically and mentally when he got hurt. You even gave up your sewing studio so he could have a playroom and game room."

"Perhaps I spoiled him..." Gudrun paused to catch her breath, looking out at the islands, she said, "His coming back to Orcas might have been God's plan. He married Rosa...she is good for him. He is doing well with the crab boat. Now they have Luke and Adam. We have been blessed...remember when I am gone that God is always good. He will get you through everything."

"I know. Now you eat. Maybe you will be strong enough to get down the stairs by the time the Lundes get here. I will help you get dressed," Arvik said and then left the room.

Oh Lord, give him strength. Keep him close to you. I am concerned about him, Lord once I come to heaven. You have given me such a good life. I cannot complain about any of it. She continued through her normal prayers for Dale and his family, for Karoline, Bjørg, Berit, and the Lundes. She thought about Berit for a moment, losing the captain about ten years ago and asked the Lord to keep her from being lonely.

Arvik came back in with a vase filled with roses from the garden. "I thought these would cheer you up."

"Oh yes, they do. Are you trying to impress me?" she teased.

"Yes. I am hoping you might let me kiss you."

She could not help but laugh which triggered a coughing and gasping fit.

Arvik rubbed her back. "Relax. Relax. You can do it." As she calmed down, he gave her a sip of water.

She leaned back on the pillows, closing her eyes and said, "I am sorry. That was funny."

As Arvik half carried her down the stairs she kept her eyes on the wheelchair below. *That is the goal Lord. Please give me the strength to get there. Please make it a good visit with*

Anna. This will be the last time I see her here on earth. Make it a joyful time.

"Alright, hold on to the newel post for a second and I will turn the wheelchair so you can sit," Arvik said.

She collapsed in the chair, leaning back and taking several wheezy breaths. Arvik wheeled her over to the window seat in full view of the entry door. He had just gotten her situated when the doorbell rang. Gudrun watched the commotion at the front door as the energy from Anna seemed to explode throughout the house. She had flowers and a basket with food. Nils waved at her as Arvik dealt with Anna's instructions. Emily stood in the corner with more baskets, waiting for a clear path to the kitchen. Gudrun wanted to laugh but was afraid of another coughing fit.

Emily started to clear the lunch dishes and the men took off to the garage to talk cars. Anna pushed her into the living room and placed her with the best view of the water.

"I am so grateful to be here. You just let me know if there is anything you need done. Write letters, things you want to go to certain people...anything," Anna said as she settled into a chair next to her.

"If I think of anything. Most of it Arvik has taken care of. Maybe letters to Karoline and Berit."

"Sure. How about a call to each of them?"

"Oh...too much..." Gudrun had to pause for a breath, "money."

"A gift to you from me and Nils, please let me do this for you." Anna gave Gudrun a long look.

Gudrun could feel the fatigue take over as they chatted about their children. She asked Anna to help her onto the window seat for a nap. As she lay back against the pillow she said,

"You and Nils do not have to stay on the island. Arvik and I will be fine."

"Nonsense. We are fine at the Eastsound Inn. Emily will give you both your privacy. It will free up Arvik to have her cook for you. Nils is Arvik's best friend. He wants to be here for him once you..."

Gudrun's eyes fluttered open. "Oh that is good. Arvik will need him when I am gone."

"Yes, and Nils knows what to do."

༝

Yesterday seemed so long ago. A disappointing day as her body no longer allowed her downstairs. Arvik had brought the wheelchair upstairs so she could make it to her study. They had sat there for several hours in the morning propped up against the pillows, enjoying the view, talking, and dozing. Dale, Rosa, and the boys came just before lunch. She got to hold baby Adam, and Luke had curled up beside her with the Jesus picture book he had taken out of her bookshelf.

Such precious moments, Lord. Thank you for the phone calls with Berit and Karoline last night.

The calls had not been long. Hearing their voices and saying goodbye meant so much to her. Anna and Nils had come for lunch and stayed through dinner although they were careful to give Arvik and her time alone. She had taken a long afternoon nap in Arvik's arms on the window seat.

Today, Lord...will I join you in eternity today? You seem so close...please allow me one last visit with my grandsons. One last time to hold and cuddle them. Bless Anna and Nils for all that they are doing. I am so eager to be with you. I ask for strength for those I am leaving behind, especially my dear husband.

Dozing off to sleep again, she dreamed of being cradled in big arms and carried away.

"Gudrun. Gudrun." Arvik gently rubbed her hand. "Rosa brought Adam and Luke."

Arvik helped her sit up a bit. She could see Rosa holding Adam. Luke jumped up on her bed and cuddled in next to her. She motioned for Rosa to bring the baby and she laid him next to her.

Putting her arm around Luke she said, "Luke bow head. We pray." She wished she could have continued in English but her strength gave way and she switched to Norwegian. "Lord I ask you to bless these boys, make them men after your own heart. Men who love your word...Please Lord give them godly women for wives...In your son's name, Amen."

Fatigue demanded she close her eyes. She could feel Rosa kiss her on the cheek. She heard her whisper, "I love you." Then Luke's kiss, a muffled, "love you." They left the room.

Arvik moved in close beside her, holding her tight. She could feel her Lord calling her home. Joy filled her heart as she followed His call.

Norwegian Words with English Definitions:

badedrakt = swimsuit

bakeri = bakery

bunad = expensive, hand embroidery national costume

fotball = soccer

frokost = breakfast

gata = street

hardanger = a white on white geometric embroidery

Himmel = heaven

Hilsen fra = greetings from

hytte = cabin, cottage

kveldsmat = late evening meal

krumkake = Norwegian waffle cookie

laks = salmon

lapskaus = thick meat and vegetable stew, sometimes made with reindeer meat

lefse = soft flat bread, can be buttered with sugar
and cinnamon between

lunsj = lunch

marsipankake = almond cake

middag = large late afternoon meal.
Served around 4:00 or 4:30pm

Norge = Norway

Norsk, Nordmann = Norwegian

Post = Post Office

potetstappe = a type of mashed potatoes

potetballer = bacon soaked potato ball

sirupsnitter = Norwegian cookie,
main ingredient is English syrup

skål = toast

småkake = small cookies

smørbrød = sandwiches

sol = sun

urtesalt = baking salt herb

vaffel = waffle, can be heart shaped; vafler = plural

venninne = girlfriend

Vi trenger badedrakt = we need to have swimsuits

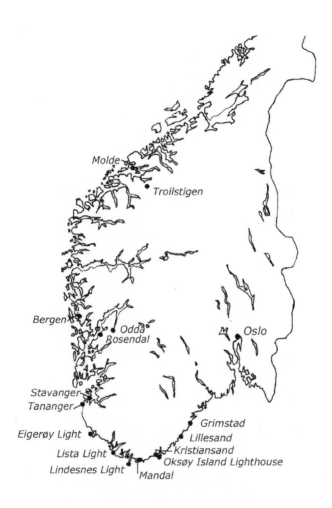

Molde
Trollstigen
Bergen
Odda
Rosendal
Oslo
Stavanger
Tananger
Grimstad
Eigerøy Light
Lillesand
Lista Light
Kristiansand
Oksøy Island Lighthouse
Lindesnes Light
Mandal

Southern Norway

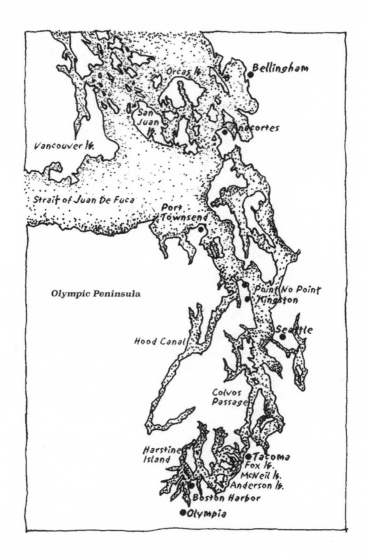

Puget Sound

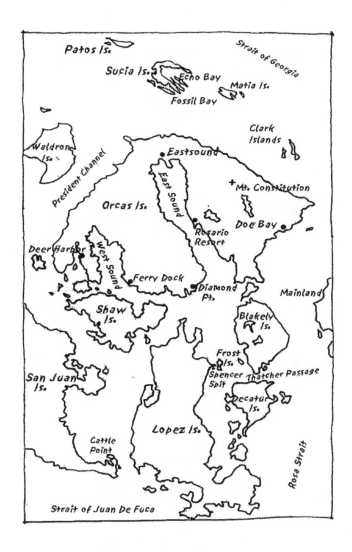

San Juan Islands

Verses:

(New American Standard Bible)

Psalm 46: 1-2   "God is our refuge and strength, a very present help in trouble. v2 Therefore we will not fear though the earth should change, and though the mountains slip into the heart of the sea."

Philippians 4:13   "I can do all things through Him who strengthens me."

Psalm 42:8   "The Lord will command His lovingkindness in the daytime; and His song will be with me in the night, a prayer to the God of my life."

James 4:2c-3b   "You do not have, because you do not ask. v3 You ask and do not receive because you ask with wrong motives."

Psalm 23:1   "The Lord is my shepherd, I shall not want..."

1 Samuel 18:1   "Now it came about when he had finished speaking to Saul that the soul of Jonathan was knit to the soul of David, and Jonathan loved him as himself."

Hebrews 11:1   "Now faith is the assurance of things hoped for, the conviction of things not seen.

Psalm 46:10   "Be still and know that I am God." (KJ)

2 Corinthians 6:14   "Do not be bound together with unbelievers; for what partnership have righteousness and lawlessness, or what fellowship has light with darkness?"

Psalm 73:26   "My flesh and my heart may fail; but God is the strength of my heart and my portion forever."

John 3:16   "For God so loved the world, that He gave His only begotten Son. That whoever believes in Him shall not perish but have Eternal Life."

The Real
Gudrun Sagen

Gudrun Sagen, the main character of *The Things Hoped For,* depicts a young woman focused on Jesus. Though shy in nature, she has a quiet courage and an adventurous spirit. While the story is fictional, the character's name is real.

The real Gudrun was born in 1884 in Molde, Norway with the maiden name of Sylte. She married Ole Sagen in 1908. In 1911 they had a son, Arne, and in 1918 a daughter, Sigrid. Both the fictional character and the real Gudrun had fathers who worked in the fishing industry.

Though the real Gudrun Sagen never left Molde, she too had courage. Many times during the WWII Nazi occupation of Norway she allowed members of the Norwegian Underground (one of them her son, Arne) to bed down in her house.

When the Norwegian King Haakon VII, and Crown Prince Olav hid in Molde, along with the government gold, the Nazi's retaliated by bombing and burning the town to the ground. Gudrun and Ole lost their house in the bombing and lived in their 12' x 10' one room cabin in the alpine meadows far above the town. Gudrun, Ole, and Sigrid spent at least one winter there, with no insulation in the walls. Sigrid would ski into

343

town to find food wherever it could be found. The cabin still stands today.

Despite never having a lot of this world's possessions, Gudrun was known for her generosity. Her grandson, born in Seattle, remembers living in Norway for two years as a preschooler. Every week she would walk with him down to the stores and she would allow him to pick out one item – anything he wanted: candy or a toy. He always went to the hardware store for more wood and nails and built a child's version of a model city in her back yard. That grandson is my husband, Stanley Jørgen Lønseth.

Gudrun Sylte Sagen passed away in 1968 in Molde from complications from her life long struggle with Asthma.

The Johansen Family Saga

Book One – *Leave It With Him*

Book Two – *Cares Of This World*

Book Three – *Anchor For Your Soul*

Book Four – *The Things Hoped For*

For more about the author or to read her weekly blog go to:

elizabethlonsethnovels.com